P9-DWF-205

ALSO BY JO BAKER

The Body Lies
A Country Road, A Tree
Longbourn
The Undertow
The Telling
The Mermaid's Child
Offcomer

The Midnight News

Baker, Jo, author.
Midnight news

2023
33305257200554
ca   05/04/23

The Midnight News

Jo Baker

ALFRED A. KNOPF   New York

2023

THIS IS A BORZOI BOOK
PUBLISHED BY ALFRED A. KNOPF

Copyright © 2023 by Jo Baker

All rights reserved. Published in the United States by Alfred A. Knopf,
a division of Penguin Random House LLC, New York, and distributed
in Canada by Penguin Random House Canada Limited, Toronto.
Originally published in hardcover in Great Britain by Phoenix Books,
an imprint of The Orion Publishing Group Ltd., London, in 2023.

www.aaknopf.com

Knopf, Borzoi Books, and the colophon are registered trademarks
of Penguin Random House LLC.

Library of Congress Cataloging-in-Publication Data
Names: Baker, Jo, author.
Title: The midnight news / Jo Baker.
Description: First edition. | New York : Alfred A. Knopf, 2023.
Identifiers: LCCN 2022052790 (print) | LCCN 2022052791 (ebook) |
ISBN 9780593534977 (hardcover) | ISBN 9780593534984 (ebook)
Classification: LCC PR6102.A57 M54 2023 (print) |
LCC PR6102.A57 (ebook) | DDC 823/.92—dc23
LC record available at https://lccn.loc.gov/2022052790
LC ebook record available at https://lccn.loc.gov/2022052791

This is a work of fiction. Names, characters, places and incidents either
are the product of the author's imagination or are used fictitiously.
Any resemblance to actual persons, living or dead, events
or locales is entirely coincidental.

Jacket images: *Southampton Row, London, April 1941*
by Ernest Boyce Uden © Imperial War Museums/Bridgeman Images;
(earrings) Van Rossen/Alamy
Jacket design by Jenny Carrow

Manufactured in the United States of America
First American Edition

For Rebecca
because you know why

"... the wicked had stayed and the good had gone ..."

ELIZABETH BOWEN, *The Heat of the Day*

The Midnight News

Late

S orry, sorry, sorry."

Charlotte has been scanning the pavements these past twenty minutes, between glances at her watch and at the posters of the new releases, and yet Elena still appears out of nowhere, in a pistachio linen dress and crocheted gloves, straw hat clutched in her hands. She's looking flushed and irritated.

"There you are!" Charlotte says.

"I am so sorry."

She pulls El to her, holds her slight frame close, breathes in her scent: roses and lemon sherbets and cigarettes—essence-of-El. She is warm and slightly damp in Charlotte's embrace. Charlotte lets her go, looks her over. That familiar unkempt beauty, like a scruffy Snow White. Her impish green eyes. And, today, a line between her brows.

"What's wrong?"

"Just that I'm outrageously late," El says. "And after treating you so abominably, putting you off and putting you off, I wasn't sure you'd wait." El claps her hat back on her head, then digs her hands into her pockets, squinting in the low September sun. "I'm so sorry, Lotts. Can you ever forgive me?"

"Already have. Always will."

"You're too good."

"*Au contraire,*" Charlotte says. "Shall we go in? We can still catch the feature."

El glares up at the grand frontage of Tussaud's Cinema, as though it were to blame for the afternoon's delays and frustrations. "You know, to tell you the truth, I don't really want to spend what's left of the day sitting in the dark."

"It is glorious," Charlotte says, touching her own hat brim, the better to shade her eyes. "The park, then?"

"Yes. Why not?"

Charlotte offers her arm. They walk along, linked, skirts rustling together, in the drenching honeyed sun. Omnibuses and taxis and vans rumble by; the air tastes of traffic fumes. Charlotte asks about work, about family, about any fun she might have had, and though El replies, she seems somehow out of step, at one remove. They turn into the shade of York Gate, past the cool white-columned façades, and Charlotte looks sidelong at her friend. That line between her brows hasn't gone away.

"D'you know who I saw recently?" Charlotte tries.

"No?"

"The Astonishing Vanessa."

El brightens. "Vanessa Cavendish?"

"Is there any other Vanessa worth the mention? She was giving her Ophelia. You know, those Shakespeare matinées at the Vaudeville?"

"Was she good?"

"Was she *good*? She was heartbreaking. Beautiful. Brilliant. Everything one would expect."

"I'm glad for her," El says. "She's earned it."

They cross the road and enter Regent's Park; the air is cooler, cleaner here. The greenness soothes the eyes.

"I managed not to loiter round the stage door and swoon all over her," Charlotte says. "I took myself straight home, dignity intact."

"I'm sure she would have been pleased to see you."

Charlotte laughs. "She wouldn't have known who I was." Two years their senior, Vanessa Cavendish had moved through the stuffy clamour of school with the otherworldly elegance of a wading bird, intent on something no one else had even thought of looking for. "Do you remember what she said, when her parents wanted her to be presented as a deb, and do the season, but she was pegging away at auditions, determined to get a first job?"

El snorts.

"I loved that," Charlotte says. It was a phrase too filthy and outrageous to be whispered in its entirety by the drop-jawed Lower Fifth of the day, or even said out loud now, in public, between the two of them, all grown up at twenty. Gaps had to be left. Words mouthed rather than spoken. "I really loved that."

They pass the boating lake, the water glimmering.

"Still," El says, "you should have said hello."

"Oh no. I don't think so."

"You should," El insists. "You should have told her she was wonderful. People never mind being told they're wonderful."

"She wouldn't have known me from Adam, and I'm not sure I could have borne it."

"You might be surprised. You had your own glamour about you at school."

"Ha!"

But Elena wasn't, it seems, joking. She adjusts her hat, becomes impatient, pulls it off again and fans her face with it. Her cheeks are pink blots in an otherwise pale and waxy face.

El had been in Paris, acquiring polish, while Charlotte had been wearing a little off in London. She'd dashed back from France when it became clear that war was coming; they'd knocked around happily for those quiet early months of the war. And then things had become suddenly hard and real. Charlotte had had the awful news about Eddie, and then El had become so busy. She has a junior post at the Ministry of Supply; by her account, it's just a fetching-finding-and-filing kind of job, but it seems to devour her every waking moment. This is the first time Charlotte hasn't been put off, let down, or plain stood up in months. Charlotte's father had secured a senior position in the same department when it was formed; he, by contrast, seems to have plenty of time to do just as he pleases.

"They're clearly overworking you," Charlotte says.

El gives the kind of wry shrug that suggests a common understanding, but really Charlotte has no idea.

"That's what Mother says," El replies. "But then, as far as she's concerned, any work is too much work for me. She considers me constitutionally unsuited to it."

"Has she told you that you'll spoil your eyes?"

"And my complexion." El lifts a gloved hand to her flushed cheek. "How's yours?"

"My complexion?"

"Your work."

"Dull. Which, coincidentally, is also true of my complexion."

"I don't believe you," El says. "If you're there, it can't be dull."

"No defence of my complexion then?" Charlotte asks.

A small cheeky smile, which does Charlotte's heart glad.

"Believe it or not," Charlotte goes on, "some things are beyond even my capacity for nonsense. But it's work. And a wage. And that still has a certain charm to it. It keeps the wolf from the door."

El draws breath, but doesn't speak. Charlotte squeezes her arm to her.

"What is it, duck? What's wrong?" she gently asks.

"Oh," El says. "I'm just out of sorts. I'm sorry; I'm not the best company."

"No, my dear, you absolutely always are."

They pass the tethers of a barrage balloon; it hangs high above the park, casts a long shadow. Sheep crop the grass. In the allotments, the old fellows move from plant to plant like bees. The first leaves are on the turn.

El taps Charlotte's forearm with her free hand. "Do you know what I miss most right now at this moment?"

A tug of grief. Because what Charlotte misses most right now is Eddie, and it seems Eddie hasn't even crossed El's mind. But Charlotte plays along, says what she's supposed to say: "Oh, I love this game."

"What I miss most right now, at this moment, is having you come and stay the night."

"Just like we used to," Charlotte says. "Sweets till we're sick, cigarettes smoked out the window, and scaring ourselves witless with ghost stories."

"I was thinking more gin and confidences."

"I'm free tonight."

"I can't tonight."

"Tomorrow?"

"Sorry."

"Oh well," Charlotte says, trying not to feel quite so crushed.

Still arm in arm, they follow the strains of music towards the bandstand, passing men in uniform, men in city suits; Charlotte can feel the slide of eyes over her, but doesn't look back. And neither, she notices, does El; she's all tucked away and inward.

Charlotte can't quite let it go.

"Can't you just, you know, *do* less?" she asks. "Change roles? If you had a word with him, I'm sure my father would—"

"I wouldn't dream of asking."

"But he's your boss, isn't he, more or less?"

"It wouldn't be appropriate. I have three or four bosses to go through before him. I really can't ask him for anything."

"Well, just you wait till he wants something off you, then you'll know all about it."

El nods but doesn't speak. Charlotte shouldn't have brought up work again; it doesn't help. She ushers the conversation back onto a more cheerful tack.

"Well, we simply must find the time somehow. So long as I let Mrs. Callaghan know in advance, I'm not going to get into bad odour at my digs if I'm out overnight. And as for you, you need a change. You clearly do. You're not exactly in the pink."

"Just too much going on, that's all. Sometimes I feel like my head is full of flies."

"You know what." Charlotte turns to El with sudden conviction. "We both have to get some proper official leave; you must be overdue; I know I am. Then we could dash up to the house in Galloway."

"Would that journey count as really necessary, though?"

"I don't see why not, if the property needs checking on, to see it's secure and up to scratch on ARP. And if we're up there anyway, who'd even know if we indulged in a bit of hiking and swimming and a thorough raid of the wine cellar . . ."

"That," El says, turning to Charlotte with at last a proper smile, "sounds like very heaven."

Charlotte beams. There she is. Got her back. "Sooner rather than later, then. We must make a proper plan. It's only a matter of time before the old place gets rented out, or requisitioned."

"Yes. Let's. Just give me a couple of days—"

"You clear the decks, and we'll go. Now that I've thought of it, I believe I shan't be able to get through the winter without it."

They both fall silent, move into shade. They pass the gun emplacement, where men from an Anti-Aircraft Command unit are working. One of them straightens up, wiping his hands on a rag. He's just a lad, maybe not even twenty, and Charlotte has never seen him in her life, but this conjunction of uniform with a light athletic build and a certain easy vigour can catch her like this sometimes. Right in the solar plexus. It sends her staggering back to Eddie, on her doorstep in battledress, popped by to say cheerio.

"Although," Charlotte says, blinking, "I'd understand. If you really are too busy."

El squeezes Charlotte's arm. "No, we'll do that, Lotts. That's what we'll do. I promise."

But Charlotte hears the silence underneath the words, and feels the swelling space between El's life and hers, and knows that since it's been this difficult to snatch an afternoon in London, then a few days in Scotland will be close to impossible.

"I wonder, should we see if they have ices?" Charlotte asks.

"You, my dear, are a genius."

Charlotte returns to Gipsy Hill in the cool evening. On Woodland Road, Mrs. Suttle picks green beans in her front garden. Children pelt past, all nailed boots and flying pigtails; one of them—little Hedy Ackerman—turns to give Charlotte a wave, not looking where she's going. Charlotte flinches; the child will surely fall and hurt herself. But Hedy turns away and runs on heedless with her friends, and Charlotte, breathing the scent of late roses from Mr. Pritchard's garden, pushes through her gate, walks up the tiled path and in through the front door.

This place is just familiar enough to be comfortable, but still strange enough to notice: the smell of malt and boiled milk and wet wool; the back window with its panes of wine-red and green and amber glass, now crisscrossed with gummed scrim; the pert but lazy progress of the grey cat along the cream-and-terracotta tiles.

Mrs. Callaghan, who is settled in at the telephone, cardigan wrapped cosily round her solid self, is listening to her sister up in Liverpool, who rings weekly from a telephone box on the corner of Edith Road. The telephone set, like the hot-water geyser and the glass-fronted bookcase stocked with cloth-bound book-club classics, is a relic of Mrs. Callaghan's much-missed and often-cited Better Half, who was, Charlotte has been told, always Interested in Things.

Mrs. Callaghan raises a hand in greeting, continues with her oohs and mms. Charlotte waves in reply, leans in to lift the notepad from the hall console. The notepad is scrap paper stitched together with wool, so that messages are recorded on the inside of a tea packet or flour bag, or have a strip of yellowed envelope-gum down one side. It forms, Charlotte thinks, a slowly changing collage of Mrs. Callaghan's days. There is a note for Mr. Gibbons, from his sister in Southampton, telling him that all is well and not to worry—even though she's never met the woman, Charlotte feels a stab of concern for her down there in a coastal zone—but there are no messages for Charlotte. Which is how she—on the whole, generally, most days—prefers it, so she can't gripe about it now.

She puts the pad back, joins Mrs. Callaghan in a farewell wave, and climbs the stairs, through the music playing from Mr. Gibbons's rooms, to her attic. He has lovely things, Mr. Gibbons does. Lovely music, lovely clothes.

Charlotte unlocks the door with her own key, locks it behind her, drops her bag. There is still something wonderful in this. She sinks down on the edge of her bed, runs her fingers over the flowered rayon. Fifteen square yards of bare boards, sloping distempered walls, and a cast-iron fireplace where Charlotte can toast a teacake when so inclined. It still feels like a miracle, that she can pay her ten shillings a week and have the skylight room all to herself.

She kicks off her shoes, unclips her stockings, tweaks them off, then washes them in her basin and drapes them over the back of her chair to dry. The only problem is that weekends can be long.

Get yourself married, her sister would say.

Get yourself out to Longwood, her father would say.

Charlotte shudders.

To think she could be holed up in El's room for gin and confidences, if it weren't for all the other things that El is busy with.

Barefoot, she climbs onto her bed to fit the blackout card over the skylight, then hops down to pull the blind and curtains over the front casement.

She will turn up someone. Do something. Tomorrow.

If only go and see *Hamlet* at the Vaudeville again. And this time, maybe loiter at the stage door afterwards, and tell Vanessa Cavendish she's wonderful.

She steps into her slippers, grabs her cardigan and patters downstairs, past the now-untenanted telephone, all the way to the basement kitchen, from where she can hear the wireless muttering. A cup of Horlicks and a bit of chat off Mrs. Callaghan. She can depend on that. That's guaranteed.

The Saturday

The problem, Charlotte supposes, is that she had only looked so far as Friday, and the flicks with El.

She could try and rustle up Janet today, but their friendship thus far has been almost entirely office-based, blooming over typing tips and Chelsea buns, and it seems daunting to barge her way into a married woman's weekend uninvited. Especially as Mrs. Janet Fuller's husband is a vicar; weekends must be particularly busy for vicars and their wives. But it's certainly high time Charlotte called on her godmother. It's always fun to hear about the fun Saskia's been having; almost better than having fun oneself, since Saskia's is always of a higher order. Saskia knows everyone, has been everywhere, has old friends and former lovers all over Europe. Charlotte, on the other hand, seems to hang on to so few people.

When she lifts the telephone, though, there's no dial tone. She leans through Mrs. Callaghan's private parlour door.

"Telephone's on the fritz."

Mrs. Callaghan is sunk deep in her armchair, intricate knitting spread on her lap, her lips paused in an "o" of concentration. She is a splendid knitter, Mrs. Callaghan, a creator of bright and lacy confections, but only ever seems to wear the one cardigan herself, a long, dull-green matted affair, which looks like it has been grown, rather than knitted, in a damp back yard.

"Oh dear," she manages to say, around the code of knit and purl running through her head. "Not again."

"I'll try the box on the corner. Do you need me to pick anything up while I'm out?"

"I have a hankering for plums, my dear. If you can get any."

Charlotte steps out into the sunshine. She turns to look down the road, even though she's going in the opposite direction. She's been here a year, but the view still delights her. On a good day, when the air is not too thick, she can see all the way to the river, pick out the wharves and warehouses, the windows golden with sun, the dome of St. Paul's rendered by distance small as an Iced Gem. Even when the fog is dense, she can still glimpse spires and rooftops and the tips of cranes. And now, hanging above the city, there's the great herd of barrage balloons that catch the light and gleam silver.

It is something to see the capital laid out like this; something one would never lay eyes on from the window of a slinking Daimler or a flat in Mayfair. But people don't come to this part of town any more, however good the views. Not her people, anyway. The Crystal Palace had become unfashionable, a place of gimcrack diversions, long before it burned to the ground. The locals carry on quite contentedly in their half-forgotten resort town on the edge of London. And Charlotte does so too, confident that she will never bump into anybody that she used to know.

The nearest telephone box is occupied by a young woman. One worn sole presses against the glass panels behind her, her free hand plays with the fraying flex. She's clearly settled in, so Charlotte does a slow circuit of the Triangle. At the greengrocer's, she buys seven apples to last the week and a pound of plums for Mrs. Callaghan, eight pence in total, then a bar of honeysuckle-scented soap at the chemist's for thruppence. She considers the autumn hats that have landed like migratory birds in Dolly Varden's window; even with hard saving on her part, she won't be able to achieve one of them this season. At Arundel Cycles, there's a beautiful Claud Butler with bamboo veneer wheels, which is as far out of her reach as Vanessa Cavendish had been when handing out herbs on the stage of the Vaudeville. Jewel-coloured coats are being applied to mannequins in the window of Maney & Cummings and Charlotte really shouldn't even look; it only makes her feel all the more hopeless and acquisitive. She buys cigarettes and spare batteries for her torch, and tries to satisfy herself with these small purchases.

At the next cluster of telephones, all the boxes are occupied, and a small queue has formed along the pavement. She walks on.

The loose end of her day trails before her; she follows it along the street and back to the tip of the Triangle. From here, the park dips down the hill, and beyond that the city fades to green; out there lies the Weald and the Downs and then the sea, and, then, Occupied France. It's not so very far away, the skin between these worlds; it's not so far that Eddie went.

She bites into an apple, sucks at the juice. A truck pulls up at the park gates, and a sentry checks papers. Her thoughts, though, follow Eddie's last footsteps into blood and darkness. Only a handful of his battalion, the 1st Ox and Bucks, were to make it back, and he was not among them. In her heart, instinctively, she still does not believe it— it was not like him to have been unlucky; he'd brushed off the debris of every previous misadventure with a grin. He could be relied upon, could Eddie. Their den in the attic, their camp in the woods, ice-cold swims in the lake at Longwood or the sea in Scotland. Sneaked cigarettes and wild rides on the back of his Norton. He was indispensable. And they had both rather assumed he was immortal.

The sentry peers, takes a step towards her. Charlotte realises how this must look, her standing there, watching the come-and-go of vehicles. She raises her bitten apple in salute, and moves on. The soldiers have settled in the park like ants, taking over a large part of it, streaming in with matériel and out in search of more, making everybody uneasy. Nobody knows quite what they're up to, and one mustn't seem too interested; it is to be hoped the Germans won't become interested either.

Charlotte heads towards the next clutch of telephone boxes. One, at last, stands empty. She posts her apple core into a hedge, pulls the door open. The box smells of stale smoke and the handset is greasy with pomade, but there is a dial tone. She holds the receiver away from her ear, feeds in coins and spins in the code, then El's number. Because you never know, El might just have time to squeeze her in for morning coffee or a flit round the shops. Charlotte needn't actually buy anything. She waits.

There's no answer. Still no answer. She presses the button, and her coins cascade.

But she'll try Janet, while she's at it. And then, if that's a bust, there's still Saskia. She fishes out her address book.

This time, the call is answered with startling promptness, by the vicar himself. Charlotte has met him once, when he came to pick up Janet from the office. He is a surprising kind of a husband for Janet: tall, immaculate, reserved, beautifully well-spoken; whereas Janet is all anxious fuss and careful monitoring of her aitches and her els. Sometimes Janet's manner of speaking is so cautious it's as if she's only just now learning how to talk. Charlotte, though, can match the man consonant for consonant. She has consonants to spare. A barrel full.

"Good morning, this is Charlotte Richmond speaking. May I speak to Mrs. Fuller, please?"

"Who is this?"

"Miss Charlotte Richmond. From work."

"I'm sorry. Who?"

"Charlotte Richmond. From Mrs. Fuller's work. I'd like to speak to her, if I possibly could." She manages not to sigh. He is, after all, a busy man; he has responsibilities. It's a poor parish. He does a lot of good there. They both do.

"Oh. I see. Good morning," he now says. "What can I do for you?"

She grits her teeth, drags a fingertip across a pane, leaving a streak in the dirt. "I'd like to speak to Janet, please."

"Can I ask what this is in relation to?"

"Oh nothing much." For goodness' sake, is he keeping the poor woman in purdah? "I just wondered if she'd like to meet for coffee."

"*Coffee?*"

Christ on a bike. "Coffee. And a walk. If she fancies it."

"I'm afraid that won't be possible."

Charlotte shifts her stance, sets her jaw. "Maybe if I could just speak to her—"

"Oh, she's not *here*."

Unseen, Charlotte allows herself the indulgence of rolling her eyes.

"She's never here on a Saturday."

"I see."

"She's on the church cleaning rota, and then there's Mothers' Union at eleven, then she has Wolf Cubs at two—"

"Ah."

"She's Akela."

"Akela. Right. Well, thank you very much, some other time then."

"Yes," he says uncertainly. "Some other time."

Charlotte pulls a face at the receiver, dumps it back in the cradle. She picks it up again, feeds in more coins and tries Saskia's number, but the call does not connect, so she dials the operator.

"Could you try Chelsea 3647 for me, please. I can't seem to get through."

"But, madam—"

"Mm?"

"Are you quite certain this call is strictly necessary?"

"Yes," Charlotte says. "I am. It is."

"You see, I'm sure you're aware, but just to bring your attention to the current guidelines. We're under instructions to keep the lines clear in case of emergency. For vital communications."

"Five minutes," she says. "Two would do it. I just want to check on my godmother."

"I'm sorry. But the rules are there to keep everybody safe. The invasion could have started, and none of us would be any the wiser, if the lines are all clogged up with people checking on their godmothers."

"I see." Charlotte rubs the glass clear, peers out at the soft September day, in which nothing, really nothing very much, is happening at all. "Do you think it has?"

"I'm sorry?"

"The invasion, has it started?"

"It could have. That's my point. It *could* have."

"Any invasion worth its salt, there'd be all sorts going on by this time of the morning, don't you think? Or they'd have wasted the best part of the day. There'd be shelling. Gunfire. There'd be dispatch riders zooming past, and trucks and tanks on the roads and planes roaring overhead, parachutists falling from the sky, all that kind of thing. They'd have rung the church bells by now, wouldn't they? That's what they're supposed to do, in an invasion."

"That," the operator says, "is beside the point. The point is that people like *you,* who carry on regardless of the consequences, while the rest of us exercise a modicum of restraint—"

"All right," Charlotte interrupts. "Keep your hair on."

She hangs up.

She shoves her remaining coins back into her purse, then pushes out of the phone box. A breeze stirs the turning leaves, bringing a first cool thread of autumn with it. She kicks a loose stone, sending it rattling along.

Some people, she thinks, are just bloody loving this war.

Charlotte has been trying to make the best of it. She settled down with the treat of the new Norman Collins, and for a while this worked perfectly well, but she now finds herself instead thinking of waterfalls, or, more particularly, of one waterfall, the one up in the woods behind the house in Galloway, and the sound it makes when it's in spate in spring, meltwater churned to milky coffee, the sound that you can hear from all the back rooms of the house, that rushes at you when you open a window and let it in, along with the sweet wet air.

Her own skylight is propped open to let the London afternoon swirl through, all smuts and dust and fumes. She can hear traffic going past at the top of the street—vans and motorcars, the clop of horses and creaking drays and carts—and she can hear children playing, and music from someone's wireless, and she feels pretty much content. This is not so bad, after all. This is perfectly all right. But she can also hear a waterfall, and there are no waterfalls round here.

She puts the book aside, goes to the front casement and peers out into Woodland Road. It takes a moment to work out what's different. The grocer's on the corner is closed, the blinds down and awning rolled in. Mr. Pritchard is on his knees in his small front garden, Ilse and Hedy are playing hopscotch on the pavement, and Mrs. Suttle is lugging a bulging string bag down the street. And all of that is entirely ordinary. But Mr. Pritchard's trowel is forgotten in his hand, and he's twisted round uncomfortably to look up at the sky. And Mrs. Suttle has stalled in her tracks, her mouth open. And Ilse and Hedy, who live with their aunt, Miss Beck, just down the road, are frozen at the hopscotch grid, Hedy stopped on a square, Ilse holding her pebble as she waits her turn. They are all looking up, over the tops of the houses, into the distance.

Charlotte cranes round but can't see what they're seeing. She leaves the casement, climbs onto the bed and shoves the skylight wide, leans out. A pigeon stares at her with an eye the colour of fire, then flaps away. The waterfall is louder here. She scans around. To the east, a swarm of insects hazes the sky. A dark central core; a shimmer of continual silvery movement around the edges. For a moment she can't make any sense of it, doesn't know what it is that she is seeing.

And then she knows.

She drops back into her room. She slams the window shut. And then a siren starts up, the sound catching under her ribs, squeezing her lungs. So this, after all, is it. You have to stay calm, don't you; it's important to stay calm. She grabs her cardigan, her coat, her bag—rummages through identity card, purse, keys, ration book, lipstick, toothbrush—her gas mask in its cardboard box, and her Norman Collins. All of this juggled and slipping, she fumbles her door and races down the stairs.

On the landing below, Mr. Gibbons is pulling on his greatcoat, steel helmet dangling on its strap over his arm.

"Oh my word," she says.

"You get yourself tucked up tight now."

A quiet kind of man, slight of build, fond of music and biscuits and good clothes, and never any trouble to anybody, he now finds himself in charge. He sets his helmet on his head and stands aside. She clatters downstairs ahead of him.

"What about you?"

"Up to the post," he says.

He opens the front door and lets in the outdoors; the sirens squeeze her tighter. The air is thick with the drone of planes.

"Good luck," she says.

He touches his brim to her, his expression grim, then slips out, closing the door behind him.

Charlotte heads for the basement kitchen. Mr. Gibbons has made a list, all up and down the street, of who lives where and whether there is a baby or a blind person or an invalid in the household, and where they intend to shelter in the event of an attack, so that any rescue party would know where to look, and when to stop looking, when the time comes. And now the time has come.

Mrs. Callaghan is already installed in her kitchen. She's making tea. She had taken the precaution of having the wireless moved down here, where it will be, she says, company for them. As Charlotte passes close by the walnut cabinet, the programme crackles and the voices break up.

"Was that me?" Charlotte asks.

"I don't think so."

They both regard the electric light as it yellows and fades. In the first flurry of preparations, Mr. Gibbons had pasted over the basement windows with gauze, and then painted that over with blackboard paint. He also built a sandbag wall around the area out front, and then, just to be sure, boarded over the back window entirely. He was very thorough. But it does mean that there's no daylight here, so if the electric goes, then they're down to a battery lamp and their torches.

"Meter?"

"I just put a shilling in."

The wireless stays a gritty fuzz; Mrs. Callaghan switches it off. "We'll try and catch the nine-o'clock bulletin. Got your mask?"

Charlotte holds up the box.

"Good. You don't want to forget your mask. Holy terrors, them'uns. My Cedric knew fine rightly, he always said. He'd seen the worst, he had. So he knew."

"Where's Lady Jane?"

"Shot down here half an hour ago, hair all on end. She's hid behind the washboard."

There are some people who bustle and talk their way through fear, and Mrs. Callaghan is such a one. She talks as aircraft thrum closer, as she puts the tea cosy on the pot, turns off the gas at the meter, and unfolds the deckchairs which Mr. Gibbons helpfully brought in from the shed. She is outraged at the slightest thing (awful how that canvas has faded) as well as weightier issues of the day (sure, what is there to bomb down this way after all? Unless it's them soldiers up to something in the park; she'd lay good money that it is. Why they can't do whatever it is they're doing somewhere there aren't so many people is beyond her).

Charlotte, though, goes still, and quiet. When Mrs. Callaghan settles herself in her deckchair, a blanket over her knees, and gets out her rosary, Charlotte just perches at the kitchen table and traces the woodgrain with a thumbnail; and when the bombs begin to fall, distant for now, but streams of them, cascades, each single one of them punching a hole right through the old life into a new and uglier one, and the lights flicker, and Mrs. Callaghan whimpers, Charlotte silently takes a step aside, a step away from herself. She becomes the girl in a story that she is reading, a girl who is by turns clever and foolish and cunning and kind and occasionally downright bad, and who makes mistakes and sometimes even gets away with them, and who need not be judged so very harshly, or in truth be judged at all, because once you take that step away you can see how it all fits together, how it all makes sense, and you can forgive almost anything.

"There's the sighreen," Mrs. Callaghan says. "All clear. Thanks be to God."

Charlotte lifts her head like someone waking, though she had not been asleep. Here they are, still. Here they are. And she does not go all to pieces, it turns out; she can hold her nerve. Some of the old strategies are useful, after all.

"Half past six," Mrs. Callaghan says, peering at, then listening to, then winding her watch.

The cat emerges from behind the washboard. Mrs. Callaghan clicks her tongue to call her over, smooths her fur with strokes from skull to tail-tip.

"Turn the gas back on for us, lovie?" Mrs. Callaghan asks. "We'll have a cuppa, eh? I'm parched."

Charlotte turns on the supply, lights the gas under the kettle. The flame is feeble. It'll take a month to boil a kettle on that.

"I'll go out for a bit, I think; see what's what."

She opens the front door on an early twilight. It feels untimely, wrong; like waking to snow in June, or to roses blooming in January. Off to the right, the sky is flushed, as though the sun has set in the north today. Her neighbours are gathering in the street, all staring off in that direction. Charlotte moves to join them. There's a bonfire-night smell in the air. She looks towards the centre of the city.

Where the docks and wharves and warehouses had glinted in the sun and elephant balloons had hung in the air above St. Paul's, there now burns a solid mass of flame. Boiling black smoke rises, spilling across the sky, cutting out the sun. A few remaining barrage balloons writhe, wounded, and as she watches, another collapses to the earth, pulled down by the flames. And from everywhere, from near and far, comes the sound of bells. She turns to see a fire engine flash past the top of the street. Every appliance from all over the city must be racing towards the flames.

This is the end, she thinks; this must be the end of everything.

Saskia. High up in her mansion flat in Chelsea.

Janet. Just across the river, in half-rotten Battersea.

El. There's that power station just a few streets over from her house in St. John's Wood. They might have gone for that. Oh God.

Charlotte's thoughts spiral out from there to her colleagues in their cramped corner of the Ministry of Information. Stella, who's always rushing off to meet her fiancé—Charlotte doesn't even know where Stella lives; Mrs. Denby, who treks in and out daily from the northern suburbs, which might mean she's escaped this; but, goodness, poor Mr. Jackson, the doorman at Saskia's building . . . there is just so much glass in that lobby; it's not right that an old man should be expected to guard a place like that, it doesn't even need guarding. Her thoughts then shift to people she doesn't exactly know, but whose lives glance against hers: the woman at the flower stall at London Bridge with her rheumy eyes; the barrel-bodied fellow behind the refreshment room counter at Victoria; and that slight young man she sometimes sees in Russell Square, who sits on his one particular bench and feeds the birds and thinks nobody notices. The idea any single one of them should just stop is not to be borne.

Her family, though; they'll be fine. She's confident of this. Her father and stepmother might be in the flat in Mayfair, but most likely they are out at Longwood; either way, they'll remain unscathed. They always do. And she can't imagine a disaster striking Francesca, not in Surrey. This is the thing about her people: whatever happens to the world around them, they are always and forever perfectly all right.

She spots Kaatje Beck standing on the pavement just outside her front gate, her arms around her nieces' shoulders, their clothes bright blotches of colour on this grey afternoon. The girls had arrived here from Belgium mute and saucer-eyed, with not much more than the clothes they were wearing; since then, Miss Beck has managed to dress them cheerfully—though on quite what it is difficult to imagine—and teach them the bones of English, which the influence of local playmates has fleshed out beautifully. The girls had lost that fearful look.

They had, Charlotte thinks, been happy here. They had been her evidence, that even when dreadful things had happened, it was still possible to get on with life, and be more or less all right.

And now this.

Miss Beck notices her approaching, turns her dark eyes away from the burning city.

"I'm sorry," Charlotte says.

Miss Beck shakes her head; she doesn't have the words.

"How are you, girls? Are you all right?"

The girls peel pale faces from their aunt's flanks. That look is back.

"Don't worry, Ilse," Charlotte says. "Hedy, don't worry."

Even though you fled this once already. Even though you left your parents and your family and all your friends, and everything that was familiar and loved, only for the monster to chase you here.

"They've been training for this." Charlotte has to clear her throat. "It might look bad, but they've been training for this. So we mustn't worry overmuch. It'll be all right. You'll see."

Miss Beck squeezes the girls closer. "That's right, girls. Listen to Miss Richmond. It will all come right."

But the look she gives Charlotte is one of dread.

Back in the house, Charlotte lifts the telephone receiver. The line is dead, of course. She hangs it up, goes down to the basement and Mrs. Callaghan, and accepts a cup of tea, which is not as hot nor strong as one might wish, but she is grateful for it.

"Is this from your ration?"

Mrs. Callaghan wafts the concern away, but Charlotte spoons some of her leaves into Mrs. Callaghan's tin.

"What should we do?" Mrs. Callaghan wants to know. "What do you think we should do?"

Where does one start? The chaos up there in the city is too vast to take in, too overwhelming to imagine. One couldn't make any difference to it. There will also be smaller pockets of harm all over town, but where to go, and what to do when one gets there? Charlotte has read the leaflets and been to the training sessions, but that's very much what to do when a bomb lands on your doorstep or someone nearby has a broken arm, and that's not the case right now. Nothing has really happened here. Anyway, it's long been established that Charlotte is not in any way useful. If she tried to help, she would only get in the way, and so the best thing for her to do is nothing, and so that is what she does. It doesn't feel good. It doesn't feel right, when so many people are in such desperate trouble, and so many others are racing to help them.

She goes with Mrs. Callaghan, though, keeping her company as they reclaim the rest of the house. She eases the doors open and peers in cautiously; she half expects the rooms beyond to be wiped out and nothing left but a fizzing void, like a radio tuned to static. But everything is, disconcertingly, just as they had left it. After that, Mrs. Callaghan tries to settle to her knitting, but instead frets about her sister, and that her sister might be fretting about her, and can't decide whether it would be all right to go out looking for a working telephone, in the hopes of getting through to the box on Edith Road in Liverpool and some kind soul fetching her sister, or if that would be unhelpful to the War Effort. And what if their own line gets fixed while she's out, and her sister rings up then, and they miss each other? And so Mrs. Callaghan stays put and slips stitches and frets about this moral and logistical complexity and sniffs and dabs her nose.

Mr. Gibbons does not come home. And soon, after everything, this Saturday takes on a wet Sunday feel: one cannot go out, one cannot settle to anything, one cannot be of any use, and the prospect of tomorrow promises no relief from the outrage and the grief and the worry and the ennui.

Charlotte retires early to her room but doesn't try to sleep. Sleep is not her friend these days; she doesn't feel easy in its company. It takes French leave at night, then ambushes her out of nowhere on the Tube or in the cinema, dragging her down to places that she doesn't want to go. Instead, she opens her skylight and leans out again among the chimney pots and pigeons. The birds coo and flap, hundreds of them crowding together; they must've fled here from the flames. The air reeks of burning; it's getting dark, but above the city, the sky is coral.

What use blackout now, she thinks. And where were the guns when they needed them?

You see them everywhere, driven round on trailers, set up on flat rooftops; they'd walked past the Regent's Park AA emplacement just yesterday. And yet she didn't hear a single shot fired in defence. They must have their reasons; you don't really know what else might be going on. The RAF will be up there, harrying the raiders, and the gunners can't risk hitting our boys; maybe falling shells are considered too much of a danger to the population below. But if that's the case, they should have thought of it already; why bother setting up all these guns if they can't risk firing them? Was it just to reassure us? To make us think we are defended? So we don't *all* run away from London? So we don't all huddle in the Underground and refuse ever to come out again?

Charlotte rubs at her arms; they're rough with goosebumps. The hair stands on the back of her neck. That faint thrum in the air, the tingle in the skin. The waterfall again, where there is no waterfall.

No, dear God, please, no.

She stares so hard that the sky seems to break apart, become at once liquid and granular, twisting and spinning like curdled milk in coffee. She can see nothing. But then a siren, distant, winds itself up into a wail, and another joins it, and another, and another, the fear tightening on her with each step closer to where she stands, leaning out her roof window, staring at the sky.

They're coming back. Already. It's about to start all over again.

She ducks back down inside her room, slams the window shut, grabs her things and races down the stairs. She catches Mrs. Callaghan just turning off the hissing wireless.

"The programme's interrupted," Mrs. Callaghan says, with false brightness. "Though I spect we shall catch the midnight news instead."

And Sunday

Charlotte lurches awake. Silence. Sunshine in her face. She presses her eyes, remembers dragging herself back upstairs to bed in the dark, after the all-clear sounded around five. She didn't even put the blackout up last night.

She checks her watch; it's nearly eleven now. Sleep had coshed her, but was mercifully dreamless. Perhaps after a day like that, the dreams had fled, knowing themselves outgunned.

She washes and dresses quickly—her bluebell-blue skirt, her good silk blouse, her summer coat. She lifts the telephone on her way past; it's still dead. She's not surprised. There are far more urgent problems today than a faulty domestic line or a damaged suburban exchange.

A blue tit picks insects off Mr. Pritchard's roses as Charlotte passes, heading for the bus stop. She's going to do the rounds. The Hartwells first, to see El. The scenes play out in her head, of relief and hugs and cups of tea. This then explodes into smoking ruins, blood and broken bodies. She waves these visions away; all will be well. All must be well. The Hartwells are a constant; they must tick on forever undisturbed. When she's checked on El, she'll go down to Chelsea and call on Saskia; it's been far too long already. Somewhere along the route, she'll find a working telephone and have a quick word with Janet. Or at least be informed as to what's keeping Janet from having a quick word with her. The important thing is to know that she's all right, and will be back in the office on Monday. And after that, Charlotte will be really brave and ring up her father, and let him inform her how marvellously well they are managing, and how ridiculous it is that everybody else is going to pieces. And Francesca. She'll have to call Francesca and hear about the trouble she's having with staff; a chronic complaint that's become acute since all the little treasures have found themselves jobs in factories, or enlisted.

And on Monday, she'll buy a bunch of whatever's looking fresh on the flower stand, and a bun from the café man, then she'll wander through Russell Square, just to be sure that the boy has returned to feed the birds. She'll go into work one way and back the other, to be certain of them all.

There are still buses, so the world hasn't ended. Only a handful of passengers are dotted about the lower deck. Charlotte makes her way to the back. The city reels past her window. Through the grey-green fog of mesh, it looks murky, seasick, but still recognisable; Michaelmas daisies and chrysanthemums brightening front gardens, the trees turning towards autumn; smartly painted front doors and polished windows. Then there's a stream of ash-faced figures pushing laden prams and handcarts along the pavement. But these are images from France, Belgium, Holland; they're supposed to be in black and white, not in London and in colour. Charlotte lights a cigarette. Her hands are trembling.

The bus turns abruptly; this is not the usual route. Here, the net curtains stir in the breeze, and the front gardens sparkle with glass, and all the leaves and flowers have been ripped away. Then another turn, and another. The light fades from the day, and the smell finds her. The smell of dark places, broken drains, plaster dust, and burning. A constable stands in the road, directing them down another side street; ashes fall on him like snow.

Charlotte looks out on a wilderness of broken brick. Two women, each with a bushel basket on her hip, pick through the rubble. The way they move reminds Charlotte of farmworkers on the estate in Galloway, when they're gathering in the freshly dug potatoes. The nearer woman lifts something from the ground; it's pale, but gleams gold. She drops it into the basket, shakes her fingers out. It's only then that Charlotte realises what she's witnessed. They are gathering up bodies. Or rather, bits of bodies. That was a severed hand, still wearing a gold ring. Then the bus lurches on, and they peel dizzyingly out across a bridge into open sky, over water. Below her, barges drift at odd angles, smouldering. Then they are back in the hot darkness of the far bank, and Charlotte takes another drag of her cigarette, and thinks: We are done for, all of us. We are destroyed. All it took was just one day.

But El's part of London, it turns out, is not yet at war. It's an ordinary Sunday morning here. The Hartwell house is a peppermint, smooth and fresh. Not a crack in the stucco, not a single broken pane. And it's occupied and awake: smoke coils from the chimney pots and the drawing-room curtains are open. Charlotte hadn't realised how much fear she'd held at bay; she's now limp with relief.

She rings the bell, settles back, waiting under the protection of the portico. All will be well. All is always well when she is here. The first time, she was twelve years old, fetched from school along with Elena at the start of the autumn half-term holiday; Mrs. Hartwell had driven her cracking four-speed Wolseley Hornet herself. The place had looked like a doll's house after Longwood; all up and down and no sideways; as though the front might open up to show all the tiny furniture and fittings and the servants on the stairs.

And Mrs. Hartwell was so very *present;* inviting one close for a tête-à-tête or whisking one on towards the next delight, as though the whole of life were one whirling dance. The buzz of friends; the children's friends as well as the parents'. Older brother Clive bringing the whole rugby team back after practice, kitbags dumped in the hall-way; "Tea please, if you would, Lily." Poor Lily, having to rustle up tea for fifteen, twenty if the reserves came too. El noodling away at the piano, or at her clarinet. Mr. Hartwell, an older father, genially handed out sixpences, and could even, Charlotte was shocked to discover, be teased. These parents asked questions, they listened to replies; you could say what you thought and they didn't laugh. And when the time had come for Charlotte to go home, the Daimler idling in the street, Mr. Parkin staring dead ahead in the driver's seat, Charlotte had been wrapped in Mrs. Hartwell's fragrant embrace, had had a kiss bestowed upon her forehead, and had gone as stiff as a broom. She had felt those arms around her and the warm print on her skin all the way home. Longwood, with its dog-legged corridors and pinched windows and rooms opening off rooms, was cold. In the winter drawing room, her mother had offered a cool cheek and had hoped that Charlotte had not picked up any bad habits, and her father had spun the ice in his glass and added, "Or fleas."

Charlotte had smiled at the joke. She'd said, "They were all very nice, in fact."

Her father had raised his eyebrows, made no further comment.

"They make their own money, darling," her mother had explained. "They can't be *very* nice."

Now, though, the front door of the Hartwell house is cracked open and the maid appears, a solid aproned presence on the threshold.

"Morning, Lily. Is the family at home?"

Lily gives a not-really-necessary bob. "No, miss, I'm afraid not."

"They're out, are they?"

"Same as yourself, miss. Out and about."

Charlotte supposes it makes sense. With many of the phone lines down, much of London's unbombed population will be chasing around the city to see how their friends are holding up, only to find they're off doing the same.

"But everyone's well, Lily? Everyone's safe. That's the main thing."

"As you say, miss. Shall I take a message?"

"Not to worry. I'll ring up later. When I can."

"Good morning, then, miss." Lily is already closing the door. There's the sound of her hard shoes on the tiles.

Charlotte lopes down the steps, but pauses under the tree; its branches reach up towards El's window. The blackout is still in place, even though everybody's up and out; Lily will catch it for that.

But it is a relief to know that all is well, and that the house will continue to tick on, with Mrs. Hartwell the turning cog at the centre of it all; that Lily will go on running up and down the stairs; that Mr. Hartwell will snore of an afternoon with crumbs strewn down his waistcoat; that Clive will still drop his kitbag and expect tea for twenty; and that El will spin around that so-familiar room, while beneath her whirling feet still lies their secret cache of sweets and cigarettes, of gin and confidences. That's good enough for now.

. . .

Charlotte sways along in the brown soup of the Underground, and then climbs up into the daylight at Walham Green and heads along the Fulham Road. One of the wonderful things about her godmother Saskia is her capacity for living beautifully: if there is orange pekoe tea to be had in England, Saskia will have charmed some into her caddy; if almond thins are still being baked in these trying times, Saskia will have a dozen laid out in a translucent fan on a plate hand-painted by a friend. And there will be some new enthusiasm, purchase, or girl—there always is—just as there'll always be sunshine on warm parquet, gorgeous clothes, portraits, masks, maquettes and *objets trouvés*—all the joyous clutter that clouds around her godmother.

Charlotte spins in through the revolving doors. Mr. Jackson has embellished his usual livery with an ARP band; a helmet hangs with the keys behind his desk. The floor-to-ceiling windows have all been pasted with gauze, but still she doesn't like it. The old fellow shouldn't have to stand here, in mausoleum gloom, just waiting for it to explode around him.

"Very glad to see you, miss."

"You too, Mr. Jackson. Still standing, I see! Good good good."

There's a congratulatory feel to the encounter. She'd like to shake his hand, but they do look sore; swollen joints stretch his gloves.

"Well, I shall just pop up to Lady Bowers then, if I may." Now it comes to it, she feels quite giddy at the prospect. She shouldn't wait for a disaster to prod her into this.

"I do believe she's in, her and her companion. Though the lift is broke, I'm sorry to say."

Charlotte thanks him, races up the stairs. A new girl, then. She does like to meet the new girls. It will be interesting to see who Saskia's beguiled into her bed this time; she favours the heavy-limbed daughters of good families, and has cut a swathe through them across half of Europe. There had been a story, not completely understood by Charlotte as a child—though she had known from her father's arch tone and her mother's silence that it was one of those bright, sharp-edged things that he'd bring out to cause discomfort—that Saskia, when she was young, had fallen head over heels for a brainy grammar-school type, who had in the end preferred bad food and hard sums at one of the Oxford women's colleges, to larking about in London with Saskia and the fast set, and that this had left Saskia bereft. Which, if true, went some way towards explaining Saskia's subsequent profligacy of the heart.

The building is undamaged by the raids, but the loss of younger staff is showing; the stair carpet is trailed with dirt and the brass bannister is smudged and dull. It's only three floors up, but by the time Charlotte gets to Saskia's door she has to stop and catch her breath. It's a tad concerning.

She hears voices coming from inside the flat. Definitely home, then. She brushes down her coat, then raises a hand to knock.

The *tone,* though. She hesitates. It's not quite an argument, but the tone is not quite *nice.* There's a low, insistent, anxious murmur—this is Saskia's voice, but not Saskia as Charlotte has ever heard her before— which the other cuts across. The words are inaudible, but their tenor is clear: forceful, admonishing. Saskia counters, louder now. The other voice barks back.

Charlotte's hand drops away from the door. She should go. Take herself across the river and see how welcome she might be at the Fuller house on their busiest day of the week . . . But she *wants* to see Saskia; she hasn't seen Saskia in an age. She wants orange pekoe tea, almond thins and accounts of Saskia's glamourous fun; so she makes a radio play of her arrival, shifting her weight from foot to foot, clearing her throat, flapping her coat around. The voices stop dead. She raps on the door.

Movement, footsteps, and the door sneaks open. A pinched face, sallow skin, a sharp, officious air. Charlotte instinctively steps back.

"Can I help you?" the woman asks.

"Uh, good . . ." Charlotte peers at her watch. "Afternoon. Yes. Is Lady Bowers at home?"

"We're not expecting visitors."

We? That's a tad proprietorial, from a new girl. "I won't stay a moment. I came to see Saskia."

The woman cocks her head. "Pertaining to what?"

"Pertaining to how she's getting on, after last night." Ridiculous. Charlotte calls past the woman, into the flat: "I may come in, mayn't I, Sas? I don't bite, do I?"

A voice calls from inside the room: "Oh, is that you, Lottie dear?"

"Certainly is!"

"Come on in, my darling, come on in. Don't mind Mary; she doesn't bite either."

The woman pulls her face out of its scowl and manages to match Charlotte's shallow smile. She opens the door.

The bones of the apartment are just as Charlotte remembers them; the white floor-length curtains, the amber sheen of the parquet, the low occasional tables and the yellow brocade chairs angled towards the rosy bars of the electric fire. Beyond that, everything is changed. Dust spins in shafts of light. The room smells stale. The remains of breakfast are lying out on the sideboard—or perhaps several breakfasts, and maybe lunches, teas and dinners too. Other surfaces are clustered with cups and glasses; the ashtrays overflow with lipsticked stubs. It's the same place, but the place is not the same; it is as though Charlotte's fairy godmother—now rising unsteadily from one of the brocade chairs—has herself fallen under some kind of spell.

"Charlotte, my darling."

Her voice is unchanged, rich and warm. Her face, though, seems to be suffering from the same malaise as the apartment—the structures still sound, but the surface seedy and neglected. Her eyes are dull, her skin has coarsened, and her make-up is creased and clotted; it was clearly not applied today.

Charlotte, moving towards her godmother, is at the same time monitoring her own performance, trying not to let the shock show. Because this is not like Saskia; she likes a drink, but stone-solid drunk by lunchtime? No.

Saskia lays her long white arms around Charlotte's neck and pulls her close. She inhales the smell of her godmother's stale perfume, cigarettes and booze, and sour skin. Charlotte fights the urge to push away.

"So you've come all this way just to see little old me?"

"Wanted to make sure you're still alive."

"Very good of you, dearest. So few people bother. Well, as you see, we are scraping by, scraping by. Here, let me look at you . . ."

Held at arm's length now, the two women consider each other. Charlotte maintains a smile as Saskia's eyes explore her face, and a greyed hand comes up to cup her cheek.

"Beautiful, my darling. The very spit of your dear mother."

People say this; Charlotte doesn't see it.

"Come, sit, sit." Saskia waves Charlotte towards the couch and returns to her own seat; she retrieves her glass, smudged and warm-looking, from the clutter.

The new girl, Mary, stands just inside the door; she watches everything.

"Tell me, darling," Saskia asks, "where have you been hiding your-self all this time?"

"Under a stone."

"Very wise, very wise. Safest place for you."

"The shelters can get a tad frowsty, don't you find?"

"Oh, this old city is just altogether too full now, I should say."

"Do you think? It seems to me half-empty nowadays."

Saskia widens her beautiful bloodshot eyes. "Oh yes, our people. *Our* people have gone. But, darling, the *others;* they just keep pouring in."

"Ah."

"And we're not even interning them any more, did you know that? All these *soi-disant* refugees. All they have to do is say they're Jews and they're let go anywhere they please. It seems we're too polite to even ship them off to Canada any more. Did you hear?"

"After the *Arandora Star* was sunk, Sas. You can't just push people off in boats across the Atlantic. Not now it's full of wolves."

"But we'll still send our children, the poor mites."

"Their parents have the choice, I believe."

"Well, it's all very vexing, I say. Who even really knows who any-body is any more?"

"I'd say the bombing's more of an immediate worry."

"Ah, but how do they know *where* to bomb?" Mary interjects. "The enemy's intelligence seems to be excellent, don't you think? Almost prescient. It's like they *know*."

"Oh, I dare say they do know. A decent map—what would that have cost before the war? Three shillings? Any sense and they'd have stocked up on them when they were first hatching their plans. And then there's the Thames. What a giveaway. Good luck blacking that out."

The new girl makes a moue, dismissive. Rattled, Charlotte's thoughts stretch back to earlier that summer, when she'd been in the first throes of grief over Eddie. Saskia had scooped her up and brushed her down and blown her nose and taken her out for tea at Fortnum's, a silver vase of white freesias on the table, and Saskia entirely herself, her concern profound, her support unyielding, even though she herself was clearly wracked with grief for that darling foolish boy. Drinking, yes, but by then it was teatime, and that was just a solicitous *coupe de champagne* to soften the jagged edges. Nobody got drunk. There was none of this jarring disagreement. Saskia seems so changed since then. These have been strange times, and they've affected people in strange ways, but this is stranger than most. Charlotte blames—look at her there, leaning in the doorway pouting like an adolescent—the skinny, awkward, why-is-Saskia-with-her-anyway girl.

"What have you been up to yourselves?" Charlotte asks, hoping for insight, but also simply to shift the conversation from this kind of unedifying gossip. Everybody knows it doesn't help. They're told so often enough.

"Oh, surviving! Barely surviving! It seems to take up all one's time these days."

Then Mary pushes away from the doorjamb and patters across the room, heading for the bedroom door, which Charlotte now notices is standing ajar. Mary must just have noticed too, and realised that Charlotte has, from her seat, a prime view of the more intimate chaos beyond. The bed a tangle of sheets, underwear strewn over a chair, drawers half open, wardrobe gaping, papers all over Saskia's bureau, and what appears to be a microscope—one of Saskia's new enthusiasms, no doubt—sticking out of a continent of correspondence. It's such a mess in there, you'd think it had taken a direct hit.

The door shut, the young woman returns to her post, her expression at once ingratiating and defiant.

"Aren't you ever going to introduce us, Saskia?" the creature says.

"Oh my goodness. Where are my manners? Mary dearest, this is

Charlotte Richmond, my god-daughter; you remember me talking about Charlotte. I talk about you all the time, darling. And, Charlotte, this is my dear friend Miss Mary Clarke."

Mary moves in with hand extended. "With an 'e,' " she says. "Clarke with an 'e.' "

Charlotte half-rises to take her hand. It is thin and dry, sticks wrapped in autumn leaves. Charlotte seats herself again, smiling from her godmother to her godmother's baffling friend.

"Pleased to meet you," Charlotte lies.

"I am so glad that you have," Saskia says. "I've been dying to see you, darling, dying for you girls to meet, but one gets so wrapped up in one's own affairs, doesn't one?"

"One does."

"Shall we have a drink?" Mary asks.

"Oh. Why not? If you'd like. What d'you say, Lottie?"

"Shall I call Florence?" Charlotte asks. Florence could whisk away some of the dishes, empty the ashtrays and maybe even open a window and let in some fresh air.

"Goodness me, darling. Florence is long gone. Mary's all the help I need."

Mary demonstrates this by fetching the decanter and a glass from the sideboard. She hands the glass to Charlotte and gives her a splash, then pours a healthy measure into Saskia's smudged tumbler, then just a whisper into her own. She perches on the arm of Saskia's chair, plonks the decanter on the floor, then gently spins her whiff of drink.

"Cin-cin." Saskia raises her glass.

"Your excellent good health," Charlotte says.

"Cheers."

Charlotte sips spiced rum, licks the burn from off her lips, glancing from Saskia to Mary and back again. She just doesn't get this.

"So what do you do, Miss Clarke?" Charlotte asks.

Saskia answers for her: "Oh, Mary gets up to all sorts of mischief."

Mary's lips twist, but Saskia carries on, unconcerned.

"We met . . ." Saskia's expression crumples with mirth. "Would you believe it, we met at the glove counter at Derry & Toms. D'you remember, Mary?"

"Naturally."

"It was her hands I noticed first."

"It would be, on the glove counter," Charlotte says.

"She has the nicest hands you can imagine."

Quite deliberately, Mary puts her glass down and folds her hands in her lap so they can't be seen. She meets Charlotte's gaze steadily. A shop girl too; not Saskia's usual type at all.

"You don't work, I take it," Mary says.

"On the contrary, I am kept quite busy nowadays."

"Oh really. I wouldn't have thought you'd have needed to."

Mary can think what she pleases. "I'm at the Ministry of Information. Home Intelligence."

Which sounds quite grand, so long as Charlotte doesn't mention what she actually does. Let Mary consider it a necessary veil of wartime discretion.

"Mary has *causes*," Saskia announces.

Mary gives Saskia a quelling look, which Saskia wafts aside.

"We both do—we *share* causes. I mean, I've always had *interests,* but she's just so practical and useful. She wants to help all sorts of people—unwed mothers, alcoholics, the mentally defective. She's a force of nature."

Charlotte raises her glass. "Good for you."

"I do think we are called upon to do more than just take care of ourselves," Mary announces. "We owe it to our fellow creatures, when faced with these times of great upheaval, to do what we can to change society for the better."

"How very true," Saskia says. "Such a wise head on young shoulders."

Charlotte has the feeling that she—her vapid, flawed and impractical self—is being very deliberately and precisely needled, and by someone who doesn't even know her. She watches as Saskia leans against Mary, looking up at her. Charlotte sees affection there, and intimacy, and something else too, that Charlotte cannot quite at this moment name. Next time, she thinks, she will definitely arrange to meet Saskia away from home. Lure her out to Fortnum's for tea; feed her tiny sandwiches and cakes; keep her sober; keep her away from this strange and stuffy ménage for an hour or two, and pick away at it a bit, find out what's going on.

"Speaking as one of the mentally defective," Charlotte adds, "may I say how delighted I am to hear that our interests are being taken into account."

Saskia gives out a great hoot of laughter.

Mary glares from Saskia to Charlotte and back again, annoyed to be excluded from the joke.

"My darling god-daughter," Saskia explains, "did a spell in the loony bin a while ago."

Mary makes a *fancy that* kind of a face, bottom lip pushed out, eyebrows up. She looks Charlotte over.

Go ahead, Charlotte thinks. Have a good old gander. Bloody tourists.

"But darling Lottie's being facetious, of course. She's not *defective*. If anything, her problem is that her capacities are *too* strong, I think; she's forever being carried off by them, to all kinds of strange places. Aren't you, darling?"

"You are too kind, Sas. You always have been." Charlotte tips the last drops of rum onto her tongue. "I don't deserve you."

"Ah, darling."

"No one does. You take care of yourself, do you hear me? Pleasure to meet you, Mary."

Charlotte pushes herself up from her seat. She gives a nod to the new girl, in the hopes there'll be a different new girl soon.

Charlotte closes the apartment door behind her, rests her forehead against it. She blows out a breath. She's about to turn away, but then the voices start up again. The same pattern as before, but with greater urgency. Saskia wheedling and anxious; a few dismissive words from Mary, then Saskia's complaint resumes. Charlotte rolls her forehead against the wooden panel in a slow negation: no orange pekoe tea, no almond thins, no charmed and fragrant atmosphere. Slovenly, contrary, and ugly-drunk; this is not *her* Saskia. The only consolation is that Saskia's romances never last, even when the girls are loveliness itself. So, really, all Charlotte has to do is leave them to drift apart, or to implode. Then Saskia will be rid of Mary Clarke and can begin to live beautifully again.

Charlotte peels herself off the door and plods down the stairs. She's fuzzy with rum, a headache starting. She descends into the still pool of the lobby.

"Safe home now."

"Cheerio, Mr. Jackson."

She spins out of the revolving doors into brilliant low sun. Shielding her eyes, she descends the steps. The stale indoors hangs queasily around her. She'll go straight back to her digs and have a bath, if Mrs. Callaghan will let her. And if there is gas to heat the water. And water to be heated. She turns towards the Tube, and blunders straight into someone. Strong hands catch her by the shoulders, stop her in her tracks.

"God. Sorry," Charlotte says. "I couldn't see a thing for all this light."

He's solid. A slab of grey herringbone twill. He lets go of her, and she ducks past him, too embarrassed to look him in the eye. He'll think she's a drunk, stumbling around in broad daylight, smelling of spiced rum. It is all so sordid and depressing. She wants urgently to be home. Never mind the bath. Lock herself in her room and not come out till Monday. She hurries down the street without a backwards glance.

He, though, stands on the corner, and watches her go.

The Boy Who Feeds the Birds

The chaffinch weighs nothing. Its claws barely pinch his thumb; its head tilts to keep one bright eye trained on him as it jabs at the broken biscuit; the tiny stabbing in his palm makes him smile. It grabs a crumb, then flitters off. On the path, sparrows hop and pick at flakes of pastry that he's scattered. He has to be discreet, keeps an eye out for police, or for anyone who looks his way too long; there'd be hell to pay if he's caught feeding the birds. Well, there'd be a fine. But he loves their trust, their greed, their fragile beauty. One must find one's happiness where one can, and he finds it in the quiet, illicit dispensation of crumbs.

Someone is coming down the path towards him. He brushes his palms off and the birds scatter; they tweet their protest from the bushes. He pulls his memoranda book from his pocket. Honest, Officer, just taking a breather, just jotting down a few musings; what birds? Oh, those birds! Terrible nuisance, aren't they?

He doesn't look directly, but detects as they come closer that the figure isn't dressed in dark Peeler blue. He gets an impression instead of lush colour. But even then, you never know. An ordinary citizen will sometimes go out of their way to give you trouble.

He looks up. And it's her. His heart goes still. The girl. The honey-coloured girl is coming towards him. She moves with that easy loping gait of hers; she wears a bluebell-coloured skirt and cream silk blouse, underneath a leaf-green summer coat.

Beautiful.

Mustn't stare.

Where's that pencil? He searches through his pockets. If he can just scribble something in his notebook; just to have something to do. Pencil. Pencil. Pencil. Where is his godforsaken pencil?

He has tried all his jacket pockets, and is reaching into his left trouser pocket—though why would anyone keep a pencil there just to get stabbed in the thigh?—when she stops directly in front of him. He slides his hand from his pocket, and lays it over the other, which is resting on the memoranda book. He looks slowly up.

Dear God, let her not be one of those people who'll go out of their way to tell you what you're doing wrong. That would be so disappointing.

Her eyes are unusual; a clear light brown, like milkless tea. He has never been close enough to notice before. She has a funny kind of look about her, at once determined and exhausted and concerned. And then she smiles. A huge guileless smile, full of pleasure.

"There you are," she says. And she sits down beside him.

There, undeniably, he is; he has never felt more so. Never felt more wedged into the reality of his body. Never more aware of the distinctness of this bench, this patch of gravel, these shrubs and plane trees. His black clothes. Her.

"I *am* glad to see you," she says.

"Really?"

He can smell her now: honeysuckle, to match the hair. He's seen her come and go but has had no more expectation of being noticed by her than by the kingfisher that skims over the canal. She smooths her skirt, smiles round at him. She seems—bizarrely—to be delighted by his presence. This is impossible; it must be a dream. His teeth are going to fall out into his hand. Next thing will be that he's back at school, naked, and late for an exam.

"I've seen you here, feeding the birds—"

"Just crumbs." He fumbles to defend himself. "What I give them, it's no use to anyone, whatever the rules may be."

"Oh yes. I didn't for a moment mean to imply . . ."

The birds have begun to bob closer again, shaming him. His cheeks burn. "They depend on us, the city birds. They have for generations. To stop feeding them, all of a sudden . . ."

"I never thought of it like that before." She grips a ringless hand over each knee, watching them. "They are dears, aren't they? I wish I had something to give them."

So she is not, thank goodness, one of those people.

"Do you live round here?" she asks, gesturing to the smart town-houses, the baroque hotel, the general genteel loveliness. He almost laughs, then sees that this is a genuine question.

"Not so far away," he says, and coughs to cover his amusement. "I used to come here for the museum. Now it's closed, but I still come here. Habit, I suppose. It's one of the things I miss most, of all the changes. What about you?"

"What do I miss most?" She fixes a strange gaze on him.

"I mean . . . No, I mean, you must work round here?" And then he bites the inside of his cheek. It's not that he even stared, when she was walking by; he just couldn't help but notice. He was always well aware that her loveliness didn't have anything to do with him.

She gives a nod towards Senate House, where it peers out over a row of brick-and-stucco. "In that mad ziggurat over there. Just can't quite face going in yet."

"Oh yes," he says. "Me too."

"You work for the Ministry?"

"No, no. Just that I can't face work sometimes."

She sighs. "I die every day out of sheer boredom. And yet . . ." She gets to her feet. "Once more unto the breach, dear friends."

"But what was it?"

She looks at him, nonplussed.

"What did you want?" he asks.

"Oh," she says. "That was it. That was everything."

"What was?"

"Just to see you. After this weekend, all the mayhem and misery, I was just glad to see you here again. Like nothing in the world had changed."

"I see." It's a job of work to keep a grin from splitting his face in two.

A cuff tweaked back from a golden watch. "Yikes. Back to the typeface. Cheerio, then."

"Cheerio."

She gives him a wave, and dashes away.

The birds scatter, chirp irritably. He watches her go, her coat rippling, her honey hair escaping into curls beneath her light summer hat. She clangs out of the far gate. And then she's out of sight.

It's only then that he realises he's been holding his breath. He picks up his memoranda book and spots the pencil. It's where he always keeps it, tucked into the spine.

"Ha."

Grasping the back of the bench, he heaves himself to his feet. He slips his frail right hand deep into a coat pocket, still smiling to himself.

Well, that was one hell of a day, and it's not even nine o'clock yet.

He limps away, along the path, towards the far gate, heading for work, and home.

Slight Comforts

O h good," Charlotte says. "You're here!"

"Yes, thank God, we made it through. Though some poor souls . . ." Janet's eyes widen to convey unspoken horrors. "Perhaps I shouldn't have come in, in the circumstances. There is so much to be done in the parish . . . But this is war work too. I can't neglect it."

"Certainly not. We depend on you."

Janet looks grateful. She tucks her hands in under her thighs. Her maroon costume is well brushed and tidy. Charlotte knows she's also exercising extraordinary self-restraint in not once glancing at her watch while Charlotte hangs up her coat, then unpins her hat and attempts to tidy her unruly hair.

Stella joins them, with a nod, in a hurry but not quite late, looking as clean and fresh as a snowdrop. They say good morning, Stella already busily organising her desk, though it never looks anything other than organised.

"But it was bad, then?" Charlotte asks Janet. "I thought it must have been bad." Where Janet lives in Battersea, the streets are stuffed to bursting; all the decent houses have been subdivided into tiny lodgings, cheap terraces are crushed stuffily close. You couldn't drop a teaspoon in Battersea without hitting someone.

Janet slides her hands out from underneath herself to show them; lace cuffs fall away. Her nails are broken to the quick, strips of livid nailbed showing. The skin is scratched and scabbed. "You?"

Charlotte wafts the question aside, aghast. "You were digging people out? With your bare hands?"

"Clearing work, rather than digging. Those terraces just collapse like cards. I should have thought to bring my gardening gloves."

"Oh goodness."

"I came in early to have a wash at the sink here. We've no hot water; no gas. My hair—" She grimaces, touches it with her sore hands, her cuffs falling back.

"Looks lovely," Charlotte says. It's powdered with pale dust. "Have you slept?"

"Not really."

"Maybe you should go home, Jan. Get some rest."

Janet twists to look over her shoulder to the cubbyhole office. Mrs. Denby's dark shape moves around behind the partition. She's sorting out the morning's work.

Janet drops her voice: "I'll get more rest here."

Mrs. Denby emerges. The folders, each one stuffed with documents, look fatter than ever. It seems a kind of mythological torment to Charlotte, that each day she must work her way, sheet by slender sheet, through the whole lot, only to be presented with a new and thicker heap the next morning.

"What about you, though?" Janet asks.

"We escaped it. We're just spectators so far."

Charlotte beams at Mrs. Denby, who slides a heap of typing into her in-tray. Janet is already tamping together sheets of carbon paper and foolscap folio. Stella is fondly dusting her machine, emerald glinting on her finger. Her fiancé is a sound engineer at the BBC; she is proudly apologetic about the terrible myopia that prevents him from enlisting.

Charlotte lifts the leatherette cover off her machine and folds it away. Tedium hangs in the air, along with the dust. She leafs through the top few sheets. Regional reports, transcribed by hand from the telephone, to be typed up in triplicate. She prefers these to the forms—all those numbers, she's forever catching herself transposing digits or missing tabs and having to cross bits out with a row of Xs. It gets messy and embarrassing. These narrative reports of daily life in the provinces are much more easily transcribed. The domestic woes of housewives in Barrow-in-Furness; the rumours of enemy parachutists in Hull. Children have been flying kites in Scarborough, and some concerned individual wonders if this really should be allowed. Charlotte can't see why they shouldn't fly their kites, the poor things; let them grab what fun they can.

These reports, with their glimpses of different, fretful, scattered lives, might be preferable to the forms, but she is dashed if she understands to what official use they can be put. Not that that's any of her business. She's here to type. So she sets herself to the task. At least the handwriting on this first one is clear. Suspicions of fifth-columnist activity in Worcestershire: a copse, recently cut back, has been shaped to resemble an arrow; where it's pointing, though, the reporter simply cannot say.

It's pointing, Charlotte thinks, to your lost marbles, chum.

She taps in the heading, and the date, then she says: "Did he tell you I telephoned?"

Janet's hands go still. "Pardon?"

"On Saturday. I rang you up. Seems like a different world now, doesn't it?"

"I wish I'd known," Janet says.

"Didn't he say?"

"No. But then we've been so busy."

"It was nothing. I just wondered if you might like to go for a walk, or for coffee, it wasn't much of a plan. And it all seems so frivolous now, doesn't it?"

"That would have been nice, though."

"On Sunday, I thought I might call again just to see you were all right, but somehow I just got . . ." Incapacitated. Lowered. By calling at my godmother's. The light blinding in the street. Blundering into that brick of a man. "Well," Charlotte says. "You know."

"It wouldn't have mattered. I couldn't have got away." Janet bites her lip, eyes on her work.

Things must be very hard, Charlotte thinks, but she doesn't know what to say.

"That's pretty," Charlotte finally manages, inadequately, meaning the silky off-white cobwebs of lace.

"They were my mother's." Janet turns her hand to consider a cuff. "Funny what you can still find at the back of a drawer."

"The old things really last, don't they? New stuff's just not the same."

"Very true."

"I don't have anything of my mother's," Charlotte says.

Janet turns to her. "Not a thing?"

"Father had a bonfire."

"He didn't!"

Charlotte nods.

"No!"

Charlotte goes on nodding, but turns to her work, scrolls her papers in. When she looks up, Janet is still staring at her, sceptical, outraged. Helpfully distracted.

"Literally?" Janet asks.

Charlotte raises a cautionary finger to her lips, looks pointedly towards Mrs. Denby, who is bustling round the outer office, and then at Stella, who is already halfway through her first item.

Janet narrows her eyes at Charlotte, not knowing if it's all right to be amused.

And Charlotte's happy enough to have diverted her, even if it's only for a moment. She finds her home keys, straightens her back and neck, rolls her shoulders down and raises her wrists so that she's sitting like the lady in the illustration, at least while she remembers. Janet often has to remind her: adjust your wrists, back straight, or you'll regret it. It's tiring, but it saves you from the worst of the wear and tear.

Charlotte starts to type—slow, syncopated, a dripping gutter to the continuous pattering of rain from the others. She has to think about every single keystrike at first, but then she falls into the typing trance, becomes the unconscious conduit of information from one piece of paper to another.

For a while, all is going well, but then a finger slips and hits two keys at once, and the mechanism jams. She peers in at the metal tangle, picks at it with a fingernail and the hammers fall back into their designated slots. She wipes the inky fingertip ineffectually up and down her blotter, leaving a grey smudge.

Janet is pretending that she hasn't noticed; she is sitting beautifully upright, her wrists elevated in cascading lace, her eyes on a handwritten report and fingers dancing over the keys.

"At lunchtime," Charlotte says, "how about we buy Chelsea buns at Clarence's, and go and sit in the Square?"

Janet's shoulders slump; her wrists dip. She speaks without looking round. "I would *adore* that."

· · ·

At lunchtime, the offices decant themselves down the stairs and out into the squares and streets of Bloomsbury, where errands are run and lunches taken. A breath of air, a bun, a cigarette and a good long chin-wag is just what the doctor ordered. That, and maybe a blob of hand cream.

Stella's dashing off to meet her fiancé, as always, at Fitzroy Square, halfway between Broadcasting House and the Senate, so that they can share a meat pie and be happy. Charlotte, however, does not even get as far as the main doors. From the turn of the stairs, there's the first sight of the lobby, and a familiar figure waiting there. She stops dead.

"Oh God damn it all to hell."

Janet's gloved hand stalls on the bannister; she peers down too.

"Isn't that Sir Charles?"

Charlotte turns to her: "Janet, I'm so sorry."

"No, that's quite all right; I understand—"

"Can we postpone?"

"Of course. Of course we can. It doesn't matter."

"We'll do it tomorrow. I promise."

"Don't worry," Janet says. "Tomorrow will be just as good."

But Charlotte is already clattering down the stairs. Is she late? She better not be late. But how could she be late for something she didn't know was happening? If she'd known about it, she'd have written it in her diary in block capitals and double-underscored it—and she'd have been fretting about it ever since. Her father is an important man; more important than ever, now that there's a war on. He doesn't have the time or patience to be kept waiting by a scatterbrained daughter. There is no way she would let herself be late for him.

"Hallo, Daddy."

"Hallo, Lolo."

He opens his arms, and she steps in and is obliged as ever to kiss him on the lips and be prickled by the copper wire of his moustache. She steps back, smiles, and manages not to wipe the wet away.

"Not dead yet then?" he asks.

"Ha ha, not yet, no."

"Took a pounding though, your neck of the woods, I'll bet."

"We were lucky; we escaped the worst."

"Still determined to keep slumming it, then?"

Gipsy Hill is not a slum. It might not be Mayfair, but it's not a slum. There are roses growing in the gardens and the kids play in the sunshine and what slum ever had a more-than-decent milliners, she'd like to know? But she just laughs a light social laugh. Ha ha.

"Well then, luncheon." As though this had already been agreed. "I know a nice little place, just around the corner. You'll love it."

"Sounds marvellous."

He offers her his arm; she takes it, dazed by the swerve her day has been forced into. Outside, she spies Janet havering on the pavement. Janet will forgo the Chelsea bun along with the chinwag, drop her pennies into a charity box, and be faint with hunger by mid-afternoon, if she's left to her own devices. Janet, she fears, is really no good at all at being good to herself.

Charlotte's father presses her arm tight into his flank, reveals creamy teeth. She stretches her lips back too.

I do not want to do this, she thinks. I really do not want to do this at all.

"Lovely," she says.

Really, I should just kill myself and have done.

He has ushered her into so many restaurants just like this one—all starched linen and mahogany, a table that is already considered his— that one would think it was his life's work to accrue deference from as many different sets of waiters as possible. Charlotte, as usual, finds herself wondering what he thinks she will particularly love about it.

As they are being seated, he's telling her a story about his new secretary, pausing impatiently every time the maître d' or sommelier addresses them. Wine is ordered, tasted, approved of, and glasses filled. Then a waiter stands at her shoulder. Charlotte stares at the menu.

"The lemon sole, please."

Her father's lips bunch. He orders the veal kidneys, which must mean that veal kidneys are the correct dish for a man in his position, at luncheon.

"And the *pommes dauphinoise,* and the *épinards aux oeufs,* for the young lady."

The waiter murmurs, and is gone.

"You need to put some meat on your bones," her father says, and then resumes his story.

His account does at least suggest he spends *some* time at the office. Efficient, the new girl, he'll give her that, but quite extraordinarily plain, and so mouse-like as to make old Parkin leap screeching onto a chair. Charlotte smiles, though she has never known the Longwood housekeeper to be anything other than brutally efficient in the dispatch of mice. And—you'll like this, Lolo—one day when the secretary had just scurried out at the end of a meeting, Monty had said to him, *Did you ever see a nose like it?* And he himself had replied, quick as a flash: *I hear she's wearing it for a bet.*

"Ah ha," Charlotte says. "Ha."

But bet or no bet, it seems he'll be stuck with her forever; it's hardly likely she'll get married and leave them, not with her looks.

"Unless perhaps she meets another mouse," Charlotte cravenly suggests.

He slaps the table, laughs.

She hates herself.

The food arrives. The sole swims again in butter. The waiter heaps her plate with strata of cream-soaked potato, a mound of spinach clotted with egg. She holds up a hand to stop him.

"That all?" her father asks.

"That's plenty."

His lips press thin. He accepts a share of the vegetables, then falls to, slicing into a chunk of kidney, prodding potato, vigorously chewing.

She looks down at her plate, daunted. If she could avoid wasting the food he's ordered, she would. But it's too much and too rich and she's not used to it. As a cook, Mrs. Callaghan makes a marvellous knitter. Charlotte's been living on bread and cheese and apples—and lunchtime buns from Clarence's—along with an evening mug of Horlicks ever since she moved into Woodland Road. She lifts a fork, straightens her napkin, sets her fork down again.

". . . I don't know why you don't come out to Longwood," her father's saying, between mouthfuls. "What with the kitchen garden,

Parkin's poultry, and game from the estate, *we* don't go without. I see no reason why a daughter of mine should." He looks her over again: hair, eyes, complexion—she could almost see him lifting her lip with a thumb to examine her teeth.

She picks up her fork, teases a few flakes off the fish, posts them between her lips; the fibres separate between tongue and hard palate. She swallows.

"I know," she says. "But, you see, it's so hard for me to get away."

He smiles, his lips wet with wine. Oh yes. Her job. "I'll have a word."

She stalls. "But pulling rank, Daddy. That's not good for morale."

He grudgingly accepts this. She watches as he spikes a creamy slice of potato, then slides it around his plate, sweeping up sauce. "Well, Francesca had the children out with us for the whole of August, you know—swimming in the lake, tea on the lawn, just like the old days. Frannie is blooming, by the way—though she's always been more robust than you; you're more like your mother."

Charlotte untangles a spinach leaf from the adhesive clag. She inclines her head, still not seeing the similarity, but acknowledging the reproach. She pushes crumbs of egg and a twist of green into her mouth, and chews.

"Do make sure you ring your stepmother and get it organised; Marion would love to hear from you. You can cook up plans between you."

"Yes, I will." She won't. She scrapes back her chair. "Excuse me a moment, would you?"

He sets his cutlery down. She weaves through to the ladies' lavatory. She locks herself in a cubicle, sits, sinks her forehead into her hands.

She is a cold and sneaking thing. She doesn't deserve to be happy. But not for *diamonds* is she going to island herself out at Longwood now. Not even for Mrs. Parkin's bread-and-butter pudding and certainly not for cocktails at five and dinner at eight and wine and more wine and everyone either getting drunk or being drunk or being hung-over or getting drunk again. Not that she doesn't like a drink, but there's a drink and then there's drinking—hard, determined drinking. And his friends, dear God, his *friends*. She closes her eyes, sees drawing-room sofas draped with slender women, men standing in stark columns in their dinner suits. Sometimes she'd surprise them in strange corners, louche regroupings. The light, irritable laughter of grown-ups. The dawning awareness that she would always be an intruder there. Even hiding out on window seats or in the rhododendrons was fraught; the things she'd overhear. At night, she'd listen to the sound of footsteps, of doors opening and softly closing. Longwood. Even the name of the place fills her with discomfort. They are welcome to it, and to each other; her father, his friends and Marion. Charlotte was sent away to school aged seven. She has really only been a visitor since.

She washes her hands, then reapplies her lipstick, digging a matchstick around in the almost-empty enamel case and smudging colour on with the wooden tip. She really must get a refill, but there's always more urgent demands on her finances. She glares at her reflection. She will do. She will *do*. She will have to do. She is all she has.

"Are you finished?" he asks, gesturing at her still-full plate as she seats herself again.

"Sorry. I'm just not—"

"I see."

He abruptly waves the waiter over, etiquette demanding that he stop eating when the lady does. Still, there's nothing left on his plate when it is removed but smudges of dark bloody sauce.

"And how *is* work?"

An unasked-for café crème and a plate of petits fours are placed in front of her.

"Oh, you know," she says, and turns the cup round in the saucer, stomach swilling.

"No, I don't, or I wouldn't ask."

Stupid. To have presumed. "Well, I suppose I mean to say, it's fine."

"Fine?"

"It's just typing."

"But what you're typing—is it interesting?"

It's risky, but she says: "It's Home Intelligence, Daddy. You know I can't."

He hesitates, on the verge of taking offence, but then laughs. "Yes. Well done."

"Tell the truth, though, I can't imagine why they bother collating half this stuff."

"There's more to it than meets the untrained eye, no doubt. Speaking of which . . ." He signals for the bill, and starts to tell her about his own self-trained eye: he's been setting up a photographic lab in the maid's room at the Mayfair flat. He can still get his hands on the chemicals, thanks to his connections; the censors won't let a fellow publish, but someone has to make a record of this time. He has also begun a series of family portraits: Marion, Francesca, and the children. He'll blow them up and hang them alongside the Gainsboroughs. He'll do her too, when she comes to Longwood.

She doesn't even blink. "Lovely."

Back out on the street, he tweaks his fingers fastidiously into driving gloves. Silence is risky, but so is pretty much any topic of conversation, should it catch him the wrong way. She fumbles for something uncontroversial to say, and all she can think is how nauseous she feels, and how much she misses Eddie; how it would change the whole tenor of the day to have him here, to wait stony-faced and arm in arm until Father turned the corner, then stagger away laughing their socks off at the awfulness of it all. But all she can really manage now is not to throw up her eggs and cream and butter and wine and fish and spinach and potatoes and petits fours and café crème all over her father's shoes. Then he'd be *really* put out.

"Oh," she asks, hopeful that she's lighted on a neutral subject, "how's El getting on?"

"El?"

"Elena Hartwell. You know, my old friend from school? She's toiling away at your place. She's really putting in the hours."

"I wouldn't know," he says. "I don't look after the children."

Her cheeks flush.

"Though, Lolo, if you don't mind. There's something you can do for me."

"Oh?"

He reaches into an inner pocket, brings out a stocky buff envelope. "Drop this off at your godmother's, would you?"

"Happy to. What is it?"

"I asked you for a favour, not a game of Twenty Questions."

"Sorry." Though that's not how you play Twenty Questions: if it were, it'd be called One Question, and wouldn't be much of a game.

"Unless it's too much trouble."

"No. Of course not, sorry, no. Any excuse to see Saskia."

She hates herself. Hasn't she already said that she'll do it? And yet here she is, apologising and cajoling, as if she were the one asking him a favour.

He hands the package over. The envelope is sealed with a string-and-button fastening. By the shape and feel of it, there's a small box inside.

"If you must know, your mother asked that Saskia be given a piece of her jewellery."

"Oh. Which one is it?"

"I had Marion pick something out."

The package is light; the box is small; there are no links slithering around inside. It must be a pair of earrings then, or one of the brooches.

"I leave that kind of thing entirely to you ladies." He buttons his gloves. "Do make sure you put it directly into Lady Bowers's hands though, Lolo; I insist on that. One can't be too careful, nowadays. You know what people are like."

People are like the old couple at her local post office and their anxiously precise weighing and stamping of parcels; people are like Jim the postman who whistles Mozart on his rounds; people are like that tormented secretary of her father's; people mostly work hard and they do their best.

"I will. Directly."

She slips the package into her handbag, twists the clasp shut, and gives him one of her best smiles.

Charlotte tackles the envelope as soon as she gets back to her desk, picking the string off the paper button, sliding the box out onto her palm. She knows this box. It used to sit on her mother's dressing table. She flips it open apprehensively, as though it might sting. Inside lie her mother's favourite earrings, a pair of perfect black pearls. She fiddles one out and lifts it to the light, remembering the soft glint of it against her mother's jaw. They were *actually* her mother's, a twenty-first birthday present from her parents. All her other jewels were part of the Richmond family collection, and of these she was only ever a temporary custodian. They'd gone to Sir Charles's second wife, Marion, on their marriage. Anything else that Charlotte's mother personally owned—her clothes, her '78s, her sheet music, her Picture Posts and paperbacks—was disposed of. Not a bonfire—probably not a bonfire—but, to be fair, she doesn't know for certain and it may as well have been. What remained in her mother's rooms when Charlotte next returned from school was only what had always been there, old furniture patinaed with the wear of generations. Her father, apparently oblivious to the implications, had always said that his first wife had had appalling taste, but since she had only been able to exercise it in the most flimsy and impermanent of ways, it's impossible for Charlotte to know if this is true. The pearls, though, would suggest otherwise. Her mother loved them, and they are beautiful.

And there is no damned way that Saskia is having them.

"Oh," Janet says, sitting in at her desk next door, her cheeks rosy with fresh air. "What've you got there?"

Charlotte holds up a pearl, dangling from its hook, for her to see. "Rescued from the flames," she says.

"Your mother's?" Janet asks. "Oh, that's wonderful. Oh, how wonderful for you, my dear."

Charlotte is touched by her friend's delight.

"These remembrances," Janet says. "They do matter. They come to mean so much to those of us who are left behind."

"They do," Charlotte says. That's about as much as she's prepared to admit.

By the time Charlotte shoves her way in through her own front door, the sky is fading and the siren could start up at any minute. She is gasping for a cup of tea, but some things are more important even than tea. She sinks down on the rush-bottomed chair in the hall and unhooks the telephone receiver from its cradle. Oh joy; there's a tone. She dials the code for St. John's Wood, and then Elena's number, and listens through the clicks and fizz as the connections are made. El is the one person in the world who will understand quite how awful lunch with Father can be.

Lily answers. In her mind's eye, Charlotte can see her there in the Hartwell hallway, with its chequerboard tiles and blue-and-white vases. Charlotte doesn't even let her finish reeling off the whole greeting.

"Hello, Lily. It's only me. Can I have a word with Elena?"

"I'm afraid nobody can come to the telephone at the moment, miss. If I can just ask you to leave a message."

This conversation will flash back into Charlotte's thoughts throughout the years that follow. It'll come to her out of the blue, when she's walking the dogs on the beach, or cooking supper; or when reminded by an instance of her daughter's own hauteur or scrappiness. A bolt of what she said to poor dear Lily on the telephone that day, how dreadfully Lily must have felt it, and how Lily could not, literally could not, say a word in response. But right now Charlotte is oblivious to her own patrician tone and her impatience; her head is swimming with fatigue and frustration and grief and lunchtime wine, and what she really wants is El. And so she says:

"Look, it's *me*, Lily. Not the grocer. So don't give me any of your old nonsense. Be a good girl and go tell El that Charlotte's on the line."

There is a sob, then a deafening clatter.

Charlotte jerks the receiver from her ear. When she returns it, she can hear running footfalls, muffled voices. Then the receiver is swept up.

"Hello?" Mrs. Hartwell's voice.

"Hello, Mrs. H, it's me, it's Lottie. Whatever's going on?"

"Oh, Lottie, darling. Oh my goodness. Oh my dear."

"I'm sorry, I didn't mean to upset Lily—but whatever's wrong?"

"No, of course not, you weren't to know. I should have telephoned you, but we are at sixes and sevens here; we haven't had a moment, we're quite beside ourselves."

And then a voice speaks out silently, inside Charlotte's head: *Brace yourself, Lotts.*

"What is it, Mrs. H? What's wrong?"

"It's Elena, my dear. I'm afraid it's the most dreadful news."

It's one of those tricks the brain plays upon itself: a protective loop that imprints, on the moments before knowing, a foreshadowing that was never really there at all: even the very worst of news loses some of its sting if it doesn't quite seem new. So Charlotte knew; of course she knew; she's known it all along; and yet it can't be true.

"No," she says.

"My lovely Elena. My girl." Mrs. Hartwell's voice breaks.

"No."

"Saturday, darling; those awful raids."

"No."

"I am afraid so."

"The house," Charlotte counters.

"What about the house?"

Charlotte had waited outside, on Sunday morning—just yesterday. "You're fine. It's fine. It's still standing—you're still there."

"She was caught out, away from home."

"No, but . . . There are shelters."

"If you can get to them in time . . ."

Oh God.

But Charlotte keeps reaching, grasping: "It must be a mix-up. A mistake. Lily said that you were fine. That you'd gone out."

"I didn't know what else to say, my dear."

"But you can't—" Retract that. Change things without permission. Pull the rug out from right under my feet. "She can't be."

"Lottie, darling. We have her here. Our doctor came straight from his night shift at the hospital to see her. She's up there in her room."

"But, Mrs. H—"

"I understand, my love." Mrs. Hartwell's voice is becoming more insistent. "We don't want it to be true either."

In the Woodland Road hallway, Lady Jane flicks past, a whip of grey around the corner to the basement stairs: there must be raiders on their way. But Charlotte doesn't move. Like a fool, she'd been walking around all this time as though things were more or less all right, not knowing that the worst had already happened. She can't help but feel the chill of exclusion; she had not been told, she had not been invited in, she had not been allowed to join their circle of grief. She had not been wanted. Because times like that are for family. And she has only ever been almost-family.

"Listen, darling. Why don't you ring me again when you've had a chance to . . ." Mrs. Hartwell founders, struggling for words. "When you're feeling better?"

"The funeral?" Charlotte thinks to ask, before Mrs. Hartwell can hang up. She is hollow, empty. She could float clean away.

"I'll send a card. I'll let you know. And please make sure you . . ." Mrs. Hartwell hesitates. "Darling. I hope you don't mind me saying. I know how much you loved her. But please don't let this set you back."

The enervating wail of a local siren; Charlotte's skin crawls. Down the line, from all those miles away in St. John's Wood, she hears its fainter echo. Raiders spotted at either end of London.

"Because, darling, you know that that's the very last thing Elena would have wanted."

As though it matters if Charlotte is set back. As though any of that matters now at all.

"I'd best go, Mrs. H," she manages. "I hear the sirens; they'll cut the call soon anyway."

"Good luck," Mrs. Hartwell says. "And God bless."

"You too."

Charlotte hangs up, swipes at her eyes. She digs for her purse, to leave a coin for the call.

Mrs. Callaghan's sitting-room door cracks open. "Did I hear that Moaning Minnie start up again?"

She means the siren; of course she does.

"Think so." Charlotte keeps her face averted.

"Oh love, what's wrong?" Mrs. Callaghan comes through to her.

"I . . . That was . . ." She has to clear her throat.

"Oh no," Mrs. Callaghan says. "Oh no. C'm'ere, sweetheart."

Charlotte leans into Mrs. Callaghan's embrace, the cooking smells and matted cardigan and soft cheek and tickly grey curls. She stands there awkwardly, not crying. The setting sun through the stained-glass window casts coloured patches over them. Their nearest siren howls again; they stiffen in each other's arms.

"Come downstairs. You're in shock. Tea and biscuits. You'll feel a bit better after that."

You told me about her cardigans and boiled meat, but you never told me she was kind.

El?

A flutter in the corner of her thoughts, as though somebody had waved.

Is that you?

Mais bien sûr.

Charlotte rubs her forehead, dazed. Mrs. Callaghan coaxes her along towards the stairs.

"Come on love, come down."

In the basement kitchen, Charlotte sits at the table while Mrs. Callaghan makes the tea. Charlotte's eyes fill and spill, and for the lack of a clean handkerchief, Mrs. Callaghan hands her a tea towel straight from the drawer. Charlotte tries to compose herself; she presses under her eyes with the cloth, dabs her nose. Mrs. Callaghan sets a cup of tea in front of her, balances a piece of shortbread on the saucer, then settles at her side.

"Who was it?"

"My best friend," Charlotte says.

"Oh my goodness," Mrs. Callaghan says. "Oh my wee dote."

But isn't this what you always wanted? El asks. *Now we're tucked up nice and cosy together. No one else is getting in the way.*

You're guilt, Charlotte thinks. You're shock. You're grief. You're not El. You're a symptom. If I ignore you, you will go away.

Rude.

I will not let this happen.

I can just sit quietly; I'll be no trouble to anyone. In the dark space of Charlotte's thoughts, El sets a bentwood chair down, and sits herself upon it. Crosses her knees. Folds her hands on top of them, alert and at ease.

I'm not going back there again.

He'll never find out about me. How could he?

Somehow he always does.

Firewatching

Tom catches himself staring at the window. The panes have been overlaid with protective wire mesh; when he focuses on his book again, a honeycomb of light laces the page.

Her warm and breathing presence at his side. The colours and the scent of honeysuckle. *I am glad to see you.*

Him in his rusty black, limp hand on his lap, smelling no doubt of his work. *Just crumbs. No use to anyone. Whatever the rules may be.*

Tom sucks his teeth.

Other readers look round at the noise—a pale man with caterpillar eyebrows, and a woman carrying a stack of books that reaches to her chin—so he shifts himself as though easing out some pain, picks up his pencil and frowns studiously down. Students are scant before term starts, but Silence in the Library still applies.

No wonder she dashed straight off to work. You'd hardly hang around for conversation of that calibre. Oscar Wilde, he ain't. That was Monday; it's Thursday now. He hasn't glimpsed her since.

But to have been seen. To have been spoken to, by her.

His gaze drifts back to the window, the latticework of glass, and the glorious sky beyond.

The bell sounds; the library is closing. He's here on the goodwill of the very kind Miss Garrett, librarian, but doesn't yet have borrowing rights and certainly must not take the mickey, so he fumbles his things immediately away in his bag, hampered by the coloured flares across his vision. It has been a muddled start to things. Transferring from King's when King's closed down; not knowing yet whether his scholarship will survive the transplantation, or when term will begin, or if it will begin at all. Letters go unanswered or refer him elsewhere.

The truth is that no one knows how best to proceed. And so, for the time being, nothing happens, and keeps on happening, and yet he must carry on as if something eventually will. He reshelves the bound volume of journals and pauses at the main desk to say thank you and cheerio, all the while cursing himself for wasting time.

Outside, he's dazzled by the sun. If term ever does start, how will he even manage to keep up? The war is a monster that eats time. It swallows ordinary hours whole, gobbles up the days, devours entire lifetimes in an instant. And yet here he is, squandering what time he has managed to scrape together for himself, daydreaming about an impossible girl.

There is no seat free on the swaying, packed-tight Tube, and so he dangles like a puppet from a strap. It hurts, and the press of people makes him uneasy. Crowds are not necessarily malign, but they are careless. He can get knocked off balance so easily.

I'm almost glad it happened while there are still proper coffins left, Mrs. Clack's eldest, George, had told him yesterday—one of those conversations that sticks with him and won't be shifted. *They say they'll be using cardboard next, and God help us, even shrouds, and the idea of Mum going off to the hereafter in nothing but a sheet . . .*

Tom said he didn't expect that it would ever happen. Best not to listen to rumours. That's what Hitler wants, people to be scared and unhappy. George mustn't worry; they will do Mrs. Clack proud. As proud as they can, within the current constraints.

But he knows their local borough council has already bought eight hundred pairs of sheets from Peter Robinson's in Oxford Street, to be used as shrouds, and has commandeered almost all the open ground remaining in the area, including squares and parks, as burial places. They are expecting utter devastation, and he cannot say a word. His lips are sealed, his eyes wide open. It is a horrible foreknowledge to possess.

He resurfaces at King's Cross, makes his way home. The family business is run out of an old livery stables; *Hawthorne and Sons, Undertakers* is freshly painted in sober navy and grey. Tom's older brothers were part of the outfit before they enlisted, now his father has had to take on two older gents, well past call-up, to help.

Home is the three-storey flat-fronted terrace adjoining the shopfront. Tom hesitates on the pavement. Go inside, and there will not be a moment's peace until he goes to bed. Every movement scrutinised, every flinch and frown. College, by contrast, is a release: nobody knows him, nobody watches, nobody's concerned. He takes a deep breath and lets it go. He eases open the door, lifts his left foot and then his right over the threshold.

Nell lollops down the hall towards him, all idiot grin and propeller tail.

His mother calls out from the parlour: "Is that you, love?"

"Just in," he says. "Off to help Dad."

Fliss comes bounding down the stairs with a book and her pigtails bouncing. "Hello, stupid."

"Hello yourself."

He pulls a pigtail fondly, sidles past the dog and goes out through the yard, to the offices. He looks in on his father, who is scrubbing down the back room in his shirtsleeves. The smell of the room, its chemical, bodily scents; that doesn't change from one tenant to the next. There is nothing can be done about that.

"The fellows gone?"

"Off home. They get tired out."

Tom hangs up his bag and pulls off his coat, but his father bats him away.

"I'm almost done, son. Don't spoil your good clobber."

Tom is already thinking of tomorrow's as an old-fashioned interment. Bird-boned eighty-four-year-old Elsie Clack, whose fingers, laced over her thin chest, were already blue before she died, is lying in her own bed two streets away. She is to be laid to rest alongside her husband, who died sixty years before. Elsie wasn't best pleased to have outlived the custom of plumed horses; cars were, she had unarguably asserted, not the same thing. Cars don't have plumes at all.

At the tea table later, his mother, Belsie, asks inevitably, "Are you all right, son?"

Tom manages not to grit his teeth. "I'm fine."

"Are you sure? You don't seem all right."

"I had to leave something unfinished; you know what that's like."

"Any news on that front?"

She means college. She means the scholarship.

"Not a dicky bird." All he can do is wait, and work, and try not to care too much either way. No one from his family, or from his school, had ever gone to university; it sometimes seems more natural that he shouldn't either. At dark moments, the war is just the inevitable thing that came between him and his prospects. Anything else was just too good to be true.

"They'll sort something out," Belsie says. "Don't worry."

She does worry, he knows this. But she also holds a complete and unswerving faith that a degree will set him up for life: that those letters after his name will mean clean dry work, a warm office and a secretary to make the tea, so that when Stanley and Raymond get back after the war, they can take over the business, Frederick can take a step back, they can let the old fellows go, and all she will have left to worry about is Felicity.

"I just want to get on with it," he says.

"I know, love."

His father is half-asleep at the table, his head propped on his fist as he chews. Under the tablecloth, the dog lays her giant head on Tom's lap with a sigh, and thumps the floor with her tail. Directly across from him, Fliss chews and chews on gristle and gives up and drops the grey morsel out into her hand and is tutted at but says "Pardon" and so is forgiven. She slips her fist under the table and clicks her tongue to Nell, who turns to whisper the delicacy off the girl's palm.

Disgusting, Tom mouths at her.

I know you are, she whispers back.

"What were you working on?" his mother asks lightly.

That essay he was almost reading: "*The Mass Psychology of Fascism.*"

"Yuck," Fliss says.

Belsie gives Fliss a quashing look. "So how does that work then?" She folds her arms and settles in.

"Ah," he says. "Yes. It's complicated, and I'm at the early stages, so . . ."

"You can tell me all about it another time."

"Exactly. Yes."

Tom reaches for the salt. He can feel his mother's eyes on him, as she follows the sea-creature splay and curl of his fingers as they wrap around the salt cellar, then guide it towards him across the tablecloth, steering it to his left hand to be used. He chafes at this scrutiny. He knows that she can't help it.

Later, he smooths a book open on the table and turns pages with his left hand. He'd like to go up to his room, but it's cold there, and retiring this early would elicit comment and concern. Fliss takes herself through to the front parlour to practise her violin. The scraping scales and arpeggios rise and fall over the allegro tick of his mother's knitting and his father's gentle bass snores. If she keeps practising, Belsie says, then one day Felicity will be quite the musician. But today is not that day.

Later still, they pull out the thin mattresses Belsie has sewn from old blankets and ticking, from where they're kept in the cupboard underneath the stairs. They make up beds in the hallway. This is the safest spot in the house, a good solid structure; not much glass to fly around, the warden said. Fred has cut a piece of board to fit the fanlight. It doesn't feel like much, against bombs that can throw a bus into the air or reduce a building to dust.

They'll have to squeeze Stanley and Raymond in too, when they're on leave, and Belsie says she doesn't quite know how they'll manage it. But sufficient unto the day; for the time being, the older boys are off at training camps somewhere out there in the dark countryside and are temporarily safe.

Tom pulls on his overcoat and drops a kiss on his mother's cheek. She touches his arm, catches his eye. Doesn't need to say, but says it anyway:

"Be careful."

"I'll be fine," he says.

He goes out the back way. As he turns to shut the gate, he can see her still standing there, at the window, her face just a pale oval. He raises a hand to her, pulls the gate closed. He heads out to the night's fire watch. It is such a relief.

Pearls

S he knows it instantly now, that prickle in the skin. It's confirmed
by a siren, and then others, closer, taking up the cry. You can track
the raiders up the river by the sirens' wail.

Nothing too local yet, though; so Charlotte stays put. She tries on
the earrings again, looks at herself in the dressing-table mirror, turns
her head to watch the black pearls dangle at the crook of her jaw. Janet
worked through lunch today, so that she could leave on the dot of five
and be home in good time for the raids; no time for a bun and a chin-
wag or even a chat on the way down the stairs. In a way, it was a relief
to just work parallel with her, and with silent Stella. It has become
difficult to maintain a conversation. Or, rather, to maintain a second
conversation. There is constant chatter in her head.

What are you going to do with them anyway?

The voice is so clear; it's El's exact accent and intonation. It's as if
she's there, perched on her bentwood chair, just out of Charlotte's line
of sight, in any room that she happens to be in. Still in her pistachio
linen dress, blooming with summer heat, hands clasped on crossed
knees.

Well, I'm not giving them to Saskia, that's for sure. She'd only lose
them. Or pawn them.

Or drink them.

Ha.

You can't wear *them.*

I can. I can round here. Who's to know?

*One day your father will ask Saskia if she was pleased to get them. And she'll
have no idea what he's on about.*

It took him six years to get around to this. Six years since Mother died. How urgent can it be?

And yet you can be sure that it'll all come back and land in your lap, and then you will be sorry.

I'll say she was drunk; that, at least, has the benefit of being true. She was drunk and must have lost them and forgot she ever had them. And one day they'll be dead, and then I can wear them whenever I like.

What about Marion? She's only twenty-seven.

When Father's dead, I won't ever have to see Marion again.

Look on the bright side. That's my girl.

Weren't you supposed to be sitting quietly being no trouble to anyone?

Charlotte unhooks the earrings, then slips the silver wires through the holes in the satin-covered backing. The planes' thrumming grows. She clips the box shut and places it on her dressing table, climbs on the bed and opens the skylight. She emerges head and shoulders among the slates. And there it is, to the north-east: a migraine distortion in the air. A swarm. Really quite close. She should get to shelter.

What was it like? Dying?

Private.

They say it's awful to die alone, but I don't think I'd want an audience. I'd certainly prefer not to have Mrs. Callaghan blubbing all over me as I give up the ghost.

You're unkind about Mrs. C.

She is a touch vulgar.

Oh dear me, Lotts; now you sound like your father.

Ouch.

It tells you something, what someone choses to remark upon. It says as much about the speaker as the subject.

You have a point.

She's kind.

Yes. She is kind. She's kinder than I am.

The air is filling, becoming fat with noise. Low C on a cello, rising out of everywhere and all at once. Glints of silver kick off the planes; she can pick out individual craft. They are very close. And then she hears, or feels, she's not sure which, a great thwack, as though a giant racquet had just fired a ball into the air; she turns, searching. From somewhere off to her right, shells whistle up into the sky. A gun emplacement. They're firing back.

"Yes!" She bounces on her toes. She waves. They won't see her from there.

Do you think you might go down now?

I'm all right here.

I'm not sure you are.

I'd prefer to see it coming. If it comes.

It can't look good, you know. I mean, in the scheme of things. Watching from an attic window, while you natter away with the voices in your head.

Oh come on, El, not voices. Voice. It's only you.

Slippery slope, Lotts. And it's not a distinction most people would bother to make.

Charlotte leans on folded arms, crosses her ankles, settling in. She knows it's dangerous. Both the lingering, and the talking. But there's a strange peace in this. Bombs fall across the city, and shells lurch up to meet the planes, and the earth rumbles, and the evening sky is patched with sudden lights, but it doesn't touch her yet. And El is here.

If you went down to the kitchen, you could talk to actual living people.

In a bit.

She'll be worried, Mrs. C.

To the east, a stick of flares pop and fall, burning white and beautiful.

Beautiful?

Yes, beautiful.

You are mad, after all.

El huffs up and drags her chair away.

Then a plane swoops, engines screaming, directly towards Charlotte. She drops back through the window, falls flat, covers her head. Everything shudders; the glass in the window rattles. The aircraft passes over. The roar softens. Just one, a lone raider, maybe off course. And further off, bombs begin to drop. She feels the thud and shudder. Someone else is copping for it tonight.

El?

The chair dragged further away, turned towards the wall.

I'm sorry, El.

El?

When the all-clear sounds at six the following morning, Charlotte is still awake, staring at the paling sky.

El, are you there?

Come back, El.

I miss you.

Bodies

This place is still lovely, even battered, even pitted with ruins; fine white dust boils in shafts of golden light. Tom makes his way along the pavement, trying to shed the weight of his morning's work. They'd collected bodies from the local mortuary for burial. Except they weren't really bodies. They have brought back three sealed caskets—decent solid caskets, thanks be to God—with labels pasted onto them. He knows these names; these are local names, but the caskets feel all wrong; the weight of them too flat, too even, the balance off. The mortuary workers had been uneasy, apologetic. *We put in more or less enough to make a person,* he'd been told. *That's the best that we can do.* And there were rows and rows of these caskets at the mortuary, already nailed shut, labels pasted on. All identified by identity cards or possessions; there being nothing else identifiable about them. His father felt it badly too, but, seeing how it afflicted Tom, insisted that he take a breather. And so Tom had gone to breathe in Bloomsbury.

He would love to escape all the way to college. An eternal afternoon in the sun-warmed library is how he imagines Heaven now. But even if he could get there, with the Tube and buses so disrupted, the state he's in, he'd just fall asleep on folded arms. Jolt awake with nightmares. And he can't stay away from work that long.

Here, the lunchtime streets are lively with office workers freed from their desks; everyone's still dressed for summer; coats are light and diaphanous; ladies' hats are impractical confections, as though nobody is prepared to acknowledge the tilt towards autumn; that winter, with its long, enemy-accommodating nights, with rain that drips through damaged roofs and wind that tugs at patched windows, will soon be here.

He takes himself through the gate, into the square, to his particular bench. He has a splinter of broken biscuit in his pocket; he teases it out in tiny bits along the arm of the seat. The birds come and pick up one speck and then another. What's tiny to him becomes substantial in their beaks.

Back to the typeface.

He looks up, looks round. She isn't here. Lives do veer off so suddenly these days. She could still be loping round these streets and to and from her work; she could just as easily have been rehoused, redeployed. Injured. In hospital. Or worse.

He looks at his watch; he can't stay away much longer. Dad will need saving from himself. He hauls himself up from his seat, coaxes his limbs into movement. He'd just like to know that she'd made it through. That would do. That would be plenty. But it seems he will have to live with the uncertainty.

He goes to cross the road, negotiating that awkward moment of the kerb, the shifting of his weight briefly to the untrustable right side. Then, when he's safely descended to the cobblestones, he looks up again, and there she is, walking down the far pavement. Just the width of the street between them. He goes to raise a hand, then hesitates.

Something has changed. She's in winter plumage: a dull green heavy coat, a black fedora shading her face. She's hurrying along, her shoulders hunched; she's clutching her bag to her belly. And then she's past, the pale exposed nape of her neck between coat collar and hat brim.

She got through, but she's not unscathed. It's easy enough to imagine what might have happened. He sees such things a dozen times a day.

That afternoon, they have three funerals to attend to. Not the nailed-shut caskets; those ones will go in the earth tomorrow. These should be more comfortable. But he finds himself fascinated by an old woman's eyelashes, the way that some have faded to white and some have not. He feels a sympathetic ache for a middle-aged man whose great slab of a belly almost touches the coffin lid. He finds himself welling up over a youth of fourteen or so, simply because of the bloom of blond hair on the boy's upper lip that almost merited a first shave. He has been brought up to this; he should be able to accommodate it all with equanimity. Dealing with the dead should not hurt him. But now each new death seems to scrape him raw.

He wants to help her, but what he can do is precisely nothing. He doesn't even know her name; and who is he, anyway, to blunder in on a private grief? But somehow her sadness seems to have made him all the more vulnerable to everybody else's.

That night, he creaks down to meet Nell's wagging welcome; he buries his face in her neck and rummages his hands into her loose skin. Dope-eyed, lolling, she breathes her stale doggy breath on him in bliss. His brow, hidden in her scruff, is knotted, and there's a tightness in behind his eyes that's almost like the start of tears. This idiot, darling dog. Her simple love.

Clive

Elena with her green eyes and freckles, peering at you out of a crooked thought. That look of hers, at once far off and intense, that made men fall head over heels for her, and of which she seemed entirely oblivious. Elena with her dark plaits, the ends either damp or crispy from having been chewed, and whose clarinet smelled of bad breath. Elena with one perpetually droopy sock right up until the Upper Fifth, when she, along with everybody else, discovered stockings. Elena, who couldn't wear a lick of mascara without smudging it. Elena, their brilliant, beautiful, scruffy little elf.

Not this doll. Not this. A doll lying in its box, hair set like wax, face precisely coloured in.

What have they done to you, my love?

Charlotte has to mesh her fingers together to keep herself from ruffling the hair out of its setting-lotion wave. From wiping the red from those seagull lips. There is too much powder on that translucent skin. El lies in the box, but she's also sitting in the corner of Charlotte's thoughts, craned forward, hat fanning her flushed cheeks, watching.

Bit of a new look. What do you think?

I don't think it's really you.

In the front parlour, where El's coffin rests, vases of chrysanthemums and late roses have been set on every surface; the air is thick with their scent. The wallpaper is an old Morris print; twining branches climb over the walls so that El seems to lie like a princess cursed to sleep until she's kissed. Clutching the edge of the coffin, Charlotte dips her head in and awkwardly touches her lips to Elena's cold forehead. The smell is bloody, alien and antiseptic. She straightens up.

Aren't you supposed to wake up now?

Ha.

"She looks perfect."

Charlotte jumps; Clive, El's brother, is leaning in the doorway. Charlotte hasn't seen him in, what, a year?

"I'm sorry," he says.

She arranges her face for him. "It's all right. I was just having a quiet word."

He comes over and stands beside her, hands resting on the coffin rim next to Charlotte's. He is so like Elena in some ways: the dark hair and pale skin, the canny looking-at-you-sideways green eyes. He, though, has their father's yeoman's physique, built for the plough and the spade, now held in uncomfortable abeyance in the factory office. Seven years El's senior, he had been always impossibly older, benevolently detached. And now, she notices with a pang, he has begun to lose his hair.

"I was thinking how much you must feel it," he's saying. "It was pretty much my second thought, how you would feel it. So soon after losing your brother too. You poor thing."

"If you're going to be kind, Clive, I can't answer for the consequences. It's not going to be pretty."

"All those schemes and games and nonsense—you and Elena. I mean, all that *time.* You grew up together, the two of you."

Charlotte smiles suddenly; her eyes brim. "Shut up."

"More like sisters than just friends, how easily you rubbed along together."

"That's not," she says, "my experience of sisters."

"God," he says. "For God's sake."

His knuckles go white, his nails digging into satin. She lays a hand on his arm. He stumbles to her, presses his face into the crook of her neck. She rubs his back.

Over his shoulder, she sees Mrs. Hartwell stop in the doorway, caught by the sight of them together. Her look is sharp, assessing. Charlotte doesn't know how much Mrs. Hartwell knows, but she must have some idea. She pushes Clive gently back.

"Clive."

Clive wipes his face, straightens himself. "Sorry. I just—"

"It's all right."

"I'll go and—"

"Yes, do."

His mother touches his arm as he passes, gives him a look. There's an edge of warning to it, but whether that's to do with his giving way to tears or being caught in that embrace, Charlotte doesn't know. Not that it matters; none of that matters any more.

Mrs. Hartwell joins Charlotte at the coffin side. They look down at the small body. Put off by the paint on El's face, Charlotte finds more reality in her folded hands, the tormented musician's fingers, the blunted nails, their tininess; these hands are as they've always been.

"I'm so sorry, Mrs. H." Her voice sounds dusty; she clears her throat. "I am just so sorry."

"I know, my dear. We all are too. We are quite, quite devastated."

Charlotte's thoughts take a step back to Eddie; their father's sour and explosive grief. For the first while, it wasn't safe to be in the same room as Sir Charles, but neither was it safe to leave. They had no body to bury; there was no coming home from that last adventure. And so Edward lies out there, somewhere by the still water, under the flat sky. And her father can't forgive her for it.

Mrs. Hartwell lays her hand over Charlotte's. "Come and have a glass of something, before we go to church."

Charlotte nods, still looking down into the coffin.

I don't like to leave you, El.

El drags her chair closer: *Don't worry, Lotts. You can't.*

A polite cough. Charlotte turns to see the undertakers in the hallway. A sandy-haired man in his fifties with glinting wire-rimmed glasses, and a younger one, lean and angular; his slate-blue eyes are fixed on her. She knows him from somewhere, but he floats free from context and she can't think where she's seen that face before.

"Good afternoon," he says.

"Good afternoon," she replies, and goes to take her winter coat from Lily.

Clive climbs to the pulpit to deliver the eulogy. His sister, Elena Rose; always up to something, always persuading him into some kind of mischief or nonsense. Her musicality. Her talent for friendship. He chokes on this last phrase, and stops entirely, standing mute in the pulpit.

The vicar climbs up, lays a hand on his shoulder; Clive descends. He slides into the pew next to Charlotte. His hand fumbles for hers and clamps it hard.

Outside, afterwards, in sunshine, she catches sight of her father and stepmother looking expensive and detached. Her father has never once had a good word to say about the Hartwells. *Made their own money; bought their own furniture; ridiculous line of work for a grown man;* how their ears must have sizzled. Presumably, he's here to represent the Ministry, and Marion's come too because she's stapled to him. Her stepmother gives Charlotte a played-to-the-gallery moue of sympathy, then stares at Clive, who is one of the four pall-bearers carrying El's coffin to the hearse, and then back at Charlotte; her plucked-away-and-pencilled-back-on eyebrows go sky-high. What, she's asking, is going on there? When all Charlotte did was sit beside him. All she did was hold his hand. At his sister's, and her best friend's, funeral. But the worst is always to be assumed.

Get your mind out of the gutter, Marion.

Charlotte bites her lip and turns away. The flare of anger is a useful counterweight to misery.

Another funeral party is already massed in front of the church, so they have to leave by the side gate. She spots Mrs. Hartwell talking with their old family doctor; they stand so close that their foreheads almost touch, his ginger-grey hair *en brosse,* hers in sculpted salt-and-pepper waves, Dr. Travers's hands wrapped around hers as he murmurs consolation. The hearse stands waiting in the road; the coffin is slid inside. Charlotte catches eyes with the young undertaker again. He's talking to his colleagues, two older men; seeing her, he leaves them with a murmured instruction, and comes towards her. She notes his limp, speculates, in that queasy intrusive way one finds oneself stumbling into nowadays, that this must be why he's not in uniform. She's expecting some guidance about form, to be told, more or less, what to do. But then she sees his expression. It's not the usual muted concern of the profession; he looks as afflicted as any mourner. As he comes closer, there's something about the set of his lips, the way the light catches on his cheekbone. And she remembers him.

"Oh," she says. "It's you. The boy who feeds the birds."

He hesitates, almost a flinch. Then he peers theatrically round for eavesdroppers. "You'll get me into bother."

She drops her voice. "I won't tell a soul."

"I just wanted to say. I'm sorry about your friend."

"Thank you."

"Dreadful thing to happen."

"Yes."

"They seem a lovely family."

"They are. They've always been very kind to me."

"I'm glad," he says. "You'll need that now. You'll need each other."

And none of this feels forward or presumptive to Charlotte, even though it's stripped of the usual formalities and platitudes. It's honest. It's kind. She discovers, in this moment, that she likes him.

"We haven't been introduced."

"I'm sorry." He tucks his hands behind his back. "Thomas Haw-thorne. Tom." He slightly bows.

"Charlotte Richmond."

She proffers her right hand. He hesitates, then moves to take it in his left. A flicker of surprise, but she doesn't say anything. They clasp hands, then let go.

"Would you like a peppermint?" he asks.

It turns out that she would. He hands her the roll. She thumbs one out and goes to pass the packet back; he waves at her to keep them.

"Oh I couldn't."

"Please. I only keep them for these occasions. A taste of sugar's soothing, many people find, but I don't have much of a sweet tooth myself."

She pops the mint into her mouth, tucks it into a cheek: "That's why you always have biscuits left to give the birds."

"It's only ever crumbs."

"Your secret's safe with me," she says, the sweetness spreading from her cheek. "I promise."

The trees at the cemetery are blasted bare, and there's a sharp smell of sap from their broken branches. The road outside is partially closed and

a policeman is waving traffic round a crater. The water main is empty-
ing itself into the pit, so that the sound of tumbling water continues
softly throughout the interment, as though Elena is being buried at
Versailles, or in the Jardin du Luxembourg, and not in East Finchley.

Charlotte stands loyally beside Clive—Marion and her presump-
tions can go hang—who holds a bunch of dark pink tea-roses. She can
smell his wholesome scent, of coal-tar soap and cigarettes, as well as
the painfully lovely roses, and the mint tucked into her cheek. Mr. and
Mrs. Hartwell lay velvet red dahlias onto the coffin. They move haltingly: ten days have aged Mr. Hartwell by a score of years. Clive steps
forward and lays his bouquet down. The blooms look rich together,
bloody, beautiful.

The vicar speaks. The undertakers lower the coffin. There are com-
forts to be taken from these rituals, Charlotte supposes, but she hasn't
found them yet.

The parents, and then the brother, drop earth into the grave. Mrs.
Hartwell clutches her husband's arm and turns away. She is white-
faced, dry-eyed. The mourners begin to disperse, the undertakers gather up their gear. Charlotte notices Thomas now, as he goes
about his work; the way he keeps his right hand close to him, curled
at his side, the way he moves, with care and neatness, but unevenly.
That twist to his lips, the way he took her right hand in his left. He's
whippet-lean, his bones clear at wrist and cheek. This is more than just
a limp, it seems, this fine asymmetry of his.

Clive takes Charlotte's hand, strokes it with his thumb. He's pale
as paper. He releases her hand and offers instead his arm. She takes it.

Behave yourself, El says.

You're as bad as Marion.

Well, we all know what you're like.

They move away from the graveside. Charlotte, arm hooked
through Clive's, feels the warmth of the sun on her skin, and then the
cool of the blue shade. She watches rabbits lollop away across the soft,
cropped grass, and fuchsia blooms nod in the new breeze; out in the
street, water cascades into the crater, and the workmen, for a moment,
stop and take off their caps, and stand silent, as the black-clad company
go by.

The world keeps on doing an extraordinary job of being beautiful, she thinks, even without you in it.

She could have made her excuses as she left the cemetery; the Hart-wells would have understood. But she let herself be dragged along by the weight of convention, and now here she is, sipping sherry and making small talk and it's unbearable. She clutches her glass and moves through the crowded rooms and it feels like wading through brambles.

"There she is."

The morning room had seemed mercifully empty, but her father and Marion had been lurking unseen on a settee; they swivel round as she comes in, and then get up and come towards her. Pincered, Charlotte is obliged to acknowledge them with the press of his lips on her lips, and the prickle of his moustache on her skin. His hand on her waist. The kiss of air near Marion's powdered cheek.

"It's awful," Marion says. "Just awful."

"Yes. It is."

Apparently this has all affected Marion very deeply. Charlotte keeps her face steady as her stepmother details her distress, inwardly reflecting that a ship leaving Liverpool need only change its course by just a smidge and end up in Newfoundland rather than Buenos Aires. Just as, if the Richmonds as a family had sent their daughters to Roedean instead of Downe House, Charlotte might never have known Elena at all, and have been spared this misery along with all those joys, and would have had to endure instead the chagrin of being able to remember her stepmother in school uniform.

Thank heaven for small mercies, eh.

Marion turns away, distracted for a moment by Lily's appearance with a sherry bottle.

"Safely delivered?" her father asks.

Oh, Lotts, he's on to you already.

Don't be daft. How could he be? "Into her own hands, as you said."

Look at you. Not doing what you're told. Lying to his face. What's got into you?

You.

"She was pleased to get it, I don't doubt."

"Mm-hm. Yes." She screws her attention to him, ignoring El. "Very."

"Any message from her?"

"Just. Thank you, really; you know Saskia! She's so scatty. But I could see she was very pleased. Touched, you know."

He'll see her, eventually.

I'll jump off that bridge when I come to it.

"Good," her father says. "Good."

"How's the brother holding up?" This from Marion, who's returned to them with a brimming glass. Her father now holds out his and watches as the liquid is poured in. Lily's plump cheeks are an unhealthy puce. Charlotte feels a pang of guilt, tries to catch her eye, but Lily's not giving anything other than sherry away.

"He's taken it hard," Charlotte says. What else would Marion expect?

Sympathy.

"Poor boy. I know only too well how this can affect—"

This is almost certainly going to be about Eddie, about how hard all of that was for Marion. And despite her best efforts, Charlotte finds she cannot bear to hear what her stepmother knows only too well.

"Excuse me a moment, would you? I must just . . ."

She leaves them to fill in the rest of the sentence for themselves.

In the back garden, Charlotte lights up a cigarette; she is just shaking out the match when Clive comes out of the French windows to join her.

"Hell in there," he says, with a jerk of the chin towards the house. He gets out his own cigarettes. They listen to the rumble of conversation; a peal of laughter.

"The strain on the nerves," she says. "It comes out in all sorts of ways."

"Nevertheless."

They stand and smoke, gazing across the lawn at the Beauty of Bath tree. Always the first to fruit, it's covered with tiny, red-veined apples that need picking and packing away for the winter.

"Did El tell you, I've taken a leaf out of your book," he says.

"Oh? Which book is that?"

"I've struck out for myself. I've taken a flat, over in Marylebone, with a pal."

"Oh, good for you."

She loves the Hartwells, unequivocally, but she can see how clammy it might get, to be Clive; to be twenty-seven, running the family business and still living at the family home, when every other man his age seems to be off doing far more thrilling things. But jam and cordial manufacture is still vital. A little sweetness is valued now more than ever.

"They'll miss you," she says.

"If I hadn't moved out already, I'd never have got away at all."

A family will clamp shut like a cockle when it's hurt. She takes a drag on her cigarette. "You need your independence, though. They'll understand."

"What about your place? Are you happy there?"

Happy is not an easy word. But: "It's glorious. I love it. If I stick my head out of the skylight, I can wave at the Germans as they pass."

"Delightful."

"And there's a cat whose hair stands all on end when the planes are taking off in France, so we always know when they're coming and can be ready to say hello. My landlady grows her own cardigans, she has rows of them coming along nicely in the back garden. And all the food she serves is boiled. Even the biscuits. The other lodger there, I've never seen him in the same shirt twice; he must be the best-dressed air-raid warden in all the country."

Clive laughs, and this is gratifying, but then there's a wash of guilt. He must have felt it too: he squints back at the house, the laughter from which had irritated him just moments before.

"So you're having a high old time," Clive says. "South of the river."

"Sorry. Not really."

"No, good for you. I mean it. If nothing else, this has shown us that life is so damned short, and that the end can come at any time. What your Edward did—"

"Don't."

"No, but I mean, what he did. When he didn't have to. When he could have, with his connections, got something, well, you know, out of harm's way. So, to have enlisted, to have chosen the hardest path—"

"I do know, Clive."

It comes out sharper than it's meant. But it silences him, so that's a start.

She sucks her cigarette down to the end and tosses it into the flower bed, where the roses are falling all to pieces.

"Thing about Eddie was," she says, "he always expected to get away with it."

Unless—and this is the persistent sneaking fear—he didn't. Unless he'd been pushing and pushing all those years, and then finally broken through. Found his escape.

"I suppose so," Clive says.

"Your flatmate," Charlotte asks. "Is he around much in the day?"

"No. Long hours, in fact—"

"Sir Charles and Marion; they still here? Did you notice?"

"They were getting their coats when I came out."

"You want to show me your flat, then?"

Clive passes a hand over his thinning hair.

"All right then," he says. "Why not."

Charlotte leaves first, having made the necessary farewells. Halfway down the street, she becomes aware that someone's following her. Couldn't he have given it five minutes? He'll start tongues wagging. They may as well walk together now; it would look stranger if they didn't. She stops, turns.

Oh.

No Clive. No one there at all. Just the ghost of movement, where someone has turned the corner and gone.

She tuts at herself, turns back, heading for Acacia Road Tube.

Clive arrives at the station before she can even exhaust the contents of the leaflet stand. He takes her by the elbow and together they descend.

She sways beside him on the Tube, hanging from the same rubber ball. He looks doughy and determined.

El leans in, elbows on knees, chin in palms, eyes narrow: *But why?*

I don't know what you mean.

You don't want *him.*

I want something. I need something.

But not him.

Let me be.

They climb out onto Marylebone Road. She detaches herself from Clive's arm. She hasn't been out this way since that Friday afternoon ten days ago—a lifetime and no time at all; she hadn't known that things had been this bad. There's too much light here. Too much empty air. Workmen are clearing ruins: timber onto one wagon, brick onto another. Windows are boarded up, or new glass is being freshly puttied in. A chalked sign on a breezy shop reads *More Open Than Usual.*

She walks through all of this beside Clive, broken glass crunching beneath her feet, her jaw set. But when she reaches the cinema, she stops dead. The same façade, the same posters, but beyond the gaping doorway is a roofless, tangled mess. The back wall, with its proscenium arch, still stands; the curtains and the fire screen hang in tatters. All of it exposed to daylight, the magic and the glamour all now fled.

"We've had a lively time of it," Clive says.

"So I see."

He goes to walk on, but she doesn't move.

"I'm a few streets over this way, so . . ."

She shivers, stirs herself, follows him along.

At Clive's building, the windows remain conveniently unbroken. The stairwell smells of gas and the treads are worn, uncarpeted. Frosted glass gives a muted light, so that when they pass a man coming downstairs, Charlotte need only turn aside, a hand up to her hat brim, so as not to let her face be seen. On the second landing, Clive keys open a door, leans in, holding it open. Inside, he pauses to lock it behind them, and leaves the key in the lock, and she scoops up his hand, and pulls him towards her, and then his mouth is on hers.

Remind me why?

"Do you have a thing?" Charlotte asks, leaning away.

He stops. "Oh God. No. Damn it. Damn."

He chews his lip, reddened with her lipstick, glancing back and forth, wondering where best to dash for prophylactics: his flatmate's bedside cabinet or the local chemist.

"Half a tick," she says, pushing him gently away.

She locks the lavatory door behind her and washes her hands. The soap is Imperial Leather, veined with grey and retreating round its stamp. Outside, she hears a door open and close, the creak of furniture. Perched on the lavatory seat, she rummages in her bag, then slides her knickers down. She clicks open the enamel case, takes out the springy rubber cap, slathers it with Volpar gel, then folds and twists and slides it up inside herself, and follows it with another squeeze of gel. She can, after all, dodge some of the consequences. She can get away with being bad.

He's sitting on the edge of the bed when she comes in. He has taken off his jacket and waistcoat. She moves astride his lap, skirt riding up. The look on his face.

Charlotte dips in towards him, feels the warmth of his body against hers. His arms come around her and she is held. A moment's peace. She unbuttons his shirt and sinks her face into his throat and slides a hand around his flank, enjoying the warmth and life of him.

El would never have told him directly, Charlotte knows she wouldn't. But that doesn't mean he doesn't know. Because people talk. They don't necessarily mean any harm by it; sometimes they might even mean well. Perhaps a word of caution, from his mother; Elena's little friend Charlotte, son, make sure you steer well clear, she's not your kind of girl at all. The kind of warning that might set a man thinking, that might have a rather different effect to the one intended.

He slips her blouse from her shoulders; she stands up again to undo her skirt and let it fall. She unclips her stockings from her suspender belt, rolls them off. He watches; she feels the pull of his desire. He at least doesn't seem to mind the absence of meat.

She should not be doing this. She knows perfectly well that she should not be doing this. She knows where it got her before, and she knows that it could get her back there again. And yet.

He fumbles the covers aside, and they sink back into the bed.

He's clumsy, needs to be led. When he climaxes, she feels glad, but remains coldly present. He rolls aside, to lie on his back, arms flung wide, like he's just fallen from the sky. She scoops up her clothing and returns to the bathroom, to let his stuff slide out of her, and to add more gel, leaving the cap in place. Her need is gone. It's not fulfilled, but she's past it.

It doesn't help.

Don't.

You think it will, but it doesn't.

Just don't.

She emerges, dressed, her face and hair tidied, from the lavatory. She could just slip away without a word, but instead she goes to find him. She'll be polite. This is Clive, after all; there's no way she can avoid him forever, and the interest to be paid on rudeness is compound. She can't afford it.

He's in the tiny kitchenette, making coffee on the gas ring, shirt-sleeves rolled, smoking, looking domestic and relaxed. He kisses her on the forehead.

They drink their coffee in the sitting room, from demitasses patterned with red and yellow poppies.

"I like your china."

He turns his cup round as though seeing it for the first time. "Came with the place." And this seems to remind him. "So, what do you think? D'you like it? Worth hanging on to?"

She looks round at the flowered paper, the windows veiled with net even on the second floor, the bookcase supplied with the requisite set of Waverley Novels. There are dainty things dotted around: a venetian glass ashtray, an empty crystal vase, a china shepherdess. Children's voices rise up from the street below, and there's the ongoing rumble of traffic and then a sudden crash as some nearby ruin falls or is pulled down. It's as though they're not inside a flat at all, but perched on a high shelf, feet dangling, fingers hooked over the edge.

"Oh, I would hang on to it, if I were you," she says.

"You like it then?" He leans in with boyish enthusiasm.

"Very much so. I love this part of town, you know. Fond memories of the place." She drains her coffee. "Though unfortunately the Luftwaffe also seem quite keen."

He laughs. She takes out her gloves, snaps her bag shut. He registers these preparatory-to-leaving moves.

"Shall we . . ." he says. "Would you like to—cocktails perhaps, or dinner?"

So maybe he doesn't know. Or maybe he knows and doesn't mind. Look at him, the great afflicted thing, all twisted up and wrung out. His green eyes so like El's, but softer, and so sad. No mischief in them.

"Yes," she says. "Let's."

She opens her bag again, fishes out her address book, writes the exchange and prints her number, then carefully tears out a strip of paper. She hands it to him.

Really?

Well, he did ask nicely.

Clive grasps her wrist, pressing her watch into her flesh. He pulls her in towards him for a further kiss. She waits it out, then straightens her wristwatch and her hem.

"Well," she says. "Must dash."

He goes ahead to open the door for her. "I'll ring you."

"Do."

She clips down the stairs. She should have left from the cemetery. She could have been home by now, drinking Horlicks in the kitchen with Mrs. C. That would have been a far better way to spend the dog-end of this awful day.

On the Marylebone Road, pigeons scrat and strut. Leaves tumble down the gutters, yellow and half-yellow and tan. The tarmac glitters with bits of broken glass.

Kill yourself.

Kill yourself and have done.

"Shut up."

She said it out loud, and someone has noticed. Their eyes snag. The gentlemen's outfitters behind him has just been reglazed, the putty still visibly thumbed; assistants are redressing the window. He's a bulky man, his skin deeply lined, a cigarette between his knuckles. His eyes are pale marble-grey; his look is strangely blank. She's sure she's seen him somewhere before, but then London is getting like that. The pool is shrinking. Everyone's swimming in smaller and smaller circles.

"Excuse me," she says. "Not you. Private conversation."

He touches his hat.

Charlotte hurries on. She feels stupid. She feels exposed. She clatters down the steps. She has to pull herself together. She really has to pull herself together. Before she starts to make a real nuisance of herself. But now El's talking, and it's difficult to ignore her. She's talking, talking, fit to burst.

Don't you think— El's leaning in, intent.

Don't you think it's funny—

Don't you think it's funny that I died—

Don't you think it's funny that I died in an air raid—

Don't you think it's funny that I died in an air raid and I didn't have a mark on me?

Cold

Tom takes the letter with him. There is something sacred about it, this headed paper, its thick, creamy, pre-war texture, its air of officialdom. It's as though he has received a message from another world, admission to which is promised, but is yet again to be deferred. The start of term has been postponed to mid-October. He begins to doubt that it will ever start at all. Just last week, Mr. Churchill had spoken gravely about a significant mustering of enemy ships. Meanwhile, the air raids intensify. Invasion is expected. He tries not to think what would become of him, particularly him, should the enemy win. He keeps his penknife sharp.

In Bloomsbury, the locals pick around the edges of chaos, sweeping up broken glass, sorting through torn books and scattered papers. When they speak, the words are disjunctive, staccato, repetitive, as though even language cannot be expected to hold together any more.

He thinks he spots Virginia and Leonard Woolf, whisking past in a car—the lady's unmistakable profile, a sweep of silver hair. But there is no further sign of Miss Richmond, Charlotte; not yet, at least. He gets caught on certain faces, clothes; he would know her in an instant, but still deludes himself with something about the way one girl walks, or someone else's hair. It's stupid. He knows it's stupid. He barely knows her; he has no right to be concerned.

He goes to his bench. Birds flutter up, bob around, flutter away again. He hadn't thought to bring anything for them today. He spends an hour fretting and getting cold. His right leg stiffens, his hand contracts into a ball. He unpeels his fist, ripples his fingers; he has to stare at them to make them move. His toes have slipped entirely out of existence. He turns his right ankle and glares at his boot, willing the toes inside to curl and uncurl. What am I going to do, he thinks; what am I going to do? Every night the raids, and every day the dead, and the college wants to wait till things get better, but every day everything is worse.

And it's getting late now. His mother will be furious.

I am stuck, he thinks. I am stuck deep. I have to pull myself out. I thought I had a handhold, but it's slipping out of reach.

The light is fading, the birds have given up, and the raiders will be along at any time. He shifts himself from the bench, staggers his first few steps, then walks on, hunched and sore. He'll have missed his dinner. Mother will be incandescent. He doesn't want to go home. He goes home.

Belsie opens the door before he's even reached the top step. "Where have you been?"

"Sorry."

"No, but where have you been?"

He is impatient, his body is tight with pain. "Nowhere really."

Her face softens, seeing his discomfort. She puts her arms around him, says, "Oh, you silly boy."

She helps him through into the kitchen, where the range is belting out heat. He wants to shrug her off, he wants to cry, he wants to run away from here. He lets her sit him down in her fireside chair.

"Don't put your feet on the fender," she says, just as he knows that she was going to, "or you'll get chilblains, and then you will be sorry."

She bustles to get the dinner that she'd left aside for him. He hates that he puts her through this. He hates that she puts herself through this. This fierce, angry, inexhaustible love. He'll drown in it.

Paper

It is a grey drag of a week. Charlotte can hardly lift her eyes to even look as it crawls by. She can't bear to read the newspapers or hear the radio. Janet brings a sandwich and eats it at her desk, leaves with a regretful wave while Charlotte's still typing. Charlotte wonders if Janet's really being dictated to by the Luftwaffe's schedule, or someone else's; sometimes her husband is waiting outside, substantial in his clerical black-and-grey, glancing up at the building, then down at his watch. When Janet appears, foreshortened by the angle, feet darting out in front of her, he offers her an arm and she takes it, and they march away at such a fierce pace that Janet seems almost to fly.

Even coming back to Woodland Road of an evening no longer occasions pleasure. The view out across the city is holed and blackened, hung over with a dirty fog. Mrs. Callaghan is on edge and loquacious; Mr. Gibbons is always out. As Charlotte climbs the street, El climbs with her, summer hat swinging in her hand.

I can't bear that there is still all this life ahead of me and you're not in it, El.

You never know; you could be shoved off your perch tonight.

True. But still. As long as I live. There'll be no you at Christmas, or on our birthdays, or at the house in Galloway, or any Friday night or Sunday afternoon.

I was mostly busy anyway.

And now I feel like I've been permanently stood up.

Buck up, old thing. I'm always here. And you do know other people.

Which reminds her of the tube of peppermints; she fishes it out of her bag, untwists the paper and eases the top sweet out. The mint is only slightly soft; the sweet cleanness of it is a consolation.

See. I am bucking up.

The hallway is cold and dim. Charlotte leafs through the telephone messages—the name "Hartwell" written in Mrs. Callaghan's lovely board-school hand makes her heart skip, but it's just a message from Clive. Charlotte keeps doing this to herself—manages to overlook, for just a fraction of a second, the fact that El is dead, and has to face it afresh all over again. Such lapses are due, no doubt, to the continued chatter in her head.

Don't you think it's strange, with all those bodies, those bits and pieces dropped in bushel baskets; don't you think it's strange I looked so—

You were slathered in make-up.

But whole, *whole enough to have an open casket. Clive said that I looked perfect. So don't you think it's strange—*

Clive has left his telephone number so that she can call him back. She tears the page out, slips it into her pocket as Mrs. Callaghan emerges from her sitting room and asks her, "Be a pet, dear, and fetch the old newspapers for the paper drive, would you? Only the Scouts said they'd be along for them."

The old newspapers are stacked on the kitchen dresser. Charlotte scoops them up and balances them on a hip to leave a hand free for the bannister as she climbs. At the top of the stairs, the pile slithers apart and papers begin to fall. She grabs at them, but they slip away. She dumps the stack on the floor, scrambles round on hands and knees for the strays, then slaps them down on top. Her attention's snagged by a photograph, exposed by this reshuffling. She kneels back, picks up the paper, turns it over, reads the article. Then she fumbles round to sit on the second-to-bottom step, the pile forgotten, just this one paper in her grasp.

The photograph is a studio shot, lush and creamy. Make-up perfect, hair flawlessly set; shoulders and collarbones bare, and there's a slick of pale satin evening gown beneath. The Honourable Miss Vanessa Cavendish. The only Vanessa worth the mention. And she's exquisite. Even in school uniform, she'd been fascinating; like a deer spotted in a clearing, you couldn't move or look away until she'd left. But it was never just her beauty that marked her out; it was her certainty. She had been known not to give one single damn what her parents thought about what she did or who she did it with; not about her success in school dramatics, nor her intended career on the stage, nor her indeed intending a career at all. And of her parents' attempts to launch her as a debutante in the season of '36, it was common knowledge all across the school that what she'd actually said was, "Fuck Queen Charlotte and fuck her fucking ball."

This is her professional headshot. And this is her obituary.

Charlotte reaches towards the telephone set; she'll ring El . . . but no, she can't. Her hand drops back.

The obituary speaks of frost in May—a bud nipped off before it had the chance to fully bloom; that readers who had had the good fortune to see her Ophelia at the Vaudeville will understand what a loss Miss Vanessa Cavendish's early death, in a recent raid, has been to the world of theatre.

Charlotte has to read the notice five or six times to glean this much.

There's a bang at the door. Charlotte looks up. A rattle-rattle-rattle of the door knocker. The paper falls limp in her hand.

"Get that would you, love?" Mrs. Callaghan calls. "Save my legs."

Charlotte gets to her feet, opens the door.

Two youths stand on the doorstep; a third, out on the street, hangs off the handles of a perambulator stacked high with waste paper. They don't look like Scouts; they look like they've mugged a Scout and div-vied up his uniform between them. One wears a battered khaki hat, the other a grubby shirt, and the third has a woggled necker dangling round his skinny neck. This is almost certainly a racket. Charlotte really doesn't care.

"No hurry then," the first lad says, with a nod to the pile on the stairs.

She sets down the obituary on the hall console, scoops the rest of the newspapers up and tips them into the lad's arms.

He points at the remaining paper. "What about that one?"

"Not that one."

"C'mon, miss, we all have to do our bit."

She picks up the obituary, folds it tidily, then tucks it under an arm. "Go on, you little bleeder, sling your hook."

His eyes go wide. "Gob on you like a docker. Shocking."

The boys laugh. He races down the path, dumps the papers in the pram and the three of them careen off down the street.

"You're welcome!" she calls out after them.

She closes the door, sinks down on the stairs, and smooths the one remaining paper out again.

Vanessa Cavendish.

Elegant, talented, utterly self-possessed Vanessa Cavendish, who always knew exactly where she was going and how she was going to get there, and would not let anyone stand in her way. Watching her succeed had been genuinely thrilling. But she's dead now, and at twenty-three. How can this have happened to someone as astonishing as her?

And then another voice; this one modulated, resonant. It breathes the words into Charlotte's ear, but could carry, with the intimacy of a whisper, all the way to the cheap seats in the gods. Vanessa Cavendish, dripping wet, her hair tangled and teased through with flowers and herbs, steps into the light, and says:

The same way it can happen to anyone, you dope.

Room

Charlotte lies in bed. Daylight, Saturday. Above her, the early haze clears, and the sky becomes an intense autumnal blue. Cloud begins to gather, but no rain specks the skylight.

Mrs. Callaghan creaks up the stairs, taps on the door and asks if Charlotte needs anything. Charlotte rolls her head on the pillow, and just about manages—*Impressively*, El offers, *given the circumstances*—to thank her, and to say that she doesn't need a thing.

Which takes all the effort she can muster, because, right now, Vanessa just won't bloody shut up, and it's eating Charlotte's brain into holes.

It's not that I'm surprised *to find you living like this, Richmond. It's not that* unusual; *the French have a term for it:* la nostalgie de la boue—

It's not mud.

Nor am I surprised to find that you are being deliberately obtuse. I'm merely saying that I understand the attraction of undemanding company. How lowering one's standards can appeal. No need to be on your best behaviour, or even your second best—

Oh for goodness' sake.

Now, I myself had a lovely mansion flat, you know. Potted Stilton in the pantry, furs slung over the backs of chairs. Ferns and orange-shaded lamps, and the parties—oh my word, the parties. All my lovely people. Noel on the piano having us all in stitches. Gin fizzes and rum fizzes and whatever fizzes we could get our hands on. I'd pour myself out of bed and into my dressing room and it would be full of flowers. Always full of flowers.

Don't you think, Lotts, offers El's milder voice, pushing Vanessa gently aside, *that you're letting her take up a bit more space than she really merits?*

Merits? What do you mean, merits? I merit all the space I want. All of it. I can fill a space like no one else. I'm known for it.

You barely knew her, Lotts, El says.

Which is why it's so particularly galling to find myself stuck here—Vanessa pulls her sodden robes tighter round her—*in this cold and poky dull hereafter, all cluttered up and tangled and miserable.*

A gull cruises overhead, between Charlotte and the clouds. The clouds are filthy, yellowish.

Now I call that mean, says El.

You protest a lot, Hartwell, for someone who hadn't had a spare moment for Richmond here in months.

Well, there's a war on, El says. *I've been busy.*

You know she's fragile. And you just dropped her, just like that, cold. You did it again and again. You did it so many times. And you know what happens to fragile things when you drop them. You can get away with it once perhaps, but—

She never complained. El gets up from her chair, scrapes it into shadow.

Charlotte rolls on her side.

You left her sitting alone at café tables. You phoned up to cancel just as she was stepping out the door.

You don't know any of this, Vanessa. You weren't there. Lotts never complained. She never said a word.

She doesn't complain. She's been trained not to.

It doesn't matter, Charlotte thinks, cheek on pillow, eyes wet. I didn't mind. I always understood.

Did you? Vanessa asks. *I mean really understand? Because nobody's that busy, are they? People have priorities, that's all. And either you're a priority or you're not.*

Later, Mrs. Callaghan taps again on the door.

"No thank you," Charlotte says.

But the handle turns and Mrs. Callaghan comes in, moving with a kind of hunched-tiptoeing motion, as if this will disturb her lodger less.

Charlotte shoves herself upright, tries to tidy her hair.

"Sorry—"

"Sorry," Mrs. Callaghan says too, at almost the same moment, and stops there, a cylinder of a woman, in her matted green cardigan and her broad shoes, not knowing where to put herself.

"What is it, Mrs. C.?"

"Just, sweetheart." Mrs. Callaghan decides that it's all right to sit down on the edge of Charlotte's bed. "Couldn't you come down for a bit? Have a cuppa, listen to the wireless with me? For the company?"

"I'm not feeling too clever at the moment, Mrs. C."

"All the more reason."

"I'll come down in a bit."

"All right then," Mrs. Callaghan says. "Mind you do."

When Mrs. Callaghan closes the door behind her, Charlotte lies straight back down again.

Vanessa, now, is laughing.

Oh shut up, Vanessa, do, El says. *Do you think any of this is easy for her?*

I imagine not. I imagine that if you start as the daughter of a baronet, it takes a good deal of effort to get yourself into such a situation. A skylight room south of the river, at ten shillings a week. With a hobgoblin for a landlady.

Vanessa Cavendish, I had no idea you were such a bitch.

Me, a bitch? Oh dearie me. I don't think so. You just don't want to acknowledge the truth.

What truth?

Shut up, Vanessa. Charlotte, make her shut up.

Charlotte presses her eyes.

I miss you, El. Whatever else is true. I miss you. I thought I missed you then, when you were always busy, but it was nothing in comparison to this. I really should just kill myself and have done.

Don't, El says. *Don't even think it. I hate it when you think it.*

Think it all you like, Vanessa says, *just don't do it. Where would I go then?*

Burning

Tom is making his way back from fire watch. It has been a volatile night, the sky lit up with incendiaries and flares, the ground quaking. His own patch had been overlooked; he'd managed to grab a few handfuls of sleep here and there, but still he's shattered. He catches sight of a neighbour, Mr. Sargent, on the turn for home, and would prefer not to have to talk to him, it being sufficiently hard work right now just to put one foot in front of the other. At first, Mr. Sargent seems to be of the same opinion, giving him a nod and walking on. But then the older man stops mid-stride, and turns back, waiting for Tom to catch up. Mr. Sargent works in the print room of the *Mirror,* on the same street as the college's main building, so they are neighbours there too. He usually has the grime of work about him, smells of oil and ink and hot metal. Today, though, his face is smudged with smuts, his eyes sore and red. He reeks of burning.

"You heard?" he asks.

Tom is in no mood to chase oblique questions around. "No."

"Caught a packet, early this morning."

"What?"

"We went to help. They've got an appliance now, so . . ." Mr. Sargent's look conveys both concern and the conviction that people are better off not developing fancy notions, since it'll only lead to disappointment. "All those chemicals going off in the laboratories. Like fireworks."

"Thanks," Tom mumbles, and hurries home.

He leans in through the front door, calls down the hallway. "I'm off out. Have to see to something."

His father emerges from the kitchen.

"I won't be long," he lies.

He claps the door shut and heads straight for the Tube.

Holborn station, he's relieved to find, is still open, though malodorous from the night before. The platform is ranked around with bunks and being swept of cigarette ends and ticket scraps. There is a scorched, electric feeling to the air. Tom steps onto the teak slats of the escalator, and is lifted towards the street.

All down Fetter Lane, there's not a window left intact; buildings stand like chimneys, blackened and hollow and open to the sky, the floors and ceilings burned away. Fire engines are stationed in the street, and the exhausted, blackened crew scroll up hoses. In Greystoke Place, he gapes up at the smouldering hole in the roof; the doors stand open on darkness, and fire hoses slither in. He picks his way uneasily over the coils. The two top floors of Breams Buildings are a charred mess, but the fire has been stopped from descending any lower. There's a WVS van; firemen, wardens, and dog-tired volunteers are drinking tea from paper cups.

This is where his classes were to have been held. This was his handhold. This was how he was going to haul himself up and out, and set off into the world.

"You one of our lot, son?" a man with an ARP armband asks.

Tom is about to explain, but gives up, disconsolate. "Yes."

"Give us a hand then. Go on up, they'll make good use of you."

He is ushered in through the dark doorway. The floor is pooled with water. His interview was at King's; this is the first time he has ever set foot inside the building.

"Right on up," the fellow says.

Tom hauls himself up the stairs. The smell is dreadful, acrid, chemical; he tugs his scarf up over his nose and mouth. The treads are wet. He takes them one at a time, the right foot lifted to meet the left before the next step can be attempted. His dreams wash over reality: he's climbing the stairs, surrounded by lively young people; he knows them all and they know him; they're clutching books and talking, happy to be shaking off the dust of their day jobs, dazzled by the brightness of their widening horizons. But he is climbing the stairs alone in the dark and stink and wet, and the horizon has collapsed down the next step he has to haul himself onto.

It's cold; there's a draught on his face. The light increases, the breeze sharpens, and he is out on a landing. Ahead of him, under the teeth of a broken roof, figures pick their way through the wreckage. He steps forward.

"Watch it!" someone calls.

He looks down; there's a dizzying thirty-foot drop to the floor below. He clutches at the doorjamb. A woman comes towards him, as though walking on thin air. But then he sees the narrow metal joist beneath her feet; a series of them span the void. That's all that's left of the laboratory floor, along with a dark frill of charred wood around the edges. She's tightrope-walking, clutching something to her: an ivory arch as big as her torso.

"Good man," she says, stepping onto the landing. "Here you go."

She leans the object into his arms. He wraps his right arm deliberately round it, the left supporting its weight from underneath. It is warm, smooth and heavy.

She says, by way of explanation: "Killer whale, lower jaw. Juvenile male. To the library, would you, and give it to Miss Garrett, stat?"

"Right you are." He dare not look anywhere other than in her smoke-sore eyes.

"Not good with heights?" she asks.

He goes to shake his head, but that's worse.

"Just scoot straight down then. Unless you're one of those awful looters trying to steal my specimens. I do hope not."

Could there really be that much of a black market for marine-mammal bones? "First year Psychology," he says, "though I haven't started yet."

"No, you wouldn't have. I take it you know where you're going?"

"To the library? Yes."

"Good chap." She's about to turn away.

"But, miss . . ."

"Hm?"

"These were the laboratories, weren't they?"

"Yes." She tucks back a fallen lock of hair. She's about to say something else, but there's a furious exclamation from the other side of this vertiginous space. She flinches, raises her voice over the emphatic swearing. "Please excuse Dr. Simons. I'm afraid he's lost some valuable apparatus. He's a tad put out."

"Oh."

"He made it all himself, so I told him he can jolly well make it all again. Meanwhile, the library, if you wouldn't mind."

He carries his jawbone downstairs, passing other recruits who are climbing up: young women in berets and headscarves and tam o'shanters and men in duster coats and great coats, all looking tired but determined. He's nodded to, and returns the greetings over the whale's front teeth.

In the library, he tips the bone carefully onto the desk.

"Ah, thank you, Mr. Hawthorne." Miss Garrett looks it over. He watches her get out a brown-paper label and write on it in tidy, tiny fountain pen. She still speaks in hushed librarian tones, which, for some reason, he now finds moves him almost to tears. "How are you today?"

"Tip-top," he says grimly, determined not to cry.

She makes a sympathetic face. "Shocking, isn't it. Could you put that on the trolley for me, do you think? Save my sweater."

The book trolley is already laden with boxes, bones and trays, all carefully labelled, but there is still space for him to shuffle in the jaw-bone. He raises a hand in farewell to Miss Garrett, teeth gritted, eyes wet. He doesn't expect to see her again.

Outside, he accepts a cup of tea from the WVS van, eases himself down on the steps on the fringes of a group of students.

A bag of broken biscuits is rustled under his nose. He looks up. A young woman with a felt cap and soot-streaked cheeks; she jiggles the biscuits earnestly. He takes a piece, thanks her.

"What's your discipline?"

"Psychology," he says. "Or it was going to have been."

"Oh my."

A fellow leans in: "Why they were still storing chemicals up in the roof there, I have no idea."

"That's the thing with these genius types," the biscuit girl says. "They can be so awfully dim."

Tom gulps down what's left of his tea over the lump in his throat. He crumples up his paper cup, drops it, and struggles to his feet.

"Are you off?" the young woman asks.

"Work," he says.

Others nod, understanding.

"See you again," someone calls.

"See you."

He almost certainly won't. He steps awkwardly over hoses, weaves between stacked chairs and desks left aslant across the street. When this war is over . . . but he quashes the thought. When this war is over, what space in the world will there be for men like him?

Shadow

Charlotte knows the way the world will retreat, if she lets it. She knows the way it will become indistinct if she doesn't keep forcing it into focus. Colour will fade and outlines blur so that it is like—though she didn't have the analogy available the last time round—looking through the gauze-pasted window of a bus.

So she forces herself to notice. To be in the world as it unfolds around her; she refuses to let it slide past at one remove. The milk float at the turn of the street; the way the horse's breath steams; Mr. Turner dodging back and forth with bottles, the milk almost luminous-blue in the half-light. She hears a door go and turns back to see Ilse Ackerman coming out of her house, in her mulberry coat and navy knitted cap. Ilse will be heading to her morning job; she has that purposeful, determined look about her, but brightens when she sees Charlotte waiting. She races to catch up.

Then Charlotte notices the figure. A grey, masculine shape, following along behind Ilse. He seems to be keeping pace with her, at about six yards' distance. A shadow man. But when Ilse darts across the street, the figure stops in his tracks. Charlotte could swear he's just noticed her there, waiting, and realised Ilse is not alone. Whatever the reason, he then turns and slips into the alleyway between the houses, and is gone. Ilse, already talking, skips up to join Charlotte, but Charlotte leans to look past her, at the entrance to the alleyway; it's screened by the mad tumble of a rose bush.

"What is it?" Ilse turns back to look too.

"Nothing." Charlotte ushers her along. "Just thought I saw someone."

"Oh, I know!" Ilse says, eyes wide. "London's got *so* many people in it."

Charlotte smiles. "Is it quiet, then, where you come from?"

And the girl falls to talking about the prettiest town in all the world, with its castle and its church and its deep cold river, and its sensible houses with only one family in each, and the markets they have and the fairs, and the dancing. But Charlotte's only half listening; her senses are trained on the space behind her, the nape of her neck tingling. At the corner she pauses, looks back. The street is empty. But she doesn't like it.

Charlotte walks Ilse all the way to the café where Ilse helps set up before school, and works behind the counter at teatime, and gets to take leftover scones home with her. It's directly opposite the station.

There are more people here. None of them stop, none of them so much as dawdle, nobody seems remotely interested; everyone's in a hurry, rushing for their trains. Charlotte was probably imagining it anyway. But the café is still in darkness, and she won't leave the child alone.

"I love your coat, by the way," Charlotte says.

"My auntie made it." Ilse smooths it down, gratified. "Out of a blanket."

"She's so clever. Do you think she'd make me one?"

Ilse grins, revealing a quirk of dentition, a raised incisor that will no doubt fall into place when she's fully grown. She must be thirteen, Charlotte thinks, fourteen at most. For God's sake.

"If you can get the fabric, she can make you *anything*."

"I have a ratty old rayon bedspread. What about that?"

"Magnificent! You'd look like a queen."

Charlotte laughs. "You know, we should walk together every morning."

"Oh, *rather!*" Ilse says it just like an English child.

"All right then." Charlotte tweaks the peak of the girl's knitted cap so that it puffs up, then slowly sinks. "That's agreed. Don't work too hard now."

Ilse grins. She knocks on the door, and Mrs. Watson lumbers up from the back of the café to let her in.

Charlotte pauses at the haberdasher's window, watching the reflections as they pass behind her. Commuters to the City, an exhausted woman pushing a perambulator, two perky women in uniform chattering away. And one man—her heart stalls—in grey. Grey coat, grey trilby. He lingers at the newsagent's stand, while everybody else just whips by, grabbing whichever paper best matches their opinions and dropping their coins. The paper seller accosts him; he's obliged to choose a newspaper and rifle out coins. Then he looks at her. He stares across the street at where she's standing, by the haberdasher's window. She goes cold. That broad face. Those pale eyes. She knows him.

Then he turns away and goes into the station. The paper seller drops the money into the cash bag at his waist. The man in grey does not come out again.

You do realise this is not normal?

I know him, El.

Lotts. See sense. How many men in grey coats and hats are there in this city?

But I know him.

You must pass a dozen such every time you leave the house.

But I *know* him. Those eyes.

To assume this means something, some malign intent. Well, that's just—

After your funeral, El. After . . . Clive. On Marylebone Road. He was there. He heard me talking to myself. And I thought I knew him then; I was sure I'd already seen him before.

Remember what my mother said. Don't let it set you back.

Sound advice. I don't deny it. But this isn't that. This is something else.

If you say so. But he's gone now, so what are you waiting for?

For a train to come and go each way.

And then?

Then I'll go down to the platform. And if he's still there, I'll know he isn't waiting for a train.

She buys her ticket, picks her way down. There's a cluster of passengers further along the platform; she can't see if he's among them. Nearer by, there's an elderly gent with a small dog on a lead; a slender young man in Air Force blue smoking outside the lavatory. She peers into the waiting room, where the piebald cat sleeps and two middle-aged women confer, turbaned heads together. She turns and scans the far platform. A train recently departed, it fills up again with a trickle of bankers, brokers and clerks. Each of them quite intent on their own business, sealed into their trajectories, heading for whatever's left of the City this morning. None of them are him.

A train pulls in at her platform. She puts her back to the wall, watches. The cluster breaks into a stream and boards the train—no sign of him. The women bustle out of the waiting room and get on board; the old man lifts his dog and the airman throws his cigarette aside. Doors are clapped shut. The train slides away. Her gaze skips to each pasted-over window as it passes by. Vague shapes, that's all. There is no way of telling individuals apart, through the gauze and paint. But her platform's empty now anyway. He's gone.

I saw him in Marylebone, and I'd seen him somewhere else before that, and now I've seen him in the street where I live.

Vanessa's vibrant tones throb through her head: *Cold sores.*

Oh God, not you again.

Shingles.

What are you on about?

Syphilis.

Excuse me?

You might think you're better, but they linger in the system. The moment you're a bit off, a bit below par, they'll creep back out. Before you know it, there you are, scabs on your face or a rash down your chest or your nose half rotten and falling off.

Must you?

I'm only telling you the truth. It's not as though anybody else will. You always were a misfit, no real friends apart from Hartwell, at odds and angles with everybody else. Came as no surprise to me to hear they'd locked you up the first time round. All it took was a teensy bit of pressure then. And how much more pressure is there now?

And then El: *Shut up, Vanessa, do. Lotts, don't let her get to you.*

Charlotte chews a nail. She shifts against the wall.

I know it hurts, El says. *I know it's hard . . .*

You don't know, El. You can't. You never lost you.

. . . but you need to do normal things.

I know.

So get on a train and go to work. There's one coming now.

I know.

Because if you can't actually be normal, then just act normal. Till you start to feel normal again.

I know. I don't want to. But I know.

Eddie, she thinks. Eddie. Are you there?

Eddie. Take my side. Stand up for me.

There is nothing from him. There's just the dark, and cold, and distance. No voice speaks back to her.

The train pulls in.

Go on, El says. *Go on.*

She pushes away from the wall.

She is rattled to Victoria, where she is swept along with the flow of passengers, past cordons and boarded-off bomb damage, and then down into the Underground. She hangs from a strap, swaying, all the way to Warren Street, where she slips off the train and climbs, blinking, into the light. At Senate House, she attaches herself to the tail end of the staff ingress, and somehow manages not to be late, and to have got all the way to work without having noticed anything very much of her journey there at all.

Janet's desk is empty when Charlotte arrives. It remains empty, the leatherette cover still on the typewriter, as the clock ticks round to nine o'clock. And Janet is never late. She is almost pathologically early; she arrives early and works through lunch and leaves early. But, come to think of it, she has been off now for a few days. She wasn't in on Monday; she wasn't in on Tuesday, either.

When Mrs. Denby hands over her stuffed-fat folder, Charlotte gives her the best smile she can manage.

"When are we expecting Mrs. Fuller back?" she asks.

Mrs. Denby's eyes widen. "I wish I knew; we really need her. But I haven't had a moment. I'll telephone her now."

But Mrs. Denby perhaps does not get through; she certainly doesn't report back, and then she's off to a meeting with Mrs. Adams, and the dust cover stays on Janet's machine all day.

Charlotte will ring Janet up when she gets home tonight. She'll brave the vicar. And then Charlotte's thoughts spin off from worry about Janet, to Saskia and Mary swaying on the brink of chaos in Chelsea, to Mr. Jackson staunch at his post in that deadly lobby, to the flower seller and the café man, and thence to Tom, the undertaker's boy who feeds the birds, and Ilse, who walks to work in the morning dark, and how vulnerable everybody is; how impossible it is for her to keep track even of the people that she actually knows, let alone a whole city full of people.

Instead of marching to the Tube that evening, she crosses to the Square, goes in through the gate and follows the path around the lawns and gardens. His bench is empty; she sits. The boy doesn't appear, but the birds do. A chaffinch perches on the arm of the seat. Sparrows land and hop around, cock their heads at her. Pigeons flap over.

"Have you seen him?" she asks the chaffinch, but the chaffinch just turns his head to stare at her from the other eye, and then flutters off.

A gentleman with a fox terrier tips his hat to her, and she says good evening. It's getting chilly. Leaves shower down in the breeze. She stays put; she crosses and recrosses her legs, lights a cigarette, taps a dangling foot. She shivers. It will take God knows how long to get back across town, the way the trains are, and the light's already fading. And she really doesn't want to have to shelter in the Tube, where it's all straying hands and noisy bonhomie and muffled crying till morning. She thumbs the roll of peppermints in her pocket, puts another in her mouth.

I hope you are all right, she thinks. Wherever you are, whatever you're up to. I do hope you are safe.

She gets up from the bench; the birds scatter. She heads for the Tube.

Everything feels rickety and unstable; the ground seems to be sliding away from underneath her feet. She no longer feels sure of anything at all, other than that she would have liked to have seen Thomas Hawthorne, the boy who feeds the birds.

She peers both ways along the empty street before going in through her front door. Mrs. Callaghan, arms bundled with belongings, halts on the turn of the basement stairs.

"Yellow's up; Mr. Gibbons just telephoned to say," Mrs. Callaghan calls back to her. "I'm going straight down."

"Be with you in a minute."

"Oh, and there was a call for you."

"Oh?"

"That young man again. Mr. Hartwell."

She hesitates. "Did he leave a message?"

"Just to say he'd rang. And that you can still reach him on that number." A knowing mischief in her eye. That young man you're courting, Mrs. Callaghan is clearly thinking.

"Right, yes. Thank you." Charlotte still has his number crumpled in her pocket, but she can't ring him now, even if she wanted to, not with a yellow warning up.

That's classy. Vanessa flips her weedy hair back over her shoulder. Using an air raid to excuse a general lack of decency.

"Are you coming down?" Mrs. Callaghan asks.

"I'll just fetch my things."

Charlotte races upstairs. It's quickly learned, the list of objects one cannot be comfortable without. She drags her dressing gown on over her clothes and grabs her gas mask and her handbag and her book, then bundles up the quilt off her bed. The earrings are in her dressing-table drawer. She hesitates a moment, then slips the box into her pocket.

The next day, she arrives at work in a blur of fatigue. Janet's type-writer still squats silent under its dust cover. Charlotte leans across the empty desk to wave at Stella—has she heard anything?

Stella's lips compress. Her eyes fill. She nods.

Janet, Charlotte remembers, prefers a rose-red to a pillar-box lip-stick, James Stewart to Cary Grant, sticky buns to cream cakes; she had lost her parents young, was married to a vicar, worked in Home Intelligence, and had no children. This is more or less the sum total of what Charlotte knows about her friend. She liked Janet, she really did, but their interactions, she now comes to realise, had been almost pathologically superficial. Janet died in an air raid, in the early hours of Sunday. That she had barely a mark on her is supposed to be some comfort to them. That, as Mrs. Denby reports, she must have gone gently, after all.

Charlotte sits at her desk, Janet's empty chair and shrouded typewriter just beside her, head bent over the cup of sweet tea that Mrs. Denby had ordered up for them especially.

A scabbed hand lands on the back of El's bentwood chair. Lace floats and flutters.

Gently, my eye.

What?

Gently, my eye, my foot, and arse.

A gaping mouth; a Chelsea bun stuffed in whole. El swivels round to look up, recoils. The next words come out clagged and sticky, spraying crumbs:

Everybody fights for the next breath. Tooth and nail. The body wants to live.

Janet?

Around her mouthful: *Afternoon.*

It's not like you to be so . . .

What?

So, well, forthright. Unrestrained.

The gloves are off now. I don't fucking care. The gloves are off.

El glares round at her. *Perhaps you could moderate your language?*

I won't moderate anything at all. Look where that got me.

"Are you all right?" Stella asks.

Charlotte nods. Head in hands, she stares down at her cooling tea.

Not you too, Janet. Not you too.

She has the number of the plot written on a slip of paper so that she would not forget it. These things are dealt with so much more quickly already; there was no time, apparently, for the usual formalities. Even for a vicar's wife. But still, Charlotte thinks, as she gets off the train at Clapham Junction, he could have let them know; Charlotte would have wanted to have been there. Though what Charlotte would have wanted must be of limited interest to a man in his position. He must have so many pressing needs to consider, before he can even get to wants.

She carries a bunch of Michaelmas daisies and goldenrod bought from the flower seller by the station, who remains defiantly unscathed. It's been a grey day, and now, as she makes her way towards the cemetery, it's getting dark. She can hear aircraft, and the crump of guns, but it's all fairly distant, and she feels safe enough for now, shrouded round and cut off by the gloom.

She walks the gravel paths. The graves are still raw, spade-cuts clear in the turf. There are no headstones yet, and some of the numbers are missing, and some seem to be out of sequence. She counts up along a row, then counts down from the other end, and there's a bunch of yellow chrysanthemums lying on the plot she thinks is probably the right one. They're half-rotten, petals scattered on the grass. She takes off her gloves, crouches, picks up the faded flowers and lays her bunch there instead.

I'm sorry, Janet. Don't even know if that's you.

Appreciate the effort, nonetheless.

You seem more mellow now.

Touched you bothered to come.

I miss you.

I'd hardly think so.

Well I do. I do miss you. It's not the same without you here.

Charlotte stands, clutching the rotten flowers. She goes to look for a compost heap, and her eye catches on movement. She stops, stares. Nothing. She moves on, and catches a shiver again, in the tail of her sight. She spins round, chasing it—headstones, tombs, a stone angel, yew trees.

Imagining it, El says.

Losing it, says Vanessa.

Ghosts? Janet suggests, peeling apart a bun and posting a piece between her teeth.

Charlotte takes a step, and as she moves, her line of sight shifts, so that a nearby headstone slides across one further off; beyond that, an angel emerges between shrubs and slowly slips across her field of vision. Parallax, isn't that what it's called? Parallax shift. School wasn't particularly concerned about science, but she remembers that.

She fixes her eye on an obelisk, walks, noting a stone cross slide in and out of sight behind it. It is hard work, just to be sure of what she's seeing. She dumps the flowers on a compost heap. Her hands are tacky with plant-rot and sweat.

Not mad, though. Not even imagining it. It's an optical illusion. It could happen to anyone.

The day has already taken three more steps down into darkness by the time she's left the cemetery. The evening is filthy, soupy; passers-by loom up out of the murk and are gone, their faces cadaverous and startling.

I'm so sorry, Janet, that you're gone.

I'm not that bothered. Or that gone.

But I wish you'd had more fun while you were with us. You needed someone to coax you into it, and he didn't do it, and I didn't do it enough. He whisked you off from work to more work and you barely got to say a word.

And he didn't even bother to let us know that you had died.

Charlotte rubs at her temples. She makes her way towards Clapham Junction, joining a thickening stream of people hastening to catch their trains. She remembers the bushel basket, the young woman, the severed hand lifted from the ground that glinted gold. Elena lying in her coffin like a painted doll.

"Yellow's up."

There are more people here, moving faster, dashing past her, slipping by, all rushing in the same direction. It takes her a moment to realise what was said. Its significance. A yellow warning.

If that's right, then she has less than ten minutes before the sirens sound, maybe ten more before the aircraft are directly overhead. Chances are it won't be a false alarm, not here. They keep coming for this area. Hammering it. Here is one of the worst places it's possible to be.

There's a crowd outside the station. She jinks around at the back; it stretches all the way into the ticket office, and up the stairs beyond. People pile in behind her; ahead of her the crowd shuffles forward, but only inches, just closing up spaces. And there's that prickle in the air, at the nape of her neck.

What's that phrase that keeps popping into your head?

Not now, El.

Then she hears, yelled from the station, "Last train out!"

There's a wail and groan from the crowd, and an onward swell, and she's shoved up against the woman in front of her, cheek pressed into her coat. Her heart flips like a hooked fish.

What is that phrase, Lotts? You keep saying it to yourself.

Charlotte stumbles. The breath is crushed out of her. They're not all getting on that train. And staying here is a really bad idea.

Searchlights slice the sky. Then thick, sickening thuds—far too close. Yelps and shouts and the crowd surges. She staggers, puts a hand on a stranger's back, pushes hard, just to keep some space between them. As her sightline shifts, she sees him. Quarter profile, not looking in her direction, but still unmistakably him. Bulky, grey, pale-eyed—the shadow man. Her heart goes still. Everything slows. She turns away.

"Excuse me."

She eases herself between the people next to her. "Excuse me."

They do their best to let her pass, glad to have one fewer person ahead of them. She edges along, apologising, pushing, then pitches out into open space. She sucks down air.

Now she's stuck here, in Battersea, with a yellow warning up.

She bites down hard on instinct and she walks away.

Stupid.

Stupid.

Stupid.

Someone must know where to go, but there's no one to ask; away from the station, the streets are deserted. If she can just find a warden's post . . . She hurries on.

The planes drone closer; the bombs thud like running footfalls. There is no tried-and-true method, no rule of thumb with a raid; you can't count it out like the seconds between the lightning and its thunder. Then the sky floods white. They're dropping flares.

Now what was it that you kept saying to yourself?

Not now, El, Christ's sake.

Not now. That's my point exactly. That's exactly what I mean.

Ahead of her, the power station shows its belly to the sky. To her right, the gathered railway lines slide away in polished curves. And then there's the river; she can't see it from here, but she knows it snakes along nearby, shimmering and treacherous. She turns about, pinned by the impossibility of it all.

Is this what it's like?

But Janet just sucks her teeth.

You don't know? You don't remember? You said it wasn't gentle.

I know just about as much as you do, duck. Janet turns her face away, as though she can't bear to watch. *That's all any of us know.*

A whistle right through the air above her; Charlotte drops to a crouch, flings her arms over her head. A clang; she stiffens. No explosion; she looks up. A metal cannister has hit the ground only ten feet away; and then, as she watches, another one falls, and then another, a dot-dot-dot of silver down the street. There's a moment's pause. She thinks, these have come all the way from Germany. She thinks, somebody made them in a factory. She thinks, somebody loaded them onto a plane. And now there they are, lying there along the street in Battersea. Then the nearest one gives off a hiss and stir, a sound like dry leaves blown by the wind. Then there's a fizz of flame. The light is silvery and strange. And then, after all that she has read and been told, about the proper way to deal with incendiaries, with a cool head, a shovel, and a bucket full of sand, she backs off, turns, and runs.

She has just made it under a railway arch when the ground buckles and the air thumps her back. She staggers on. Everything ahead is washed with a weird orange glare: gap-toothed streets; a crouching, solid church. She looks back; the heat hits her face. A bank of flame. Something big—a gas main or fuel store—has gone up.

She staggers on towards the church.

The door clangs shut behind her. She is in a shadowy space. She takes off her gloves and wipes her cheeks and tries to catch her breath. The noise of the air raid comes buffered by thick stone walls and boarded windows. Her footfalls ring out on the stone floor. The nave is deserted, but from somewhere nearby comes the murmur and whiff of humanity. She finds herself staring up at a crucifix. Frail ribs and hollow belly, waxy skin; beads of blood drip from the crown of thorns and from the iron nails in hands and feet. She shivers. The things you have to do just because your father says you should.

"Can I help you?"

She turns towards a familiar voice. The vicar is frailer than when she last saw him, his complexion liverish in the yellow light. Mrs. Parkin, in her West Country way, would say that he was hanging; Mrs. Callaghan would say that he looked awful failed. Charlotte knows well enough how grief feels; now she can see how it looks.

"Good evening—"

He doesn't recognise her. "I heard the door," he says. "It doesn't do to linger above ground. You can sit out the storm with us."

The neighbourhood has packed itself into the crypt like meat in a tin. Men, women, children, cats, dogs and canaries, three-tier bunks with huddled sleepers, benches, deckchairs, piles of belongings, cases, blankets. Trestle tables have been set out down one end, and a makeshift kitchen cobbled together; women are busy preparing tea and sandwiches. Charlotte rubs her arms; it's cold down here. And the smell. Base notes of bodies, breath and old clothes, and over that, the chemical, faecal stink of Elsan closets. The raid goes on above; she can feel it through her body, feel the pressure change in her ears; the planes' drone is still there, in the background, like the hum of a factory.

He leads her over to one of the tables, where a woman and small child look up at her with matching pairs of china-blue eyes, then shunt along the bench to make room, the woman scooping up the child onto her knee.

"Thank you," she says. She takes off her hat and gloves, slides in beside them.

Then he rests his palm for just a moment on Charlotte's crown. She stiffens, startled. Then he lifts his hand and walks away.

"I don't know you," the woman says.

Charlotte touches her hair uneasily. "No, I'm not from round here."

The woman widens her eyes: Then why be here at all?

"I knew his wife," Charlotte says, with a nod towards the vicar.

"Oh dear."

"I know."

"I'm sorry."

"I came to leave her flowers."

"That's nice."

"I didn't think for a moment I'd get stuck."

"No one ever does."

"You could get evacuated, though, with the little one," Charlotte says. "You could be somewhere lovely now instead."

"We did. It wasn't. We came back."

"Oh?"

The woman rolls her eyes. "Those people and their charity."

"There." He's back, places a cup of weak tea and a paste sandwich down in front of her.

"You're very kind." She leans out of the way. "Thank you."

"Man cannot live by bread alone, but that's where we like to start."

His hands are scraped and scabbed, she sees, just like Janet's had been.

"I was very sorry," she says, "to hear about Mrs. Fuller."

His jaw tightens. "It has been a difficult time. We miss her every day."

Oh I bet you do, Janet hisses. *At the tea urn, in the parish hall, when the church needs cleaned.*

"Make yourself comfortable," he says. And then he weaves away.

The raid continues. The woman holds the child's head pressed to her, a hand over her exposed ear. The girl keeps drifting off to sleep, but at every impact, she startles back to wakefulness. The woman tries to soothe her, her own nerves jangling, a desperate edge to her voice.

"He's a good man," Charlotte says experimentally.

A sceptical eyebrow. "Do anything for you, he would."

"Anything?"

"Near as makes no difference. He'll wash your feet for you, if you let him."

Charlotte was going to sip her tea, but stops short. "Wash your feet?"

"Maundy Thursday, he's there with a big bowl of warm water and a bar of Lifebuoy."

"Is that . . . done?" Charlotte no longer goes to church, except for funerals. But she can't recall the officiant at school chapel ever soaping up two thousand wriggling schoolgirl toes, or the vicar at Longwood scrubbing his parishioners' horny heels. And the feet of Battersea must be a stale and calloused lot. An image of her own, slippery with soap; his fingers sliding between her toes. She puts the teacup down. "Why would he do that?"

The woman shakes her head. "I tell you, if there was a decent municipal shelter, we'd be there, like a shot."

Charlotte's about to press this further, but the woman looks down at her child, who has finally fallen asleep, long eyelashes on pale cheeks.

"Will you scuse me, love? I better get some kip too, while I can."

And so Charlotte, her questions still only half-formed, slides out from the bench. She watches the woman carry her child over to the bunk, where her possessions—a small suitcase and a folded blanket— are already stowed.

With no bunk of her own, Charlotte returns to her seat and pillows her head on folded arms. She closes her eyes, screws them up tight as the ground jolts and rumbles: the giants are playing football tonight. They're crashing into buildings, kicking bits off them, sending things flying. In the crypt, a baby cries and cries. A woman murmurs prayers. A thud, a rush of masonry, someone says, "Fuck," and someone else says, "That'll be the station," and then someone else starts to argue, "It was further off than that," and there's a pause, and the pause stretches, and Charlotte begins to breathe softly, and a blanket is laid over her shoulders. It smells of body and smoke, and a hand rests again on her head, and the words are murmured:

"God bless you, child."

The slow shallow beach in Galloway, distant fog, still water. She is swimming with Eddie. He's talking, laughing, wet hair slicked back, his skin paper-white, his body delicate as a frog's. This is ours, he says. This is our ritual cleansing; every year, we forgive ourselves, we bless ourselves, we make ourselves anew. He ducks under, crashes back up. Cos no other bugger's going to do it for us, that's for sure. He pulls away, strong strokes, and the fog creeps closer.

Wait for me. Eddie. Eddie. Wait for me.

But just stillness in the water, grey meeting grey.

And then a foghorn sounds, and she turns, foundering, searching, but no sign of him, no sound of him, and she cries out for him, but her voice cracks and fails and she starts awake. The long level keening of the all-clear, filled with mourning for the night that went before.

She peers at her watch. It's half past five. She sits up and the blanket slides off her. She scoops it up and folds it, and looks round the crypt, to the piles of clothes and blankets and bodies and belongings, the people stirring, gathering their things, getting ready to go. There is no sign of the vicar.

Charlotte makes her way upstairs, back into the main body of the church, still in blackout. There he is, on his knees at the altar rail, a hunched shadow, head bent onto folded hands, deep in prayer. She does not know what to make of him; this discomfiting, devout, charitable man.

Charlotte manages to flag down an early bus and climbs up to the empty top deck. It takes her on a devious route through streets unused to traffic, past curtained bedroom windows, scraping the canopies of trees, all the way to Euston. From there, it's only a short walk to the office; she arrives an hour before it opens. Her muscles ache, her head swims; she feels fogged and anxious, as though she has something important to do but has forgotten what it is. She takes herself to the nearby corner café, where she orders a cheap breakfast of mushrooms on toast, and sips her tea, and wonders how much of a wash and brush-up she can manage in the office ladies' lavatory.

She's already waiting outside when the janitor unlocks the main doors; she darts through with a "Good morning," but without catching his eye, and rushes up the stairs. In the mirror she sees a ghoul: skin and hair grey with dust, eyes rimmed with red. She washes her face with hard soap, dries it on a loop of towel that's already crisp with use. She scrubs her teeth with a corner of her handkerchief, powders her shiny nose, dabs on lipstick, combs out and repins her hair. It feels sticky. She still looks a fright. She tries a smile, but that's even worse.

She rises from her desk as Mrs. Denby bustles in, taking off her gloves.

"Good morning, Miss Richmond! First one in today, I see!"

And then Mrs. Denby's expression changes as she takes in Charlotte's appearance.

"Are you all right?"

Despite every determination to be calm, Charlotte's voice wavers. "I went to see the grave."

"Ah."

"I got stuck out there. In a raid. I mean, in a shelter. In the thick of it. It was pretty bad."

A hand on her arm. "Do you want to go home?"

Charlotte clears her throat. "I'm better working. And we're . . ." She was going to say *already one short,* but that feels flippant. "We've lost Janet. So."

A sympathetic squeeze. But that just makes it worse.

"All right. If you're up to it."

Mrs. Denby sidles into her tiny office and lifts the telephone. Charlotte, as she readies her typewriter, can hear the older woman dialling; then the whirring stops, and the handset is set back down. Mrs. Denby returns to the doorway.

"Oh, Miss Richmond."

"Charlotte, please—"

"Charlotte. Dear. I'm sorry. But one thing."

Charlotte sits up straight. "Yes?"

"About your work. I'm sorry. This is not a good time. But then it never is. I've been meaning to say." Mrs. Denby comes over. She rests a hand on the desktop. Her nails are pearly-pink, beautifully buffed. Her clothing—a moss-green suit and oyster-coloured blouse—is immaculate.

Charlotte is suddenly more conscious than ever of her physical self. The smell of the shelter lingering about her. Her crumpled clothes and the grit in her hair and her clown-like powder and lipstick. The sheer unmanageableness of her face.

"Yes?"

Mrs. Denby grimaces sympathetically. "Because, you know, forewarned is, I think, forearmed."

"I see." Charlotte looks away.

"Well, the problem is, you see, your speeds. You are just very *slow;* I'm sorry to say it, but it's true. And your accuracy, if I'm honest. I know you don't have your RSA certificate and so we shouldn't expect too much from you. But, forgive me, I also know that Mrs. Fuller was helping you. I didn't object to that. I admire your sticking at it. Especially as you're not, well, very good at it. I admire your tenacity. But accuracy is an issue. We catch some of your mistakes, but perhaps we're missing others. And if the errors started to stack up. Well, then we would be in a pickle, wouldn't we?"

Charlotte nods. She supposes that we would.

Mrs. Denby lays a hand on her shoulder. "Because the work matters, my dear. Decisions are made on the basis of this work. Decisions that might change the course of, well, everything."

The guilt is grey; it bubbles up inside her, seeps and sticks.

"I don't wish to further upset you. It's been a truly horrible time. But I do know you're not brought up to this. Ladies of your background, well, they volunteer, don't they? They fundraise, they oversee, they organise. They don't type."

Charlotte knows that this is true. She has to fight the urge to get up from her desk and run out of the room. She can't run away from this.

"Just a word to the wise, my dear. You *can* do better, I know you can do better. But you need to do it"—Mrs. Denby drops her voice to a whisper at the upcoming expletive, even though it's only indicated by its initial—"PDQ. If you want to stay."

Charlotte's voice sounds small. "I want to stay."

"All right then. Good. We are agreed."

Mrs. Denby's tone is encouraging, but Charlotte only feels a dragging shame. Stupid, stupid, stupid. Of course the work matters. Every figure, every comma, every rumour and complaint; it must all add up to something. Just because she doesn't see the sum total herself doesn't mean that other people aren't frantically working it out. And for her, too, personally, the work is essential. Everything depends on it. Her rent, her train and bus fares, her lunchtime bun, her ability to meet her own eye in the mirror, and tell herself that she can be allowed to live another day; all of this depends on her earning a wage, and being able to continue to evade her father's efforts to impose an allowance on her. Just because they let her do this work doesn't mean it doesn't matter.

Mrs. Denby squeezes her shoulder. "Good girl."

"Thank you," Charlotte says, with new determination. "Thanks."

When Stella comes in, Charlotte barely speaks to her, so brutally conscious is she of her own deficiencies. She only murmurs to Mrs. Denby, and then only about work. She feels that there's a haze around her, white and necrotic, like the pale halo around a wound. Three women that she loves have died. A grey figure creeps along in the corner of her eye. And she is failing at the simplest of tasks. She chews and chews and chews on this all day at work, in silence. She chews on it all the way home on the train. She can't keep chewing on it forever, by herself. And there is only one person left that she can think of who can be supposed to care.

Café Bleu

It turns out it has not been so long since she last saw Clive, after all. He doesn't seem particularly put out. He's not to know how entirely she had intended to avoid this, or that she had to search her pockets to find and flatten out his crumpled number before calling him.

Soho, for goodness' sake, though.

The place itself is just this side of acceptable. Noisy, convivial, the waiters overfamiliar; there's an accordion propped up behind the counter; God help us, someone might even start to play. All the clientele are couples, lovers. And then there's her and Clive.

"Well, you do look lovely," he says.

She manages not to say *Really?* She's shattered, and in terms of tenue has gone for uninviting: a simple black dress, already old when the war broke out, with a newish cream collar and gloves. She could teach Sunday school dressed like this. She wears the black pearl earrings, too, defiantly. It's not like she's going to bump into Father in Soho. Or if she did, that'd open up such a huge kettle of fish that a pair of purloined earrings would pale into insignificance. Clive fills out a navy suit and white shirt and there's a flash of gold at his cuff when he flags down a passing waiter. He asks for a Scotch and soda; she orders one too.

He's looking well, El says.

Is this him? Janet wonders. *Oh, I like the look of him. He has a bit of substance to him. Looks like he knows how to enjoy himself.*

He's fat, Vanessa opines, barely looking up. *And scant of breath.*

"I was glad you telephoned," he says.

"I'm sorry, yes, the phone's been out, and then what with work . . ."

"Oh yes, I know. Everybody's busy."

The waiter brings their drinks; he drains half his glass. Charlotte sips. She wants to tell him how women that she loves seem to be dying like cut flowers. She wants to tell him about the shadow man lurking in her street. That it's hard to concentrate on anything, to be sure of anything, because of the voices in her head, voices that even now are commenting on her posture—thank you, Vanessa—making her adjust herself, sit straighter, hold her head up nicely—or rattling on about him—*Solid meaty fellow like that, something to get your teeth into.* Charlotte wants, she really wants, to ask him, don't you think it's strange that everyone said El died in an air raid, but she looked so perfect. She can't blurt it out just like that, but she can't find a reasonable, sensible, not-at-all-crazy way to say it.

But Clive's talking anyway. He's telling her how difficult things have been for him. How his parents lean on him more heavily than ever, now that El is gone. How work has become next to impossible. How his father still believes that he's in charge, but refuses to accept wartime regulations. He can't stand it that the bottles are unbranded, that the family name is gone from the labels. He can't stand it that the company is now producing what he calls an abomination. He tried to smash a whole batch of the new cordial just today. He doesn't understand the limitations they're working under. And rhubarb cordial is really far nicer than it sounds. Charlotte should try it.

"I will."

"It's so good to talk to someone who knows us all, and understands," he says.

She gets out her cigarettes. He hastens to strike a match for her.

"How are they holding up otherwise?" Charlotte asks, dipping to the flame.

He lights his own cigarette. His lines deepen.

"Father," he says, "barely speaks now. I mean, he shouts at work. But he doesn't talk at home any more. Not to Mother, or to me."

A slick of guilt spreads through her.

Lord, she's so solipsistic, isn't she? Vanessa flicks back her dripping hair. *Thinks every single thing is to do with her.*

"And your mother? How is she?"

"Busy," he says.

"Busy?"

"Almost manic. She announces that they're moving up to Rydal.

She packs things up, and then they don't leave, and then she starts to need the things she's packed, so she unpacks again."

"You think they will go?" To the house by the wide water, the beech trees whispering.

"I hope they do, it'd get Dad out of the way."

I could get to like it here, Janet says, swilling down Scotch and soda between chunks of Chelsea bun. *Do you think he'll buy us another drink?*

Ask him what you need to ask him, El murmurs. *He's my brother. He's a decent man, whatever indecencies you might have committed upon him. He's known you since you were twelve years old.*

Charlotte shivers.

"Goose walk over your grave?"

She looks up at his face, its roughly sketched traces of El. She looks down at her hands, entwined on the tabletop, playing with her cigarette.

"Don't you think it's odd," she tries.

My God! Your cuticles! Vanessa barks.

Charlotte darts her hands under the table. Cigarette smoke now rises from her lap.

"Don't you think it's odd," she says again, carefully.

And your fingers are so yellowed. You need a cigarette holder, if you really must smoke, though I consider it uncouth and it's certainly bad for the skin. You wouldn't catch me dead—

Charlotte shakes her head, trying to clear it.

"Don't you think," she begins again, looking up at Clive. His expression is still, contained. As though he is withholding something. But she sets the words down carefully, one after the other, as though standing dominos in a row. "That it was odd."

Spoonfingers, Vanessa adds.

Spoonfingers? Charlotte blinks.

From typing. Broad and flattened at the tips. So common.

Give over, Cavendish, El says. *For goodness' sake, let her speak.*

"That El. That her body. Was so intact." She gains momentum. "I mean, you said so yourself. You said that she looked perfect. And after a raid. And when you think what can happen in a raid."

Clive leans away. There's a sliver of concern to his look, along with a sliver of disdain.

She recognises this expression. She's seen people look at her like this before. "No, why would you? I don't know why I even—I didn't mean for a moment—"

"Charlotte."

She falls silent.

"I understand," he says.

She widens her eyes, raises her eyebrows. You do?

"I know how difficult all this is for you. You must be beside yourself. I know I was. I am. I wanted to say . . ." He leans in again, and drops his voice. "That afternoon, when we . . . We were both upset. And things like that, they can happen, when one's in a state like that. But I should never . . . It was wrong of me. I took advantage of the situation, I took advantage of you."

Her cheeks flush hot. She lifts her cigarette . . .

Hands!

. . . and takes a long drag. Clive talks on.

"And I wanted to apologise. For that. It's not something I would normally have done. It was entirely out of character. I am quite ashamed of myself. I should not have, I never would have done a thing like that at all, if I had not been so distressed."

She grinds out her cigarette, shunts her seat back.

"You're not going?"

She should have left him well enough alone.

"I seem to be."

She walks through the busy bar, slips past the blackout curtains and opens the door into the Soho night. The shadows are thick and busy. Limbs and shuffling and breaths. Girls stand on the corners, in almost darkness. She follows the white lines painted on the pavement, hurrying to the Tube.

Did we have to leave? Janet says. *I liked it there.*

She replaces the earrings in their box, returns the box to her dressing-table drawer. She brushes down her dress, hangs it up, puts away her gloves and collar. She stays in on Friday evening. Where would she go anyway? The raids remain at arm's length. The gas and electric stay on, so she puts up the blackout, lights her lamp, gets out her portable

Olivetti and her *Pitman's Business Typewriting,* and she practises. She's aware of the distant wails of sirens and the pounding far-off bombs, and the music rising up through the floor from Mr. Gibbons's gramophone, and the warm smoulder in her fireplace, and in their own way each of these things is comforting. The exercises take over. She fills pages densely, flips them, scrolls the paper back in and starts again. It helps. It helps to think she is securing her position. It helps to quieten the voices in her head. She taps and taps and taps; the clock ticks, the fire fizzes and the music rises. Mr. Gibbons has a romantic ear; Schumann softens the arrhythmic clatter of her work.

Charlotte bumps into him—Mr. Gibbons, that is—later, on the landing, when she is slipping downstairs for a mug of Horlicks before bed. He is on his way back from the bathroom, a towel folded over his arm, impeccable in a burgundy quilted dressing-gown, forest-green pyjamas and soft leather slippers. A lady really should not comment, but she has long since abandoned any notion of being a lady.

"I have a weakness for beautiful things," he confesses. "I could have a flat of my own by now if I hadn't bought so many shirts."

Saturday she spends in coffee shops and at the pictures. Watches footage of the survivors of the *City of Benares;* lifeboats being picked up at sea. Children in their nightclothes in tiny boats. It doesn't help. She chews her nails. Clive keeps muscling back to the surface of her thoughts.

I don't know why you're in such a stew about it, Janet says. *You were taking advantage of him too.*

Difference is, Vanessa says, *that he's honest. Whereas madam here has her delusions. She thinks all the men want* her, *for her irresistible self. When all they really want is a—*

It's fair play, El says. *Take advantage of each other. Go right ahead. No harm done.*

Charlotte would go and see Saskia and be comforted, if Saskia was in any state to offer comfort. Maybe she'll pop round on Sunday, see how things are going. That particular storm might have blown itself out by now.

But on Sunday, inertia claims her. It is as much as she can do to rinse out her blouses and stockings for next week, and hang them up to dry. Officially, her rent includes laundry, but Mrs. Callaghan boils everything she gets her hands on. Which does rather explain the state of that cardigan. Then Charlotte has to wash her hair, and that takes ages, the sink rimmed with dirt even after two rinses, and the water running cold so that the soap flakes don't properly dissolve; she dries it by the fire that evening, and thinks of Saskia, and how what she really wants is Saskia as she used to be, not Saskia as she is now, and so Saskia remains unvisited.

What about my old man, Janet offers.

What about him?

You could go and talk to him.

I don't want to talk to him.

He's good at that kind of thing. Consolation. Probably.

But Charlotte doesn't want to talk to anyone.

That night, when her light's extinguished, she takes the blackout down and watches the tracery of searchlights, listens to the planes and the bombs and the guns. The sky is dirty orange. She hears Mr. Gibbons clatter down the stairs and clap the front door shut. Mrs. Callaghan will be huddled up with Lady Jane. Charlotte could join them in the basement, or even Mr. Gibbons, out at the wardens' post, but she can't bring herself to move; her head is full of noise, and she's befuddled, tongue-tied, her thoughts scrambled by constant interruptions. She can't bear to inflict herself on anybody else.

When the raid fades out, and the all-clear sounds, and morning is near, she hears Mrs. Callaghan emerge from the cellar and do her rounds of the house, reassuring herself that all the rooms are still there. She listens, breathing, outside Charlotte's door for a moment, before moving on. Charlotte hears, too, Mr. Gibbons's return, hears the front door open and close, hears the weary climb to his room; she hears the sounds of him getting ready for his day's work, hears him leave again. Then she turns over and stares at the wall.

Doing Better

When she pauses in her work to correct her posture and ease out her neck, Charlotte spies Mrs. Denby peering at her through the panels of her cubbyhole. She raises a hand. Mrs. Denby smiles encouragingly. Charlotte's speeds are up; her accuracy is improved. Charlotte feels no pleasure in it, only an abeyance of guilt. But the work helps. Work, obsessive work, takes up some of the space that would otherwise fill with grief. But the moment her concentration slips, the voices crowd close, demanding her attention.

Often, on the way home of an evening, Charlotte thinks, I could just stop here, on the street. I could just lie down here and never move again. On the pavement. Outside the station. Huddled in that corner. Nobody would mind. But she drags herself back to Woodland Road, and straight up to her room. Not a word to anyone. She sets her Olivetti on the dressing table, drags herself in, scrolls paper. Neck and shoulders tight from the day's work—

I told you to sit properly.

She adjusts her posture, leafs through her Pitman's. She'll have to buy the next book in the sequence, or begin this one again, and do the same old exercises all over again, just better.

A bell is ringing downstairs. She carries on typing. The noise drills hard. Telephone. It will not be for her. Not even Clive calls her any more.

But when the bell cuts off, Mrs. Callaghan can be heard climbing steadily to the attic. There's a tap on Charlotte's door. Charlotte gets up, opens it.

"A Mrs. Thorpe on the telephone for you," Mrs. Callaghan says, holding on to the door frame, rather out of puff. She doesn't believe in shouting up the stairs.

"Oh no."

"Oh, would you rather not . . . ?"

"It's my sister."

Charlotte hasn't mentioned her sister before. Not her name, nor the fact that she has one. Whereas Charlotte knows all about the trials and triumphs of Mrs. Callaghan's sister, up there in Liverpool. Mrs. Callaghan's eyebrows rise.

Family, Janet says, round a mouthful of chocolate—where on earth did she get chocolate?—*is overrated.*

If you could all be quiet for a moment, ladies, please.

She slips past Mrs. Callaghan, clatters down the stairs, hand skimming the bannister. She lifts the receiver and shepherds the voices back, squeezing a door shut on them. They protest, and they're still there, twittering and complaining, but they're not right in the core of her thoughts, for now at least. If Francesca were to notice anything amiss, then Charlotte really would be in trouble.

"Frannie?"

"Hello, Lolo."

"Frannie! How are you? How are the kids?"

"We're all quite well, thank you. As well as can be expected."

Francesca's husband had enlisted with what Charlotte had uncharitably thought of as indecent haste, and so is currently crunching on sand and swatting flies in Africa. Which, Charlotte imagines, may in many ways be more comfortable than being married to her sister. But this is not generous, and she must behave herself. So what is the correct thing to say here, now, to Francesca? And what is the right tone in which to say it? She mustn't appear excessively gloomy. Nor must she seem too bright and breezy. That would really put Francesca's antennae up.

But she doesn't have to worry about that, because Francesca just steamrollers on:

"Thought it better that you hear it from me, Lolo."

"Hear what, Frannie?"

"It's about your godmother, my dear."

Her heart goes still.

"I'm afraid there has been some dreadful news. It has hit Father particularly hard. He is quite, quite devastated."

"Saskia?" Charlotte reaches for the wall. She finds herself looking down at her half-broken shoes, her belly swelling and contracting as she tries to catch a breath.

There always was a chance that this kind of thing would happen, Francesca explains. When people put themselves in harm's way like that. Saskia should have known; she should have got out of London, like anybody else with any sense. Lord knows she didn't *have* to be in Town; she didn't have to be anywhere in particular at all.

"She was her own worst enemy, when you think about it."

"Not the Luftwaffe then?" Charlotte finds herself saying.

Francesca doesn't seem to notice the tone. "She hung on in Chelsea far too long."

But Saskia was the last person left that Charlotte could go to, and know that she was loved. Given time, Saskia would have been herself again; she'd have split with Mary, she'd already left a dozen women far lovelier than her without a qualm; but she was not given time.

"Funeral?" Charlotte asks.

Family funeral, Francesca reports. Up in Salisbury. Saskia's brother had already sent for the body.

"How," Charlotte asks, "did you find out?"

"Father heard. You know him. He hears everything. And the poor darling, he was so badly affected; he's beside himself. So I said I'd ring you. Though I do hate to be the bearer of bad news. Especially after your little friend—"

"El."

"Yes, Elena Hartwell." That class distaste. "Especially after she—"

Charlotte cuts her off. "Thank you, Fran. Thanks for letting me know."

They say goodbye. Charlotte sets the telephone receiver back down in its cradle. She feels brittle and transparent, as though rendered into glass. She'd break into a thousand pieces if you rapped her with a knuckle.

And she remembers. That's when she first saw him. Outside Saskia's flat. She ran right into him in the blinding sun. The shadow man.

And he was in Battersea, the evening she went to visit Janet's grave.

And he was there, in Marylebone, the day of El's funeral.

And he was on her street, the morning she'd walked Ilse to the café. She'd thought he was following Ilse, then. But now she sees things differently.

He could have been there long before she had any inkling he was there. He could have been there that Friday afternoon, when Charlotte had strolled with El round Regent's Park. He could have followed her to work for weeks, watched her eating buns with Janet in the square. He could have followed her to matinées at the Vaudeville, and Vanessa.

He finds out who I love, she thinks, and then he kills them. He uses the raids to cover up what he's done.

And then Saskia leans in against the back of El's chair. She's wearing furs, holds a champagne coupe between her fingertips. Her voice is languid, rich and stirring. *Don't let yourself get run away with, darling.*

Even if that is what's happening, El says, *it wouldn't be your fault.*

You really shouldn't go loving people without their say-so, Vanessa adds. *It was none of your business to be loving me.*

But Janet just raises an eyebrow, speaks around a boiled sweet: *Prove it.*

How on earth would I prove it?

Scene of the crime, Janet says, crunching. *That's where you'd start.*

If it is a crime at all, El adds. *And not just an accident of war.*

Darn

U p there is the window onto Saskia's drawing room, the curtains still open, the blackout not put up. If it really was a raid that got her, then it didn't happen here. Nothing at all has happened here; the building, the whole block, is, so far, untouched by war. It makes it all the harder to believe that Saskia is dead.

Oh, I am though, darling. Dead as the proverbial dodo. There is no doubt whatever about that.

If I had known, Charlotte thinks, that that was the last time that I'd ever see you.

What?

I'd have dragged you out of there and into the sunshine. Peeled Mary's clinging hands off you by force.

You really didn't like her, did you?

She wasn't doing you any good at all.

Did it ever occur to you that perhaps I didn't want to be done good?

Charlotte steps off the kerb, steps back as a couple of girls whizz past on bikes, and then waits as a horse-drawn flatbed trundles by, laden with furniture.

Mr. Jackson's face does an uneasy reshuffle when he sees her; the bland politeness of his job is broken by recognition, and then a muddled sequence of sadness, affection and sympathy, before returning to restrained formality.

"Dreadful news, Miss Richmond. Dreadful. We're all very sorry, I'm sure."

She takes his proffered hand and holds it gently: those swollen joints. "Me too."

"It'll be an awful loss for you," he says.

"It is. I'm—"

A basket case? Vanessa offers.

"I'm coping. Just about. I wondered, Mr. Jackson, is Mary in? I tried telephoning, but there's no answer."

"Miss Clarke? Oh no, she doesn't live here. She was only ever a visitor."

This news is at once a disappointment—whatever she thinks of Mary, it would have been so useful to speak to her, to hear exactly what had happened from the horse's mouth—and a relief. So they weren't living together; they weren't as entangled as all that.

"Would you happen to have a phone number for her? Or an address?"

"Sorry, no, that's not the kind of thing . . ."

"Do you know what happened, though?"

"Dreadful, dreadful."

"Yes, but what actually happened?"

"Well, I couldn't tell you exactly." He's flustered, embarrassed by the intimacy of death. "I wasn't on that night. When I came back to work the next day, the news was that Lady Bowers had been caught up in a raid, and that we'd lost her. The poor girl, Miss Clarke, was so upset, and I was shocked; we didn't really talk about it."

"You don't mind if I go up, Mr. Jackson? Just for a moment. Before the place gets stripped."

Charlotte closes the door behind her, locks herself in. The place is in chaos, but that's not new.

What are you looking for? El asks.

Mary Clarke's phone number, or address. And anything out of place. If Saskia didn't die in a raid, if the shadow man came for her, then there might be something here to indicate it.

But everything is out of place. The hallway is a chaos of heaped correspondence and discarded hats and coats. She peers into the kitchenette, where the sink is piled high with crockery and glasses. Opened tins and empty packages lie on the counter of the House Proud. And the whole place smells. It smells of cigarettes and booze and a general sulphurous uncleanliness.

My, you are so judgemental, Saskia says. *I really had no idea.*

Charlotte opens the bedroom door. The bed is still unmade, the eiderdown thrown back, the lemon-yellow sheets creased. She smooths out the linen, tucks in the coverlet. It seems wrong to leave such things so exposed. On the bureau, there's a slithering island of papers and art materials, the microscope an incongruous mountain peak in the middle of it all. She pulls back the chair and sits down.

We did have fun, Saskia says. *Whatever you might think.*

I'm glad to hear it. But it didn't really look like fun. It looked seedy.

Charlotte shifts the papers into piles, tidying as she goes; no sign of an address book.

Seedy can be fun. You don't understand what we had together.

And I don't want to, thanks.

It was special.

I'm glad for you. Shut up.

Charlotte peers into the microscope; it's empty, but there's a box of pre-prepared slides to one side. Petal, fern tip, flea. The most recent of Saskia's many expensive enthusiasms.

The papers are mostly bills, for the stationer, the grocer, the milliner and the doctor; there are also unfilled prescriptions for liver and nerve tonics. Saskia's letter-writing pad emerges from underneath the heap. Charlotte flips through it; there might be a note, an unsent draft of a letter to Mary from which she can scavenge the address; but its pages are blank. Then she spots the blotter underneath; it's curled and looped with fragments of Saskia's handwriting, where she has flipped her correspondence over to dry the ink. Charlotte carries the blotter across to the mirrored wardrobe, holds it sideways against the glass. She makes out the ghosts of words—*darling, can't, the, faded*—but they don't add up to anything useful—no suggestion of a telephone number, not even a scrap of an address. She dumps the blotter back onto the desk.

Still a delicious mystery, aren't I?

A rummage in the bureau drawer reveals Saskia's ration book, chequebook, paying-in book and passport, along with bundles of old letters. She unties the ribbons; other new girls, different times. Maybe there were qualms after all.

Where left to look? Handbags? Pockets? Charlotte opens the wardrobe doors, shifts the silks and wools, making the hangers chime. The clothes give off the scent, still, of the woman Saskia used to be, rich and sensual and complex. Charlotte has to stop and swipe at her wet eyes. But then she scoops bags off the shelf, upends them; old invitations and folded handkerchiefs and the scent of beautiful evenings tumble out. She digs in pockets and finds hairpins, a stray leather button and a handful of crisp dark rose petals. The base of the wardrobe is filled with neatly stacked shoeboxes. Charlotte gets down on her knees and pulls off lid after lid—gold evening shoes, walking brogues, a pair of cream satin slippers, worn to grey threads on the toes.

This begins to look like prurience now, Richmond, Vanessa says. *What on earth do you expect to find here?*

I don't know, Charlotte thinks. I don't know.

You need to learn to leave people alone. You need to let them rest in peace.

But she *was* mine, Charlotte thinks, stroking the stained satin slippers with her thumbs. She was mine for a while, at least.

You told Mr. Jackson that you'd be a moment, El says. *And you have been an age.*

Charlotte wipes her eyes. She gets to her feet. All of Saskia's glittery things—her hair clips, pins, brooches, earrings, necklaces—all paste, naturally, but tempting, and still worth a decent amount—are still there. Nothing has been stolen, as far as she can see, by Mary or by anybody else. And there is nothing at all of Mary's here. No hint of her. You'd think Saskia had died all alone in alcoholic disarray.

The sitting room. The carved African mask, the books, the exquisite pencil sketch of Saskia as a young woman by Augustus John. Charlotte can see nothing out of the ordinary. She swipes a finger over the sideboard and leaves a clean streak behind. She crosses to the window, leans back against the sill and considers the room from the other side.

And then she sees it.

The rosewood table by Saskia's habitual seat. It's cluttered with smeary glasses. And that's quite normal. And yet. There's something different about it. She paces over, crouches to bring her eye level with the tabletop. It has a patterned edge; lozenges and triangles in pale and dark veneer. It's silky and beautiful. It's also ringed with careless cups and glasses. She runs a fingertip along the surface and leaves only a smudge; her fingertip comes away clean.

No dust.

She shifts to kneeling, lifts aside the glasses, looks the table over. Is that a *dent*? And one of the pale lozenges—she picks at it with a fingernail—has come loose. She shifts the table aside. And there, underneath, until now concealed, is a fresh-looking scrape on the parquet. She sees the table knocked over, skidding, dragging something sharp—a shard of glass, a scrap of broken china—across the polished boards.

So we liked a drink. Sometimes we drank too much. So what? These things happen.

Yes. But.

Charlotte peers under the armchairs and sideboard. Not a glimmer of glass, not a shard of china anywhere, not a speck of broken anything. And there's no Florence now to clean up after them. Charlotte brushes off her hands. Sits back on her heels.

So someone sent the table flying, and then tidied up very thoroughly. And *then*—and this is the strange bit, this is the bit that sticks like a poppy seed between her teeth—someone gathered up other dirty glasses, and placed them on the table, to disguise what they had done.

Maybe Saskia was trying to hide a drunken accident. Maybe Mary was trying to cover up some carelessness.

Maybe.

But whoever it was, they were thorough. And nothing else here has been done thoroughly in months.

This is not the natural warp and weft of life, Charlotte thinks. This is a darn on it.

Charlotte closes her eyes.

She sees the white sheepskin rug that used to lie in front of the electric fire. She sees herself, as a small child, sitting not so much on, as in, this rug. It's vast; a cloud-continent, from the centre point of which she watches her mother, who's lounging with Saskia on the pristine couch. Her mother's shoes are kicked off and her legs are curled underneath her, and she's chattering away. Then she throws back her head and laughs. And this, to small Charlotte, is astonishing.

Charlotte opens her eyes. Was the rug here the last time she visited? She can't be sure. Any number of cigarette ends, glasses of wine and cups of coffee might have been dropped since she had sat in it as a child. It might just have become shabby, grey and unwanted.

Or.

It might have survived long enough to be stained with blood.

That's quite a leap, Vanessa says.

Oh, do put a cork in it, Vanessa, Janet snaps. *You're no help at all.*

Stained with blood. Rolled up and sneaked out of the building. So that it didn't give the game away.

Just supposition, El says. *You can't know.*

No, I can't know. But it's something to consider, isn't it.

Charlotte locks the door on the stale mess. She presses her forehead to the panel again. The only sound now is her own ragged breathing.

I miss you, Sas. I can't bear this. Did I bring this trouble to your door?

Saskia, in silence and in furs, raises her shoulders, lets them fall. She doesn't know.

I wish you were in there, you know. Even if you were pissed as a fish. I wouldn't mind. I wouldn't mind if you were never really mine again at all, if I could just know you were still here. I just wish I'd had a chance to talk to you properly, before you'd gone. That we hadn't left it like that. I can't bear that there will never be afternoons with you again, no more almond thins, no more orange pekoe tea. No more living beautifully.

If I could have done differently, darling, I would.

Charlotte returns the key to Mr. Jackson.

"Anyone take anything from the apartment, do you know?" she asks.

"Just Miss Clarke; she fetched away her things. Why? Is something missing?"

"I don't know. I was just wondering."

"About the funeral . . ." he asks.

"It's in Salisbury. The family have brought her home."

"Ah." Salisbury is simply too far away these days. "I never knew she had a family. There were only ever friends, and there was you."

But family has a way of elbowing through at times like these. People who barely bothered with you in life will come scuttling up to claim your bones. Leaving everybody else—everybody who was there when things were difficult or beautiful or just ordinary—with a wound in their lives, where you've been ripped away.

Fog

He's heading towards his bench in Russell Square. He moves slowly, fatigued and sore. He has come out to take the air, to feed the birds; he hopes to cheer himself up a little, to clear his thoughts. But with the college in ruins, he cannot help but find the prospect bleak. It's as though he is stuck on a sheer peninsula, fogbound, nothing to be seen beyond his fingers' ends.

Which is why to spot her now is such a jolt. She's wearing the dark winter coat from the funeral, and her simple black fedora, and is rushing along at a tremendous lick, her head down and shoulders up.

He changes course, moving towards her, bright and unselfconscious, crunching over gravel and onto grass, back onto gravel again. Her brow is knotted and her eyes fixed on the ground. They're close now and she still hasn't noticed him. His grin fades.

"Good afternoon," he says nonetheless.

She jumps. Stares at him.

"I'm sorry. I didn't mean to startle you."

For a heart-sinking moment, her expression is entirely blank. Then he sees recollection dawn.

"The boy who feeds the birds," she says.

It's discomfiting, to see exactly how she sees him.

"Thomas Hawthorne," he says. "Tom."

"Yes. Sorry. Mr. Hawthorne. Tom."

"Miss Richmond."

"Charlotte."

"I saw you, and I thought, well, look who it is. And then I thought that you didn't look quite the ticket, and I hope you don't mind, but I wanted to ask if you're all right? You were so kind as to enquire after me following that first weekend of raids. And I thought, well, I mean, that awful loss. Of your friend. So . . ."

She watches him with those clear brown eyes, while he rattles on like some kind of fool. All this time he'd been hoping to bump into her, thinking what he'd say, and this is the best that he can do? Rubbing her face in all her grief. He should shut up. He should go. He'd better go.

"I am sorry to intrude. I'll leave you to your walk. I do apologise."

She tucks a stray curl back into her hat. And then she smiles.

"You," she says, "are a sight for sore eyes."

He has to keep reminding himself not to stare. The snug is just murk and shadow; the only light is from the yellowed window and it falls only on her. He lifts his drink but sets it down again without sipping. He's not used to strong drink, or pubs; finding himself at a loss, he had just ordered the same as her. Port, it turns out, tastes like Ribena mixed with vinegar and is about as unpleasant as the look the landlady gave them; she must think something truly vile is going on, this beautiful young woman drinking in the daytime with a man like him. The husband, though, seems prepared to overlook it for the sake of their custom. None of this—other people's perceptions of them, to which he finds himself exquisitely attuned—appears to be of any interest whatsoever to Charlotte. She turns her glass idly, slowly rolling the stem between her fingertips, the light and the liquid both staying put as the glass moves. Her head is cocked, almost as though she's listening, though the public house is deathly quiet. And then she starts to talk.

She speaks slowly, as though each phrase is assembled with considerable labour. She tells him about the people she has lost. Best friend, colleague, school friend, godmother. How it seems that everyone she loves is dying.

"I am so sorry," he says. "I can see how it would seem that way."

Because, loved or not, everyone is always dying. But he knows fine well that to be reminded of that offers no consolation. "What about your family?"

A sudden, direct look: "Them? They're fine."

"That must be some relief."

"Oh, they're indestructible. Hitler would quake."

"But they will help—they'll be a comfort to you, at this difficult time."

She laughs.

He doesn't understand.

She leans in closer, wets her lips.

"You remember El, my friend, Miss Hartwell?"

"I do." Truth be told, he's never forgotten a single one of them, the persons that he and his father have conveyed to their final rest.

"And what did you think of her?"

"What did I think of her?"

"I mean, what did you think of how she looked?"

He sits back, disconcerted. What he remembers most is the pervading sense of wrongness. The already dressed-and-painted corpse, the mother bleached and stiff, the whole household thrumming with shock. Everything jangling and out of kilter. Elena Hartwell had washed up in the first flood of Blitz bodies, before he'd even heard the term "Blitz." He'd found her unsettling, to say the very least.

"I don't like to comment on that kind of thing," he says.

"But did you see any injuries? Any bruising?"

"We don't *examine* them."

"But still, you might have seen—"

"Her mother laid her out," he says, blushing, annoyed with himself for blushing. "If that's what you mean."

She brushes this aside: "My friend Janet. They said she barely had a mark on her."

The light is fading outside; the gas mantle has yet to be lit. Her face is shadowed now, but her eyes glimmer.

"Go on," he says.

"When you think how a person can be, well, quite blown to pieces. I've seen that too, after the first big raid. So isn't it a bit strange. That they both weren't."

"The most densely populated city on earth is getting hammered nightly with high explosives," he says. "That itself is strange. And strange things are bound to happen."

But she's gone distant again, her thoughts turned inward.

"If there were anything untoward about it," he continues, "if you're thinking that it wasn't what we thought it was, then some official, someone medical—a doctor, a nurse or an ambulance driver—would have noticed, I can assure you. And if her family had any doubt at all, they could have raised it at any stage. But it was all certified and registered. Her mother passed on the disposal form to us. The paperwork was quite correct. It's not a free-for-all out there. Not yet."

"This form you got; does it include the cause of death?"

"No, it doesn't. It never does."

She sips, frowns, peers at her drink; maybe it's not supposed to taste quite like that. "But I can't help wondering . . ."

"Wondering what?"

"If it's my fault."

"*Your* fault?" He almost laughs.

But she's serious. She leans back, turns her face aside. Her profile, against the dark panelling, is stark and angular. He's struck by how different she is now, to the lively young woman in the leaf-green coat, in the September square. Has she changed, he wonders, or is it just that he is beginning to know her?

"I think I make the bad things happen," she says.

"No—"

"Honestly I do."

"It's the war," he says. "How could it be you?"

He has seen grief take people in strange ways. Guilt is commonplace. As is anger. Sometimes blame, of self or others. But, for the life of him, he cannot see why she would think herself *responsible* for this.

He moves his glass aside, leans his left elbow on the table. "Let's be sensible. Let's think it through."

She sits up straight now, like a child. "I'd like that."

"Some of your friends have been killed. And that's desperately sad. I don't discount that. But unless you have a side-line piloting a Heinkel on the QT, it has literally got nothing whatsoever to do with you. Hundreds, thousands, of others have died in the raids, and each of those deaths is a terrible loss, but you wouldn't hold yourself responsible for them."

She has been nodding along, but is clearly just waiting for him to finish.

"But, you see," she says conclusively, "somebody's following me."

He sits back. "Really?"

"Yes."

"Because, the blackout," he says, "it can make people nervous."

"Don't patronise me. I won't stand for it."

This jab of acuity makes him straighten up. "No. Sorry."

"It's a man. He wears grey. I've seen him in various places. Marylebone. Chelsea. On my own street, in Gipsy Hill. He follows me, and my friends die."

It is possible; people are capable of terrible things. Fear slithers through him. "Is he here now? Today, I mean?"

"Don't think so. It's not all the time."

"Have you told the police?"

"No. Nor shall I."

"But it's dangerous."

"I know how it sounds. And anyway, they're already at full stretch. You think they could spare a man to follow a man who might be following me?"

"What matters most is that you're safe," he says, leaning in. "So if you really do think—"

"Who's safe?" she interrupts. "Nobody's safe."

He can't argue with that.

"Anyway," she adds with a shrug, and a determined sip of port, "my father would find out."

"Why would he? And why would it matter if he did?"

"He's Sir Charles Richmond. You'll have heard of him."

"The MP?"

"That's him. I can't sneeze without him knowing about it."

"I don't see how it would be wrong, you talking to the police. He'd want you to."

"I'd be making a nuisance of myself."

He's about to dispute this, but her jaw is set and her tone was blunt. "Let me help."

She lifts her glass. "How?"

"I can ask around. I mean, ask other undertakers. About the state of the bodies. I mean, we know about Miss Hartwell, but I could find out if there was anything at all moot, or contested, or open about the circumstances of the other deaths."

She brightens, astonished. "Would you do that for me?"

What a pleasure it is to be needed. "Yes."

She fishes out a notebook and tweaks the pencil from the spine. She writes, tears out the leaf and spins it across the tabletop to him. He sees, neatly printed there, the names and dates of death of her friends, and—aside from the Cavendish woman, Vanessa, with whom she couldn't have been that close—their addresses. Beneath this list, her own address and telephone number.

He folds the page carefully and slips it into his wallet. He keeps his face steady. The fog has lifted; turns out there is a world there after all, solid ground, and even a pathway across the plains; all he has to do is scramble down to join it.

"It's getting dark," he says. "I'll walk you to the Tube."

As if he were a man like other men are men. As if he could defend her. Though company, a witness, might be enough to put an attacker off.

He meets the landlady's glare with a polite touch of his hat brim.

Outside, their breath stirs the fog. They walk together, and this murky, cold evening, a prelude to a night of terrors, feels to him like Christmas had felt when he was a boy; there's a magic in it, a magic that specifically includes him.

He would like to be able to offer her his arm. He is more than usually conscious of his limp. She pays no particular notice to it; she just adjusts her pace to match his. He sees the low blue light of the Tube station.

"Perhaps it would be better if I saw you all the way home?" he says.

"You wouldn't get back yourself, though, not before bully-off."

"It would be safer for you, if you had company to your door."

She gives him a wry look. "But what if you were next?"

"We barely know each other. I daresay I'd be fine."

"Get yourself home," she says. "Your people will be worried."

She holds out a gloved hand. He notices that, this time, she has offered him her left. Their hands meet neatly, equally, clasp, and then they slip apart. Then she turns and walks away, into the fug and hum of the crowded station, joining for a while its night-time population, with their bundles and their babies and their birds in cages and their bedrolls spread on concrete.

He flexes the fingers of his left hand, spreads them.

Have a bit of sense, Hawthorne.

Because whatever else is going on, however strange it seems, he must be honest with himself. His family won't ever let him feel it; school made a hero of him; college welcomed his intellect without reservation. But he sees strangers' looks; the men's assessing, the women's pitying. He has been jostled, jeered and beaten. He knows what he is. And if he had been in any doubt at all, her offering of her left hand to meet his must remove it. She knows what he is too.

As Charlotte is rattled away in the underground dark, her shoulders sink, her forehead softens. She has an ally now at last. She no longer feels so torn to pieces. All the voices, while she was with him, had drifted and dispersed. He listened to her; her concerns were not dismissed. This is new.

She thinks: Follow me, you shadow man, if you must. Just don't you dare follow that sweet boy home.

Close

Charlotte rings Saskia's brother, up in Salisbury, herself, since Tom's professional circle does not extend that far. She has not met the brother since she was a child, but remembers him as tall, benign and mellow; an aristocratic giraffe.

"That was the thing about Saskia; she always went her own way," he says.

"That's very true."

She hears the suck and hiss of a cigarette down the miles of telephone wires. Gets a glimpse, in her mind's eye, of a giraffe smoking a black Sobranie.

"It is a shame about the rushed arrangements," the giraffe says. "It was literally the last train that would take a coffin. If we hadn't got her out when we did, she'd have gone in some anonymous London plot, and that's the last thing she would have wanted."

"No, you're right. She'd have hated that."

"She always thought so highly of you, dear; she thought of you as a daughter, I know she did. Because . . . well . . . you know . . ." He abandons even this slight attempt to acknowledge the realities of his sister's life. "But if you wanted to come up, I could show you the old place, her room, all the old haunts."

"I'd love that," Charlotte says, "when I can get away, I'd really love that."

"So ring again and let me know when you can come—"

"Ah, but . . ." It's awkward, but she has to ask, before he can hang up. "What about Mary? Did you see her?"

"Mary?"

"Mary Clarke. Her particular friend."

"Well then, no, I wouldn't know." He sucks on his cigarette again and hisses smoke away from the receiver. He will not be drawn.

"And Saskia. I can't help thinking. I just hope she didn't suffer."

"One feels it dreadfully, doesn't one?"

"But did she look, at all, at peace?"

"I can put your mind at rest. She looked as she always did," he says. "The only difference was the wicked spark had gone."

Her hand is shaking when she dials the Hartwell home. She feels grubby, having finagled information out of Saskia's giraffe, and now, after what happened with Clive, to be inserting herself back into the Hartwells' grief. But when Mrs. Hartwell answers the telephone, there's a real warmth and solicitousness: so good to hear from darling Lottie, they talk about her often; they think about her all the time. How is she bearing up, how have things been out that way, because, by all accounts, it's hellish down there, south of the river. Charlotte feels reassured, emboldened.

"We're all right at the moment, thank you. Nothing too close to home so far."

Though there's a series of craters like a giant's footprints across the cricket pitch, leading up to a ruin where once a pleasant villa stood; the Luftwaffe were aiming for either the army works in the park or the nearby railway lines, and missing, or they did an excellent precision job of destroying one nice house and the prospects of next summer's cricket season.

"Come for tea then, why don't you," Mrs. Hartwell says. "Nothing fancy. Not that anything is fancy any more. When can you come? Sunday?"

It is only after the arrangements are agreed, Charlotte has hung up the receiver and is making her way up the stairs, that she identifies the familiar discomfort she had felt throughout the conversation. This has happened before; this has happened so many times. All these last months, when Elena had cancelled on her at the last minute, postponed, or simply forgotten, or was not, in fact, at home when Charlotte called for her as arranged—Mrs. Hartwell would invite Charlotte in, or invite her round, and ply her with tea and cake and cheerful conversation. It was always a slightly melancholy substitution, but Charlotte had been grateful for it then, as she is now. It is even kinder and more generous of Mrs. Hartwell to think of Charlotte at the moment, with all she must herself be going through.

Oh, she thinks of others all the time, El says. *It's pretty much all she ever does.*

Still. She's nice.

Nice.

What? She is. Isn't she?

That night, the raids are an irritant Charlotte confines to the edge of her thoughts, until a solitary plane bumbles and drones overhead and a bomb comes whistling down. She balls up, hedgehog, in her bed.

So this is it, she thinks.

Now what is that phrase again?

Irrelevant, El, is what it is.

The windows rattle, the bed bucks underneath her, the walls suck in, then belly out. Her ears pop. She bounces to her feet, grabs her dressing gown and slippers, and runs helter-skelter down the stairs. She bangs into the basement kitchen, where Mr. Gibbons and Mrs. Callaghan look up at her as though she herself is a high explosive landed at their feet. Mrs. Callaghan is clutching her rosary; Mr. Gibbons holds his box of records in his arms. They sit in a pool of light from a battery-operated lamp, their upturned faces haggard; Lady Jane stands rigid in the recess underneath the sink, her tail bolt upright, her hair on end, yowling quietly to herself. Charlotte is struck for an instant how like a Caravaggio this all looks: she should have brought something with her, a prop—the severed head of John the Baptist; a grubby Cupid's bow; some grapes that are clearly on the turn.

"It's a wild night the night," says Mrs. Callaghan, though she only manages to get it out at the second attempt, after clearing her throat.

Mr. Gibbons releases one hand from its grip on his record case, indicates the deckchair folded against the wall. There's a blanket neatly laid over it, waiting for her. A thud, and the house shudders. They flinch. There's a rush of falling glass across the floor above their heads.

"Oh dear, that'll be the hall window," Mrs. Callaghan says.

Mr. Gibbons looks up at the ceiling.

"I hope not," Charlotte says. "It was lovely."

"Settle in, petal, why don't you." Mr. Gibbons wafts a hand at the deckchair again. Charlotte goes to fetch it.

"Night off?" Charlotte asks him.

"Four nights on, four nights off. I was hoping for a bit of kip."

Charlotte sets about unfolding the chair and rattling it into place. She can feel the vibration of the planes in her teeth.

"I can't remember," Mrs. Callaghan says, "when I last had a proper night's rest."

She pours a cup of black tea from her thermos and hands it to Charlotte. Charlotte thanks her.

"I don't sleep much anyway. Not well. Even without all this going on."

Mrs. Callaghan looks surprised. "Unusual in a young'un. My time of life you expect it."

Charlotte raises her shoulders. She shouldn't have said. She can hardly explain that she has slept too much already. She's not prepared to open that particular can of worms in this company. She's been happy here; she's been made welcome. It's the one thing she hasn't tainted yet.

"I suppose I'm just made that way."

Mr. Gibbons opens a biscuit tin and offers it across. "Garibaldi?"

Charlotte thanks him, takes one, bites off a chunk of biscuit, chews. Along with their battery-operated lamp, their deckchairs, blankets, flasks and tins, Mr. Gibbons has brought his portable Grafonola down, but it is not playing.

"The only disadvantage is," he explains, and then another bomb screams past, close enough to make everybody stiffen and go silent, "the needle skips."

"Mr. Gibbons has been reading to me, until this all got a bit distracting. *The Death of the Heart,* it's called; I'm quite enjoying it."

"Oh, she's an Old Girl," Charlotte says, unthinkingly.

"Who is?"

"Elizabeth Bowen."

They both look at her blankly.

"I mean, she went to my school." Charlotte feels her cheeks go warm.

Mrs. Callaghan and Mr. Gibbons exchange *who would have thought it* looks.

"No one went to my school," Mr. Gibbons says.

Mrs. Callaghan slowly shakes her head. Hers either.

"Shall we continue?" Mr. Gibbons asks. "Would you mind?"

"Do."

Mr. Gibbons clears his throat. He reads determinedly, and with lively modulation. The raid moves away; the noise and shocks become fainter. They all stay where they are. They listen, senses bristling, till the all-clear sounds.

Mr. Gibbons puts the book aside.

"I'd better go and report in," he says. "See what can be done. Not much chance of sleep now, is there."

"Hold on a tick," Charlotte says. "I'll come with you."

Cold air billows through the broken window. That distinctive sour, sooty smell. Her slippers crunch on shards. About as effective as you'd expect it to be, the latticework of gauze-and-gum it had been stuck together with. She runs upstairs, dresses. Sweater, slacks, sturdy brogues and coat. She grabs her torch. Mr. Gibbons is waiting at the foot of the stairs, his greatcoat and helmet on, glancing at his watch.

They step outside. The foul air catches in the throat; it stings the eyes. She can't see a thing apart from Mr. Gibbons; it's like walking out into the worst fog she's ever seen.

He switches on his torch, offers her a hand, and she takes it. It is warm in its woolly glove; reassuring. He leads her out into the road. There are others out here: she hears snatches of conversations, the odd word, figures pass; she chases after them with her torch beam.

Hundred and twenty, she hears someone say. It's like a secret code, coordinates. *A hundred and twenty-two, a hundred and twenty-four.*

"All right?" asks Mr. Gibbons.

"All right," she says, her voice choked with dust.

They inch along together; her eyes stream; she wipes her cheeks with her free hand. They move towards the blur of flame and movement.

Images are caught in flashlights, and in the hot light of the flames. Figures with steel helmets scramble up a landslide; others work like pistons on stirrup pumps; others run heavily, hunched, lugging buckets of slopping water. Flame climbs a staircase into emptiness; it licks at a party wall. A hundred and twenty. A hundred and twenty-two. A hundred and twenty-four. Flashlights catch on flowered wallpaper and a brass bedstead. A hundred and twenty-two is gone. A hundred and twenty and a hundred and twenty-four are broken-backed, collapsing into the hole that a hundred and twenty-two has left.

"What do we do?" she asks, swiping at her streaming eyes.

Mr. Gibbons steers her towards a fellow in a helmet like his own.

"Evening, Arthur."

"Morning, Sidney."

"Any chance of an appliance?"

The other man shakes his head.

"What's the plan then?"

"Keep at it ourselves, till help arrives."

"All right then. What do you need?"

"Shift water or shift rubble. It's up to you."

For a while, Charlotte is in a neighbour's scullery, a mirror image of their own, filling buckets at a tap and handing them on. She has no sense of time passing. She hefts bucket after bucket into the shallow stone sink; the tap putters onto zinc or enamel; she swings full buckets out again; they fill agonisingly slowly; the water pressure is low. She is nudged aside and told to take a break. She wipes her face and goes back out into the street.

Help has arrived while she was indoors. Cars are pulled up on the cobbles, and a rescue party picks its way over the scree. They work methodically. They gather up and hand off bouquets of dusty laths; they lift aside beams with great gentleness; baskets are filled with broken brick and plaster, passed back and emptied out of the way. She moves to help, carries away whatever she is handed, and then returns for more. Later, retying her coat belt, she finds one hand is wet; blood is darkening her palm. She sucks on the cut, tastes dust and blood. She remembers what Janet had said, about wanting her gardening gloves. She carries on.

A WVS van arrives. She is offered a paper cup of tea. A sandwich.

She shakes her head at the sandwich. The tea is warm, and weak, and she drinks it down without a pause; she had not noticed she was thirsty.

From time to time, they stop work so they can listen. There are faint noises: a cat's mewling, a fall of grit. The sky brightens. They find Mrs. Suttle and for a moment there is a flurry, but then the rescuers fall silent. They lift her body out. This is at number a hundred and twenty; and it is only then that Charlotte thinks, a hundred and twenty-two is Kaatje Beck, it's Ilse and Hedy. She takes a few brisk steps across the road and throws up into the gutter, then she wipes her mouth and turns back to rejoin her small effort to the whole.

A small corpse is lifted from a cavity, pink nightgown patched with dark red blood. Then an adult woman in a daffodil-yellow wrap, hair dangling. Ilse is carried out last; she lies limp as a sheet, her face a dark mess. Charlotte remembers how Kaatje Beck would call them from her front step; how she would sing out their names, *Ilse, Hedy, teatime,* in her precise English, and the girls would come running to her.

Later, locked into the bathroom back at home, trying to run a bath, Charlotte is haunted by the image of those stained ragdoll figures, of Miss Beck's bright robe against the grey-black chaos. The gas pops and putters; the water comes out lukewarm; she runs a couple of inches and then it gives out, so she strips, climbs in, scrubs at herself with a flannel. She soaps and then tries to rinse out her hair with water that by now is cold and already dirty. She scrubs her nails, soaks them. They won't come clean. Her hand smarts where she cut it.

She tries to comb out her hair, but it's rough and sticky with the dregs of soap. She pulls and pulls and pulls, and then she lets go of the comb, leaves it hanging in her hair, covers her face with her hands, and sitting there, naked in the cold, shallow bath, she cries.

She only stops when she hears footfalls on the landing, and then a gentle knock.

"Are you all right in there, Miss Richmond?"

She wipes her face, clears her throat and reaches up to extract the comb. She says: "Yes, fine, thank you, Mr. Gibbons. I'll be out in just a minute."

"No rush. No rush at all, my dear. So long as you're all right."

Charlotte wipes and rinses the grime from the bath, then dashes up to her room in her dressing gown. She squeezes her hair as dry as she can with a towel, then coils it up and pins it into a chignon. She finds a sticking plaster for her hand, clips off her broken and snagged nails, still stained with dirt, then paints lipstick onto pale lips, drags eyeblack through her lashes. Pinches her white cheeks. She sprays on perfume. She isn't properly clean. She doesn't feel as though she will ever be properly clean again. She can still smell it; a blink and she's back in it. The thick air, the blood, the burning. The bodies carried from the ruins. Ilse, Hedy; Miss Beck standing on her step to sing the girls in for their tea.

She remembers what she'd said to them, after the first big raid. *They've been training for this . . . So we mustn't worry overmuch.*

Stupid.

So fucking stupid.

What a stupid fucking thing to say.

She can't even close her eyes; everything is seasick. She should go to work. She has to go to work. She can't not work.

She comes upon Mr. Gibbons in the hallway. He's fitting a sheet of lightweight ersatz glass where the beautiful old window used to be. It doesn't smash so easily, Windowlite, so that's something in its favour, but it's not lovely. In the yellowish light it casts, she considers her good winter coat, abandoned over the bannister earlier this morning. It has become a vile vagabond thing, stinking, filthy with dust. There's her own blood on the belt and blotched down its skirts.

"Are you all right, Miss Richmond?" Mr. Gibbons asks, brushing off his hands.

"It's just, it's my only warm coat."

He sucks his teeth at the state of it. "Dear me. Well, you might have one of mine."

"I couldn't possibly."

He rests a hand on her shoulder, just a moment. He doesn't say, I know what you are feeling, I feel it too, that this is all so bloody awful, you can't face another day of it, and yet we must. He says, "You'd be doing me a favour. I'm quite ashamed how many coats I own."

.   .   .

She slides into a Crombie. Charcoal-grey wool, lined with pale blue watered silk, it's warm but lightweight, and it falls from her shoulders to just below the knee without pinching or constricting anywhere in between. The pockets—multiple, beautifully finished, and capacious—are a revelation.

"My *word*," she says, turning in front of his wardrobe mirror.

"There is a more mannish cut in women's clothes these days; it doesn't look out of place on you at all."

"Oh my goodness." She admires the fall of the fabric, the clean neat lines. "I feel at home in it already."

And she does. She tweaks the collar up and admires the blue felt backing; she ducks her face down and inhales the masculine scents of cologne and cigarettes.

"Thank you, Mr. Gibbons," she says. "I will take good care of it. Thank you."

He wafts her words away, smiling, gratified.

"Would you check on Mrs. Callaghan before you leave?" he asks.

"Certainly."

"Only, she's taking it hard. She was fond of those poor girls."

Mrs. Callaghan is in the kitchen, her eyes red and puffy, the kettle steaming faintly on a weak flame, and her knitting abandoned mid-row, needles splayed among the breakfast things.

"Oh, Mrs. C."

"Them poor wee'uns," Mrs. Callaghan says, dissolving. "That poor woman."

Charlotte squeezes her shoulder. "Shall I make you a cuppa?"

"Kettle won't boil." She blows her nose.

Charlotte could be so easily tipped back into tears again herself. "Not like you to stop mid-row," she says, of the knitting.

"It was for the little one. For Hedy."

Mrs. Callaghan sniffs. Charlotte drags out a kitchen chair and sits.

"I'll unravel it," Mrs. Callaghan says. "I'll start again."

Charlotte takes a work-hard hand in both of hers.

"I have to get to work, Mrs. C. But I'll be back afterwards and we can . . ." What? What could they do that would in any way begin to dilute this misery? "Read. I can read to you. Or we can listen to the wireless together. Or play gin. Or drink gin. Whatever you'd like."

Mrs. Callaghan looks up at her, sore. "Thank you, love. You're a good girl."

Inside Charlotte, at these words, there's a terrible collapse. If she doesn't go now, she will make a dreadful show of herself. She gives Mrs. Callaghan's hand a quick squeeze, says, "See you later," and bolts for the stairs.

As Charlotte leaves the house, her lips bitten hard between her teeth, the smell hits her again. It's thicker outdoors, but she's carrying it with her anyway. On her clothes, on her skin, and in her hair. And inside her too; it has become part of her.

Are you there, Hedy? Ilse? Kaatje Beck?

But there is no reply from them. They don't join the clamour in her head. Because she knows what happened to them. She knows it wasn't the shadow man.

Cornflower Blue

Charlotte stops just inside the ornate glass doors. Customers bustle past her, then disperse and slow down, to wander the maze of glass-fronted, glass-topped, mirror-backed counters; the place glitters under frosted glass lampshades big enough to take a bath in. She has been here before, many times, but she'd never noticed how much glass there was until now. She has to fight these newly acquired instincts, take hobbled steps past customers picking over trays of scarves and lipsticks, a woman choosing a new powder compact, a man considering a gift of carnelians. The glove counter at Derry & Tom's is where Saskia met Mary, and the glove counter is at the back, but her body wants urgently to be elsewhere.

She pushes on through images of exploding panes, flying shards, blood; she reaches the back of the shop and clutches the countertop. A customer turns her wrist to fasten the button of a kidskin glove. The girl behind the counter comments on its neatness. A pleasing transaction is made. Where have they been, these people? Have they not seen what the world can do?

You're here too, moron, Vanessa says. *You can't talk.*

"How can I help you, madam?"

She can't be much more than seventeen, with pretty puffs of strawberry-blond hair. Her expression manages to be at once bright, expectant, and bored. She is very much not Mary Clarke.

Charlotte clears her throat. "I'm looking for—"

The girl impatiently indicates her wares. This is, after all, the glove counter. "Day or evening?"

"Day?" Charlotte offers.

"Size?"

"Six and a half."

"Colour?"

If anything, she needs a lipstick. "Blue, perhaps?"

The girl opens drawers and lifts out boxes; she fans them on the countertop.

Charlotte eases off her own cream cotton gloves, realising only now how worse for wear they are. And how rough her hands. Her palm stuck with peeling Elastoplast.

The shop girl certainly notices too, the gloves and the ragged mani-cure. She looks, and then looks away, but doesn't say anything. It must be a fairly common sight now. She offers Charlotte a pair in navy suede, with cream pansies embroidered on the back. Charlotte touches the silky flowers. The dye will surely bleed the first time that it rains.

"Is Mary not working today?" She sets the gloves back in their wrapping.

"There's only me," the shop girl says.

"Are you new?"

"I've been here three years now. Ever since I left school." The girl slides another box towards Charlotte. "What about these? We used to call that Prussian Blue, but now we call it Midnight."

Charlotte picks up the gloves. Dark doeskin. Beautiful. "Do you know Mary?"

"Mary who?"

"Mary Clarke. She works here."

"Not on gloves, she doesn't. Do you like them?"

Charlotte does, but can't afford them. "Do you have anything in a brighter shade? Not sharp; I mean, a nice bright soft blue."

"Bright *and* soft?"

"Cornflower," Charlotte says. "Delphinium?"

The girl sighs. She shuffles boxes. "We're finding there isn't much call for that kind of thing. Ladies are opting for more sober shades that don't show the dirt."

"Are they?"

The shop girl manages not to roll her eyes. She turns back to her cabinets, bobs down to rummage.

"Maybe my friend Mary is on at a different time to you?" Charlotte asks.

"I'm full-time," the girl says, over her shoulder, conveying a world of weariness. She dumps a stack of packages on the counter. "I don't know if these would count as cornflower, but they're what we've got."

"I really thought my friend was working here."

A pointed look. That's some friend, if you don't know where she works. "There's me," the girl says. "And there's Miss Howard." She gestures to a stately woman in black, with an enormous, festooned bosom and stone-grey, high-piled hair who's moving between the counters, surveying the shop floor with a stern eye. A creature from another era, and nothing like Miss Mary Clarke at all.

The girl unwraps a package. Charlotte lifts the gloves out. Not quite cornflower blue; a touch more purple, more like harebell, or periwinkle. The leather's butter-soft; they're gently frilled at the wrist. Delicious. She wants them. She can't afford them.

You said the glove counter, Sas; you said Derry & Tom's.

You must have got the wrong end of the stick.

Wouldn't be the first time, Vanessa murmurs.

"I'll take them."

"Excellent choice." The girl's now cheerful, satisfied, tucking the gloves back into their tissue-lined box, writing out a receipt.

"Perhaps, though, madam, it occurs to me, you might have mistaken the shop? We're not the only department store on the High Street. There's Barkers and there's Pontings too, just down the way. You might try there?"

"Thank you. Yes. Good idea."

The gloves cost seven and six. Charlotte will have to skip lunch for the next few weeks. It's not like she's got anyone to eat Chelsea buns with now anyway. She slips across a dismal penny for the girl, who receives it with reasonably good grace.

Saskia raises her champagne glass and sips. *You're going about this all wrong, darling.*

Well, what do you suggest?

Go home, pour yourself a nice glass of something cold and—

Oh, for goodness' sake.

She tries Barkers. It's still functioning despite the building works, begun before the war had started and now on hold for the duration.

Its unfinished state now seems entirely in keeping with the rest of the boarded and tarpaulined city. She even tries Pontings.

The House of Value! I wouldn't be caught dead!

She finishes this trawl of Kensington High Street with thankfully just the one additional pair of gloves, but having also fallen for a lipstick refill—*framboise*—in Pontings. It leaves her with an awkward hole in her finances, and no closer to finding Mary Clarke.

When she gets her purchases back to her room, she slots the lipstick into her case and colours in her lips at the mirror, then slips on her new gloves.

Lovely, but foolish, given the parlous state of her finances.

Nonsense, darling, Saskia says. *You have to treat yourself sometimes. Now I'm not around to do it any more.*

Peachy

Charlotte hasn't been here since the funeral, when everything was shifted around and crowded and at odds with itself. The rooms are now returned to their former state: carefully aligned islands of polished wood and plump upholstery are set on seas of carpet; beautiful things—porcelain, paintings, ruby glass—are placed for visitors' contemplation. The tea table is covered with white linen. There's a vase of marigolds standing in a patch of sunshine, and the smell of baking in the air. But this all feels strange too; differently strange.

"My dear," Mrs. Hartwell says. "Come in, come in; you do look pale. Are you all right?"

"I jinxed us, I'm afraid. Our neighbours took a direct hit. Four dead, at least, that I know of." She breathes in, she breathes out. "Two of them were children."

"How very sad." Mrs. Hartwell shifts the vase unnecessarily, smooths the cloth on which it stands, repositions a cushion. She doesn't want to think about dead children, and who can blame her. "Maybe you should move away. We are thinking of decamping to the house at Rydal."

"Oh yes."

"But Lily is in open rebellion. She finds it rather rustic for her taste."

Lily, though, is humming to herself as she comes up the corridor. She sidles into the room with a tray. Mrs. Hartwell moves the marigolds aside, and Lily sets the tray down on the table. The good china tea-things. A plate of scones and a conserve dish filled with something purplish-brown.

"I wonder what we have here?" Mrs. Hartwell dips a spoon in, watches the preserve drip back.

"I think it's plum, ma'am. I had a taste and I think it's plum."

Mrs. Hartwell stoically transfers dark syrupy stuff onto her scone. "You'll forgive me, Lottie, but I feel it's only right I try first, before subjecting a guest to the experience. We have had a few surprises."

"That time with the chutney, ma'am," Lily murmurs.

"Exactly."

Mrs. Hartwell gives a polite shudder, then bites her scone, chews and considers. Charlotte watches, baffled—not by the unlabelled preserves, which come straight from the factory and are both perquisite and occupational hazard—but by the levity, the normality here: the sunshine and marigolds, the unchecked humming, the easy conversation, as though there has been a decision made not to suffer. Charlotte, with her scabbed hand and her sore heart, now inhabits another world. She didn't know that this one still existed.

"Plum, Lily, yes," Mrs. Hartwell says. "Or possibly damson. Anyway, it's definitely jam, not chutney. Do go ahead."

Charlotte spoons some jam onto her plate.

"And your work, my dear, at the Ministry," says Mrs. Hartwell, not looking up from her scone as she subdivides it. "How is it?"

"Oh, I'm afraid I'm not very good at it."

"I can't believe that."

"It's true. I am trying, but—"

"No," Mrs. Hartwell says abruptly. "I can't believe that you aren't brilliant at whatever you turn your hand to. Elena always said, you know, that you had twice the brain she had, and that was half your trouble."

Charlotte sits back, can only raise her eyebrows at Mrs. Hartwell.

Did you, El?

But El has retreated. She's silenced in this place.

"Oh, I know you muffed your examinations," Mrs. Hartwell's saying, "but who could blame you? Given the time you'd been having. And what does an examination say about a person anyway? Next to nothing. Take Clive, for instance."

Charlotte raises a napkin to her lips. "Clive?"

"I mean, the boy's terribly smart, university and everything; we insisted on it, before he started at the firm. He's clever, you know. But he's also a complete and utter dunce."

"Is he?"

"Mm. Just recently, for example; he's been mooning around, making himself miserable. I'm pretty sure it's all over some trollop on the factory floor. He hasn't got a clue about that side of things at all. And my Elena; dear Elena. Smart as a whip, she was, but we both know that she didn't have the sense to put her umbrella up when it was raining."

Not a word from Elena. She's turned aside, in shadow.

"You, though, Lottie dear. I know you've had your troubles. But you also . . . Well, you're tenacious. Do you remember Peachy?"

"Peachy?"

"The Dandie Dinmont we had when you were girls?"

"Oh, Peachy." Charlotte had never really understood the appeal of that gimlet-eyed bolt of fluff and fury.

"She'd set her mind on something and it'd be the devil's own work to stop her. You remember the stairs up to the nursery here? Far too steep for her short legs." Mrs. Hartwell sips her tea. "She'd launch herself at them, fall crashing back, and then she'd just pick herself up, have a shake, and fly at them again."

So this is how Mrs. Hartwell sees her: as a ball of intransigence, flinging herself at impossible obstacles, failing, picking herself up and flinging herself all over again.

"Your mother always said—" Mrs. Hartwell begins.

Charlotte stalls, returns her cup to its saucer. "What did she say?"

Mrs. Hartwell presses her lips together in sympathy. "That you could have been anything at all, if you hadn't had the misfortune to be born into money."

Charlotte's eyes go wide. She has to pretend to cough, to disguise a laugh.

"What's that, my dear?"

She shakes her head. How dare her mother leave this petard planted here, with Mrs. Hartwell, of all people, to explode all these years later in Charlotte's face? What insight could her mother pretend to possess? Money or no money, she herself did nothing with her life but leave it with as little fuss as possible.

"I was wondering—if you don't mind me asking, Mrs. H."

"What's that, my dear?"

"I was wondering, you see, and I am sorry to ask. I wanted to talk about Elena."

"That's only natural, my dear. We all miss her."

El, on her bentwood chair, shifts uneasily.

"About the circumstances of her death," Charlotte says.

Mrs. Hartwell moves her cup and saucer a little to the left. "In what way?"

Charlotte clears her throat again. "Just, I wonder, if there might have been some kind of mistake."

She won't want to talk about this, El suddenly announces.

"Mistake?"

She won't want to even think about this.

"You see, I've lost a few people already, due to the bombing." It sounds inadequate, she knows it does.

"So very sad."

"And the thing is, I just can't make sense of it."

"I know. I understand."

There's something quelling about Mrs. Hartwell's tone, but Charlotte carries on: "Because I've seen what an air raid can do. I've seen the damage done, to a human body. But. El looked . . . nothing like that. And so I wonder . . ."

"What do you wonder?"

Charlotte's cheeks flush hot. "I mean, I think it was you who laid her out, who made her up, so I wonder, did you see anything that might suggest something else had happened to her? That she might, for example . . . that someone might have . . ."

Mrs. Hartwell lays a hand on the tea table, rings gleaming. "I can put your mind at rest. She died in the raids that Saturday."

Charlotte sits back. "Sorry."

"Look, Lottie," Mrs. Hartwell says. "I understand, believe me, I do. But it will do you no good, no good at all, to pursue this line of thinking. If you allow one of your *idées fixes* to take hold, it will only make you . . . well, you know what it will make you."

Charlotte blushes fiercely now. "It's not like that, Mrs. H. Honestly. It's just eating away at me, to think there might be someone out there still, on the streets, who did Elena harm, and we don't even know—"

"Our own family doctor," Mrs. Hartwell interrupts, "who'd known her since she was a baby, who'd delivered her, for goodness' sake. He confirmed the cause of death. There is no doubt whatsoever. I wish I'd thought to tell you at the time and save you this distress, but I didn't for a moment imagine you would go off on such a wild ride as this."

"But what if—"

"Charlotte." There's hardness here, suddenly; there's anger just beneath the surface, like a razor blade pressed into soap. "Stop it."

Charlotte sits back. "I'm sorry, I didn't mean—"

Mrs. Hartwell lays her hand over Charlotte's. "My dear. You have been under a lot of strain. The recent loss of your dear brother, and then your dearest friend, not so long after—well. The most important thing, my dear, the crucial thing, is that you do not risk your equilibrium. You must try and remain rational. You must not give way to fantasies."

"I will. I mean, I won't. But I haven't been—"

"You must get on with the business of living, my dear, just as Elena would have wanted you to."

Charlotte's throat is tight. She understands. She has been warned. When she speaks again, the words come out like a child's: "You won't tell him, will you?"

Mrs. Hartwell makes a pantomime show of innocent incomprehension.

"My father," Charlotte says.

"We needn't mention it to anyone, my dear. Dismiss it from your thoughts. And try and be—well, *accepting*. There is nothing that could have been done differently; there is nothing now to do; there was no way to escape this. We must learn to live with it; we all must."

Charlotte looks down at her tea. "I am sorry, Mrs. H; I'm so sorry for upsetting you."

Mrs. Hartwell squeezes Charlotte's hand. "Darling, none of this is your fault. Remember that. Not one bit of it."

Charlotte's face feels full and heavy. Lily is rung for. She retrieves Charlotte's borrowed coat without comment, and helps her on with it.

"Remember," Mrs. Hartwell says. "You're always welcome here, my dear."

"Thank you."

"We count on seeing you, as often as you are able. You are almost family, my dear; that hasn't changed."

"Thank you."

Mrs. Hartwell scoops up both her hands, squeezes them. "You've been a motherless daughter too long, and now I am a daughterless mother. We'll have to help each other along, won't we?"

Those old hazel eyes, with their glint of El's green.

"Yes," Charlotte says. "Yes, we will."

She kisses Mrs. Hartwell on her powdered cheek, then steps, blinking, out into the street, hands stuffed improperly into the pockets of the Crombie.

She played the card, El says.

Charlotte's blinking in the sunshine, blinking back the tears.

The card?

The Poor Mad Charlotte card.

Charlotte tuts. That's not fair. Your poor mother.

Surefire way to get you to shut up, though, isn't it.

Charlotte fishes out her cigarettes, lights up. Is everybody equally awful about their mother?

Everybody's own mother deserves it. But everybody else's mother is delightful.

God, El. I do miss you.

And then Janet's voice jabs in: *Now that is true.*

What is?

You miss Elena.

I miss all of you.

But you miss her so much more than anybody else. She takes up so much space—

On the contrary; I, for one, am surprised to find so much space has been accorded me, Vanessa says. *I barely knew you. Two years below me, not even in the same House at school. I really had no idea.*

—while I'm squeezed into a corner and can hardly get a bloody word in, Janet huffs.

Saskia's patrician drawl: *Perhaps if some of us weren't quite so vulgar when we do speak—*

No surprise that Mrs. H wanted rid of me. Who wouldn't. Dragging her back into all that. Do you think she'd tell Father though?

You do realise, Vanessa asks, *that you're asking the voices in your head?*

That's what's keeping me sane. Having you lot to talk to.

A figure at the corner of the street, a grey shoulder angled towards her. Charlotte stops dead.

No.

In broad daylight. The shadow man. Solid now, firmly present, built like he's been carved out of an old tree trunk. He's smoking, his face turned aside, as though innocently waiting for someone who'll be coming down the other street. Well, she knows better.

Mrs. Hartwell's admonishments clunk through her thoughts like cog teeth. She must not risk her equilibrium, she must remain rational, she must not let this set her back, she must not give way to fantasies.

But he is not a fantasy. Look at him. There he is. He's trailed her here, now, for Christ's sake, *here,* back to El's house again. She floods through with adrenaline.

"Hi! You there!"

Are you mad? El shrills.

Evidently, Vanessa says.

Oh for Christ's sake, Janet snaps. *Don't be stupid.*

Charlotte marches towards him. What's he going to do to me in St. John's Wood in the middle of the afternoon? It's not his way. He hangs around in the blackout. Catches people unawares. He's a coward and he won't dare touch me here.

He's pretending not to have noticed her; he taps ash, his face still turned away. But she's not going to stand for it.

"Hey! You there! I mean you. Hey!"

He reacts slowly, turning to look at her. Broad features, deep lines, heavy brows and those pale blank eyes. *Who, me?*

"Yes, you. I see you."

"I see you too."

She stops a few feet short of him, out of reach.

"I know what you're doing," she says.

He slowly shakes his head, eyes blank; no idea what she is talking about.

"Don't give me that. I know what you're up to. I am on to you."

"Are you?"

"You bastard. You're a killer, clear as day."

Those cold marble eyes. "You want to be more careful about the kind of things you say."

And then he throws his cigarette stub into the gutter, and walks away. His back is a slab of grey herringbone.

Charlotte stutters after him, a few steps. Falters. But. But.

He just carries on walking. And then he turns the corner and is gone.

But.

That was quite the performance, Vanessa says.

But that was him. The man who killed you all.

In the dark space, there's a pregnant silence.

Then El says, *If you say so, Lotts.*

Oh for Christ's sake. You lot are no bloody use at all. Don't you know him when you see him?

Well no. We don't. How could we?

How could you not?

You'll have to figure that one out for yourself.

Rue

When the office is empty at lunchtime, Charlotte slips into Mrs. Denby's cubicle and lifts the telephone directory. There are two dozen M. Clarkes—with an "e"—listed, and Charlotte places call after call. Of those that do pick up, none of them are Mary, and only one of them is a woman, Margaret; all the rest are Michaels and Marks and Malcolms. It was always long odds, that someone of Mary Clarke's age and class would be found this way. If she has access to the telephone at home, it's more likely to be listed under a landlady's name. Whereas those charities—what was it Saskia had said? *Unwed mothers, alcoholics, the mentally defective*—there's still a chance of turning her up at one of them. Charlotte flips again through the directory, but then hears footfalls approaching down the corridor. She shelves the book, dodges back to her desk, and is looking blamelessly busy when Mrs. Denby returns from lunch.

She can't telephone from home; she's only ever home out of office hours. So the following lunchtime, she ducks into Mrs. Denby's office again and finds within the space of ten minutes half a dozen charitable organisations that Mary Clarke might have been involved with. She telephones them all. One of them does in fact have a Mary Clarke on the board, but is not about to put a stranger in contact with her; particularly since this Mary Clarke is eighty-two and has gone to live with her daughter in Hertfordshire for the duration.

Charlotte gives it up as a bad job, goes back to her desk, lifts the next report, just as Stella whisks back in from her lunch break, rosy-cheeked, her lipstick worn off with sausage rolls and kissing.

Why would you lie to me, Saskia?

Did I lie, or did you not listen?

I could do nothing but, the way you were rattling on.

I said I'd met her at the glove counter. It was you who assumed she was a shop girl, and not another customer.

She might be on to something there, El says. *You can be a dreadful snob sometimes.*

I'm not.

Oh you are, Janet howls. *If you weren't, washing your stockings in rented rooms and earning your own living and consorting with the lower orders wouldn't seem so damned glamorous at all.*

Charlotte cranes her neck, pretends to look for something in her in-tray, muttering to herself, cheeks burning.

She makes her way to the far end of the platform, then lights up a cigarette. It's already crowded, but passengers are still arriving, filtering round each other and round the shelterers' encampments, filling up every space like water pooling between stones. She idly follows the progress of a woman in a tobacco-coloured box coat and a burgundy beret, but then loses sight of her. Charlotte, twining and untwining the loose ends of the day, smokes. The platform thickens with people. Then the woman slips back into her line of sight. She's standing five yards or so away, queasily close to the edge of the platform. Those colours really do nothing for her complexion, Charlotte vaguely thinks. Then the woman raises a thin hand to her beret.

"Mary?" Charlotte wonders aloud.

The woman seems to flinch, but does not look round.

"Mary?" Charlotte drops her cigarette, grinds it out. "Is that you? Mary!"

Charlotte moves towards her. "Excuse me, excuse me—"

People shuffle, they tut and murmur, but they can't move out of her way. There's no space to move into.

"Mary! Hey! Mary!"

Thwarted, Charlotte stands on her tiptoes, peers left and right, steadying herself on the shoulder of the man next to her, ignoring his *do you mind* look. Catches sight of the woman again, or rather her beret; she's turned towards the sound of an approaching train. She's the only person who isn't either already staring at Charlotte or glancing round to see what all the fuss is about.

"Come on, Mary, don't mess around! I just want to talk to you!"

But there's a rush of dirty air, the shriek of brakes, and the train thunders in. Doors are opened and passengers stream off, then more press on board. Charlotte, sidling and dodging, unable to get closer, can see movement behind the painted-over windows, sharper colours and shapes through the squares that have been left clear.

"Excuse me, please—"

But she can't get through. The train is too full; not everyone can get on. Doors slam and the carriages slide past. Through one clear square of window, she glimpses a young woman in a burgundy beret, her face staunchly profile. Then she's gone, and Charlotte is left behind on the platform, with the other unsuccessful travellers and the night shelterers, who look at her and murmur.

And again, may I say, that was quite the performance.

Shut up, Vanessa. I do not give one single damn.

Charlotte lights up another cigarette, ignores her audience.

She looked different though, didn't she. Mary Clarke. Charlotte can't quite put her finger on it, but she looked different.

Perhaps she looked different, Saskia says, *because it wasn't her.*

It was her, Sas. It was. The way she wouldn't even look at me. When everyone else was frankly gawping. It has to mean something.

A madwoman was yelling at her, Vanessa says. *That's what it means.*

What do you know about it anyway?

Vanessa brandishes her herbs. Tosses her sodden hair. *I know mad. I've played it. There's rue for you.* She offers a wilted stem. *You must wear your rue with a difference.*

Charlotte rolls her eyes. This isn't *poetry*. I'm telling you. She cut me dead. That's something. That's information.

If it was her, El says.

No, Charlotte says. Not you too. I don't need that doubt now. I won't stand for it. I know what I saw. I'm not at the end of my tether. Not quite yet.

Breath

When she telephoned, Charlotte was told by the receptionist that while she could in principle make an appointment with Dr. Travers, there was in fact nothing available for a fortnight, so Miss Richmond should probably try elsewhere. The poor man, the receptionist said, with a trace of Midland vowels, is terribly overworked. When he's not looking after his own patients, he's volunteering at the hospital, which is more than anyone could reasonably expect of a man of his age, who should, by rights, be having a quiet time with his pipe and slippers. But then he was an army doctor in the last war; they are a breed apart, the old soldiers, she says. Don't you think?

"Volunteering at the hospital?"

"That's right. And St. Stephens are very glad to have him."

"An example to us all," Charlotte says, grateful.

She follows a pair of auxiliary nurses, in capes and caps, up the steps; one of them passes the weight of the door to her. Inside is a bustle of preparation. Behind the counter, a nurse presses her forehead, telephone receiver at her ear. *Yes, yes I know you said, but we need it now, it's five-forty already . . . Well, if it doesn't get through before kick-off then . . . well, yes I understand but . . .* Charlotte could wait and ask, but if she asks, she could be told no, so she just assumes a purposeful air and strides down the corridor.

Really, Lotts?

Don't you want to know?

She follows the clink of crockery and the sour-coffee-and-soup smell to a cold and steamy canteen. She scans the room. Nurses coming off shift, blinking over cups or somnolently eating sandwiches. A porter, blue coat unbuttoned, is sipping soup from a spoon. A cluster of orderlies move away, and from behind them a man in his sixties appears. His grey hair is tinged with ginger; he has a white coat on over a rusty tweed suit. She remembers him from the funeral, his hands clasped round Mrs. Hartwell's, their heads together. As she approaches, he looks up at her with tired eyes. An empty pipe lies cold beside an almost-empty coffee cup.

"Dr. Travers?"

He looks blank. "Have we met?"

"Nearly. I know you have a long night ahead of you, but could you spare me five minutes? I need a word."

He looks at his watch. "I could."

"Another coffee?"

"Please."

Charlotte returns from the serving hatch with two green institutional cups of moderately warm, moderately stewed coffee. Dr. Travers swills down his cold dregs and reaches for the new cup. His hand faintly trembles.

"Thank you. So where did we nearly meet?"

She clears her throat. "At Elena Hartwell's funeral."

"Ah. What was this word you wanted?"

"About her. About El."

"Patient confidentiality, I'm afraid."

"I know. It's not a . . . a medical question, as such."

He knuckles an eye, waves for her to continue.

"I just wanted to know, if you don't mind me asking, were you there when she died?"

"No. I got the message as I came off shift. I went straight round."

"To the house?"

"Yes."

"That's where you saw her? In her room?"

"Yes, in her room."

Charlotte sees the satin bedspread and the carpet with its twining roses; the tree whose branches tick-tack against the window. El lying like a cursed princess.

"So she wasn't even brought to a hospital?"

"I don't believe so, no." He lifts his pipe and examines it.

"Isn't that a bit, well, strange?"

He pauses for a moment, and then he says, "Do you know how many people died that week? The week Miss Hartwell died?"

"No."

"Neither do I. I don't know if anybody does. Not even the government. They certainly haven't published total figures yet. I don't expect they ever will."

"I understand, but if she—"

"Forgive me, Miss . . . ?"

"Richmond. Charlotte Richmond."

"Forgive me, Miss Richmond, but I don't think you do. I don't think you possibly could understand. You really can have no idea what we deal with here, after the sirens go." He gets out a tobacco pouch from an inside pocket, begins filling his pipe. The scent is woody, sweet. "I work in triage. I've still got enough pep in me for that, even at my advanced age. When casualties come in, I examine them and decide what course of action's to be taken. And it's the same pattern every night, I can tell you, once the bombs start falling. First we get the walking wounded, these are people with injuries just beyond the skills of a first aid post. So you have the simple fractures, wounds that need stitches, minor burns. We sort them out, and we send them home, or we send them on to a rest centre if they've lost their homes. And we'll just be finishing up with them when the second wave starts crashing down. These are patients who come to us by ambulance, or by car. We'll be dealing with nasty, messy breaks, then; with crushed limbs, punctured lungs, with serious, extensive burns; we'll be injecting morphine with far greater frequency; and there will be hopeless cases; one has to accept that. Sometimes all one can do is try and make them comfortable. And then the third wave hits. That's when the dead start to arrive. It isn't meant to happen, but it does. A rescue party loads a casualty onto an ambulance, and the nurses here unload a corpse. All we can do then is find their identity card, tie a tag and add their name and number to the list. And after that, it's hell till morning. And all the while, the electricity is off and on, sirens are screaming, and we're taking hits ourselves."

He lifts the pipe, lights it, sucking at the bit.

She says, "I'm sorry."

"Difference is, you knew where you were, in the last war. I mean that quite literally. There was a line, and we were on it. We were there to stop them getting through. To push them back, if we could. That was hell too, I'm not saying it wasn't hell. But it wasn't *here*."

"I'm sorry," she says again.

He blows blue smoke aside.

She hesitates. "Forgive me, but—one last thing. You say about those terrible injuries you have to deal with every night. But Elena. She didn't have anything like that. She looked, well, perfect."

"That sounds like a medical question."

"Not really."

He closes his tired eyes. "But, yes, I see. It's disconcerting."

"What is?"

"To be fair, plenty of doctors go a lifetime without seeing it, or they did before the war."

Charlotte leans in. "Seeing what?"

"To speak in general terms, you understand, not about Miss Hartwell."

"Naturally."

"Years ago, when I was newly qualified, I was called to the scene of an explosion. Vauxhall Gasworks. Nasty job. There were a good few casualties, along with three fatalities. But the dead men had no visible wounds, not even serious contusions. That means bruising."

"So what killed them?"

"I was to see it again, in the last war, the same phenomenon. With an explosion, it doesn't matter what causes it, be it coal gas or a bomb, the body makes no distinction. In the immediate aftermath of a blast— I'm talking fractions of seconds here—a vacuum forms. And what do we know about vacuums?"

A phrase surfaces: "That nature isn't keen on them?"

"Exactly. Stuff—anything, everything—rushes in to fill them. And that stuff. Well. We've had patients come in with eyes scarlet with blood. Burst eardrums. But the lungs, though, they're particularly vulnerable."

She covers her mouth.

"You can live with a burst eardrum; they often heal of their own accord. The blood will drain from the sclera eventually. But those delicate inner structures of the lungs; in a vacuum, well, the damage is terrible, and I'm afraid there's nothing to be done. Death is quick, and certain."

She looks down at the scuffed parquet floor; she holds up a hand, palm towards him. Please stop. But he doesn't.

"We're seeing it with increasing frequency. I recognise these cases immediately. I know it at a glance. Just like the men at Vauxhall all those years ago; and all those boys, in the trenches, who were rosy-cheeked and whole, but were in fact quite dead."

Charlotte sits back, wraps her coat tighter round her. She can't quite bear to look at him. "I'm sorry."

He sucks on his pipe, peers into the bowl, rubs an eye.

"If I may say, Miss Richmond. You might consider finding something rather better to do with your time, and not squander it on such ghoulish ruminations. Any death is difficult, but we shall have to get used to it. Because if one thing is certain, it's that we're not getting through this without a great deal more."

The bus jostles her through the torn-up streets of South London.

If you all just died because you died because you died. If that was all there was to it. With the sky full of fury and the world exploding all around you, and the breath ripped from your lungs—

How humiliating for you, Richmond, Vanessa's saying. *And how unbecoming. Pestering a grieving mother, shouting at a stranger on the Tube, and now barging into a hospital, for goodness' sake. I mean, troubling a doctor, now of all times. A doctor. An old soldier and a volunteer who just wanted a cup of coffee and a sit-down to smoke his pipe before the night shift.*

I'm not sure we can really say my mother was grieving, El counters. *She seemed in fairly decent spirits when we saw her.*

You still haven't spoken to my old man, Janet adds, *but I don't blame you; I wouldn't go back to that hellhole either if I could help it. But do you have to assume I went the same way as your darling El, just because it is El, and El's the be-all and end-all, the perfect friend against whom all other friends are measured and fall short?*

Whilst my darling Charlotte has many delightful qualities, and is by no means entirely loco, Saskia interjects, *we do have to recognise the possibility that the pressures and privations of this ghastly war have leaned harder on her than she is able to bear. Particularly when she says that thing you know she says . . .*

Oh yes, that thing, El says. *I hate that thing.*

That's what happens with girls like her, Vanessa chimes in. *No talent, no ability, no actual use, nothing to keep them occupied, nothing to distract them. If they're not married, they go just off, you know. Like milk.*

Charlotte grabs for the cord, makes the bell ring. She staggers down the aisle. She should just give up. She should just give in. She is making a terrible mess of things. She is the nuisance that they always said she was. She should just kill herself and have done.

There it is. That thing.

I'm sorry. I just miss you all so much.

There are other people still, El says. *There are other people you could love, if you'd just give yourself a chance.*

Dinosaurs

Tom eases himself down onto a bench opposite the dinosaurs and stretches out his leg. It's a relief to get away from home, and this is about as far away from home as it's possible to get without leaving the city. It feels like a holiday, even though—perhaps because—it has just begun to rain.

He closes his eyes and leans his head back, the cool water speckling his face. When were they last here together, the Hawthorne boys; him and Dad and Stanley and Raymond? It must have been '37, the year after the fire, when they'd come to watch the Grand Prix. A day of sun and cloud; they'd had a great spot and been up close when Dobson had spun out on Big Tree Bend. He'd walked away from the wreck, smiling and shaking his head, which is something you now seldom see. The walking away unscathed.

The four of them had also taken a gander at what was left of the Crystal Palace, which was very little, and rather sad. Scorched stone foundations, a solitary water tower, and the Sphinxes, their paint peeling, guarding the entrances now to nothing. The fire at the Palace had seemed a terrible blow at the time, as though a whole era and a way of life had consumed itself in flame. Now it feels like a pretty toy got broken. Some lovely things were lost.

That part of the park has been sealed off by the army now. When he'd seen the stalwart chap guarding the main park gates, Tom had just continued down the road as if that had always been his intention. He'd begun to wonder if Miss Richmond had made a mistake; the wrong day, the wrong park—though what other park has dinosaurs?— and then, chillingly, it occurred to him that the whole thing might have been an elaborate joke. Dupe him into thinking he was needed, send him on a fool's errand, and then invite him to a never-going-to-happen meeting in a park that's locked up tight. Was she laughing at him even now, with a bundle of completely unscathed friends? Had he made that very easy mistake, of assuming her to be lovely because she looked it?

He had walked the length of the railings and around the corner onto Thicket Road, heart sinking, about to give up entirely, when he saw someone slip through a side gate, and followed them through. So it turns out it's not actually *impossible,* this meeting of theirs. Here is the lake, here the islands inhabited by concrete monsters. And this— the row of benches opposite three giant lizards, at two in the afternoon, is where and when they had agreed to meet.

A flotilla of ducks sails past on the lake. A moorhen flutters up and perches on a statue's scaly neck.

He checks his watch again; still a few minutes shy of two o'clock. He gets his book out of his pocket. He thought he might say that he saw the author motoring down Southampton Row, and how she'd looked—patrician, luminously beautiful. But really he has no idea whether a girl like Miss Richmond would have any interest in books. He does not know much about her, and has caught himself filling in the gaps with hopeful supposition. Rain speckles his page, so he unfurls and props his umbrella so he can read in the shelter of it.

Five past. In the puddle at his feet, concentric circles spread and disappear. There are a dozen different things he should be doing at home.

Perhaps she's the kind of girl who's so used to people being delighted to see her that she doesn't even notice when she's late.

A rat slips across the water, leaving a sharp "v" of a wake; he watches it climb out and shake like a tiny dog. An hour back on the train, at least, and that's if the service is not disrupted. He shouldn't have come. He really shouldn't have come. Just to sit here in the park, watching the wildlife while his boots get soggy. He has been stupid, and selfish, and taken for a mug.

Then she ducks in under his umbrella. On his right, shoulder to shoulder, stunningly present; the honey-coloured girl, whose name he's not yet used to. Charlotte. He didn't see her coming.

· · ·

Of course she's late; she's always late. She can't do anything right.

Even at school, where the furthest you ever had to go was to the playing fields, Vanessa's saying. *Used to see the two of you scurrying around after the bell had gone—*

I did try and shake her off but she was like glue.

Charlotte winces. Oh El.

My god-daughter has many good qualities, but knowing when she was not wanted was not one of them. She'd come round my flat when I had a girl there, never so much as a by-your-leave, and just be there, just assume . . .

She steps over a milky puddle.

There he is, says Janet. *That lovely boy.*

Waiting for you like a dog in the rain, Vanessa says. *Got him well trained already.*

Not trained. Not trained at all.

She skips the last few steps, closing her own umbrella and ducking in under his.

"Sorry, sorry," she says, shaking her brolly out.

"Oh, there you are!"

"Sorry I'm late." She turns her wrist to show him the stray minutes that have slipped away.

"Barely," he says, happily closing his book.

"But I've only come from just around the corner, and you've come all this way. It's disgraceful."

"It's always harder to be on time when one hasn't far to go."

"But to keep you waiting in this weather."

He nods to the dinosaurs, stoically darkening in the rain. "These chaps have had it far worse than me."

"Oh, English dinosaurs can take it. Hitler doesn't stand a chance."

He laughs.

"How have you been?" she asks.

He looks at her askance, startled by the directness of her question, finding himself unable to answer it directly.

"Fine," he says. Frustrated. Distracted. Ridiculously daydreaming about you. But, "Fine. I tested the water. I mean, not the water"—the rain, the puddles, the lake—"I mean, I spoke to colleagues."

"And this kind of death, where the body appears undamaged, is not uncommon, nor considered untoward," she says.

That's blunt. He leans away, the better to see her. The rain drums on the umbrella skin, and the blueish light that filters through it reflects from her cheekbones, giving her a chilly, porcelain sheen.

"There have been a few," he agrees. "Consensus seems to be that it's caused by trauma to the lungs. My friend Joshua Staple has had a couple, older men. And Sherry & Son had a child, they said. A six-year-old girl."

"I made some enquiries myself. I'm sorry," she says. "Please don't hate me."

He's jolted again by the strength of that word, by her discomfort. "What? Why would I?"

"Sending you after wild geese."

The words seem to elide again with the scene around them; the paddling waterfowl and the dimpling lake.

"It really was no trouble to me at all."

She brushes her face with fingertips, like she's being bothered by something he can't see; a stray hair, cobwebs. "You're at university, aren't you?"

"I am enrolled."

"So you're clever."

"I haven't started yet."

"But you are clever. You must be. Or they wouldn't have given you a place."

"Well, as far as that goes." It is gratifying, her insistence. "Why d'you ask?"

"I think," she says. And then she looks at him directly. "I think I must be going mad."

He sits back, pinned. "Why would you think that?"

She says, "I've been mad before."

He considers this. He has seen her lively and he has seen her low and he has seen her anxious, but it has always seemed like a rational enough response to circumstances. But then he's no expert, and he doesn't know her well. "What was the diagnosis?"

She hesitates. "I was being a nuisance."

"That's not a diagnosis."

A slight shrug.

"Well then, what was your treatment? If you tell me how they treated you, I might be able to tell you what they were treating you for."

She bites her lip, her eyes wide and eyebrows up. She shakes her head, either unwilling or unable to speak. He feels an overwhelming concern for her.

"Let's not worry about that for now. The key thing is, you feel the same malady has returned?"

"No. It's not the same."

"So why—"

"I know I'm not quite right," she says. "I mean, I'm not sure I ever am *quite* right. But I know my behaviour is becoming a problem. I feel . . ."

distracted

vexed

unsettled

sad

"Haunted," she says. "I feel haunted."

"But you do know," he says, wanting to touch her, knowing there's no way he could ever touch her, "that you're not remotely responsible for what happened to your friends."

Her chin crumples.

"Grief can do strange things to a person," he continues. "I've seen people taken by it in all kinds of ways. You might say grief itself is a kind of madness, one that even the sanest people have to go through at some point in their lives."

He watches her face as she considers this. There is, he thinks, a slight easing.

"I saw a woman on the Tube the other day," she says. "I was convinced I knew her. I called her name, and she didn't respond, so I just kept yelling at her. Pushing and shoving to get to her. But what if it wasn't her, I just wanted it to be? As though yelling at her would somehow make that happen?"

"Who was she? I mean, who did you think she was?"

"Mary Clarke. A friend of my godmother's. Her particular friend."

"Why don't you arrange to meet? That might help."

"I don't have her number. I don't know where she lives."

"Well then, no wonder you reacted strongly, when you saw her. Anyone would."

"I had been trying to get in touch. It felt like I'd somehow conjured her up."

"Forgive me, but how were you trying? If you had no means?"

"They'd said that she was involved with a number of charities; I'd been ringing around, but nobody knew anything about her."

Charlotte gets out her cigarettes, offers them. He raises a hand in refusal.

"Which ones?" he asks.

"Which ones what?"

"Which charities?"

"Oh. I wasn't told their names. They shared causes, Saskia said, the two of them. It was something they did together. They mentioned unwed mothers, alcoholics and the mentally defective. So I rang every relevant organisation I could find."

"Unwed mothers, alcoholics and the mentally defective, you say?"

"Though she was quite the drinker herself." Charlotte hesitates, then puts her cigarettes away. "Now I come to think of it."

He feels a prickle of antipathy; he can see where this is going. "You're sure it was a number of different charities?"

"What else could it be?"

"The Eugenics Society?"

"But, do they do that? Do they help people?"

"Not help, no."

She sits back. "Thought not."

"I pick up a pamphlet from time to time," he says. "I keep an eye on what they're up to. I like to stay abreast of the arguments for my non-existence."

"Christ."

"Well, you know," he says, keeping his tone light. "Know your enemy. Isn't that right."

"We should pay them a visit together, you and I. We'd blow them clean out of the water."

"What do you mean?"

"Between us"—there's a laugh now in her voice—"we'd prove

them wrong. There's you all brilliant, with your university place, and a good, kind man to boot. And then there's me, with what must be, by their lights, generations of faultless breeding at my back, and I'm a shipwreck."

He's snagged on her words. *Good, kind man* is more distracting even than *brilliant*. "You? No. You're just going through a sticky patch."

She laughs outright.

"I mean it," he says. "You don't have to drag yourself over coals for not feeling A1 all the time. There's a war on."

"Hold on though. Mary and Saskia were Sapphists. What do eugenicists make of homosexuality? Would they even be allowed to join?"

He stalls. She just said those words out loud. He has only ever read them before this moment. He knows what they mean, more or less. His cheeks flush to think of what they might mean more precisely. Skin and mouths and soft arms and hands and—for God's sake, just stop *thinking*.

He clears his throat. His face is hot. He says, casually, "It does rather fly in the face of their theories."

His face is *so* hot.

"But yes, good idea. I'll ring them. I don't have to like them. If I could just get in touch with Mary, that would, I think, settle everything." Because for all he was adamant, Dr. Travers hadn't actually seen what happened, and he was only talking about El. If she can hear it from Mary, then she would know for certain—just as she knows with Eddie, and with Ilse and Hedy, and Kaatje Beck—what happened to Saskia, and that it was nothing to do with the shadow man.

He reaches into an inner pocket of his jacket, produces a business card. *Hawthorne & Sons;* an address and telephone number in Somers Town. "Let me know how you get on. Or if you want company when you go. And if there's anything else I can do to help."

He goes to hand it to her, but then whisks it away before she can take it.

"On one condition," he says, astonished at his own temerity.

"What's that?" Her hand, in its beautiful blue glove, is extended in mid-air.

"If you ever get the merest inkling that you're being followed again, you'll go straight to the police."

She frowns, drops her hand to her lap.

"No," he says. "You have to. Or you can't have the card."

"If my father—"

"How's about a compromise, then? You tell me, and I'll tell the police."

She begins to shake her head.

"Listen. You have to understand this. You are not a nuisance. And you are not a child. Your father be damned. You're allowed to ask for help. And you can always ask me. All right?" He offers her the card again.

She reaches for it, her expression brightening. "All right."

One of the pleasures of Tom's company is the way the voices retreat from it. For most of that gone-in-a-blink hour in the park, they were at arm's length. They muttered for a bit at the start, then they stumbled and staggered and jostled in the background; El followed the others out, dragging her chair, then closed the door behind them. They were still there, on the far side of the door; the door sometimes cracking briefly open and words and phrases tumbling through, but they were in another room, not yammering right in her face. This distance persists right through the weekend, and into her Monday morning. It's a relief.

The Eugenics Society is based in Eccleston Square, Pimlico; she goes to all the trouble of sneaking in another call from Mrs. Denby's phone, and all she gets is a crackling hum. She dials the operator, who confirms that the number has been disconnected.

"Does that mean they've disbanded, the society?"

"Not necessarily."

"What then?"

"Perhaps they didn't pay their bill. Or they changed their minds and decided against the telephone after all; it's not for everyone, being at the mercy of the bell. Or they might have been bombed out. Or they might simply have moved out of London altogether; many organisations have."

"I see. Thank you."

Charlotte puts down the receiver, slips out of Mrs. Denby's office. If she breaks her journey at Victoria, she can walk to Eccleston Square from there, and see if she can rustle anything up. But there's no point even trying after work: everything will be closed by then.

At half three, when Mrs. Denby is in a meeting, Charlotte slips the cover over her typewriter and turns a pained expression on Stella.

"Tell Mrs. Denby I'm ill, would you, and had to go home?" Then she mouths the word "Monthlies," and Stella makes a sympathetic face.

The charity is housed in one of a row of fine stucco townhouses, over-looking a private garden. She tugs on the bellpull. She can hear a jangle, far off inside. Nothing happens. She looks over the brass plaque again, to be certain she's in the right place; the plate, she realises, is tarnished and grimy—it's not been cleaned in a good while.

She goes back down the steps and crosses over to the gardens. She sits on the low wall, shoulder against a lamp post, her back to the flower borders and the vegetable plots. She lights up a cigarette.

You are not a nuisance, she thinks.

Your father be damned.

She'd like to thank Tom for this. For simply being on her side; for letting her head clear and her thoughts settle. But you can't do that, really, can you? You can't say, thank you for quieting the voices in my head. And the way he blushed when things got a bit too frank for him. There's an innocence to him that's unlike anything she's ever known.

She watches the building. Scratches the itch on her palm where that cut has healed. No one comes, no one goes; not Mary Clarke nor any-body else. Nothing is done by way of raising the blackout or opening curtains, but then no lights are switched on either. She covers a yawn with a hand, wraps her Crombie tighter; she tips up the collar, dips her nose into the warmth. She tucks her gloved hands under her armpits. She rests her head against the lamp post, and her mind drifts among the dinosaurs and umbrellas and dripping rain.

Charlotte wakes shivering, in darkness.

She springs up from her perch, casts around her, panicked by the dark. She remembers where she is, but not which way she came. She turns, looking for a landmark, but everything's the same in all directions. Ghostly white stucco buildings, thick shadows. She takes a breath and lets it go, and chooses. Huddled and stiff with cold, she heads off towards a corner of the square.

On the road beyond, shaded torches bob along the pavement. Cars pass, myopic with their slitted headlamps. She comes upon the muted light of an ARP post, hesitates for half a step. She could just duck inside. Because the air is humming now. If she were Lady Jane, she'd be bolting down to the basement with her hair all on end. But the instinct to get home is as strong as hunger. She'll go straight to Victoria; shove herself into the crowds on the last train; twitch all the way around its agonising circuit south of the river; run full pelt from the station, slam through the front door and race down into the basement to join Mrs. Callaghan, to face the night at home with her. It is not as though she'd be safe there; there are no guarantees. But there's comfort. Companionship. There's Mrs. C.

Charlotte takes a turn, thinking it might bring her out onto Belgrave Road, but it's just another residential street, empty, the houses all in darkness. Her torch skims the kerbs and paving slabs. The hum is growing, becoming denser. She hurries on, takes the next left; it jinks off unexpectedly to the right. It can't be far to Victoria; it can only be a few streets away. She should go back, speak to a warden. Ask directions. She casts her beam over cobbles, railings, brick. She takes a few steps back the way she came, then turns again, uncertain, caught. The streets have become a maze.

Standing still will get you nowhere.

Thanks, El. Very helpful. I had no idea you were so clever.

If you're going to be like that. El shifts her chair round, turns away.

Charlotte carries on, following the thread of her torch. The streets are deserted. The air is thick with engine noise. The hair stands on the back of her neck and on her arms. She turns a corner, then another, comes upon a dead end that she is only certain is a dead end after running her torch along the whole T of privet and garden gates and back again to the entrance. Then she hears it, the first siren. And at the same moment, in her hand, the torch fades. She bangs it against a palm. It flickers, dies.

Damn it. Damn it. Damn.

She has an image of the new batteries she'd bought, left lying on her dressing table. Stupid. Stupid.

She casts around. Paler sky above rooftops, black pools behind railings, blank façades, patches of shrubbery. Could she bang on a door, beg for shelter? But everything has such a silenced, closed-up air.

Another siren joins the first, and then another. Searchlights slant into the sky, illuminating columns of fog, catching individual craft like raindrops. A wash of white; flares bloom above her. Then the bombs begin to fall.

For a moment she is caught, staring up, as though at some grand theatrical spectacle or natural phenomenon, as if it had nothing to do with her. She thinks, almost abstractly, I could die here, tonight. Then she feels, through the earth and the air, the first impact. And she runs.

Keep going, Lotts. You'll find the Tube. A warden's post.

Not if she gets blown to bits first, she won't. Janet bites her ragged nails.

Well, this is fun, Vanessa says.

Darling, seriously, go straight to my club, order yourself a Soixante Quinze and put it on my tab.

Thanks, Sas, but I don't know where your club is, I don't know where I am, and the dead do not have tabs.

This is a wider road now; a through route, it will get her somewhere. She peers along it, looking for landmarks. A plane shears directly overhead. There is nowhere to go. There is no cover. She watches as, a hundred yards further down the road, a bomb lands on the cobblestones. She feels the jolt of its impact. She is caught in the memory of Dr. Travers, his account of blood-red eyeballs, burst eardrums, lung tissue shredded by the vacuum's pull. Then she steps back into the side street and drops, huddling against the wall, one hand clamped over her nose and mouth, the other pressed over shut-tight eyes. She makes herself small, tiny; tiny things just bounce and roll and scuttle on. And then the world explodes around her. The ground shrugs her off. And then there's nothing. Nothing but a sharp whine in her ears. Then tightness in her chest. She can't breathe. Just darkness and dust. She can't breathe.

Is this what it's like?

Is this it?

She's on all fours. She can't breathe. But then she manages to force a breath out, and drag another in. It hurts. The air's jagged. She staggers to her feet. Her teeth crunch on grit; she wipes her eyes, spits. She stumbles on. She's lost her torch. The noise of the raid comes to her as though through a blanket, through the eardrum whine, and the street is weirdly lit by a blood-red sky. A new and different fear now grips her. She can feel it in her flesh. Someone's there.

"Who is it?" She spins back, searching, staring so hard that the night breaks into fizzing dots. "I know you're here."

There's no reply. But alongside that fear, a strange elation dawns. If this is happening, then she is not mad. She's not even wrong. The shadow man is tailing her in the blackout and a raid. Just like he did with all her friends.

"Fucking coward!" she yells at the darkness. "Be a man and show yourself."

Then the dark drags itself together, takes shape and begins to walk towards her.

She takes a step back.

Well, Richmond, you did ask.

Charlotte jolts down a kerb, staggers backwards. The figure pulls himself towards her, a lean and tar-black shade. It's not the shadow man that she has seen before, not that bulky form in a grey suit, not those marble eyes. It's not the same person at all.

"Who are you?"

The head inclines, but there's no further response; he just keeps coming, with a loose and swaggering malevolence. A bright terror grabs her, and she bolts.

The red darkness is broken by patches of vivid flame. She swerves round mounds of rubble, ducks under a drunken lamp post. She runs hard. His footfalls follow closely. Her breath rasps; her head is light. Any moment there will be people, any moment there will be help. If she can just stay one step ahead of him. Then her foot catches, and she goes flying. Time slows, but there is nothing to be done; she knows that this will be bad, both the impact and the delay. She hits the cobbles. There is a moment before the harm is registered, in which she scrambles back to her feet. Then it hits her, a wave of nausea and pain. Elbow, knee, hand. There's blood, hot and wet; her head swims. She thinks: the last cut has only just healed and now I'm hurt again. Then she turns to face what's coming. The darkness lands on her and wraps itself around her. The voices clamour in her head.

Is this it, Lotts?

Is this the bastard who did for me?

Has he always been on this island, like Caliban, just waiting for the dark to set him free?

Oh my darling. Oh my sweet girl. Don't let this happen to you.

She's dragged sideways, feet bumping loosely over cobblestones. She's suffocating. Her lungs will burst. She'll die and it will be just another death among the thousands, another body in the Blitz.

Don't be like us, darling.

Damn him, don't let him get away with it, Lotts.

Charlotte shoves, squirms, but he is too strong and too heavy, all dense fabric and lean muscle and she can't get a hold on anything. He doesn't speak; she can feel him breathing. She twists again and for an instant sees: she's in an alleyway, between high walls. A clutter of bins and crates, and beyond that, the street. But it is so far away. She is slammed back against a wall. Crushed.

It's dark in here, Vanessa says.

I know—

No, it's bloody dark in here.

Inside your head, darling. It's so dark.

Darkness is yours, Lotts. It always has been. Use it.

His face is close to hers, her head shoved hard into the rough wall behind her. She feels the force of his hands, the pressure of his body, the bristles of his moustache. His breath is tobacco and decay. This is everything that has ever been done to her against her wishes; everything she hasn't wanted but has had to tolerate. Every moist lip and every prickling bristle and every unwelcome touch and all the icy silences and every needle slid into a vein. The anger is useful, it's transformative.

He loosens his hold for a fraction of a second; she twists a hand free, grabs his hair, yanks his head back and sinks her teeth into his cheek. And he screams. He's rendered suddenly, ridiculously, human. He pulls away, taking her with him, scrabbling at her; she wrenches harder at the hair—it's thin and slick with pomade—and sinks her teeth deeper. There's blood in her mouth and she is thrilled by the salt and iron and heat. He's pushing at her, yelling at her, calling her a bitch and a whore and a fucking lunatic.

She could laugh. If she didn't have a mouthful.

She loses her grip, drops away. There's blood in her mouth, hair in her hand. She spits and shakes her fingers out.

I am going to die, she thinks, but I won't leave a perfect corpse. It's going to look like what it is. And he'll look like what he is, too; I've marked him.

Then there's a clatter beyond the end of the alleyway. She turns to see an incendiary land. Then it fizzes, breaks into incandescence. In its light, she can now see him fully. His hand is clasped over his face; she can see the dark blood between his fingers, see his angular features; see his good, clear skin, and his neatly clipped moustache, his hair all tangled and stuck with pomade. He looks, more than anything, like a young RAF officer. This is the last face her friends ever saw. She squares up to him with renewed ferocity. How *dare* he?

His fist catches her in the mouth and she's flung back. Her head cracks into brick; the pain is dazzling. She clutches at the wall, determined to stay upright. The blood pounds in her head. She can hear his ragged breathing as he moves in again. Her thoughts stretch to Tom across the night. When they find me, she thinks, you will see, you will understand, and you won't let it go.

But the blow doesn't come. She keeps on breathing. There are voices, footfalls in the road. At the end of the alleyway, a shape moves across the pale fire, and is gone.

She licks her lip; the skin is split. She touches at the back of her head; her fingers come away tacky with blood. She stumbles away from the wall, straightening her skirt, sweeping the hair off her face. Pins fall; it all comes loose. She is still alive, and that seems rather extraordinary.

Look what you did, Lotts.

My clever, clever girl.

Hats off to you, Richmond.

Told you it was bloody dark in here.

Dressing Up

A vivid, sparkling morning. Shopkeepers sweep broken glass off pavements, and there's the tap-tap-tap of nails into board. Her nose is buried in her upturned collar, her hat carefully perched on her bloodied head. She'd spent what was left of the night on a hard chair in a first aid post. Her cuts and grazes were cleaned and cups of hot sweet tea provided, and a greatcoat was bundled up and given to her for a pillow, and she dozed and was woken, dozed and was woken by conversations and explosions and the phone ringing, the wireless on for the midnight news; dozing and being handed another cup of tea and a piece of bread and margarine, being asked if she could make her own way home or needed to be taken. Clasping her cup, she thanked them and said that she could certainly manage. But she couldn't begin to articulate how grateful she was.

She tries one telephone box, and then another. At a third, she is at last able to place a call through to Mrs. Denby and explain that she was caught out in last night's raid; no, no, she's fine, she was, as they say, just lightly injured. Oh no, please don't worry, it could have been so much worse, she just looks a bit of a fright at the moment and she'd prefer not to come into the office till she's had a chance to, well, tidy herself up a bit. Yes, she honestly is fine, and she has everything she needs; Mrs. Denby must not worry and must certainly not put herself out on Charlotte's account. Just two or three days' leave at the most, she'll certainly be back in next week, full of the joys of Monday. Thank you.

She feels guilty at Mrs. Denby's obvious concern. People are, she thinks, as she replaces the receiver, more often than not, kind. It's just unkindness has a way of hitting one harder. And in the face. She touches her sore jaw, tastes her split lip. So she must make a point of noticing the kindness when it's offered.

When she gets back to her digs, she tells Mrs. Callaghan the same not-quite-lie and is deluged with sympathy, even permitted another non-regulation mid-morning weekday bath. The gas pressure is rather better today; the geyser pops and putts and roars and she sinks into a waist-deep warmth, then lies down, knees bent, and ducks her head quite under. Her hair lifts and spreads like seaweed. The water stings her broken scalp; dark clots come adrift. The grey-green ceiling is blistered with condensation. The water cools, so she can only really feel it's there when she moves and stirs it.

Why hide the truth? El asks.

It's easier.

It's like you've done something wrong.

I don't want to upset them, Charlotte thinks. I don't want too many questions.

So being injured by a blast is cause for sympathy, but being injured by a man is cause for shame.

I don't need this right now, El. I don't need to work out whether I'm doing this right. I'm just doing what I can.

But it is, she thinks, as she explores the pain at the back of her head, real. Whatever may or may not have happened to the others, this happened to her. She cannot be persuaded out of this.

Back in her attic room, she examines the evidence—her bruises, blue and pink patches that have yet to fully bloom. She pokes at her grazes, the skin around them gone pale and the flesh oozing again after bathing. She starts to get dressed, stepping stiffly into fresh underwear, her shoulders tight and sore as she fastens her brassiere. She sits down to roll on a new pair of stockings, yesterday's being in tatters, but then she stops. Music is rising through the floorboards. Mr. Gibbons is playing Debussy on his gramophone. She wraps her dressing gown over her underwear, treads back into slippers. She pads down the stairs, and taps.

He opens the door, then registers the split in her lip, frowns, opens the door more widely. He looks her over, moving round her and turning her to peer at the back of her head. He sucks his teeth in sympathy: "My dear, whatever happened to you?"

"Blackout injury," she says.

"Goodness me. What on earth did you do?"

"Fell into a lamp post."

A frown, chin tucked in, sceptical.

"Awfully bad luck," Charlotte says. "Is it your day off, Mr. Gibbons?"

"I'm on nights at the warehouse now," he says. "It's nearly bed-time."

"I see. Well, the thing is. You know how good you were, in lending me that coat?"

"You get along so well together, it would be wrong to part you. You must keep it."

She melts at this. "You are so kind. So kind, really. Thank you. And here I am angling for another favour already."

"What would that be now?"

"Could you see your way clear to sparing a girl, say, a pair of slacks, perhaps a jacket? Just for a while. I don't feel safe tottering around in skirts and court shoes in blackout, not any more. And I can't very well go dragging round the shops, can I? Not looking like this."

He stands aside to let her pass; she steps into his pin-neat room. He's opening the wardrobe, leafing through the hangers.

"The thing is to find something cut to your frame. We don't want to swamp you."

A crisp white shirt with a studded collar makes her lift her head up high. A teal-blue sweater covers her warmly from collarbones to hips. The jacket falls from her shoulders without nipping in or bulging out or riding up; it just stays there, being no trouble at all, just holding the warmth around her comfortably. No clips or bones or elastic. Nothing chafes. She unbuttons the jacket again, tries the inside pocket, then the front pockets and the ticket pocket. She slips her hands into her trouser pockets, cocks an eyebrow at herself in the mirror.

"Damn," she says.

"What is it?" Mr. Gibbons asks.

"You chaps do so well for pockets. I had no idea."

She slips the Crombie on over the top, turns herself to catch the different angles.

"Swear, soon as I get myself sorted out, I will get this back to you without so much as a speck."

"Really, don't worry at all; I have more than I really should. But what about shoes? Mine won't fit your fairy feet."

She glances down at a slippered toe. "I have a pair of walking brogues upstairs."

"That'll do nicely."

They regard her reflection together.

"Do I actually look like a chap, do you think?" she asks.

"More principal boy than leading man."

She frowns.

"No, it suits you; really suits you. Gamine, you know," he says. "But a ladies' hat is too flimsy with those lines. I have a trilby that would be just the ticket. If it won't hurt your poor dear head."

She doesn't sound herself, Tom thinks. It's an awkward situation any-way, the receiver handed to him by his astonished mother; him aware throughout that his parents are engaged in intense, whispered specu-lation just beyond the kitchen door. While it's hard to filter out this distraction, Tom is still very much aware of how bright, almost giddy, Charlotte sounds. She's nearby and would love to see him; some new development, could he spare her half an hour? Of course he could; when and where? He immediately tosses up in the air all that after-noon's commitments at the prospect of meeting up with her, but he keeps his tone neutral and formal throughout the conversation. His parents are listening, and he is just about to lie to them.

College on the phone. Yes, hopefully, good news, since they are calling students in to talk over the situation. Yes, it's all a bit last-minute, but you know how things are these days. His parents do; deci-sions have to be made on the hoof, plans are always provisional and liable to change. Everybody understands this. They send him on his way with their blessing—Dad can manage without him for a bit; he has the other fellows to help him if he needs them. This matters.

Tom is at once thrilled and mortified. It'd only take him being spot-ted by an acquaintance—and they have so many acquaintances—and a few idle words to either parent, for the lie to be exposed. He sinks down on his bench in Russell Square, in his winter coat and gloves. He chafes his hands and waits for her; he keeps an eye on passers-by. The walk took him a while; he'd hoped she'd be there already.

There's a young man dawdling along a far path, smoking a cigarette, and there are a couple of small ladies in long skirts walking their small dogs, and that's it. Not anyone he knows, so far, thank goodness.

Starlings flutter in, stop, hop, cock an eye at him. They are lovelier than they are given credit for, starlings; at a glance they look mouse-brown, but their plumage is shot through with petrol colours. The kingfisher's unassuming cousins. But he has nothing for them today.

"Sorry, lads."

His eye slides round the square and lights on the youth again, who's now reached the turn in the path. Tom knows him. Damn, that's awkward; but so long as he's moved on before Charlotte gets here . . . Where does he know him from? He's sharply dressed, slick even, hat tweaked to shade his face. And he's definitely seen Tom, because he raises a hand and strides towards him. Tom will say he's on his way to college, stopped for a rest, then if it does filter back . . . Then Tom sees the bruised jaw, the split lip. State of the kid. And there's something about that loping gait. The space between them contracts. There's a shift, as with one of those puzzle pictures, when for a while all you can see is the vase, and then all you can see are the faces staring at each other.

"My word." Tom gets to his feet.

"Hello, hello," she says.

"What on earth—?"

"This?" She touches her split lip. "Don't worry about this."

Charlotte drops onto the bench, takes off her hat and sets it down on her lap. Her curls have been razed to stubble. There's a mess of bruise and scab at the back of her head. Her eyes look huge, luminous. He sits back down beside her, winded, looking her over, his gaze then drawn back to her lip.

"It's worse than it looks," she says.

"Worse?"

"I mean, the other way round; it's not as bad as it looks. In fact, it's good."

"*Good?*"

She laughs. She's been battered like an orange that's fallen from a barrow and been kicked down the street. And she laughs and says it's good. He's scared.

She takes his hand in hers. "Don't look so worried, Tom."

"What happened to you?"

"He did."

"*What?*"

"Him. In a raid. He nearly suffocated me. We had a bit of a tussle, and so, you see. And then he ran off."

"How are you? Are you . . ." He squeezes her hand, astonished at this intimacy, not knowing what to say.

"I'll be fine."

The wind picks up; leaves drift sideways from the plane trees.

"I'm sorry," he says. "I'm so sorry. What did the police say?"

She lets go of his hand. She closes her collar against the breeze.

"You still haven't been to the police?" he asks.

She pulls a face. No.

"You don't want to be a nuisance. You don't want your father to find out. That's it?"

"That's it."

"Your head's so badly cut that they had to cut your hair off at the hospital, and what you're worried about is your father's feelings?"

A funny, furtive, dismissive shrug.

He sits back, studies her, trying to look beyond the physical harm done. The glittering eyes, the restlessness, the elation. "You didn't go to hospital?"

"They're very busy."

"My God, Charlotte."

"The people at the first aid post were lovely, though. They were very helpful. And the barbers."

He aches for her, but is entirely at a loss; he feels unequipped to deal with this. "Why did you want to see me?"

"Yes, so, what I wanted to say is now I know I was right after all. Whatever Dr. Travers might have thought. It *looks* like it's caused by a blast, but it isn't. So I'm as sane as anyone, thank you very much, though God knows how many other women—but now we know there's someone doing this, all we have to do is get the coroner to reconsider these cases—"

"*All* we have to do?"

"Mmm. Vanessa's and Janet's and Saskia's, as well as El's—though after that it will be down to the authorities to decide what to look at. And so, you see," she says brightly, "I thought you'd be well-placed to get the ball rolling. You'd know who to speak to and what to say." She leans her shoulder against his. "So, what do you think?"

"We have to go to the police."

She frowns, licks her split lip.

"You said you would," he says. "You promised, when you took my card."

"That wasn't what I was agreeing to."

"But the police would get the coroner involved. If there was a case to answer."

Her eyelids flutter in frustration. "You're not listening to me—"

"Miss Richmond. Charlotte. Please." He moves so that their shoulders no longer touch. "Listen to me. You have to stop."

Her look is excoriating. "Stop? Now? When I finally—"

"Stop acting like you're on your own," he continues over her. "When there are people who will help you."

She goes to speak, but he forestalls her again; he has to make her see reason, before something even worse can happen.

"Believe me. I know families. There's nothing I know better. I know families under strain, families in grief, families in the most devastating of circumstances. And I know that whatever happened in the past, your father will honestly have believed that he was acting in your interests, and he will want the best for you now, and will continue to want this for the future. I am sure that all you need to do is be open with him, and all of this will resolve itself. There's no need to be afraid. Of him, or of going to the police, or of making a nuisance of yourself, as you insist on describing it."

"You don't understand."

"No, I don't. I really don't. We have to go to the police. Phone your father and tell him first, and then there's no risk of him finding out second-hand. I am certain, I *bet* he will only be concerned for you. Horrified, even. He'll only want to help."

"How much?"

"How much what?"

"How much do you want to bet?"

She turns away, staring off across the autumn square. His frustration and fear distil into fury. She is so stubborn; she takes such risks; she puts herself in harm's way. And she will not even consider seeking proper help.

"Do you *think*," he asks, waving at her attire, "that this will protect you? That because you're dressed like a man you're somehow *safe*?"

She pulls a face: "It's worth a try."

"You have noticed we're at war? You have noticed what happens to men in wars? It's not a free pass. Just you wait till some lout takes you for a conchie. Or a pansy, or decides you walk funny, or doesn't like the way you're looking at them. Or not looking at them. Try it out. I should bloody know. It won't protect you. Whereas what you *do* have is you have family—"

"You're wrong."

He lets the brakes off then; the fury is invigorating. "*I'm* wrong? You're the one with the mad theories and the weird clothes and the burst lip and an actual head wound, if you hadn't noticed."

"You have no . . ." But then she shakes her head; she pushes up from her seat.

"Charlotte—"

She turns back to him. The cold light catches on her jawline, on her cheekbone, and in her shorn hair. Her eyes are glittering and wet. She has never looked so heartbreaking, or so beautiful.

"You're wrong," she says again. She reaches into a jacket pocket and gets out her cigarettes. "Right up until this moment, I didn't think I was on my own."

She turns away, and crunches off across the gravel, lighting up a cigarette.

He goes to call after her. Bites it back.

For a clever man, he can be so damned stupid.

The train comes to a halt at West Norwood; they're clearing a UXB from near the line. Charlotte joins the collective, fatigued sigh of resignation as the passengers get up from their seats and shuffle out into the cold slap of the wind. She's warmer, though, than she ever was in women's clothes. And she holds herself differently, moves differently, dressed like this. Shoulders back, head up, stride long. But she tips her hat to shade her face, the swollen and cut lip.

She can manage without Tom, she tells herself. She clearly can't contact the coroner herself; that would certainly filter back to Father, but she can try Mrs. Hartwell again. Her injuries must elicit concern; they make the argument on her behalf. And with Mrs. H recruited, she can then go back to Janet's husband. A man like that, a man of active, practical compassion; he'll know what to do, and he'll be listened to by other men. Then she can take a step back. Her father need never know it was anything to do with her, when the story hits the newspapers. She can keep that quietly to herself. And if all else fails there's still Vanessa, or rather Vanessa's people; she must have people somewhere. If the theatre is still opening for matinées, there must be someone there who knew her.

Charlotte pauses to light up. She feels brilliant and lucid and not the least bit tired; the cuts and bruises barely bother her. She walks on. Whatever Tom might say about it, this is a superpower, this male attire. The invisibility it confers; the space it claims. One is planted to the ground. One can push into a crowd without fear of straying hands. One can race up a flight of stairs without the slightest concern. Tom hasn't got the faintest idea of the trouble it gets her out of, even if it might get her into other kinds.

She straightens her hat, flinches as it scrapes against the scabs. She takes a turn for home.

There's a large Vauxhall saloon parked halfway down Woodland Road. Which is funny, because you never usually see a car here.

Must be a doctor, she thinks. Or some local dignitary come to glad-hand and commiserate.

Key into lock, then self through the door. She goes to hang up her hat. She'll go straight upstairs, get ready for the evening's show. In her thoughts, she's already in dressing gown and slippers, already sipping on her evening's Horlicks in quiet communion with Mrs. C. And then tomorrow, thanks to Mrs. Denby giving her a few days' grace, she can get started on what needs to be done. But even as she's thinking this, Mrs. Callaghan comes bustling towards her.

"Afternoon, Mrs. C."

Mrs. Callaghan makes a strange hissing noise and flaps her arms, wafting Charlotte back towards the front door. The overall effect is like being confronted by an angry goose.

"What is it? What's wrong?"

"Just go, go on, love, get you out of here."

Mrs. Callaghan darts an anguished look at the parlour door. In all of Charlotte's time here, only Mrs. Callaghan herself has ever occupied that room. She sweeps and dusts and polishes and sometimes sits in the good light to knit, but mostly she just seals it off until the next frenzy of sweeping, dusting and polishing. She keeps her husband's photograph in there, on its own side-table.

"It's them 'uns," Mrs. Callaghan whispers.

"What?"

"Them 'uns you've been hiding from."

"Hiding?"

"Hiding from, avoiding; whatever you want to call it, living here."

A flood of fear: "I wasn't hiding; I—"

"Doesn't matter. They've come for you anyway."

A sudden clarity. Charlotte grabs the old chapped hand. "Thanks."

Mrs. Callaghan returns the squeeze. "Honestly, love. Just go."

But it is too late. The parlour door opens, and light streams through. A woman steps into the hall. Slim, soignée, her hair set in a perfect wave, she wears a fox-fur stole fastened with its own bite, and her hat is a delicate confection of dead things.

"Hello, Lolo," the woman says.

It's like finding a scalpel in the cutlery drawer, or a pike circling round the goldfish bowl. Nothing wrong with scalpels. Nothing wrong with pike. Nothing wrong with her older sister, either, not as such. But not here, in Woodland Road, please, dear God, not now.

"Hello, Fran," Charlotte hears herself say. "What are you doing here?"

Other figures move into the doorway behind Francesca, blocking out the light.

Charlotte realises Mrs. Callaghan was right; she must have been hiding, because this is exactly what it feels like to get caught.

"I came to see you, silly," Francesca says.

"Is that your car in the street?"

"We're worried about you. Father and I."

"Father?" She cranes round to peer past Francesca.

"Oh, he's not *here,* you ninny. He's tremendously busy. Really, this is the last thing he needs."

"What is?"

With a waft of Je Reviens, Francesca moves closer to lay an immaculately gloved hand on Charlotte's sleeve. "Lolo," she says, "you must stop it now, you know."

Charlotte affects a nonchalant tone. "Stop what?"

"This," Francesca says, taking in with a sweep of her arm the whole life that Charlotte has assembled for herself. "This pretence."

"There's no pretence," Charlotte says.

"You're not well. We all know you're not well. You're convincing no one."

"I am in tip-top condition, thank you very much."

"Oh come on, Lolo," she says, gently shaking her arm, as though to wake her. "I mean, look at you."

The pressure of Francesca's hand forces everything into sharper contrast. The light is brighter; the shadows deepen; every action seems to slow, every word to take on a heavy inevitability.

"Would you excuse us, Mrs. Callaghan?" Francesca asks. "This is a family matter."

Mrs. Callaghan nods, gaunt. She backs reluctantly towards the basement stairs, turns down them. Charlotte wants to call after her, but "family matter" is a blank cheque; it can be used to cover anything.

Charlotte takes a step back too, so that Francesca's hand falls away. She runs her bare palm over her cropped head. She stares towards the parlour. She considers the front door. She makes calculations.

"You mean this? The Victory Crop?" she says. "I considered it my patriotic duty. Shave and save."

"Don't be ridiculous. You look like a galley slave."

"*Au contraire.* It's quite liberating. All that washing and drying and setting. All those kirby grips; all that *waste.* I don't have to worry about any of that any more. I know a fellow in Bloomsbury who'll chop the lot off for you in a trice, if you're interested."

Francesca sighs. "It's not just the hair. Or even all"—a gesture at Charlotte's injuries—"this. You know that, Lolo. It's you. It's your nonsense."

"What nonsense?"

Francesca's beautiful brow creases. "How do you think Elena's mother feels? To lose her daughter, then have you prodding at old wounds?"

So she did it, Mrs. Hartwell. She said she wouldn't, but she did. "They're not old."

"And Dr. Travers. As if a man like that didn't have enough to contend with, without your silly stories."

"He came to you?"

"He went to Mrs. Hartwell, as you might well have anticipated, if you had any sense. It upset her dreadfully, as you might also have anticipated. The poor woman was obliged to telephone Father, just to get some reassurance you'd be . . ." Charlotte can see the phrase *dealt with* almost come into being. But Francesca settles on: "calmed down."

"I see." Charlotte takes another step back, as though to examine the notepad on the hall console, but her thoughts are trained on the front door, three feet or so behind her. If she can get outside, get as far as the station, then maybe—

"And Father's in the midst of some crisis at the Ministry," Francesca continues. "Which he can't even *talk* about, the poor creature, but I can see that he is dreadfully preoccupied. And then, to top it all off, you decide now's a good time to go on one of your sprees. The trouble, Lolo, that you've been causing, tormenting these poor people. It's the last thing any of us needs."

"I didn't mean; I wasn't . . . Sprees?"

"Clive?"

Charlotte stalls. "Oh."

Francesca drops her voice: "In such bad taste, Lolo. Really. Shocking. The poor boy."

"He's not a boy." Her cheeks burn; she had trusted to his decency, or, failing that, his sense of shame. Clearly neither had been sufficient to override his need to apportion blame.

Francesca's voice drops to almost nothing; she mouths the words: "The *things* I found, Lolo. In my *little sister's* room. No unmarried woman should even know these things *exist*."

"That's private, Fran!"

"We all thought you were better. We thought you'd behave better now. But here you are again. Up to your old tricks. As though you haven't learned a thing."

Charlotte feels sick; she swallows down the terror. There must still be some chance of clemency. Some way back from this.

"What does Father know?"

"Everything. Apart from . . . your device. And I'll spare him that."

Charlotte's voice comes out dry and defeated. "Thank you."

A pause. "You know I would very much prefer not to have to do this."

"Then don't," Charlotte says. "Please."

"I wouldn't if it wasn't necessary." Francesca calls back over her shoulder: "Gentlemen?"

They come out into the hallway. Two sinewy, shaven, tight-featured men.

Charlotte nods to them as if they are old acquaintances. She does her best to keep her voice level: "Really, when it comes to it, it's just a haircut, Frannie. It's just a change of style. Haven't you seen a woman in slacks before? It's quite normal nowadays, it's quite the thing. And as for the rest of it, I won't trouble anybody again, I promise. Clive was just an aberration. A mistake. I was beside myself, after what happened to El. But I'm better now. So really we can just forget all about it and you can be on your way."

A sympathetic head-tilt. "Darling. You must realise how ridiculous this sounds?"

The hall is now tight-packed with bodies. The men take up so much space; Francesca's furs and feathers and perfume; they all take up so much space. Charlotte's chest and throat tighten.

You can't go back there, El says.

Tell her to sling her bloody hook.

Don't let them take you back to that godawful place, my darling girl.

You're the Cordelia here, Richmond, if you're anyone. And you know how things worked out for her.

"You mustn't let yourself get worked up, Lolo," Francesca's saying over the crowding voices.

"I'm not worked up. I'm entirely calm. All I'm saying is, there really is no need—"

Francesca smiles blandly, uninterested. "Come along, Charlotte dear. Time to go."

Last time was not as bad as this. Last time, Charlotte believed that they would make her better. Last time, she didn't know what that would involve.

"Shall I get these gentlemen to help you, Lolo?"

"I'm not going—"

Francesca is already shaking her head, taking her arm. "Come along now."

"I'll be good, I promise, please."

"I'm afraid we're a long way past that now."

Charlotte swerves out of Francesca's grip and makes a lunge for the door, but the men move faster and hold her back. She knows she's doing it wrong; it's wrong to resist, it's wrong to protest; it's only ever taken as proof of your deficiency. But she can't help herself: she ducks, drags, and the grip just tightens on her. Mrs. Callaghan has clambered up from the basement; she's darting ineffectually to try and get to her; Mr. Gibbons comes to a startled halt at the foot of the stairs. But she is held by the men. They're different individuals but always the same men: bland, stone-faced, stronger than they look; her memory of last time is broken and sick and fractured, but it is always the same men.

"You can't make me."

Francesca's tone is sympathetic. "I'm afraid we can, Lolo. You're not yet twenty-one. We're your family. We'll take care of you. You don't have to worry about anything any more. You'll be quite safe in Summer Fields."

Charlotte notices it happen; it's involuntary. She takes an inward step away from herself. She watches herself surrender. She watches herself walk, compliant, surrounded by her escorts, out of the house, across the street and to the car. She watches as they open the back door and manoeuvre her inside.

Because this is how to survive it; this is how she survived it before. This sideways shift, so that she becomes a bystander in her own life.

Whatever happens, it happens to this other girl they call Charlotte, and it might be sad, and nasty, and terrifying, but it affects her only in the way a story affects the person reading it. Beside her is the scraped skin of a man's cheek, outside the car, Francesca's immaculate silhouette; Mr. Gibbons is coming down the front path. "Now look here—" in rolled sleeves and braces, pale as his shirt; Mrs. Callaghan stands in her doorway, twittering like an angry robin. Charlotte feels a distant kind of regret. When she turned up here over a year ago, with nothing but a small suitcase and a desperate need to disappear, she had never thought that she would come to love this place, or leave it like this.

Through the clean glass of the car window, she sees Francesca's face blank with contempt as Charlotte's friends attempt to intervene.

"I don't know why you have to treat her so rough," Mrs. Callaghan is saying. "She has not a bit of harm in her."

Mr. Gibbons's voice is stiff with outrage: "She was perfectly all right till you got here."

And Francesca's disdain. "She can be quite convincing, I'm afraid."

All of this—the blasted-bare privet hedge and the garret window with its yellow curtains and her own room beyond, these people—it was silly of her to come to care for it all; she should have known that she couldn't keep a life like this. They have put up barriers round the bomb site; the bright girls are gone and buried in London clay; the petals are all fallen, the rosehips swelling red. She can't keep it separate; she can't stop herself from feeling it: the horror of being torn away, the urgency of this love.

"I want to stay," she cries, but it comes out messy and distorted. She bangs on the window. It is a relief, to give in. To give in to feeling, and to expectations.

"Let me stay, please; let me stay."

"Poor thing."

Francesca taps on the glass with a gloved fingernail. The orderly slides the window open.

"Can't you do anything to help her?" Francesca asks.

The man in the front passes a small leather case to the man in the back seat. A hard grip on her wrist as a sleeve is pulled back and her inner arm exposed.

"This isn't necessary," Charlotte says, shocked out of tears. She tries to pull away, but the fingers just dig deeper into her flesh. "It isn't necessary."

She watches a needle slide into her skin. She watches the plunger depress, feels the chill as the drug surges from syringe to her vein, as it flows up her arm with the current of her blood.

Her fingers fizzle out. Her legs have gone. Her face turns numb and hard. Francesca watches through the glass. The dead fox stares at her. All these eyes, of glass and flesh. The fox blinks. Her sister swims away; the man beside her blurs around the edges. The engine starts and they lurch into movement.

She slides, droops, slumps, drags herself upright again in the back seat; she won't let go. Houses scroll past. She lets her cheek fall against the cool pane. The man beside her takes up most of the seat with his breathing and his body. In front of her is the driver's shiny ear, his white shirt collar, the clipped hair at the back of his neck, all cold and pale and wintery. She watches the shift of his arm as he changes gear. Her head is syrupy, her mouth full of wet. It doesn't matter. It actually doesn't matter. It isn't happening to her.

The road is hypnotic. They cross the silvery treacherous river and slide steadily, smoothly, as though on rails. Next to her, the man's coat spreads round him in a puddle. His breath is pug breath, clogged and nasal and wet. Dead ahead is a pork joint, bristling fat rolling over collar; she can smell the crackling. Her mouth fills with spit and she can't be sick because being sick is so much worse than not being sick, but when she looks out the window now, everything's craters and boards and ruins stretching wide like the battered mouth of a giant. Her teeth chatter. Her shoulders muffle her ears. She must think of something else, hold on to something else, something clean, something fresh. Crisp air, falling leaves, a square in autumn. Tom.

She rolls her forehead on the glass. Tom. She tries to remember herself back into the argument, how it came to fizz then flare, but it slips away from her as the city slips away; there's no hope in mock-Tudor semis, market gardens, copses, in horses standing at gates, sheep studding twilight fields. She is falling out of the world again.

Hours may pass. Or minutes. Hours. The man beside her sleeps, spot-scarred temple against his window. A patch of condensation rolls out across the glass from his open mouth, and disappears, and rolls out again. Her head is clearing, though; the drug is wearing off. A cross-roads; the car slows. It seems suddenly and brilliantly clear: this is her last chance and she must take it. How much can it hurt anyway? Not as much as Summer Fields.

Her hand yanks the handle, her shoulder slams the door: but it doesn't move. The noise jerks the sleeping man awake, makes the driver twist round to glare at them.

"Chrissake, Bert. Can't you even stay awake?"

He stirs his mouth with his tongue. "She's not going anywhere."

"No thanks to you."

"How about I drive? And you sit back here with Lady Dribbles?"

"No thanks."

"Well then."

The man beside her folds his arms.

"You know what," he says to Charlotte, "usually, when you give people that stuff, they more or less roll over and start snoring."

Despite the returning sense of clarity, it's still hard to make her mouth behave itself; words are difficult to form, and come out thick and slurry. "Not much of a sleeper," she says. "Not of late."

He says, "You're safe with us, you know. Safer than you were back there in that London."

She turns to look out of the window. Safe. A row of houses, a curve of river, and then blue-grey slopes of fields up towards the cloudy evening sky. They dive into woodland; it goes on forever. They skim alongside a familiar, high brick wall. The wrought-iron gates stand open. The car slows, makes the turn. Summer Fields stands in black-out, a shadow against the star-flecked sky.

There is no way around this now. The only way out is through.

Summer Fields

The wall is fog-green up to the dado rail. Above the rail, it's milky tea. Charlotte wasn't on this ward before. It's half-empty; it seems that women are not going mad with quite the frequency that they did before the war. There's an ancient woman a few beds down, almost bald, who barely seems to breathe, and who can't really need to be in Summer Fields since all she does is lie there, quietly dying, and being no trouble to anyone. There are other women further along the ward, but the bed opposite Charlotte's is empty.

The women keep busy. They get up and get dressed. They come and go. They receive visitors in the day room. The visitors bring flowers, mop-headed dahlias and chrysanthemums that smell of death. These women have a chastened air about them. They are very properly dressed; they are very deliberately composed.

Charlotte watches them, their played-to-the-gallery sanity. The manifest embarrassment at having been such a bother, and the determination not to be a bother to anyone again. She knows what they are up to. But if Francesca—or, God forbid, if Father—were to come and visit, could she even begin to make a show of such compliance? The most she can manage at the moment is to be quiet.

Later, her suitcase—how did that get here?—is lumped up onto the foot of her bed. A nurse flings open the lid and prattles on at her like it's Christmas morning. Now that she's nicely rested, she'll get up, she'll get dressed, she'll go through to the day room and try some knitting or sewing and there's a piano too, if she plays? Does she play? She'll feel much better for it. And if that goes well, then maybe in a day or two, Charlotte can go and see Doctor.

"Osterheim?" Charlotte asks, her voice thin.

"Oh dear me, no," the nurse says. "Dr. Osterheim's gone. It's Dr. Gantley now."

Charlotte slips out of bed. On bare feet, standing beside the nurse, she peers at these possessions. She recognises her bluebell skirt, her cream silk blouse, her cardigan. Stockings, underwear, her new gloves, her grey suede shoes in a calico bag. Francesca has packed for her. Her washbag is tucked into the silk pouch-pocket in the lid of the suitcase. Toothbrush and half-rolled-up toothpaste, her lipstick, face powder and perfume. Even her hairbrush. She supposes that this was all well-meant. But—a spike of fear—what happened to the earrings? She upends the case onto the bed, runs her hands through the pouches and pockets. They're not there. She'd left them in her dressing table. Frannie will have found them, and she'll have told Father. The nurse is staring, so Charlotte starts laying the clothes back in the case.

"Where are my other things?" Charlotte asks.

"This is all we have for you."

"What happened to the clothes I came in?"

"I believe they've been disposed of."

Charlotte's jaw slides sideways. Mr. Gibbons; his beautiful things. She slams the case shut, buckles it. She hopes she gets the chance to make it up to him.

The nurse folds her lips in, raises her eyebrows. "We'll try again tomorrow, then," she says.

Some nights the sky rumbles and down low over the horizon there's a patch of pinky-orange. It's visible through the high window. Visible if she can slide the evening pill into her cheek, let it drop down the plughole with the spat toothpaste. She can never know how much of it will have dissolved before she can be rid of it, and that makes her uneasy, suspicious of herself, as though things are sneaking and slinking in the corner of her vision, and her head swims and words are hard like pebbles in her mouth.

In the mornings, she sifts through the contents of the case but cannot think of the folds of wool, the scraps of silk, the diaphanous slips of stocking, as really being clothes.

"If you'd just get dressed, then you can go and see Doctor."

The nurse is an angular young woman, sweetly nervous. Charlotte wants to be obliging, she really does; she wants to be nice to the nice nurse. And the doctor is the way out of there, she knows; they always are.

"It has to be . . ." Her mouth is slack. She dabs at her lips. "Those things?"

"You can hardly go and see him in your nightie, can you?"

Charlotte considers her nightgown, her bare feet. "I expect not."

But what about my sturdy trousers and jacket, and my nice warm sweater? What about my lovely brown brogues? She wants the clothes that made her feel like a person, and not like a present wrapped up in shiny paper, just to be unwrapped.

Something lifts Charlotte from her nightmare. She crawls to the end of her bed and tweaks the curtain back. At the bed opposite, a new arrival is being installed. The woman—youngish, dark—talks. The curtains move and billow as nurses fuss around and shush her, but she just keeps on talking. Sometimes quietly, sometimes rising to a shrill and panicked pitch, but always talking. Nobody is listening; the only concern is to make her quiet. They give her something *to help you sleep, love;* and her speech collapses like a sandcastle; the words break apart and are stirred and flattened into moans and mumbling. The nurses leave the bedside.

Charlotte drops the curtain and scrabbles back under the covers. The gaps increase between the noises; there's whimpering, and then silence. Charlotte lies back and stares at the ceiling.

"Such lovely things," the nurse says. It's a different nurse. She lifts the clothing reverently, lays each item on the bed. "Don't you have such lovely things?"

"Where do you come from?" Charlotte asks, not looking at the clothes, but at the woman's high cheekbones, her bright black-coffee eyes, her warm beauty.

"Finsbury."

"I thought you might be Spanish."

"My mum was Greek, my dad's a Scot," she says. "Now, pop your clothes on, love, and we can go and see Doctor."

Charlotte wants to help, she really does; she wants to oblige this woman if she possibly can.

"Would you like them?" Charlotte asks, and touches the wet from her chapped lips.

The nurse laughs.

"No, I'm serious. The blue would suit you beautifully."

"They're your clothes, dear."

Charlotte shakes her head.

"My dear," the nurse says. "They are. You have to stop pretending. You have to *try*."

In the middle of the night, noise stirs Charlotte back to the surface of her dreams. Her own bed-curtains are not quite closed; she leans up on her elbows and she can see that the bed opposite is empty. There's a strange keening noise.

Charlotte heaves herself up to seated, peers down the ward; the dark woman feels her way blindly along the room, moaning and whimpering to herself. She stops by the old woman who barely seems to breathe; she pulls up her own nightgown, pulls down her underwear and seats herself on the old woman's bed. One of the night nurses, having noticed something's going on, strides down the ward. It is only when Charlotte hears liquid drip onto the linoleum floor that she realises that the dark woman is urinating on the other woman's bed.

Charlotte slides back down to lie flat.

The nurse scolds, calls in help; they begin their irritated work, while the dark woman now sobs. They shift the poor old sugar-bones to a dry bed. There's a clank of the mop bucket; the jangle, flap and scuff of the bed being remade.

Charlotte says quietly, "She didn't mean to," but she isn't heard.

Charlotte calls out, "She didn't mean to; she was lost," but she isn't heard.

Charlotte gets herself up out of bed and pads across the ward. She puts a hand on the arm of the angular young nurse, who swings round with alarm, and then softens at the sight of her.

"Go back to bed, miss, why don't you."

Charlotte says, "She was confused; she thought she was at home; she thought it was the lavatory."

"Go back to bed," the nurse says again, with a warning look. And Charlotte, chastened, pads back to her bed, and gets in, and rolls on her side, and lies there with her eyes open, listening to the nurses' fading irritation.

In the morning, the bed opposite is empty. It is stripped to mouse-and-porridge ticking.

The dark-eyed nurse lifts the suitcase and opens it again. Charlotte watches the way the woman's fingers sink into the wool, the way the stockings drape like shed skins from her hands.

"What's your name?" Charlotte asks.

"Aminta."

"That's unusual."

"Not where I come from."

"Finsbury?"

Aminta laughs, gives Charlotte a sidelong look: "Are you teasing me, Miss Richmond?"

She wouldn't dream of it. "What happened to the lady opposite, Aminta?"

"Oh, you don't need to worry about that."

"She was confused. And nobody was listening."

"All you need to worry about is getting yourself better."

"Where is she now?"

"Where she can get the help she needs."

"What kind of help?"

Aminta stops what she is doing and looks Charlotte in the eye, but her tone is warm, amused: "You're a doctor now, are you? This is a professional interest you're taking?"

"No, but . . . What kind of help?"

The nurse sets the stockings down on the bed. She lays out the sweater.

"Word of wisdom for you, duckie. Worry about your own good self. That's how you'll get out of here. Do what's asked of you.

Don't make a fuss. And don't wet the bed. Your own or anybody else's."

The nurse looks from the laid-out clothes to Charlotte and back again.

"So," she says. "We'll get dressed then, shall we?"

It's a costume, Charlotte tells herself. I can put it on and I can take it off again. I can wear it but it doesn't change me. She lifts the skirt and shakes it out.

"That's right," the nurse says. "Good girl."

Fish

Dr. Gantley is a sleek man, long-limbed, with strangely hairless, shiny skin; he is buttoned to the gills in a charcoal-grey three-piece suit that has an expensive sheen to it; a watch chain loops across his barrelled waistcoat, and there is a gold band on his left ring finger. His lips are thick, his eyes prominent and lashless. A fish, she thinks; slow-moving, hanging in the cold depths.

"Do you understand why you have been placed under my care?"

"Yes." He is not Dr. Osterheim; he has that in his favour.

"Can you explain it to me," he says, opening her file, "in your own words?"

"It's best for me," she says.

"Yes, and?"

"I'll be safe here."

"Yes, and?"

"You'll help me."

"But why is that necessary?"

"Because . . ." she says, remembering what Tom had said: *That isn't a diagnosis.* "Because I was making a nuisance of myself."

"Because you have been manifesting erratic, irrational behaviour."

She sits up. "No, but I worked it out. I found evidence—"

He fixes her with his carbuncle eyes. "The killer in the Blitz?"

She hesitates. "Or," she says, "I thought I did."

"But now?"

She bites her lips together. She can't talk about this, she realises. She'll only argue herself into deeper water. "I don't know."

But she will not tug at her hem. She will not fold her arms across her silk chest. She will not wrap her cardigan tight or curl forwards over folded arms, although all her instincts are to huddle down and make herself as small and sealed off as possible.

"Your last stay with us, here in '38. When you were—"

"Seventeen."

"Seventeen. And under Dr. Osterheim's care."

She sits with even more determined, rigid niceness. Upright, knees pressed together, hands folded on her lap. She has never been as scared as she is now. "Yes."

"And I see you were treated with continuous narcosis." He adds, assuming her ignorance: "Deep Sleep Therapy."

"Yes."

"And you have had no relapses until this."

It's not a question, so she doesn't venture an opinion. She drags her attention back to his shiny unfringed eyes. How much eye contact is enough? How much is too much? She must show that she is taking it seriously, but not too seriously. That she is not frightened or angry, because what, after all, does she have to be frightened or angry about? If she's mad, then they will make her sane. If she is sane, they will let her leave. This is the game. She has to play it.

He smooths out the open file in front of him with a dry palm. "Do you remember what it was like when you were unwell before?"

"Some of it."

"Some of it?"

"I was not myself."

He looks at her a long time, then makes a note. "What do you remember?"

"I acted—out of character. I embarrassed my family."

"You were sexually promiscuous."

She looks to the chestnut tree outside the window. The leaves are almost all fallen; it's grey against the sky. She had watched this tree over Dr. Osterheim's shoulder too: bare, budding, the buds swelling and splitting and fresh green leaves beginning to unfurl. Osterheim was small, silver, sharp; his attention was like a tack; it pinned you. A young woman engaging in such extreme misconduct, he said, might lead some clinicians to write her off as a moral imbecile. But he, Osterheim, a man of faith as well as science, could not believe any case to be entirely without hope. She had, then, she remembers, laughed in his face.

"This is not the same," she says.

"Well," Dr. Gantley says, "we shall see."

"We don't have to see." She can hear the edge of panic in her voice, clears her throat. "I can tell you now. It's not the same thing at all."

He unscrews his fountain pen and writes something more in her notes. She can't see the words. She wants to say she didn't mean it, she didn't mean to contradict him; she didn't mean to sound so strident. She wants to beg him not to write anything else. She bites the words back. He flips the document over and blots it on his blotter, then slides it into her file.

"I'm not like I was back then," she tries, her tone supplicating. "I have been good, honestly. I have been doing better all this time."

He screws the pen cap closed. "I'm afraid that's not quite accurate, is it? Your problems seem more complex and intractable, if anything. Your delusions. Your . . . seductions. The games you're playing."

They have stitched her right up, between them: Francesca, her father, the Hartwells.

"But, Doctor, you see, the people who've told you—whatever they've told you; they have barely seen me of late. They don't know. They make assumptions. They're in no position to judge. None of this was a game to me."

He slides the page out of the file again. Unscrews his pen. It's agony.

"Don't," she says, reaching out as though to stop him.

A measured loop and dip and curl of ink across the page. Then he looks up at her hand. She brings it back to her lap.

He dabs a final dot in place, caps his pen. "I think we can leave it there for today."

"Today?"

"Unless you have something more to add?"

She sinks back into her seat. "Work."

He peers at her over his glasses. "Your work?"

"They're expecting me back."

"No, they aren't."

"But—"

He looks at her levelly. "Miss Richmond. You must understand that this is what is happening now. Nobody is expecting you. You're not going anywhere. You will remain here until you are better. Do I make myself clear?"

"Yes. I'm sorry," she says, chastened and afraid. "I want to be well."

What no one here knows is how good she is at being watched. She is as attuned to shifts in emotional temperature as a chameleon is to colour. These are useful adaptations in this place. She got out once before; she'll get out again.

Charlotte takes her tablets when she's given them, feels them dissolve beside her gums until she can dig out what's left and rinse it down the plughole with the washing water. She can't know how much of the stuff she has absorbed. She can't let her expression change. The staff watch her, and she watches them right back, out of the tail of her sight, observes their comings and goings, their differences and their loyalties. It's all right, so far; so far, she can cope with this. But if they decide on the Deep Sleep again . . .

A sleep that passes in a blink, but on waking you find you can hardly lift a limb, speak, or pull into focus the figure hovering over your bed. When tongue and lips are finally marshalled to ask what time it is, the answer is always a laugh. Two weeks have passed, sometimes three, and there's no knowing what might have been done to you, or how often, or by whom, while you slept.

And while she's stuck here, is he still stalking the darkness, that man, that Caliban? She feels helpless, strung out, engine screaming, brakes on full. But she will continue to put on the costume. She will play the game. She tugs at her razor crop, tries to smooth it into a parting. She scrubs and buffs her nails. She puts on lipstick and stretches her clown lips in the mirror. She strikes up conversations with the nurses, and with any patients who seem to be stamped for departure; she becomes adept at anodyne interactions regarding crochet, clothing and the weather. She keeps her distance from the most dishevelled and distressed. She knows what good girls look like, how they speak, how they comport themselves. The lipstick and the stockings and the hair. The smiles.

But in all this ceaseless company, she is desperately lonely. Her voices are all muted, a buzz from behind a door, the door rattling from time to time but locked up tight. She misses Tom. She misses park benches, shoulder brushing against shoulder, silver shoals of conversation, unlike the water-boatman words that skate around here. The memory of his presence can make her catch her breath. She hopes nobody notices.

Letter

That morning, Tom's parents fall silent as he walks into the room. On the scrubbed kitchen table between them is a letter. He recognises immediately the creamy pre-war paper, the Birkbeck crest on the top left corner.

Oh.

"It's for you," his mother needlessly says. His father sits in silence, smiling mildly.

She holds it towards him; Tom takes it, hesitates. He reminds himself of the lie; that invented meeting, at which, he'd said, the professors had talked all around the houses but in the end nothing conclusive had been conveyed. When in fact he'd been falling out with Charlotte, in Russell Square. He winces.

His father says, "Don't worry."

Tom nods. But he can't help it.

"No, honestly. Don't worry either way. If it happens, it'll change your life forever. But your life will change forever anyway, just in smaller steps. Either way, you'll get there."

His father is not known for his long speeches. After this, he shifts on his chair almost guiltily, and shoots a look at his wife. Surprised by this outpouring, she reaches for his hand and squeezes it.

"Thanks," Tom says. Better to know the worst, he thinks, than go on hoping. He runs a thumb under the flap. He won't complicate matters by asking where his father imagines "there" might ultimately be.

The letter announces that, damage to some facilities notwithstanding, courses will commence on the last weekend of October, and continue thenceforth every Saturday and Sunday, in daylight hours, until the Christmas vacation. The Governors sincerely hope that Mr.

Thomas Hawthorne will be able to join them to begin his Undergraduate Degree in Psychology.

Tom folds the letter and slips it back into the envelope.

"Good news," he says.

And then it's clamour and hugs from his mother and back-thumping delight from his father. This is the best news that he could have hoped for, news that he's waited more than a month for, but it doesn't actually make him happy. He feels instead that he is sliding down a helter-skelter and is afraid of what's waiting at the bottom and has no way to stop.

"I'll just go and put this somewhere safe," he says. He leaves the kitchen and climbs the stairs. He pulls out the top drawer of his bureau and slides the letter in with all the other crested, typewritten correspondence. The letter from King's inviting him to interview. The offer. The announcement of the closure of King's and the move of teaching staff to Birkbeck. The letter of postponement. And now this. He has been keeping an archive for himself, to prove it's real.

And there, lying to one corner of the drawer, is Charlotte's handwritten note. Her friends. Their addresses. The days they died. Her telephone number and address. So earnest and urgent and sad. He closes the drawer. He sits down on his bed. In a while, he will have to go downstairs and face his family's excitement again. But he cannot face it yet.

It can't just be left like this, in pieces on the floor. Their . . . acquaintanceship. Whatever it was. He'll have to ring her up. But if it's to be done at all, it's not to be done from home.

At lunchtime, he takes himself along to the telephone box, slows and havers, then walks on and goes to buy the newspaper, and a box of matches, and pear drops for Fliss, for when she gets home from school and is told his good news. He loves to give her sweets. It still makes her bounce up and down with delight, just like she did when she was tiny.

That night, an incendiary lands on the hospital roof and slides down the slates and he has to slither round up there with a bucket of sand and a long-handled shovel. The intense focus and activity is a release, for a while, from his preoccupations. Afterwards, he finds himself willing the raiders on: come on, come on, come *on;* send more fire at me from the sky. Because you can't be anything other than utterly present in those moments. You can't think of anything but the fight.

As the next dawn breaks, Tom finds himself peering across the city from his rooftop perch, staring out towards the south, but it's ridiculous to think that he could pick out her part of town from here, or tell what's really going on there, street by street.

He will ring her up. He has to. He makes his weary way home that morning, thinking, This is what friends do, isn't it; they ring each other up, they share their news. They forgive each other. He pauses by the telephone box again, but two of his mother's pals are chatting away nearby, baskets on their arms, headscarves knotted, and he has to nod to them and go home.

He is combing out the white beard of an elderly gentleman later that morning, when his father asks, "Are you all right, son?"

"Just tired," he says, because that's true, and uncontroversial; everyone is always tired now.

"Only you don't seem that pleased."

He had thought that he was doing a decent job of hiding the turmoil he's feeling. He had thought that he was getting away with it. "About college, you mean? I am. It's just a lot to think about."

His father accepts this. Having a lot to think about is, more or less, the point of going to college.

At dinner, his mother asks, "Aren't you hungry?"

Which makes him pay proper attention to the plate she's put in front of him. A meatloaf of some kind, breadcrumbs and lentils mixed in with the mince. Boiled cabbage.

"I don't blame him if he isn't," Fliss says, poking at the stuff.

Her mother rolls her eyes. "Give me strength."

"Just tired," he says again.

His father looks up. "The boy needs a tonic."

"Maybe he does."

Nelly ambles over and sits down beside Tom's chair and lumps her hefty head onto his lap. Tom scratches her forehead, tugs on her abrupt silky ears. She thumps her tail on the tiles.

"A half of stout of an evening, that'll build him up a bit," his father says.

"Couldn't hurt," his mother agrees.

"Me too?" Fliss asks.

"No."

He's presented with a half-pint bottle of stout that evening. He takes a sip, pulls a face. It's not as bad as the port, he'll give it that. But it's no cure for missing her.

He's passing their bedroom one evening, when he's snared by his mother's voice.

"He was happy before," she says. "He was happy enough."

"All this coming and going." His father sounds exhausted. "All the uncertainty, you know."

A silence, in which he imagines his mother slowly nodding.

"And at least we know he can be happy," his father adds.

The sound of covers rustling. "And what use is that, if he isn't any more?"

"Be fair, love. That's not true of everyone. And it's far more than they'd ever have had us expect."

A pause. Tom, on the landing, holds himself still, holds his breath.

"Do you ever think what it would have been like," his father says, "if we had given him up, like they said we should?"

Tom bites his lip.

"Always," his mother says. "All the blessed time."

He moves quietly away. He doesn't think about it himself. He sees a cot, one in a row of cots, in a long cold room. And then his thoughts close down. But the knowledge that it would have happened, if his parents had not determined otherwise, colours every single day.

On Sunday, after a night's duty, he lies listening to his family organise themselves for church, and creaks downstairs only when they're gone.

It is now or it is not at all and it is such an insistent discomfort that it must have some relief. He lifts the receiver without allowing himself to think. He dials the local code, the number. After only two rings, the landlady answers. He had been so hungry for news of Charlotte that it never once occurred to him that others might be desperate for the same thing.

"Who is this? Who's calling?"

"Thomas Hawthorne."

"Hawthorne." She says it uneasily, as if she's not quite sure herself if she does recall. "Hawthorne. Are you the one she's courting?"

"No! No. No. Ha ha. No. Not me. I was helping her with something." He gasps in air; he seems to have forgotten how to breathe. "May I speak to her?"

"She's not here."

"Then may I leave a message?"

A hesitation. "You don't know?"

"Know what?"

"I'm sorry, young man, I've never met you, and God knows I don't want to get the poor child into any more trouble than she's already in."

His skin goes cold. "What trouble?"

"She had to go. Her family came for her. And she had to go."

"Where's she gone? Home?"

"I don't know. I don't know. Nobody tells me anything. I just hope she's in good hands."

The woman's voice is cracked with anguish. He says goodbye, hangs up. But Charlotte must be in good hands, he tells himself. Her family will help her. That's what families do. Surely.

Pioneers

She is sitting opposite Dr. Gantley in his office, but she is looking at the chestnut tree. She knows that weeks have passed, because it's now completely bare. Otherwise, time is hard to track here. They have taken her watch away.

"There is a moment I can identify, before it all started to get so . . . confused for me."

"Go on."

"It was . . ." that one searing awful day, the day she found out about Elena, the day she let Janet down and then could never make it up to her; the day she stole the earrings that were meant for Saskia. "Early September, a Monday. I went to lunch, with my father," she says, and clears her throat. "He asked me to stay with him and his new wife, at Longwood, the old family home in Somerset."

"And you see that now as pivotal?"

"I think it must have been."

"And why is that?"

"I didn't want to go. But if I had gone, then everything would have been different."

"In what way?"

"I would have been safe. I would have been taken care of. I would not have . . . slipped. I wouldn't have felt that what was happening in London had anything to do with me."

She does not believe this, but that doesn't matter.

"So you chose to remain in London, in danger, over safety in the countryside."

"I see now how unsound that looks. Though at the time . . ." She shakes her head, as though baffled at herself. She has calculated this moment carefully; she has had long enough to think about it.

"Go on," he says.

"That person is a stranger now," she says. "I don't recognise who I was. I don't know what I was thinking. All those wild ideas."

An admission of any previous unsoundness of mind is not without its risks, but it is worth a try. One must be sane now, surely, to recognise that one was previously mad?

"And now?"

"I am quite myself again." She touches her hair. "Or I will be, once my hair has properly grown back."

He stretches back his lips.

"I am convinced that the best thing for me," she continues, "would be to resume my normal occupations. To go back to work, to get back to my own digs—"

"But not to go home to your family?"

She shifts in her seat. "Of course. Yes. Of course I could. Why not."

He writes something more in her file. She holds herself still; she will not complain, she will not even attempt to see what he's writing.

"I should probably explain exactly how this works, Miss Richmond. We will judge for ourselves, as clinicians, whether or not you are a danger to yourself or others, to your own or others' reputations. Only when we believe you can face the world again in a moderate, ordered, rational fashion will you be released back into society."

She does her best to keep her composure, to keep her expression neutral and calm.

Her face feels numb. "I understand."

"I hope you do. Because the whole process will be so much more comfortable for you if you simply accept this. If instead you're just looking for the quickest way out of here, you are in fact blocking your own path to recovery."

I am going to die in here, she thinks.

And she hears El's voice from the darkness; it speaks just four insistent, quiet words: *Darling, don't you dare.*

. . .

At night, when voices are hushed at the nurses' station, she watches the sky for messages from that other world, where everything can blow up in an instant, the walls collapse around you and leave you filthy, bleeding and exposed. Where that creature is still creeping round the darkness, a scar now on his face. She is desperate to know how the city is changing in her absence, if there will be anything left for her to get back to, if she ever does get out. She wants London so badly. She misses the jagged edges and the roughness and sourness, and the sunshine and rain on umbrella skins and the leaves drifting sideways from plane trees. She wants the boy who feeds the birds.

Her hair is grown to chenille softness. She slicks it aside and fixes it with a kirby grip, so that it looks like a terribly daring 'do from twenty years ago. She slides on the stockings and clips them up. She hooks the fastening of her skirt, buttons up her blouse and paints her face in the mirror.

The ancient bare-pated woman is gone one morning; her bed lies stripped. Charlotte mentions this to dark-eyed Aminta; partly out of real concern, partly out of a necessary cynicism: she wants it to be noticed that she notices. The dear old thing has been sent to the medical ward, Aminta says. Pneumonia.

"The old man's friend. And the old woman's."

The friend that scoops a frail old person up and carries them those final few paces and over the threshold into death.

Charlotte wonders if Tom is still angry with her. If only she could speak to him. She would like to explain. He, if anyone, might understand, if she just allowed him to. About her family, about herself, about the voices clamouring in her head, about how difficult and how distracting things have been. Now that she is forced into this stillness, she begins to consider fully, for the first time, the realities of his existence. What it must be like, to be born into a body that doesn't cooperate the way that other people's bodies do. She thinks about pain, and fatigue. About the frustrations of negotiating a city already full of kerbs and cobblestones and crowds and stairs, before rubble and barricades and sandbags and craters started getting added to the litany of obstructions. How every time he shakes somebody's hand, he has to choose between his fragile right and the mismatch of the left, and how he must feel it, even if what he feels is defiance. To face the world as he does, unflinchingly, and with generosity. How do you *be* like that, she wonders; how do you get to be entirely yourself, and for that to be enough for you?

She is back in Woodland Road, in the basement kitchen. Mrs. Callaghan and Mr. Gibbons are wrapped up in their deckchairs, but they will not talk to her, will not even look at her. Mr. Gibbons is angry with her for losing all his lovely clothes, and now he will have nothing to wear to the Christmas party; Mrs. Callaghan is angry because Charlotte has left the skylight room full of her things, and everyone knows her things are nasty, and have been crawling up the walls and eating holes in the furniture. She wants to apologise, she wants to excuse herself, but when she goes to speak, instead of words there pours out a siren's sad wail, which makes her feel stupid and embarrassed, and then she jolts awake to find a nurse is shaking her by her shoulder.

"Get up, miss. Quick. There's a raid on."

Wet with sweat, shivering, she slides her feet into her slippers, wraps her dressing gown around herself and ties the cord. The ward is full of firefly torches. The nurses are getting patients out of bed. There's an urgent communal tenderness to it all, the pairing up of inmates, the ushering of them out of the ward and down the stairs to the basement shelter. Charlotte is handed a young woman with wide blue eyes and a straggling plait down her back. There's a sour night-time smell off her; she's mute; she bites her lip and holds Charlotte's hand but doesn't look at her. Charlotte has steered wide of her before; this is not the kind of company she wants to be seen keeping. Her hand is ice.

"Where are they bombing?" Charlotte asks Aminta as she hurries past.

"The city," Aminta says.

She had not known that there was a city. The lawns surround the house, and the trees surround the lawns, and a wall surrounds the trees, so once you're here you can't see anything of the world beyond. Both of the times she's stayed here, she'd arrived and departed by a country road. This place has always seemed entirely separate from everything else, as though you'd come here by falling down a rabbit hole, or by being led away by goblins.

The newly discovered city is having seven bells knocked out of it tonight. The ground trembles at each impact. And the planes are circling wider, wider; you can hear them pass, jangling the nerves, making one grit one's teeth. The torch beams bob along, and the staff and patients make their fretful way down the back stairs.

"That's right," Charlotte says. "Soon be nice and cosy. Down we go."

The young woman is whimpering, trying to pull her hand away from Charlotte's. Charlotte recognises the urge; she wants to run away herself. She holds tight.

"Come on, love, come on."

But the young woman stops dead on the turn of the stairs, whimpering and glancing back, and when Charlotte tries to coax her on, she yanks her hand out of Charlotte's grip, drops to a squat and tears at her cheeks with her nails.

Charlotte crouches with her, tries to grab her wrists. "Don't do that. Please don't. Please. Come on, we have to go."

The woman shakes her head furiously.

"Take my hand. Stand up. We have to get to safety. Please." Charlotte's voice begins to choke. She feels so helpless. One of the nurses climbs back towards them. The patient is heaved upright, her hands pulled from her face, and she is told off. She goes quiet, is bustled down towards the basement. And Charlotte's left to make her way alone.

"Scuse us."

Two orderlies sidle down, carrying an old lady on a chair. Charlotte steps aside to let them pass, finds herself standing on a kind of half-landing, back against a door. The orderlies shuffle by; the old woman glares at her with sharp black eyes. And nobody follows after them. She hears their footfalls and huffing breath, and the old lady's complaints, as they descend; she hears a door swing open below, and then clap shut. She's on her own. Speculatively, she tries the handle of the door behind her. It turns. She leans her weight on the door; it opens; she steps backwards. Then she turns to face the darkness.

She's in a corridor. One side of it is entirely metal-framed glass; floor-length windows look out across lawns and woods, to where the sky is lit up crimson. So it's not entirely dark.

Fear, she thinks, is a sly and sneaking kind of thing. It'll snicker at your back for ages, but run right at it and it flaps away. Because now that she is actually doing something really dangerous, that could get her into even worse trouble, she is not afraid. She's running along the corridor, in dressing gown and slippers, past windows that at any moment could transform into a cloud of flying blades, and she is not afraid.

She rattles at the far door. It's locked, damn—no, it's bolted, at the top. She undoes it and she's out. Into night air, space. She races across gravel that crunches under her slippers, then on wet grass that soaks them. Searchlights rake the sky. She is filled with sudden conviction: she is so tiny, so unimportant, that nothing at all will happen to her. You can't crush an atom with a shoe. You can't kill a virus with a hammer. Her smallness is her strength.

Charlotte reaches the edge of the trees; she pushes through tangles of rhododendron and camellias and her wet slippers pad over fallen larch needles, and then birch twigs. There's the wall, ten feet of sheer red brick; no obvious spokes or wire along the top, but not a finger- or toe-hold to get her up there either. The trees offer no assistance; they're slender, upright and at a distance from the wall. The raid still continues; horrors are happening over there, but here is all quietness, darkness, just her own ragged breath and the crunch of her footfalls. She makes her way through the trees, heading towards the drive.

The gates still stand open. She walks cautiously towards them, and then out through them, at once thrilled and unnerved. The lane is empty, a pale gravel line curving away to its vanishing point. The hedges are high, the verges lined with dry sticks of old cow parsley and dead grasses. It's all cast in an unnatural orange light. She wraps her dressing gown tighter, shoves her hands into her pockets and sets off as fast as she can manage, towards the burning city. If she can just get herself that far, she'll disappear into the chaos; she won't be the only one wandering the streets in a dressing gown tonight. If she can find a WVS station, or a Citizens Advice Bureau, someone will front her the fare to London.

She goes to look at her watch, and then remembers, and feels a squirm of grief. She thinks, why bother with high walls, and then leave the gates wide open? But she marches on towards the flames.

· · ·

It is getting light when the van pulls in beside her. The driver is a man in his sixties; flat cap, holes in his sweater.

"Where you for?" he asks, as she climbs gratefully into the cab. It smells earthy and sulphurous; a fruit-and-veg merchants. Cabbages, she thinks, turnips.

"My sister's, in town," she extemporises. "I'm awfully worried."

He looks her over. Dressing gown and sodden slippers.

She says: "I know, I just walked out the door. I wasn't thinking, I was beside myself."

"Don't fret." He shunts the engine into gear. "I'll get you where you're going."

The lanes are winding; the light is cold and grey. The road unrolls through trees and the van pauses, rumbling, at unmarked junctions, to make a turn. The aircraft roar has faded out; the bombs no longer fall. They are not going so very fast; in fact, he seems to be in no hurry at all: he changes gear and hums to himself. Charlotte's head sinks; she drifts, jerks awake, then drifts again, feeling grateful for the distance covered at no effort to herself. She looks out for the city, for the fires, but the sky is a homogenous pink haze, and she can't orientate herself by it.

They are driving through woodland; slender trees, no landmarks at all—she feels like she is being spun blindfolded as in some childhood party game—dizzy, disoriented, a figure of fun. The driver is silent beside her, a rough-cut profile and hard-worn skin. She bites her tongue. She can't ask, *Are you, after all, one of those tigers that look like men; are you the kind that bites?* Because this still could be a kindness; this could still just be the long way round, or this could be the journey into the woods that a girl does not come back from.

Then she spots red brick through the trees. Ten feet high, no sign of wire or spokes along the top. No need for it. No need to lock the gates, either, if whoever you run into on the roads will just scoop you up and bring you back again. She grabs the handle, rattles it. The driver drops down a gear to turn onto the drive. The building looms ahead. It looks perfectly normal from outside. A Victorian gentleman's residence, with its bay windows and gables and gothic arches. The kind of place a self-made man could settle down to worship his creator. She slams into the door, panicked. She can't shift it.

"Don't worry, love, it's broke."

"You don't understand."

"I do, dearie," he says. "Can't have you wandering the streets, can we?"

He pulls past the house and stops round the back, between the garages and the kitchens. Two orderlies come out of a service door. They have the look of people disturbed at breakfast. A brushing off of hands, tongues exploring back teeth.

"This is beginning to look like carelessness, lads," the driver calls down to them.

"Devious little—"

The larger of the two men ambles over to open the cab door. He goes to take her hand, but she snatches it away, climbs down unaided. Once her foot hits the floor, he grips her just below the bicep. They're trained to do it; the grip at once lifts you and clamps you down.

She stares back at the driver. "You have no idea what you have done."

"Hey!" The orderly shakes her. "None of that."

"Take good care of her," the driver says uneasily.

"Will do."

"I don't want to find out I'm doing a wrong turn, bringing em back."

"Not at all, not at all," the smaller orderly says. "Best place for her. Out of harm's way."

It is not as it was before. She is shown to a small room, the walls distempered, the window high and barred. She doesn't know these nurses; she doesn't see Aminta. They press a tablet between her lips, hold a tin cup of water till she chokes and coughs and swallows. They strip her clothes from her and she stands shivering, all bones and gooseflesh. A gown is thrust at her and she pulls it on. The tablet leaves a chemical trace in her mouth, dust down her throat, it lodges somewhere behind her breastbone. The door is clapped shut and locked. The footsteps die away.

There is nothing in this room but a bed, a pot, and the window. She tries to drag the bed to the window, but the bed is bolted to the floor. She climbs up on it anyway, perches on the metal rail at the foot, leans across and plants her palms on the wall so she can peer out. The sky is hung with a great black curtain. Her fear balloons so big that it makes her dizzy and she can't hold on to it. Her head swims; the tablet. She steps down off the bedstead. She has to sit before she falls; she keels over to one side, and lies there.

When she wakes, it is a fight out of deep water. She struggles up to seated, heart racing. There is a patch of sky visible through the window. She was woken by footfalls and the tacky peel of wheels on lino. The door flings open and a solid, cylindrical orderly backs in pulling a wheelchair. The wheelchair has straps at wrist and waist and ankle.

"Hop in, kid," the orderly says. He has freckles like ginger nuts, and startlingly bright blue eyes. He is losing his hair.

"Where are my clothes?" Her mouth is wet and the words come out clumsily.

"You're fine as you are."

"But Doctor wants me to . . ."

The orderly jiggles the chair. "Doctor wants you to do this now."

Spittle seeps from her lips. She raises a hand to wipe it away. There must be something. There must be something she can do. To divert or mitigate or delay. To perform sanity in such a way they can't ignore it.

"Walk," she says. "I'll walk, thank you."

"More than my job's worth." A rattle of the wheelchair: she will sit, she will be wheeled. "Hop in."

She would protest, but her head seesaws. "Don't strap me down."

"Be good, and I won't have to."

She shifts herself to the edge of the bed, gets to her feet, then sinks cautiously into the wheelchair. She lifts one foot and then the other onto the footrests; her feet have turned an interesting shade of blue. She pushes her fists between her knees, holding the gown down; she has nothing on underneath.

They reverse through the cell door, spin round into the corridor and bowl along the linoleum. Her head lolls; she lifts it; it lolls again. She lifts it. Her heart thuds heavy and slow. They scroll along the long glassed-in corridor, and she turns to look at the lawn, the trees, the encircling wall, the wrought-iron gates standing wide open, the view of countryside beyond. She goes to say something, but it comes out as a wet mumble. She swallows clumsily.

"You always leave the gates open," she manages.

The orderly says, "He insists on it."

The wheelchair spins and bumps backwards through swinging doors, and then she is whirled back, dizzily, to face not Dr. Gantley's office, but an anonymous treatment room. She is parked alongside an examination table. It has straps at ankle, wrist, waist and head. She looks away.

Today, Dr. Gantley is wearing a white coat over his nice suit. Two nurses are with him; one of them is familiar.

"Aminta," she says.

"Charlotte, dear."

There is a steel trolley laid out with a tray; the tray is covered with a cloth. It all has a sickly familiarity about it. She was fourteen when Mother died. She was called out of Prep to the headmistress's office and the colour faded from the day. She caught the train home later that same day. Eddie met her at the Longwood halt, held her, rubbed her back, kept his arm around her shoulders for the rest of that godawful week. Francesca she remembers as beautiful, pale and pregnant, clinging to her new husband; her father and his friends were already half-cut at the graveside. The gathering back at Longwood afterwards; the guests already forgetting why they'd come. Laughter, records on the gramophone, dancing, stealthy night-time footfalls that Charlotte now, at fourteen, was beginning to understand. Then Francesca and her swollen belly and her Mr. Thorpe had motored back to Surrey, Eddie had packed himself off to the university, and Charlotte had waited alone at the Longwood halt for the train back to school. Their father had already roared off in the Daimler with a young friend, heading first to France, and then to Germany, and after that, well, wherever the road took them, because travel, and lively company, were known to be the most efficacious remedy against grief. Charlotte, in her school coat and hat, swaying and sick on the train, had felt a geyser build inside her. That her mother, having chosen silence while she lived, had now disappeared into it entirely.

"No," she manages.

"She's saying something," Aminta says.

"What is she saying?" the other asks.

Charlotte drags the words together. "Not the sleep," she says.

The sleep is their bullyboy; it sits on you and pins you down, and then they can do anything else they like.

The doctor places a hand on her shoulder. It is all weight and no warmth. "Don't worry; we don't do that any more."

Charlotte heaves her head round to stare at the tray. "What, then?"

He considers her with a kind of fond puzzlement, as though she is a particularly clever pet. "This is Coma Therapy. Up onto the table, please."

She wants to know what difference is there then between coma and deep sleep, but her mouth can't make the words. Inwardly, she is thrashing, frantic, running hard; outwardly, she is shackled and weighted by the drug. The nurses move to help her; she waves them back. If it must happen, then she is going to do this herself. She gets to her feet, shuffles round and hitches herself up onto the treatment table, bare legs dangling.

"You have to lie down."

She hesitates, then swings her legs round to lie on her back, stiffly, her knees pressed tight together. The gown rides up; she tugs it clumsily back down. She can't look at anyone.

Aminta and the other nurse come closer. The other nurse takes Charlotte's wrist, moves it towards a strap. Charlotte jerks away.

"It's for your own good," Aminta says. "We don't want you getting hurt."

Aminta takes Charlotte's left wrist, draws it firmly towards the fastening and does not meet her eye. The wrists are buckled down. Then the band goes around her waist and is wrenched tight.

Aminta and the other nurse take an ankle each, pull them towards their separate straps.

"No."

But the women are strong and they pull her legs apart and buckle her down. Her heart is stuttering, missing beats. She feels sick.

The nurse leans in with something; something is pressed against her mouth and she tries to turn her face aside, but she's held still and pressure is applied until she opens her mouth and lets in something cold and rubbery and dense, which holds her tongue still and now she has no chance to speak at all. She can hardly breathe. She's choking. She's going to be sick. If she is sick when this is in her mouth . . . she pulls against the wrist straps, pulls against the ankle straps, tries to bring her legs together, tries to spit out the thing that's in her mouth.

"You'll feel so much better," Dr. Gantley says, "once this is over."

She watches as her inner arm is mopped with iodine. Beyond the strap, her fingers curl into a fist; above, muscle bulges. In the crook of her elbow, a treacherous blue vein rises to the surface, like the smooth mound of a porpoise's back.

It is not her. It is just a body. It is just what she uses to get around.

But she can't take a step away from herself. The old strategy no longer works. She remains coldly present, chained by the drug to the anchor of her body.

"Nurse, the insulin, please."

She watches the doctor's hand on her arm, feels his weight on her. She watches as the hypodermic needle slides into that blue bulge, and she watches as he depresses the syringe, and she can feel the cold liquid rush into her warm blood. Her belly swells and sinks with her breath, and her eyes blink shut and the heat falls from her face and her face slicks with sweat. Her heart squeezes, slumps; squeezes and slumps; it swells huge and heavy and loose; her head swoops and slams back. Her fingers splay and clutch; she's crying out, but her mouth is jammed full and she's gagging, choking; sounds come to her as though through water; *All right, all right, that's her now;* and another needle slides into her skin. *Take her down, take her through for observation;* and somebody laughs. Blunt fingers dig the plug from her mouth. Her limbs are made of lead weights hung together with kid leather. She is shifted, dumped, draped, slumped in her wheelchair, and they spin her round to wheel her to the door, and she has just a second to lean over the arm of the wheelchair, before vomiting hard onto the floor. Swallowed spit and yellow bile and the dregs of bitter drugs hit the spinning linoleum. The nurse backsteps out of the way; there are tuts and exclamations. Charlotte's arm is so heavy, she can't even lift a hand to wipe her mouth, and no one wipes it for her, and so she is wheeled away down the corridor, a trail of yellow hanging from her lip.

They put her to bed back on the ward; she watches them lift and settle and tuck her in. Familiar nurses check on her from time to time. Eyelid pulled back. Pulse. Gown tugged down and a cold disc pressed to listen to her heart. All this dishevelment and interference accompanied with a few loud phrases, in which Charlotte is addressed in the first person plural: HOW ARE WE FEELING. DO WE THINK WE WILL BE SICK AGAIN. WE HAVE GOT OUR COLOUR BACK A LITTLE ALREADY. DO WE THINK WE MIGHT TAKE A LITTLE TEA. If we, Charlotte thinks, as she peers out of blurred eyes at Aminta, is me and this girl's body, then both of us are feeling very like death, thank you very much.

"Can I go home now?" she asks Aminta, when she has managed to sip a little tea, her mouth still feeling strange and slack.

Aminta, unexpectedly, drops a kiss on her forehead. "Don't be silly."

She has had the Coma Therapy three more times. It is once a week, she has been told, so she counts the days, the fear building so that she can't eat, certainly can't sleep, can't even attempt to perform her sane self. She can't converse with the women marked for departure; the looming treatment blocks out all the light. She's rigid and twitchy, talking to herself, coaching herself to comply, to be calm, to endure. It is not as bad as the Deep Sleep, she tells herself. It is not as bad as that. But still, each time she faces it, her body rebels. It pulls against the hands that hold it down, it wrenches against the straps. It screams and sobs. Her body knows that it won't long survive what they are doing to it. And there's no escape; the drugs slam her into the reality of her physical self and she is stuck there, heart like wet leather, like a burst football, her body slipping away into pools and rills.

As she is being wheeled out of the treatment room, she hears the doctor say, *If no significant improvement, then we have to consider the next step.* And she is scared to think what that might mean.

Her skin blossoms with bruises at wrist and ankle and belly. Over the week, the bruises change colour: pink turns to blue; blue fades to purple, green and yellow; then yellow bursts back to pink again with the next treatment. When she can get out of bed, she moves slowly, painfully; her joints are swollen and her muscles stiff. Her tongue feels fat now; her mouth is always dry. She can sip black tea but shakes her head at food when it's put in front of her. She feels constantly nauseous.

When she undresses for a bath, her thin fingers struggling with buttons, she sees that her ribcage is covered with soft downy hair like the feathers of a chick. I am growing feathers, she thinks; I am growing feathers so I can fly away. She expects some cheerfulness from El, some comeback from Vanessa, some consolation from Saskia, or just a moment's warm vulgarity from Janet. But there is not a word from anyone.

"When can I see Doctor again?" she asks Aminta.

"You see him every week."

"But he doesn't talk to me. How will he know I'm better?"

"Are you better?"

"I must be."

Aminta hesitates, then says, "He's talked about trying something else."

Charlotte knows this, but still it brings her arms up in goosebumps. "What?"

"Don't be afraid. It's to make you better."

"Not the Deep Sleep?"

"No. We don't do that any more. Not now Dr. Osterheim has gone."

"What is it then?"

Aminta sits down on the bed—quite the transgression. "A new procedure," she says. "Dr. Gantley is a pioneer."

"What is it?"

"An electrical stimulation of the brain."

"Electricity?"

"The Italians began working with it before the war. We have had some excellent results."

But Charlotte remembers the flicks and *Frankenstein,* how she and El had gasped and clutched at each other as that collage of cadavers had been jolted into life. And now they'd smash electricity into her living, sparking, fully inhabited brain? She feels an urgent concern for the voices trapped behind their door. A jolt of white. A scorching flare. She doesn't know what that might do to them.

"It's far safer than the Deep Sleep," Aminta says. "But we should have to shave your hair, just when it's growing back so prettily. So you should try and get better without it, if you possibly can."

Try? Charlotte thinks. And who's to notice if she does?

"Because, also, this new technique, with all its benefits, has a tendency," Aminta says, "to leave gaps. In the memory. And that can be upsetting."

The things she might forget. She might not just lose her voices, but also forget that they were ever there. She might forget that she's missing anyone at all. She could forget herself along with them. She could start again, newborn.

Taking Tea with the Dead

The outside world no longer imposes on her. This place is a sealed jar, a nailed-shut packing case. This safety is something to be grateful for. One must try and be deserving of it. One must try and be better.

She is colouring her face in at the vanity unit, as required, when Aminta appears and smiles over Charlotte's shoulder at their paired reflections. Aminta's complexion is warm and velvety; her eyes are clear. Charlotte's attention shifts to her own face. Her lips lacquered red. Her eyelids smeared with blue. Eyelashes scrubbed up and spidery. None of which conceals the greyed skin stretched over the bones of her skull, and her shadowed, muddy eyes.

"I have a surprise for you," Aminta says.

This is it, this is now. The electricity. Next time she sits down at the vanity unit, she might not even know who she is looking at.

"Oh yes?" She splits a hair grip between her teeth, thrusts it into her stubby fringe. Her hand, though, is shaking.

"Don't you want to know what it is?"

She lifts her eyes to look again at Aminta. "The new treatment."

Aminta's expression collapses into laughter.

"Oh dear me, no. Since you'll never guess, I'll tell you." Aminta gives Charlotte's bony shoulder a squeeze. "Your brother's here to see you, you lucky thing."

Charlotte walks down the corridor, handbag clutched in spider hands. She feels unusually calm. Eddie is dead; she knows that Eddie is dead. So he can't have come to call. But alongside this truth, another begins to take shape. In a world where a girl is expected to get better by being repeatedly shoved into and wrenched out of a coma, it could be normal to receive a visit from a dead brother. What's waiting for her in the day room is a corpse, uniform dark with the dirt of the Hauts-de-France, drumming rotten fingers on the armrests. Or, look on the bright side, he could be an angel now, rising to greet her with his shining wings folded carefully so as not to knock over the ornaments. Perhaps, and this would be even better still, Charlotte is dead now too; that last treatment finally did for her, and this is when she gets to see her darling Eddie again, in the afterlife. Though not, of course, in Heaven; the day room of Summer Fields is Purgatory at best.

She and Aminta reach the door. Eddie is waiting for her in the day room; Eddie can't be waiting for her in the day room. Both things appear to be equally true. Aminta is opening the door. Or maybe—and this comes to her as a breathtaking hope—she has already had the shock therapy, and forgotten that she's had it, and forgotten that Eddie, despite all their fears, came back unharmed from Dunkirk, and the Ox and Bucks weren't slaughtered there like calves. That she's been remembering not what happened, but what she used to fear the most.

Maybe the world is still filled with friends.

Maybe the war never came at all.

Maybe she has been here all this time, in Summer Fields, since she was seventeen. Dreaming of loss. Stuck here in terror of being sent back here.

Aminta opens the door wide. Paper chains and lanterns are hanging from the ceiling. A bunch of holly, its berries scarlet, stands in a vase on the mantelpiece. Charlotte moves into the room. There's a tray of tea-things set out on a table by the fire. So do the dead drink tea? Then, from an armchair, a figure rises, his back towards her. He is solid, bulky, as though carved from old grey wood.

"It's not Edward," Charlotte says, anxious.

"No," Aminta agrees. "This is your brother John."

He comes towards her out of another world, through fog and smoke and ruins, from the shimmer in the corner of her vision. The shadow man with the pale grey eyes. He has followed her here.

She says, "It's you."

"Yes," Aminta says reassuringly. "It is."

Charlotte lets him take her hands. His are hard and huge; they engulf hers. She looks up at his broad, deep-lined face. She has to wake up. She has to get her head clear. She has to leap and catch whatever's being thrown at her.

"How are you, John?" she asks.

"Charlotte, dearest," says the shadow man. "You look wonderful."

She sinks into a seat, as Aminta walks away, gratified, leaving them to this strange reunion.

"Tea?" he asks.

"Please."

He leans to pour it, and she catches that smell from his clothes, of London in the raids. Dust and burning and sour secrets brought out into the light.

"If you've come to gawp at the mad women," she says, and licks her rough and greasy lips, "they don't let people do that any more."

"Ha! No."

She leans in to accept the proffered tea, sets it on the table in front of her.

"Bit of business," he says. He lifts his own cup. He seems perfectly at ease. She can't make sense of this at all; her thoughts are blurred and smudged with drugs and thoughts of her dead brother.

The intercom buzzes. Aminta answers it, then calls over: "You'll be all right for a moment? I'm needed on the ward—"

"Quite all right," the shadow man calls back.

He digs in his pockets for smoking materials, lays them out beside the tray. An inexpensive chromium cigarette case. A match fold. Charlotte can't tell very much from this, other than that he isn't wealthy. He clicks open the cigarette case and offers it to her. She hesitates.

"They're not poisoned," he says. "If that's what you're wondering."

She picks one out, studies it, as if this slim cylinder of paper and leaf will tell her something, anything, about the kind of man he is. She raises it to her nose and sniffs. That sharp, heady, vegetal scent. She aches, suddenly and fiercely, for everything she's left behind, with all its pleasures and its dangers.

There's a slight shift in his expression. He seems amused. "They don't let you smoke in here?"

"It hasn't come up." She hadn't even realised that she missed it.

He strikes a match and offers it out to her. She leans in to catch the flame. Her hand trembles.

"So," she asks, "what's this bit of business, then?"

"Let's not play games."

The shift in tone is bracing. It cuts through the fog. She takes another drag on her cigarette; it hits her hard, sharpens her; it gives her time to think.

"That's rich," she says. "Coming from you. When you've been playing Grandmother's Footsteps with me for months."

"But now you're out. Left high and dry."

"I am being well looked after."

"It looks like it." He leans in, hard hands dangling between his knees. "I have a proposition for you."

Her thoughts are still short-winded; they struggle to catch up. "Go on."

"Tell me where it is," he says, "and I'll be on my way. No questions asked."

It? She balances her cigarette on the lip of the ashtray, lifts her tea by the saucer; the cup dances. She takes it by the handle, stilling it.

"I see," she says. She doesn't see.

"No one will even know that you ever spoke to me."

"Right."

"And if you *do* ever get out of here, we'll talk again. But, in the meantime, far as I'm concerned, you can see out the rest of the war in here, no more questions asked. Rest of your days, if need be. I won't cause you trouble."

"That's your proposition?"

"That's it."

She raises the cup towards her lips. "It doesn't sound like much of a proposition to me."

"It's better than you'll get from your own lot. It's better than you deserve."

She sips. Her own lot? What lot? Her family? And what then *does* she deserve? She sets the cup back on its saucer. She slides it, rattling, onto the table. She's scared.

"Who exactly are you?" she asks.

"You can call me Harris."

"I can *call* you that? Is that your name?"

"Captain Harris, if you prefer."

"Are you from the police?"

"Not exactly."

She leafs back through those weeks. What is this "it"? What can he possibly think she has that he might want? And then it dawns on her: her *work*. All those strange obsessive accounts of morale in the provinces; rumours of nuns with hairy knuckles in Kent; suspicions about tinned fish in Manchester. It had all seemed so inconsequential, so pointless. But Mrs. Denby had been insistent that every tiny detail, every figure, every full stop, was worth the candle. It *all* mattered. So something—his "it"—must have gone astray. Not by her hand, not intentionally at least, but she could quite easily have fouled things up. She wouldn't put it past her to pick up two reports at once without noticing and only type up the top one. Or to drop something in the wastepaper basket that wasn't yet waste paper. Whatever he suspects she has, she doesn't have it, but that doesn't matter; what matters is that he *thinks* she has it. And what he's prepared to do to get it. Which, since he's gone to the trouble of following her across half of London, and then hunting her down here, must be quite a lot.

Her lips unstick: "All right then, Captain Harris. I think you can do better than that."

He regards her with his grey eyes. "Better than what?"

"Better than leaving me here to rot."

"You're in no position to negotiate."

"On the contrary."

"You could swing for what you've done."

So it's that stark. He considers her a traitor, has considered her a traitor all this time. And yet she has no choice but to keep digging. If she digs long enough the hole she's in might turn into a tunnel.

"Nonetheless," she says, "if you want to know where it is, you'll have to get me out of here first."

He starts to shake his head, but she continues, certainty growing as she speaks. Because this is it. This is her last chance, and she must grasp it with both hands, or she will die in Summer Fields.

"I need to get back to London. I'll make sure you get what you want"—she'll jump off that bridge when she comes to it—"and you'll never hear another peep out of me again. I'll be good as gold."

Her breath is tight, her heart thudding. But she also feels strangely calm. Because however mad this is, it is the sanest thing that she can possibly do, in the circumstances.

"Up to you," she says, sinking back, spent. "But it's something of a last chance, this. I mean, to get it back. Because the next kind of treatment they'll give me here, it rather knocks about one's memory, I've heard. It would be an awful shame if I forgot where I'd left it."

At the top of the steps, he offers her a brotherly arm. She takes it. They pick their way down and crunch out across the gravel. The world seems impossibly huge; everything is either a million miles away or looming far too close. She shivers. Someone might yet stop them. She won't believe she's out of here till she's a hundred miles away. And he is being so damned *leisurely* about the whole thing; his unhurried confidence makes her want to scream.

But it worked its magic on Aminta. Aminta, at the gentleman's suggestion that he might take his sister for a constitutional, had merely cast an eye at the sky beyond the windows and stated that Miss Richmond would need to be well wrapped up, and that she herself would just pop and fetch the patient's outdoor things. In a few short moments, Charlotte had been handed her shoes, her periwinkle-blue gloves and her black fedora, and helped into her Crombie. It was a real joy to slide into this coat again; until this moment, she hadn't known that it had survived the cull. She now finds herself out in the cold grey day, her nose nipped, eyes watering, arm linked uneasily with the shadow man's. There is frost on the grass, and a glossy blue car sits waiting on the gravel like a dog.

"Is that yours, the little Austin?"

"It's not little."

"I didn't mean—just, that's handy you have a car."

"You thought we'd run for a bus?"

"I tried to get away on foot last time. Didn't go so well."

A moment, then he asks, impassively: "When was this?"

Time has passed so differently here. "The night they raided the city."

"Coventry?"

She looks round at him. "That was Coventry?"

"Very much so. Though it was back in November. Over a month ago."

An eternity and a finger snap. "How long does it take to get to London?"

"In the car? Depends. Four hours; five."

But they are not heading for the car. He steers her away, along the side of the building.

"What? No—"

"We'll take a turn about the place. Like we said we would. In case we're being watched."

This makes sense, though it's agonising to amble, arm in arm, along the flank of Summer Fields. The brickwork is frosted, the path patched with ice. The lawn has been dug up for vegetable plots, and there are lines of winter greens and leeks and the woody stems of Brussels sprouts.

"What vehicles do they have here?" he asks.

"There was a big Vauxhall," she says.

"Anything else? Do the doctors drive in, or do they live on site?"

"I don't know."

They round the corner to the back of the house, past the outbuildings and bins and water butts. Harris is glancing round. She watches him as he makes assessments and calculations, tries to follow his thinking. There are no cars parked in the yard; the old stable doors are padlocked; any vehicles they might have are kept locked away. Keys would have to be fetched, locks fiddled with. Cold cars, left garaged for a while: they'd be slow to start. It all helps.

"Nearest police?" he asks.

"I don't know," she says. "I haven't seen any."

"Good."

A caretaker clanks past with a bucket and mop. Harris pats Charlotte's hand where it lies rigid on his arm. She smiles thinly. It's agony, to be hobbled like this, when all she wants to do is run.

They carry on round the far side of the house, Charlotte's teeth gritted under smiling lips. They pass her ward, and the high barred windows of the secure rooms; they pass the glassed-in corridor. It feels like there's a bubble in her chest. All these weeks, the treatments, all that hopeless fear, it was all contained within these walls that she is now passing by in moments. Dr. Gantley's office is just up above them now, because, look, over there is the chestnut tree, now naked as a bone. Even if the doctor were at his window now, he wouldn't spot them. She will slip away beneath his line of sight, and he will never get to fix her. She laughs under her breath.

"What?" Harris asks.

"Just, I'll miss this place."

He does not respond. They are almost back where they'd started: there are the stone steps and the front door, and there, the small blue saloon stands patiently on the gravel. She has made her choice; she set all this in motion, and she has not the slightest intention of backing out now. But still, Charlotte, who is usually so good at reading people, finds that she has not the first idea how Captain Harris will react when she tells him the truth.

He lets go of her arm to open the passenger door for her, waits as she takes off her hat and slips onto the seat, then swings her legs in after her. He claps the door shut. She looks down at the black fedora in her lap, her breath misting the air. She tugs her skirt down and smooths it over her knees; she straightens the seams of her gloves. Her heart flutters; its beat has never been quite steady since the first Coma Therapy. She tries to calm her breathing.

He lands in the driver's seat, making the car sink and creak. He turns the key and pushes the starter button and the engine sparks into life; they slide forward, peel around the carriage circle and start off down the drive; he's driving sedately, so as not to attract attention. She stares back at Summer Fields, at its blind windows. Goodbye, you hateful place, she thinks. I wish your wards empty and your roof blown off and all your windows smashed and your beds and straps and syringes and tablets all gone up in flames.

She turns back just in time to see the gateposts slide past the window. Then they are onto the lane, cruising round the first bend, and out of sight of the house. He sinks his foot; the engine roars and the car lurches forward, spitting gravel; he stamps and shunts his way up to third, and soon they are hammering along at nearly thirty miles an hour, bouncing shoulder to shoulder. Charlotte grips the edges of her seat. They both turn to look back through the rear window. The road winds emptily away. Then a wheel hits a pothole, and the car gives a sickening crunch and lurch. They're thrown from side to side; for a moment, she believes they're done for, but he rights the car, and they rattle on, engine straining. Speed folds up the world and slides her like a needle through its pleats. Thirty, thirty-five miles an hour, in top gear. The lid is off the jar; the packing case is flung wide; she is hurtling out into the world, and it's thrilling and terrifying.

He wipes the mist from the windscreen with the back of a gloved hand. Sleet falls, and he sets the windscreen wiper going, peering out through the arc of smeared screen. When they are safe in London, she thinks, and she has her own people around her—Mrs. Callaghan and Mr. Gibbons—that's when she'll tell him the truth. He will have to understand. It is, after all, his mistake.

"When will we reach London?"

"Not going to London."

Her grip tightens on the seat. "But you said—"

"No," he says. "*You* said."

She sits back. Her heart stutters. It seems she has peeled herself off the frying pan and launched herself right into the flames.

I mean, look at the great bleeder; six foot two of meat and eyes as cold as stone.

Oh Janet, hello, you're back.

Look at those hands. Vanessa now. Charlotte does, staring at the broad, blunt fingers gripped round the steering wheel. *Did you ever see anything coarser? Imagine those wrapped round your throat.*

"Where, then?" she asks, trying to sound unconcerned.

"Phone box first. Have to make some calls."

"Then what?"

"Then we'll see."

They drive on in silence. He seems satisfied that they're not being pursued. He softens the pressure on the engine and it settles on a more comfortable note; something is rattling; the windscreen wiper squeaks with every sweep. To think that it is less than an hour since she was colouring in her face.

Which reminds her. She opens her handbag, takes out her compact. Looks at herself; the state of her. An old drab or a circus clown. She doesn't want this; she never wanted this. She rubs at her face, pulling at her eyelids, scrubbing at her lips with the back of her hand. Then something lands in her lap. It's a clean white handkerchief, folded square.

"I'll ruin it."

"Doesn't matter."

She unfurls the cloth, wipes at her lips and cheeks and eyelids.

He reaches across her into the glove box, then drops a small tin of Vaseline on her knee. She looks at it, and then at him.

"Shift anything, that will," he says.

"Thanks." She wonders what the "anything" might be that he has had to shift.

She scoops out a fingerful, warms it in her hands, then smears it all over her face; her eyes blear with it. She wipes this off, and the paint comes off with it. The handkerchief becomes an artist's rag of colour. She scrubs at her face until it becomes hot and sore. She'll rub away all traces of the paint.

He stops the car on a village green, places a call from a phone box. She watches his stillness; no gesticulation, no nodding, no change in his expression. She could get out of the car now, walk across the green to that big house, knock on the door and beg to be taken in. The only thing that's keeping her in the car is the knowledge that she looks every inch the escaped inmate. Chances are they'd call the police. Chances are she'd be turned around and marched straight back to Summer Fields.

So, she sits in the car and watches him, and he remains as unreadable as stone. She is unsure if anything at all has been decided, until he returns to the car and says, "All right."

He starts up again and drives a short distance to a petrol station on the far side of the village. It's closed, but he knocks at the adjoining house and an old man comes out to serve them, peering in at the young lady in the car. Charlotte keeps her face turned away.

The tank refilled, coupons and cash handed over, Harris sits in and unfurls a map; she can make nothing out but the fingerprints of contour lines, overlaid with patches of green and blue, before he abruptly refolds it.

"Where are we going, then?"

"Safe house." He turns the engine on, shifts the car into gear and they pull away.

"Where?"

"People knew where it was, it wouldn't be safe."

Nothing about this is safe.

Oh El! There you are at last. Charlotte's eyes fill. I missed you.

Been keeping my head down.

You can do that, can you? Come and go as you like?

Lotts, dearest. None of this is as I like.

"None of this is what?"

"Hm?"

"What d'you say?" he asks.

"Nothing," she says. "Talking to myself."

They drive on. The road passes through woodland; they cross a river. They've been on the road now for—she has no watch, can't see his, doesn't want to ask—two hours maybe? More? This is wilder country now. The light fades out into blue. He doesn't consult the map again; he must have quickly memorised the route, or know the way from here.

At a crossroads, a fingerpost stands bare, the signs all taken down. He makes the turn without hesitating. It's dark now. They judder up a narrow track between high hedges. This goes on for miles: just the blur of ragged hedgerow and two white ruts, a wedge of winter grass between them, all lit by his faint headlights, and the white blank moon. They round another bend and the hedges fall away and they're in deep woodland. Thirty yards further on, and he pulls up. There is nothing here at all. Just a clearing in the woods. Trees and rocky outcrops, fallen timber. She has made a dreadful miscalculation. She quails.

See, El says. *When it comes to it, you don't really want to.*

What?

Kill yourself.

You're no help.

Because if you did, you'd let him do it. You'd goad him into it. He'd be good at it, I bet.

Please.

He kills the engine. He swings himself out of the car, claps the door shut. Walks away.

So what are you going to do?

I don't know.

Charlotte gets out. She peers after him, over the roof of the car. And then she spots the cottage. It's on the far side of the clearing, all overgrown with moss, houseleeks, and lichen; it looks like it has grown there from the woodland floor. So there is a safe house, after all.

He's feeling around the porch roof-beams; he locates keys, unlocks the door, opens it on darkness. He turns back for her. She leans against the front wing of the car, hooks her left foot up over the opposite knee, and fiddles with her shoe, stalling for time.

"Are you coming or what?"

"Just a minute."

He lumbers back towards her. She gives up on the shoe, faces him foursquare.

"It's cold," he says. "Come in."

Into the dark space beyond the door. She doesn't move.

"You may as well," he says.

He means, there's nothing he could do in there that he couldn't do out here.

"Lookit," he says, "you put yourself in this situation. I didn't want any of this. I have more than enough on my plate already. And I'm tired and hungry and I've had a long drive, and now I just want to stop, and if you're going to be a pain about it, I'll pick you up and carry you in. So maybe you could have a bit of a word with yourself and shift your bones in there pronto, because to be honest with you, my back's not what it was, and I've been told I get a bit short-tempered when it flares up."

These are all good and valid points, and she is glad that he is speaking to her, and not just wrapping those hands around her throat. "I said London, though."

"Beggars can't be choosers."

"Fair enough. You have me there. But tell me one thing first."

"All right."

"Why me? I mean, what put you onto me, in the first place?"

"Nothing."

"Don't be ridiculous. All over London. At my heels like a dog."

His lips narrow. "You weren't in the first place. You were a late addition."

She baulks. Does he mean that Stella and Mrs. Denby have been scooped up too? Was this, or something like this, how Janet really died? But she can't believe that any of them were anything other than pristine. "To what?"

He nods to the door. "You've had your 'one thing.' Move."

She bites the inside of her cheek, and having no other choice, she slips past him, marches up to the cottage, and goes in through the open door. She stands, frozen and disoriented in the indoor blackness, but then hears him open a match fold. He strikes, and there's a scatter of sparks, then a flame: he dips it to a wick, and clunks the glass chimney of an oil lamp into place. He carries the lamp past her, kneels at a small cast-iron stove and sets about lighting it. He sits back on his heels. The light spreads. He gets to his feet, opens a cupboard.

"You've been here before," she says.

He acknowledges this with a nod.

"With whom?"

"Doesn't matter."

And what happened to them? Because this place gives nothing away. The ground floor is all one room. A door in the back wall, a ladder up to a trapdoor; a kitchen dresser and a slate sink; two square windows to the front, where the Austin is parked. It all seems very fresh-faced and honest, homely; but then they wouldn't leave blood spattered up the walls, would they? Bullet holes in the stone.

"May I use the facilities?" she asks.

"Out back. Be my guest."

She follows the slabbed path up towards the end of the garden. No neighbours, no perimeter fence; the trees stand as solid as a wall. Moonlight in the clearing. Absolute silence; the heavy stillness of deep woods.

The outhouse is half dug into the hillside and smells like a cave;

water seeps, and small ferns grow out of the unplastered walls. She bolts herself in, rests her head in her hands. Her situation, she realises, is not so radically different after all. Like Dr. Gantley's open gates at Summer Fields, Harris knows that she can't run away from here.

So she makes her way back down the path, and goes indoors.

Three oil lamps now cast yellow pools; the fire crackles, a kettle gathers a head of steam. He had been holding a can to a lamp, to peer at the label, but on seeing her, he sets it down and lifts the kettle instead, a cloth wrapped around the handle, and pours the hot water into the sink.

"Didn't make a break for it then?"

"Just biding my time," she says. "Waiting for my moment."

Impassive, he operates the pump a few times to cool the hot water down with cold. He gestures for her to wash.

She feels self-conscious at first, but he ignores her, busying himself at the stove, opening tins and banging around. There's a bar of cracked old soap; she rolls it between her palms and dips her hands into the warm water, and it is such a pleasure that she forgets herself, leans in to splash her face, soaps and rubs till her eyes sting and her cheeks feel tight. She wets her head with handfuls of water and rubs the bar of soap over her curls—it seems an age since she last washed her hair. She ducks, splashes, scoops and rinses away suds. She fumbles blindly for the scrap of towel. It is placed into her hand, startling her.

"Thank you."

While she dries her hair by the fire, he takes his turn at the sink, sleeves rolled up, collar off, quietly scrubbing and huffing. Warming through on the stove is a rough hash of tinned sardines and canned potatoes; her stomach growls at the smell.

Dried off, he brings plates and forks, and then a bottle, glasses chinking. He hands her a glass, pours a finger of whisky. She sips. It's familiar, sweetish, fine; it takes her right back to the house in Galloway.

"This is good."

"I keep a bottle for emergencies."

"I'm an emergency, then?"

"You're a turn-up for the books. I'll give you that."

He hands her a plate and fork. Crumbling salty potato, melting fish. She has a sudden, overwhelming appetite; she has to remind herself of her manners. The contents of two tins, bashed about in a frying pan, is one of the best meals that she has ever eaten.

"Where did you learn to cook?"

"This isn't cooking."

"In the army?"

"I'm not captain of a fishing boat."

She sets her cleaned plate down, wraps her hands round the glass and rests them on her lap. She leans back in the chair, eyes soft, head heavy.

"Who exactly are you, Captain Harris?"

His expression doesn't change. "Exactly what you see."

Perhaps this is true. Perhaps this is literally true. After all, he had followed her across London, and had every chance to do her harm, but he has done her no harm at all so far. It wasn't him who'd attacked her. And now that he has her all alone and far from anywhere, and suspects her of some grave wrongdoing, instead of immediately squeezing what he needs out of her and disposing of her corpse, he's heating water for her to wash, making her supper and pouring her a drink.

You like him that much, why don't you marry him?

Shut up, Vanessa.

But she will tell him the truth, she thinks, and take the consequences. The words, though, are in a terrible muddle and won't be mustered into order. Her eyes are dry and sandy. She knuckles them. Her head is heavy. It drops, and swoops, and she is gone.

Winter Woods

When she wakes in the morning, it's to birdsong, and cold light, bedclothes weighing her down. She lifts an arm out from underneath the covers and finds she is still dressed. There's pale sky and bare branches visible beyond the skylight.

And then she remembers.

She leaps out of bed, clunks her head into a beam. She curses, rubs. She climbed—was half-shoved—up the ladder to the attic. Poleaxed onto the bed. He doubled the covers back over her, fumbled off her shoes. And then a night of shallow, fevered sleep, full of corridors and spinning linoleum, and her mother, sitting with her legs curled up on Saskia's sofa, leaning in to tell Charlotte something, her black pearl earrings shimmering, but Charlotte couldn't hear what she was saying.

Now Charlotte peers down the ladder, into the room below. A square of stone floor; silence. Her clothes are crumpled, her mouth sour, and her hair, when she feels for it, is a cloud of frizz. There's no mirror up here; she does her best to smooth herself out. Then she takes a hold of the top of the ladder and reaches a foot down into the empty air, feeling for a rung.

Downstairs, the shutters are open; winter light floods the room. He's not here, but the fire has been revived and is muttering and popping; the kettle has been filled and set at the back of the stovetop to keep warm; it faintly steams. Folded blankets have been piled on the linen chest; he must have dossed down on the floor, while she slept like a princess upstairs in the only bed; there's not even an armchair here to kip in.

She crosses to the window. The car has gone, leaving darker tracks across the frost. Her heart kicks. She rushes to the door, yanks on it;

it swings open easily, making her stagger back, letting in the cold air, and the sun shafting through bare trees.

She hears the motor, then, and goes out onto the porch. The car races up towards her, perky as a terrier. It is a strange relief to see it.

He claps the car door shut, stuffs a paper-wrapped parcel under his arm and climbs the steps.

"Morning," he says.

"Morning."

She moves aside; he dips under the lintel, sets the package on the table and shifts the kettle onto the hottest part of the stove, then sets about unwrapping the groceries. A small loaf, a tin of condensed milk. From his pockets, like a magic trick, he takes out four brown eggs.

"How on earth . . . ?"

"Hens can't help themselves, can they?"

He slices bread, and when the kettle boils, he fills the teapot, then pours what's left of the water into a pan.

"Poached," he asks, "or boiled?"

Her mouth floods. "Either. Anything."

Outside, the trees creak in the frost, and birds flutter by; inside, the sounds of cooking. Other than that, there's a deep, wide silence.

The eggs are very fresh, and poach beautifully. The white is cooked to a pillow, the yolk soft and oozy. Charlotte eats eagerly, wipes her plate with a last scrap of bread.

"You done?"

She touches her lips, suddenly self-conscious. "Yes. Thank you."

"More tea?"

She peers into her cup. "No, thanks, this is fine."

"So you can talk now."

"Yes."

"There's no particular reason why you can't."

"No."

"You're not going to fall asleep or shout at me or demand to be taken anywhere?"

"I won't."

"Because I don't have an infinite amount of time, and my people do not have an infinite amount of patience. You must understand that."

And she is on her own: the voices in her head are silent. There's a collective stillness, a watchfulness from them, but that is all.

He gets out a notebook and pencil and dabs the lead against his tongue. "Go ahead, then."

"Go ahead and what?"

"Tell me where it is."

"And that's, well, that? I mean, that's it? I tell you where it is, you'll let me go? That's everything you need from me?"

"That's the gist of it. We have the whole thing tied up nice and tight otherwise, nobody's wriggling out. It's just the last consignment we've lost track of."

She lets go a shaky breath. The woods are vast; the world is empty. She has nothing whatsoever to give him, and she cannot run away from this.

"All right," she says. "I'll tell you everything I know."

She drains her tea, sets her cup aside, slides her trembling hands under her thighs. And she tells him.

She tells him about her work at the Home Intelligence Division, where for months the words went in the eyes and out the fingertips and barely registered in between, and when they did, she was at a loss to imagine what use any of them could have been. She tells him that while she is clearly not above making a mistake, whatever is now missing from the office has not been stolen by her. It may well have been misfiled, mislaid or dropped in error into a wastepaper basket and securely shredded, pulped and dispersed into a whole new ream of paper by now, but it was not stolen by Charlotte. And this is not to attach doubt to Janet, God knows, nor to Stella, nor to the diligent and dedicated Mrs. Denby. She would vouch for each of them, with her life. But that's all she has to offer him. She doesn't even know what is missing, what he's looking for. She feels dreadful to have deceived him, but she sincerely hopes he will believe that she has only ever been incompetent at work, and then, at Summer Fields, desperate. But not a traitor, now or ever.

He watches her in silence. She feels prickly under his observation. He makes a few marks in his notebook, but mostly just waits, impassively, letting her run on, until she has exhausted everything she has to say, but still attempts to fill silence with supposition and apology.

"So, you see, you have the wrong woman. Or the wrong idea. All I can think is that somewhere, in the darkness, in blackout, you got me mixed up with someone else. So it's not really my fault, is it; it's more yours."

She peters out. Her cheeks flush. The silence stretches. Then he speaks. "Explain to me your movements. Throughout this period."

"All of them?"

"Yes."

"But you were following me. You already know."

"What I know doesn't matter. I want to hear what you have to say."

It seems at first impossible to account for all that time; she begins haltingly, but soon the words are spilling, jostling, leaping over each other. He makes the occasional note as she speaks, but does not interrupt. She tells him first about himself, the shadow man, when and how she'd noticed him—though she didn't realise at the time—running into him full tilt outside Saskia's flat, and again in Marylebone, when she'd told herself to shut up and startled him into looking straight at her. She describes the time she'd walked with Ilse down Woodland Road, and then the crush outside Clapham Junction, with yellow up. She explains that her friends had died around this time, one after the other, and she'd added two and two and come up with five. She tells him about that godawful lunch with her father. Her mother's earrings that she was meant to give to Saskia but couldn't bear to part with. She tells him about El's funeral, and about going to Clive's flat, though not what happened there; she tells him about Mrs. Hartwell and the awkward tea, and the new hardness there, the determination not to suffer. She tells him about Tom, the boy who feeds the birds, who'd been her friend and tried to help her, and the huge and stupid row they'd had, and how she hasn't heard from him since; she tells him about Mary who she'd spotted at the Tube station but who cut her dead, and who she'd tried to track down, but had drawn a blank. How the Eugenics Society had packed up and scuttled off from London, and how she'd sat outside it till it got dark, and then got caught up in a raid, and about the man who had attacked her in the middle of it all—her throat constricts; this is the hardest thing of all to talk about—and how it had made her realise, once and for all, that she was right in essence, if not in the particulars, that someone was using the wider violence to cover up their own personal acts of cruelty, but that this someone wasn't, in fact, him. Though she now understands why he was following her, and she hopes he will forgive her for calling him a killer, and as she had put it, bastard. Sorry about that. She tells him then about her hair being stuck with blood, after the attack, and going to a barber's to have it all clipped off, and how kind the barber had been; and how Mr. Gibbons had lent her clothes that she'd felt much sturdier in, her hands in her pockets and her feet planted on the ground. And about Francesca turning up at her digs, now that Charlotte was considered a nuisance again. And then Summer Fields, and Dr. Gantley, and Aminta. And the treatments. The Coma Therapy, that has made her heart go skittish, and the Electrical Therapy that was coming next, that knocks great holes into your memory. A blitz, she says, but on the brain. Smoking craters and broken walls, where there used to be a fairground, or a cricket pitch, or home.

"Which is where you came in again." She looks to him, trying to gauge his response, but she can't. She takes a deep breath. "I think we have been rather at cross-purposes, you see."

He reaches into an inside pocket, takes out a pack of cigarettes, taps the base, offers the protruding one to her.

"Thank you," she says. "Thanks."

Her hand is shaking.

He strikes and extends a match to her, pushes a tin ashtray across the hearthstones towards her with a foot. He doesn't seem angry. But then he doesn't ever seem to be anything very much ever. He's not even a mirror, she thinks, since a mirror reflects your own self back. His is an absorbing kind of blankness; he takes you in and you disappear. You say something and it's no longer yours; it is assimilated.

"People don't tend to notice me," he says.

"I do rather expect trouble."

He seems to consider this. After a moment, he says, "Well," and grunts as he gets up from his seat.

"Well what?" she asks. "What do you mean? What's to be done?"

"About what?"

"About me."

He extends a hand towards her, and for a moment she's nonplussed, looking at the thick fingers and the curve of his palm.

"Cup," he says.

Oh. She hands it to him. He takes it over to the sink.

"We'll set you up somewhere," he says. "I'll make some calls."

"Set me up?"

"Some town where nobody knows you."

"What?"

He turns back to her. "It'll be nice."

"No it won't."

"It'll be safe. You can make jam and grow vegetables."

"Me?"

"Join the WI."

"I don't knit."

"I believe the knitting is optional."

"You've clearly never met the WI."

There's just a twitch of a smile from him.

"Take me home," she says. "Take me back to Gipsy Hill."

He shakes his head.

"All right, don't take me then. Just let me go. Put me on a train, or a bus. Or I'll hitch-hike. I'll walk. Just point me in the right direction."

"You can't go back."

Her stomach plummets. "But. But. I won't hide away in some godawful provincial town, knitting socks for the troops. Which is, frankly, the last thing our boys need. You can't make me. I have things to do—"

He turns away, works the pump, washes the teacups.

"You go back to your old gaff," he says over his shoulder, "your family will find you. Your feet won't touch the floor. They'll ship you straight back to Summer Fields."

He's right; she can't go home. She can't ever go home again. All that shabby resort town sweetness; the house that smelled of malt and wool, her own hearth, the music coming up through the floorboards. Mrs. Callaghan and Mr. Gibbons. Cups of Horlicks and Garibaldi biscuits. Lady Jane twining at her ankles.

She clears her throat. She says, "It doesn't have to be there. You could take me to a friend."

He turns back to her. Behind his milk-quartz eyes, she imagines a series of swift, unfathomable evaluations and calculations. She knows she is at best an inconvenience to him, and that it's only one shade away from being a nuisance. And a nuisance is just about the worst thing it is possible to be.

And then he says, "What friend?"

He drives down to the village to make a call from the post office. These things have to be cleared, it seems, with HQ.

Impatient and unable to be still, she sets about straightening up the place with unpractised inefficiency. She sweeps the floor, wipes the table and brushes the hearth, all the time imagining what it will be like to see Tom again. Somehow, in her head, it is still autumn in Russell Square, and Tom is fluttering with birdlife. Chaffinches peck from his hands, and a smart crow looks at her sidelong from its perch on his head. But try as she might, she can't summon up Tom's expression. She can't imagine what he would say. Like a dropped scarf, a thought now drifts and sinks and settles softly. It is at once comforting, and delicate, and entirely opaque; she can't look beyond it. I just need to see Tom, she thinks. That's all.

At the sound of the engine, she hurries out to meet Harris. It is a dry bright day, the ground hard, her breath in clouds; she leans in at the car window.

"Well? What did he say?"

He waves her back so that he can open the car door. "I didn't speak to him."

"So, what then?"

"We'll send someone round. You'll be billeted on them."

"*Billeted? On* them? You mean I have to go and *live* there?"

"What else were you thinking?"

That she'd see him. That she'd talk to him. That she'd make things right with him, somehow. And then she'd break her last pound on a guest house for the night, and dinner, and figure out what to do next.

"I don't know, but not that." She follows him back to the cottage. "I didn't realise you were going to do that. It's too awkward. And such a wild coincidence."

"With half of London in ruins, everybody's in everybody else's pockets. It's just what happens now."

"I wish you'd let me phone him myself."

"They'll just be told an essential worker needs their spare room, and then you'll turn up. It's simplest. You have to be somewhere, so that's where you'll be."

Her worries shift and pin themselves now to this: that she'll see Tom, but that Tom might, given the option, prefer not to see her. Certainly might not want her living in his spare room. What Tom thinks, what Tom feels, how Tom will react when she lands on his doorstep; this all looms hugely now.

She grabs her coat, hat and bag, and heads for the door. But Harris just sinks into a chair.

"What?"

He lifts his whisky bottle, holds it to the light, then inclines it towards her. "We can't go now."

"You have to be kidding me."

"We leave now," he says, "we'd only get there in time for the fireworks. Anyway, you have to give the billeting officer time to do her work."

"Oh, for goodness' sake."

"Tomorrow."

"*Tomorrow?*"

She drops her things on a chair, stalks to the window, glares out at the woods.

"There's a pack of cards in the dresser," he offers.

Her skin crawls with pent-up nerves. She scratches at her neck, and then her chin, and then rubs her forehead; she pulls at her temples. "I can't stay cooped up in here till tomorrow."

"You'll be surprised what you can do, if you're obliged."

She sits down, stands up again. Paces back to the window. The Austin's just out there, waiting patiently. She taps her fingernails on the windowsill. Damn it. Damn.

"I'm going out," she says, grabbing her coat.

"Out?" He sounds actually surprised.

"Yes, out." She reaches for the door. "Bye."

"But there is no out," he says.

"There's masses; it's huge. We drove through miles of it, re-member?"

"But there's nothing there."

"And yet . . ." She lifts the latch.

He sighs, sets the bottle down, and creaks to his feet.

She picks her way along the frozen path, her Crombie on over the blue skirt and cardigan that she'd put on yesterday at Summer Fields. Harris trails along behind her, lumbering and graceless. He's growling to himself, tripping on every exposed root and fallen branch, but he's still following. The path is barely a tracing between the trees.

The sky is pearl grey. Birch trees slope away to the left, climb to the right, studded here and there with dark blots of yew. Ahead, there is a change in density, a different light.

"What's that?" she asks.

"More bloody nothing, far as I know."

The light expands before them, becomes silvery and drenching; the woodland ends, and a lake stretches out beneath the pale sky. Charlotte, stunned by distance, steps down onto a pebble beach. On the far side of the water, hills rise up abruptly, patched with woodland, bare stone and bracken. She has not been anywhere like this since she was last up in Scotland, or at Rydal with Elena. Those weeks in Summer Fields, the dirt and distress of the time before; all of it is eased aside.

"You said it was nothing."

"It is nothing. The wet kind. Lots of it."

She darts him an incredulous look, then turns back to the water. She feels as though her edges are blurring, as though she's dissolving into this stillness.

She plucks at her buttons.

"What?"

She shies off her Crombie, undoes her cardigan.

"What!" He spins away. He stares hard at a tangle of thin willows growing out over the water. "You can't be serious?"

"Christmas morning," she says, continuing to undress, "my brother and I would always have a swim."

"It's only the twenty-second."

"There's a lake at Longwood." She unbuttons her skirt and slides it down. "Or maybe you know that already? I have no idea what you do know, in fact; I have no idea how long you were following me."

But that question is washed away by memories. That first Christmas without Mother. The house was raucous, packed and lonely; she and Eddie had sloped off to the water's edge for a secret cigarette. *Come on,* Eddie'd said. *I dare you.* Then he'd stripped off his clothes and ran in, chasing ripples out across the surface. A dive, then he'd come up and flung the hair back from his face, and he'd laughed. And when he laughed, she'd thrown her own cigarette aside, pulled off her party dress and waded straight in after him. She had not known until then how cold it was possible to be, nor how alive in her own body she could feel. This was a baptism, wild and theirs alone. She needs it again now, now more than ever.

Harris clears his throat, still staring at the willows. "Must you?"

"I must." Though she can already hear the shivery stiffness in her voice. Revealed in the cold light, her body is very thin, her ribcage downy. "You're not coming in?" she asks.

He doesn't look round. "Don't be daft."

"Suit yourself."

She wades in. The cold is so complete that her nerves refuse to acknowledge it. She wades till she is up to her waist, then makes a shallow dive to skim the lakebed. She trails her fingertips over the rocks; her chest tightens and she swims up, crashing back through the surface, gasping in air, and then letting out a great, explosive, wordless shout that echoes back from the far hills and is caught and muffled by the trees.

The cold is everything: impossible, stunning. She laughs and wipes the wet from her face. Then she swims on, spinning circles out across the water.

From behind her, clear across the water, she hears Harris's exclamation: "Oh, for God's sake—"

But she just keeps on swimming. Her toes sing out like a nest of hatchlings; her legs and arms are stabbed with tiny knives. The water, almost at eye level, is quicksilver, moved only by her movement.

"Come back!" he yells.

But she thinks, I could stay in here forever. She thinks, I am immortal here.

"Bloody fool," he calls after her. "You're going to kill yourself."

She glances back. He has dropped his coat, is peeling off his jacket, unbuckling a shoulder holster. A gun. She feels a different kind of cold. All this time he'd had a gun. She turns away. She hears pebbles clatter, hears him cursing and splashing in.

"You are mad!" he yells, and it echoes back at him, bouncing from the hillside, before it's caught and silenced by the trees: *Mad, mad, mad.*

He thrashes out towards her, making a racket, complaining furiously. She stops, treads water, waiting for him. The rest of the world has fallen entirely away. There is just this moment, and her body, utterly alive.

"You made it look like it wasn't cold," he says tightly.

Her arms stir ripples. "That's the trick of it."

She grins at him, kicks out, swimming back towards the shore.

"God's sake."

He splashes after her. She comes into her depth, wades through the shallows and onto the shore. Her skin is hard with gooseflesh; she will not even think about the cold. She glances back. A stumbling, splashing, stringy beast follows after her, hands cupped over balls, muttering under his breath. There is a wound, she sees. A discoloured patch of scar in his flank, just above his hip. Like a bite has been taken out of him.

"Cold cold cold cold cold cold cold," he says, hurrying towards his clothes.

She grins. The pale fluff still grows on her belly; she runs a thumb over her ribs. She has come home to her body. It is hers, this structure of bone and skin and blood and muscle; this tender thing; it still works for her.

She sacrifices her slip to rub herself down. Her skin flushes. She pulls on knickers, skirt, blouse and cardigan, squeezes out her hair. She slings her Crombie over it all and then crouches to roll on her stockings, shivering hard. He is still only half-dressed, his clothing sticking to wet skin, all joints and angles and long bones.

"You all right there?" she asks.

"Yes." He's shivering so deeply that he's blurred. He stretches to pull a vest over his head, and she sees again that scar: a livid violet pit. She looks away. Her sense of him has shifted again. The gun, and the wound. She feels an uncertain sympathy.

"Are you sure?" she asks.

"Yes."

That seems to be all that he can say for now.

She gives him time to get completely dressed before she looks that way again; she crouches down inside her coat and rubs her arms and legs. A clink of metal and the creak of leather: she watches as he buckles his holster back on over his sweater.

"You needn't have come in at all, you know," she says.

"I wasn't going to let you drown."

She laughs.

Back at the cottage, he crouches at the stove, swearing under his breath. He stirs the fire up and lays in small bits of kindling that will catch quickly; he leaves the stove door open for the warmth. She drapes a blanket over his shoulders, wraps one round herself.

"Well, that," he says, "was different."

He offers her a cigarette; she manages to grab one—a moving target as both their hands are shaking. They smoke and shiver and watch the flames. The wood crackles, gives off sparks; the kettle spools out a thread of steam. She hands him her cigarette, struggles out of her coat under the blanket and throws it out like a fruit peel from a tent. He moves, wincing, to ease out his wound. She turns her head and rests her cheek on her knee and looks sidelong at him. She smiles.

"No wonder they committed you," he said.

"That's not very polite."

"Whatever got into you there?" he asks.

"My brother, Eddie," she says. "My actual brother, the one I mentioned—" Perhaps Harris knows about Eddie, but there's nothing in his expression to indicate it. "He died in May. He was with the First Ox and Bucks, at the Ypres–Comines Canal."

"I'm sorry."

"I miss him every day. He was my pal. I was always in the dog-house, growing up. Eddie would stick up for me, whatever happened. Half the time, I never even knew I'd done anything wrong till he came crashing down on me."

"He?"

"My father."

There's a small pause, the tack of cigarette against lip. "He a violent man, your dad?"

"No."

"What, then?"

She clears her throat. "It's not interesting. It doesn't matter."

"It'll go no further."

He's clearly good at keeping secrets. He's a professional secret keeper. But she's never said this out loud to anyone. Even now, it feels like a betrayal.

"The summer I was eight," she says, "I had new sandals. They were maybe a bit big, but I loved them. One day I was haring up the terrace steps, late as usual, and one of the soles caught, and I went flying. I landed face-first on the paving stones. Split lip, split chin, grazed knee, blood everywhere. The sandals were ruined, and one of my new front teeth was knocked loose."

She shows her teeth, then lifts her chin to reveal the absence of scars.

"All fine now. But when I walked in through the French windows, eight years old, all blood and woe, Father took one look at me, folded his newspaper and left the room."

"What?"

"He didn't speak to me for ages. Wouldn't even acknowledge me. It felt like forever, but it was probably no more than a fortnight. But while it was happening, it was like I'd disappeared. I did a lot of embroidery that summer. It seemed like the best thing to do, to sit and do embroidery. God, I hated it. I thought he might forgive me if I was good enough, and somehow doing embroidery seemed like the most obvious way of being good. But he didn't look at me, so really it didn't matter what I did. I burned it all, every stitch, every last scrap, when I realised that being good didn't work."

"But why the silent treatment?"

"I didn't understand either, till Mother informed me. It was her job to explain how I'd made him angry. How I'd jeopardised his love. I'd been careless; I'd been clumsy. I might lose a tooth. I might have scars. Had I not thought what it would be like for him, a man in his position, to have a daughter with a scarred face and a missing tooth?"

"But it was *your* tooth."

"It didn't come out anyway."

"And they'd have been your scars."

"And I was eight years old." She hesitates. "But the thing about Eddie was, it just didn't apply to him. He'd never get into trouble. However bad he was, whatever mischief he got up to, it'd just be shrugged off. He was allowed to have scars. And that could so easily have made a brat of him; but he wasn't a brat, he was a darling. Whenever I was in disfavour, he'd scoop me up and take me off to do something fun. He was always so charming and delicious, he'd get away with anything. Until he didn't."

Harris says: "My old man had a hard hand."

"I'm sorry."

"I learned to dodge."

He squashes out his cigarette. His lips are pressed tight, his brow furrowed. She's surprised to find that, for once, she can read him immediately. There's discomfort there, though whether at her memories or at his own, she doesn't know. But something's troubling him.

Hawthornes

Harris pulls the Austin up at the corner, kills the engine.

"Here we are," he says.

Charlotte looks up at the soot-blackened terraces. She's not sure what she expected, but it was not quite this. Tom's well-spoken, confident air had suggested something altogether more substantial and leafier than this. This is just a commonplace, lower-middle-class North London street; even if it weren't dead of winter, there'd be no leaves here. A few prams have been left out on the pavement so that their thickly wrapped occupants can benefit from the outdoor—she's not going to call it fresh—air; a woman scrubs her step; a well-fed dog is taking itself for a walk. The end house, adjoined by a purpose-built shopfront and office, is the Hawthorne family home and business. Gipsy Hill may not be as refined as her father thinks his daughter's due, but it has a wholesomeness to it. This patch of the city saw its heyday when Dickens was a buck, and its age is showing in darkened brick, missing cobbles and cracked stone. But the houses are well cared for, the doorsteps scrubbed and the windows clean, and the kids swinging on the lamp post have coats on; their songs and shouts make puffs of mist in the cold winter air.

She bites a thumbnail that is already bitten to the quick.

"Day before Christmas Eve," she says. "I didn't even think of that."

"It's all agreed. They're expecting you."

"Even so."

There's a pause, their breath fogging the windscreen.

"Right." Harris claps his gloved hands together and rubs them against the cold. "Well."

She peers into the back seat, as though she might have left a suitcase there, but she hasn't got a suitcase; she has hardly any possessions left. Just the clothes she's wearing and the handbag on her lap and whatever Francesca might have left behind at Mrs. Callaghan's.

"Well," she says, "I hope you find it. Whatever it is."

"We will."

"I'm sorry if I held you back."

"I've eliminated a line of enquiry. That's something."

"You're just being kind," she says.

"I don't do that."

"That's not true. You've been kind to me."

A moment's pause. "Anyway." He nods towards the house.

"Well, goodbye." She picks at a glove seam. "Thank you."

"Goodbye."

There is nothing else for it, so she gets out of the car. All she has to do is walk up there and knock. It seems impossible.

He restarts the car, shifts it into gear, then turns it, and drives away. She watches him checking both ways at the corner. Then he's gone.

"Ah. Good afternoon," Charlotte says.

The hallway seethes with family, is festooned with streamers and looping paper chains. A girl holds the door open, pigtails dangling, violin and bow clutched in one inky hand. A slight sandy-haired man that Charlotte remembers from El's funeral joins the girl, glasses impenetrably shining. A neat woman with a wing of white from temple to chignon comes to stand next to him, looking Charlotte over with an incisive eye.

"Good afternoon," the woman says, extending a hand. "You must be Miss Richmond?"

"That's me, yes."

"I'm Mrs. Hawthorne. Pleased to meet you."

Charlotte takes the woman's cool hand. Her own hand feels grubby against it. It was a long drive down, from wherever they'd been. The past few days have taken on a quality of otherworldliness, as though a remembered dream.

But there, coming uncertainly down the hallway, is Tom.

Tom is, she sees, like his father in stature and reserve, but with his mother's sharper edge, though he is also utterly and entirely Tom. It is a simple joy to see him—she wants to wave to him past the others, claim their connection, but then she registers his expression—guarded, uneasy, not meeting her eye. She falters.

A dog noses through to greet her; a great sway-backed beast with a face like a split football, its thin tail swooping back and forth behind it. Charlotte gives it the back of her hand to sniff.

How did she let this happen? Clearly, from the looks of Tom, this is the worst thing she could have possibly done.

"Is it her?" The girl lobs the words across to Tom.

"Yes," Tom says.

"So it *is* you." The girl shifts her bow into her other hand, gestures with it like a fencer, making Charlotte lean away, out of its ambit. "We did wonder. Tom said he knew someone with the same name, and we thought, what a coincidence if it should turn out to be you."

"Some of us thought; *some* of us wouldn't leave the subject alone." Tom is glaring at the girl now, determinedly not looking at Charlotte.

"I'm sorry. This is all very awkward," Charlotte says. "I really don't know how this came about—"

"No trouble at all," the mother says, though her tone suggests the contrary. "You can hardly help getting bombed out, can you? Why don't you come in?"

The family parts to let her by. She glances back, in the futile hope of glimpsing Harris. The street is empty, but for the prams, the pigeons, and the kids playing on their lamp-post swing. He's gone for good now, she thinks. I've lost my shadow.

She steps over the threshold. The dog turns across her path, making her falter. She notices with a start that it's missing a back leg. It limps slowly along ahead of her; the family exclaim at it, cajole it along; it seems to have a talent for getting in the way.

Well, this is becoming ridiculous, Vanessa opines. *What next, the actual gutter?*

Who rattled your cage? Janet says. *It's better than many people have.*

It's decent. It's kind. It's more than Lotts has herself right now, the poor thing.

Darling. This is fascinating. You must write an account of it like Mr. Orwell did. Or a play. How the Other Half—

Charlotte shoves the voices away.

Tom, she wants to say. Tom, please look at me. There's no way that she can say any of the things she'd wanted to say. That she missed him. That she regrets their falling out. That she simply wants him back.

"Do you like dogs, Miss Richmond?"

"Charlotte, please."

The child delights at this invitation to familiarity, and now positively buttonholes her: "Do you like dogs, though, Charlotte? I *love* dogs. Ours is called Nell. She hurt her leg before we got her; she was in a pretty bad way altogether. I don't like to think about what happened, because someone must have been horrible to her, and how could anyone be horrible to her, she's such a darling, aren't you, Nelly? But we love her now and we spoil her rotten, and she does pretty well on three legs, and when you think so many people had their pets"—she drops her voice so that Nell won't hear—"*put to sleep* when all this started, she turned out to be one of the lucky ones in the end."

A warning from her mother: "Felicity."

"I like your hair," the girl, only slightly chastened, says. "It's very short."

Charlotte, dazed, runs a hand over her curls. "It was a lot shorter at first."

"Why?"

"I had an accident."

The girl's eyes go wide. "An accidental haircut?"

Charlotte laughs.

Tom stands aside to let their guest through into the back room. It's crowded with furniture and stuffy-warm. Charlotte desperately wants to bridge the gap between them, to excuse and explain, but his sister is monopolising company, and Tom is giving out no light at all in her direction; he still won't even look at her. This was such a bad idea; she should have settled for anonymity in some provincial town. Even the WI would be preferable to this.

"I had no idea," he says, as she slips past him, "that you were an essential worker."

She makes a wry face, too upset even to reply.

· · ·

He had thought that he was doing well, considering. He had thought that he was fine. His weekend classes at the college had revealed him to be at least as capable and well-informed as any other student in the room, and his accent, among the other clerks and shop workers there, doesn't mark him out particularly. It has been reassuring to discover this. Otherwise, the trick has been to always be slightly too busy, slightly too tired, so that he hasn't had time or energy to feel miserable; current times have offered plenty of opportunity for this.

He had thought about her; he doesn't attempt to deny this. He'd worried about her. He'd wondered where she was, and how she was spending her time, and if she was doing any better than she had been. He'd expected that her family were looking after her. He'd expected that all misunderstandings would have been smoothed over, all disagreements resolved. He'd assumed the man she'd been courting would be with her, as far as wartime constraints would allow. And as Christmas had approached, he'd imagined the two of them, her and this unknown suitor, out at her family home in the countryside, away from the worst of the trouble; he'd seen them happy, festive, surrounded by her family. But he didn't spend all his time pining for something he could never have; not *all* of it.

So when that billeting officer had appeared at their front door with her clipboard and breezily efficient air, and told them to expect a Miss Richmond the next day, it had been something of a shock. A sleepless night had followed; by the following morning, he had resolved that if it was indeed her, he would be glad to see her, simply to know for certain that she was safe and well, and that would be an end to it. He would not make himself ridiculous; he wouldn't embarrass her. It had been, after all, only a brief acquaintanceship; that was all there was to it. Her silence since had made that clear. He would be fine; he was determined that he would be fine. But now, faced with the reality of her, worn threadbare, in crumpled clothes and without a scrap of paint, her beauty just the starker for it, he finds himself crumbling inside. He catches that look of hers and has to turn aside. All resolve is fled. He is not doing well. He is not fine. Far from it.

The range is belting out heat. Tea is laid out on the table. The family meal has been spread even thinner to accommodate the visitor, and, in her honour, is served on the pink Woolworth's tea service that his mother keeps for best. The windows are all steamed up and the Christmas decorations, which, two days ago, had seemed to add cheer and comfort, now look paltry, dismal and exposing. He is mortified. There is no way this could not be awkward, but if his mother had known her new lodger was the daughter of a baronet, she'd have entertained her with considerably more grace, and in the front parlour. He turns away and climbs the stairs, pursued by his sister's unbearable chatter.

". . . but you can call me Fliss. Can I take your coat? And my dad's called Frederick, or Fred, or Freddy, if you like. And Mum's name is Isobel, but everyone calls her Belsie. And you've met Nell, but there's also the cat, Magwitch, but he's out and about, he's a wily old fellow and is off after the—"

"Fliss." Mrs. Hawthorne's tone is quelling. Fliss buttons her lip.

"I can't thank you enough, Mrs. Hawthorne," Charlotte tries again, flustered; it is so hot and stuffy in here. "I hope you didn't go to any trouble."

"We have the space, with our older boys in the army. It was only a matter of time." Before someone was foisted on us, her expression inevitably adds.

"I'll do my best not to get in the way. Hopefully it won't be for long."

"Do you expect to find other lodgings?"

"Yes, of course, as soon as possible . . ."

"Have you tried?"

"Well, no, not yet."

Mrs. Hawthorne smiles politely. Then: "Do put that violin down for a minute, Fliss. Miss Richmond, have a seat."

"Is Tom not joining us?"

"He'll be getting ready for the watch," Mrs. Hawthorne says.

They sit. She realises she has been given Mrs. Hawthorne's seat by the ferocious range, upright and supportive, in which a chilly woman might manage her needlework. Mr. Hawthorne sits quietly opposite her; Mrs. Hawthorne has taken a plain dining chair. Fliss goes to her music stand and flips the pages, frowning, glancing over at the grown-ups, desperate to be involved.

"In future, you might give your coupons to me," Mrs. Hawthorne says, "if you want to take your meals with us. Or you can have a shelf of your own in the larder if you prefer to go your own way."

"Thank you." Charlotte's lip blooms with sweat. She dabs it away. "I'm afraid I am all at sixes and sevens at the moment."

"Inevitably," Mrs. Hawthorne says. "A bomb is a dreadful muddler of affairs."

"So tell me, Miss Richmond, what is it that you do?" Mr. Hawthorne asks. He is such a quiet presence that it startles her when he speaks.

"You can't ask her that, Dad," Fliss says. "Not if it's war work."

"True. Good point, Fliss. Apologies."

Charlotte wafts his concern away, mortified. "Just typing," she says. "Though for some reason it does seem to be terribly important."

Tom comes in, pulling a greatcoat on over a siren suit, adjusting the ARP band on his upper arm. He looks slim and neat and practical and she wants, she *wills,* him to look at her. If they could but talk, the way they used to, before it all got so knotted and difficult. But he is different now. All those imagined encounters fall to pieces and drift away. She can't get through to him. He's sealed himself off from her.

Then, as if obliged by the sheer force of her will, he finally turns his eyes on her. His mouth twists up, and his eyebrows raise; he is simply wretched that she's here. He turns away before she can even mouth the words *I'm sorry, I'll go,* and addresses his mother:

"Mr. Hastings said to get there early; we've a training session about the new incendiaries."

"They have *new* incendiaries?" His mother tuts. She bustles to pack up sandwiches and a scone in paper, pours tea into a thermos, while he leans down to fuss the dog, just to be doing something. All this time he had only been thinking about his own pain; now that she is here, in the undeniable flesh, he has to acknowledge that he has not been having the worst of it. To look at her is devastating; it's like she's walking a tightrope: a breath of wind, a nudge, a loss of nerve, and she'll fall. He can't bear to look.

He digs his fingers into Nell's big loose cheeks and ruffles them; he kisses her head, and stays there, scratching under her chin, until he's got his face in order again.

His mother proffers the packages. He pockets them.

"Well," he says. "Good night."

"Good night," Charlotte says. "Stay safe."

He dips his head to her, ducks into the cold scullery and darts across the yard beyond.

He is so desperate to get away from her.

Kill yourself.

It would be simplest. Better for everyone in the end.

The window mists with condensation. Tea is poured and sandwiches passed. Charlotte follows him in her thoughts, out into the city streets, up onto the roofs above, where he'll be perching for the night, watching, listening, waiting for fire to fall from the sky.

"Are you going to eat that up, Charlotte? Only I'm desperate to get started on the scones."

"Felicity!"

Charlotte catches Fliss's eye and consumes her overlooked sandwich in three deliberate bites. There.

"Isn't it such rotten luck for you," Felicity says as she reaches for a scone, "that you got bombed out of your digs."

"It could have been far worse," Mr. Hawthorne says. "If you think about it, Fliss."

"Crikey, yes. Silver linings, eh?" Fliss grins admiringly at Charlotte.

"So where did you meet our Tom?" Mrs. Hawthorne's tone is light, but the lightness sounds forced. "You'd hardly move in the same circles, I would have thought."

"At college," Fliss says. "Tom said, remember? All kinds of people mix at places like that, don't they? That's part of the point. What are you studying? I'm going to be a doctor when I grow up."

"Good for you," Charlotte says.

So Tom lied about how they'd met. He gave the impression that there was more to her than there is. The park benches and the autumnal squares that she had returned to with such pleasure in her thoughts must have seemed so slight and shameful to him. And then it crashes in on her. If he knows. If he's somehow found out what she's done. About Clive. And all the other times she's done something like that, unhappily, wanting almost anybody's approval, anybody's warmth, if only for a while. Not just that she made a nuisance of herself to her family, but *how* she did it.

You're being paranoid, Lotts.

The sweaty little pixie's right, Janet says. *How would he have found out?*

Different worlds, darling. Entirely separate circles.

Thank goodness, Vanessa says.

"Fliss has to get her scholarship first," says Mrs. Hawthorne.

Fliss rolls her eyes.

"You know what happened with Tom's start at college."

"No. What happened?" Charlotte asks.

"He didn't tell you?"

"Not that, in particular."

"Odd that he didn't mention it. Just a series of delays. He transferred from King's to Birkbeck, and somehow the finances were held up, and then there were all those postponements, you know, and the bombing. It was all very trying for him, in particular, since he couldn't go at all without the scholarship. Though it all seems to be going smoothly now, thanks be to God."

"That's awful," Charlotte says. "I mean, about the scholarship. He never said."

"Oh, don't you worry, he'll get there. He might have to go the long way around, but he'll get there."

"He always does," Mr. Hawthorne chips in. "In the end."

"I don't doubt it," Charlotte says. "He's an exceptional young man."

"Yes he is," Mrs. Hawthorne replies, brisk. "We're very proud of him. And you know, the thing about that boy is, he's always simply sailed through. Exams and things, I mean, school, all of that. He's never had any trouble there. And we've found the money when we've needed to, for uniforms and books; we've managed, we've always managed to give him what he needs. My point is that, God willing"— she sits back, peers at her knitting—"the boy will make something of himself, whatever life throws at him. He was always going to."

And you're a complication, El says.

At best, Vanessa adds. *She clearly doesn't want you messing his life up for him.*

I don't either, Charlotte thinks. I really don't.

"Can I help with the washing up?" Charlotte asks, turning to Mr. Hawthorne, who has sighed to his feet and is now stacking plates; the cool empty scullery looks like heaven—but Mr. Hawthorne will accept no help, and so she is stuck instead with the purgatory of Mrs. Hawthorne's prickliness, Fliss's endeavours on the violin, and the dog's aural distress that provokes her to make complaining noises in her throat which never quite amount to a howl.

The local siren doesn't sound, though they can hear the buzz and crackle of a distant raid and the thud of far-off bombs. They listen to the nine-o'clock bulletin and it is the usual mix of puffery and flannel. The decision is taken to try for a night in their own beds. The stove is banked down. Mr. Hawthorne winds the clock. It will be Christmas Eve tomorrow. Fliss helps Nell up the stairs, a comic waggling effort; the dog lumbers into Fliss's room and harrumphs down onto what appears to be a marvellously comfortable rag rug.

"A quiet night at last," Mr. Hawthorne observes, as Charlotte passes him on the landing. "I hope you can benefit from it, my dear."

"You too," she says. For all his slight build, Mr. Hawthorne has a carthorse steadiness about him, a benign plodding-on with things. She could get on comfortably with him, she thinks, if she had the chance. For now, she is obliged to follow the rather more vinegary Mrs. Hawthorne up a further flight.

"I hope this will do you."

It is an attic room, with two beds, one of which has been made up in anticipation of her arrival; the other is bare, a stack of folded blankets at its foot. On the boarded floor between them is a blue-and-green rag rug, a near relative to Nell's. A charcoal-coloured blanket has been tacked up over the window, by way of blackout.

"I'm afraid you're very high, up here, but there's nothing else for it. The billeting office believed that it would do for you, and so I suppose it must."

"It's very nice," Charlotte says. "Thank you."

Mrs. Hawthorne looks sceptical. "I wasn't sure you'd think so."

"You've all been very kind," Charlotte says. "I'm most grateful, really."

.   .   .

Light off, key turned in the door, Charlotte moves the blanket aside to look out of the window. Twists of fog; frost gathering on cobbles and slate roofs. Moonlight catches on windows, church spires and towers.

It is indeed a quiet night, just the final sounds of family and home, the creak of the stair treads, the shift of floorboards, the dog already snoring, a murmured conversation between husband and wife, a jangle of springs as someone turns over in bed. Charlotte winds the window covering back around itself into a fat knot, so that it stays open, letting the moonlight flood in. She sits down on the edge of the bed, kicks off her shoes, lies down, pillows her head on a crooked arm. She should not have come. The mother just fizzes with dislike. The sister and the father are welcoming enough, but that is irrelevant when he, Tom, clearly wishes her a thousand miles away, or at the bottom of the sea. She shivers. The world seems so terribly empty now.

She hears the hall clock, two floors below, its tick resonating up the stairwell. She waits for the half-hour chime. Once everyone is properly asleep, she'll slip away. She can't face the fuss and protest if she were to tell them. She'll find a shelter. A rest centre. Something for the night. And then tomorrow . . . well. She blinks. She'll worry about that tomorrow. She closes her eyes. She drifts. And is gone.

When she wakes, the room is stark black and white in the moonlight, and empty. She has to leave, but there is nowhere left for her to go; there is no one left for her to go to.

Oh, El. El.

I know.

I want to see you. I want to just lean up against you, and talk. I want to hole up in your old bedroom with you and gin and cigarettes and moan and sob and hug and laugh and know that even at my very worst you still love me. I have lost his good opinion, and it's horrible, and I know you'd understand. You'd care. I *miss* you.

I know.

I give up.

Now you're being ridiculous.

But I am stymied. If I go to my digs, my family will find me, and

I'll be slammed straight back in Summer Fields. The same will happen if I go back to my old job. I have not a friend left in this city. When the chemists open in the morning, I may as well buy half a dozen bottles of aspirin and find a quiet place, a corner of a shelter, an empty building, a bomb site—

Don't be stupid. You give up now, what was the point of any of it? What was the point of any of us being friends at all?

I'm done.

You're not done. You're not nearly done. You're half-baked at best. For all you know, you might have another fifty years to drag yourself through. Or you could die tonight, whether you want to or not. Either way, do you want to spend whatever time you've got left being such a godawful drip?

Oh, El. That's harsh.

Because you're being ridiculous. You've stopped trying. You've stopped thinking. And you never stop. Whatever you might say about yourself. However you torment yourself. This is not like you. Remember the dog?

The dog?

The Dandie Dinmont. Peachy.

Christ's sake. That bloody dog.

That dog.

What about the dog?

Be the dog. Be the stubborn little mouse-hound that you are.

Like your mother said. I am a ball of bloody-minded fluff. Though I wonder . . .

Yes?

If they went up to Rydal in the end . . .

There we go.

Charlotte sits up. From downstairs, the hallway clock chimes the hour. Five o'clock already; she'd slept longer than she'd thought. Soon another day will begin and she'll get tangled up in it.

She carries her shoes, creeps down the first flight in stockinged feet. On the landing, the blackout card has been lifted down; the scrim-stuck windowpanes cut trapezoids of white moonlight on the carpet. She's about to turn to go down to the hallway, but there's movement—she stops dead, hears the front door click shut and the turn of the key on the inside, footsteps. Tom, coming back from fire watch. A stair creaks. There is no way she can face him now. She races softly back up the stairs to the attic.

From where she stands, heart pounding, she watches Tom haul himself up onto the lower landing. The cold light hits him sideways. He stalls there, caught by his thoughts or by fatigue. He is half bone-white, half blue. He reaches out to steady himself against the wall with his right hand. Charlotte finds herself caught in the shape of that hand, in the delicacy of it, the way the fingertips just rest on the wallpaper. And then the turn of the muscle in his forearm, his shoulder; the curve of his nape; the hair clipped to a haze; the way he holds his head. He is beautiful, she thinks; it has taken her till now to realise.

God forgive him, Tom thinks. He doesn't wish to call trouble down on anybody, but tonight was just too quiet. He could have done with a bit of mayhem to keep him busy. And now she's just up there, sleeping, her body soft beneath a familiar quilt. It's torture.

He is beautiful, she thinks, and he is kind, and he is clever, and she can never have him.

And as though he's overheard her thoughts, Tom is impelled into movement. His hand drops away from the wall, and takes himself off to his room. He'll stand it, he decides. He'll have to. It's better this than not knowing whether she is safe.

She listens to the sounds of him settling. She hears the dog whimper in Fliss's room, dreaming. Charlotte waits for the next quarter-chime, to give Tom a chance to fall asleep, then she makes her way down the stairs. The clock ticks in the hallway. Christmas decorations hang like cobwebs in the dark. She takes her coat and hat from the rack, the tiles cold under her stockinged feet, then unlocks the door. It is a foggy, freezing night. She slips her shoes on, steps out, locks the door behind her and reaches in through the letterbox to drop the key softly on the mat. Then she makes her way along the pavement, easing her gloves on. At the corner, she looks back. She takes in the dark house-fronts, all glittering with frost and trailed with fog. She wants to fix it in her memory, this place, this moment, his home.

Giving Up

By moonlight, the white stucco still looks wedding-cake pretty, but there are now cracks in the icing, and chunks have fallen off; a downstairs window is patched with board. The old tree still stands, its branches spreading towards the house, reaching for Elena's old bedroom window. Its tick-tacking fingertips, at night, had seemed like an invitation: Come outside, the world is out here; come outside, the world is waiting just for you. Charlotte leans against its bole now, footsore, collar turned up and hat tipped to keep in a little warmth.

It all felt so huge, El, the future; everything that was coming to us.

And it is. Look at it. What could be bigger?

But not the way we'd thought.

Nothing ever is.

I always loved it here.

I'm glad.

I always felt safe in this house.

I know.

Jealous, too.

I know.

So easy here. So safe and comfortable.

Charlotte takes a cigarette from her packet, tucks it between her lips.

I'm sorry about Clive.

You didn't have to twist his arm.

I should have been nicer to him. Or just left him well enough alone.

Nobody's perfect.

Charlotte considers this. It seems a startling insight.

It's hours yet till sunrise, but the house's emptiness gradually confirms itself. No smoke rises from the chimneys. No bread or milk is delivered. Lily doesn't bob out to salt or sweep the steps. Windows stand blank, crisscrossed with scrim, as though the house's eyes have been scratched out.

So they have gone to Rydal, after all. The lap of lake waves; wind in the beech trees; ducks locked in battle with the current where Rydal Water tips itself out into the River Rothay. There'll be no bombs falling up there yet.

Charlotte drops her cigarette-end and scrapes it out with a foot. She checks around her; quiet skeins of fog, glimmering frost. No one. There hasn't been a soul to be seen all the way here, through the dark miles of London streets. Not even her old shadow. A lonely kind of night. She ducks into the mews behind El's house; the old stables all stand locked and empty. The back gates have numbers on them for the delivery boys, but she knows it by the Beauty of Bath tree, a tracery of black against the winter sky.

The gate is bolted. A quick shufti round, then one foot up onto the door handle, fingertips gripped over the top of the wall and she's up, and then she's over, sliding down to land with a thump in the flower bed. She straightens herself out, brushes off her stinging hands. She strides up the path, trying to look like she belongs there. Inside the coal shed, her fingers fumble along the ledge where the spare key is kept.

The house is full of shadows. The grandfather clock stands silent. The electricity is off. In the drawing room, they have packed up the ornaments and paintings, rolled up the carpets, closed the blinds; the furniture stands like bulky ghosts, shrouded in dust sheets. She finds herself caught, for a moment, staring at the draped contours of an armchair, where Mrs. Hartwell had sat and told her not to let El's death set her back. How long was it, she wonders, before she'd decided that Charlotte had manifestly been set back, and set back so very far, that the only thing to do was telephone Sir Charles? Perhaps Clive felt better about himself, once they'd all agreed he'd been seduced by the girl with the dreadful reputation. By the girl who really needed locking up. By poor, mad Charlotte. But, dear God, Clive. To tell your *mother*.

She shivers, rubs her arms.

Clearly she can never see these people again. She couldn't be in this house if they were here.

But it's my house too, Lotts. Never mind them. I invite you.

Upstairs, in Elena's bedroom, death has been left to grow undisturbed. The room is tangled thick with it. Nothing has been packed away or covered up here; the bed is neatly made, the blind down and familiar curtains have been left hanging at the window. The carpet is the well-remembered riot of green foliage and golden roses. In the wardrobe, clothes still hang from silk-padded hangers. A scent of El lingers here: her perfume, her cigarettes, her body, her grown-up self. That bias-cut gown from the May Ball; the pistachio linen dress she'd worn that Friday in the park.

You always did look your very best in green.

Charlotte reaches out towards a chartreuse blouse, but her hands are grubby, so she doesn't touch. Instead, she crouches to lift out shoeboxes, pushes bags aside.

Your tennis shoes.

What about them?

She tugs them out. Greyed, rewhitened, the laces grubby and trailing.

Ha.

Ha what?

Ha, this is you.

The other stuff is also me.

Charlotte tugs off her tired suede shoes and tweaks the plimsolls on, lacing them briskly. Her toes are ice inside them.

This is you when you still chewed your plaits and played your smelly old clarinet; do you remember all the time we seemed to have back then? All that *time:* reams of it, acres, aeons, stretching out forever, a sunlit meadow for us to run in.

I grew up.

You died.

I grew up first.

And I didn't?

You weren't ever going to, Lotts. You didn't stand a chance.

Charlotte sits down on the bed, stares at her scruffy feet. It is all too difficult.

You're scared. It's understandable.

Isn't everyone? This business of living; it hurts too much.

Not just now; you always were. Since long before this war started, you've been scared the world was going to blow up in your face.

It does have a tendency.

That's not how everybody lives. Not all the time.

I'd noticed.

That's a start.

She is so tired; she is so cold. She sinks down on El's pillow. There is a faint, strange smell here, earthy and atavistic. Fully clothed, El's tennis shoes still on, Charlotte pulls the quilt around her. She can still feel the mineral silk of lake water on her skin. It was beautiful there, she thinks; she'd thought that things would be better after that. But she was wrong. She'll never see that place, or Harris, or even Tom, again. She'll just lie here, and let the cold claim her, and that will be that.

Oh no you don't. You're not leaving another corpse here for poor Lily to find.

Maybe she won't have to. Maybe the house will be bombed to bits.

Oh for God's sake, Lotts. Don't be such a lame duck. You have things to do, remember? Don't just collapse because it's difficult. Don't give up because you're sad.

Charlotte rolls her head from side to side: Enough, El. Leave me be. Let me have some peace.

It's you keeps rattling my bones. It's you won't give me peace. And you don't even bother to remember.

Charlotte turns onto her side, curls into a ball.

That's the problem, darling; I can't do anything but.

The voices retreat from her, gather behind that half-closed door. She's aware of them, conferring together, but they don't address her. Light slides past the edges of the blinds, the shadows shorten. She is so cold. She hears the milkman's horse clop past, the paper-boy's whistle. Post drops onto the mat. There's traffic in the distance. Indoors, the shadows lengthen and expand to fill the room again.

No clocks chime. And her watch, still locked in the safe at Summer Fields, ticks down, unwound. She is so cold. But it's all right. It turns out that this is what she should have done all along. It's simplest; it is, after all, for the best. And it turns out it's not difficult at all. All she has to do is wait.

But in the new darkness, something starts to scrape away at her. She rolls her head at the irritation. A rasping, scratching sound. No. Shut up. Go away. But it goes on; it intrudes. She is forced to stir. For God's sake. She tries to sit up, but her body's slack and heavy. Her mouth is dry, her stomach hollow. What is that noise? Why can't she be left in peace?

She wraps the quilt around her shoulders, goes stiff-jointed to the window; she opens the blind. The street is silent. The moon has risen. It could be midnight, it could be teatime. She has no idea. She feels utterly adrift. But that scratching noise is coming from downstairs. Metal against metal. As though, she thinks slowly, someone is trying to pick a lock.

I should not be here, she thinks. Not just in this house. I should not be in this life at all. And here I still am, still going on. And now I have to deal with this.

At least you're moving now, El says.

God's sake.

Charlotte pads out onto the landing in El's tennis shoes; even the slightest movement masks the sound, so she stops there, to listen again, before treading her way cautiously down.

Hide.

No.

If it's a housebreaker, a monster, that brute from the raids.

No. Mrs. Callaghan was right. I was hiding all that time. I'm not hiding any more.

She pauses at the foot of the stairs. Moonlight pools on the tiles. The sound is coming from the kitchen. She feels a surge of anger—glorious, resentful anger—can't she even be left alone to die in peace—and slips into the morning room to lift a poker. Then she treads silently through to the kitchen.

She absorbs the shapes of the place. The moon spills through the window: she can make out the dresser set with kitchen china, the blank window, the scrubbed deal table, the cold range squatting like a toad. And the back door, resonant with threat. She grips the poker, takes the key from her pocket, slots it into the lock. She hears a muffled exclamation as outside the pick is shoved out of the keyhole. She twists the key, flings the door wide.

"Go on, get out of here!" she yells. "Clear off!"

A dark shape stumbles back. A dropped torch casts a wedge of yellow light across the path. She raises the poker high, starts after the intruder.

"Coming round here, breaking into people's houses; what the hell do you think you're doing?"

The figure staggers, unsteady, reaching to a wall for support; it forms into a familiar, light-boned, unanticipated shape.

"Much the same as you?" he says.

She lowers the poker. "Tom?"

For a humiliating moment there he thought he was going to fall, but then one hand found the roughcast wall and he steadied himself.

There she is. Admittedly wielding a poker and yelling at him. But at least he can breathe now. He must remember not to sneak up on her again.

She peers past him, suspicious.

"I'm on my own," he reassures her. "You can put the poker down."

She lowers it. "Sorry," she says. "Sorry, I . . . Sorry. What do you want?"

To know that she is safe. This has been the most pressing need ever since the heart-stalling sequence of events that morning. He just had to know that she was safe.

His mother, having given up waiting for Miss Richmond to emerge for breakfast of her own accord, had tapped on her door illtemperedly, bearing a cup of tea, and, receiving no reply, had creaked the door open. Finding the room empty, she had clumped downstairs to let everybody know, with some concern and just a touch of triumph, that Miss Richmond had done a moonlight flit. No note. Not a word. Just gone in the night, without so much as a thank-you. How could anybody be so, well, frankly, *rude*?

Rude was not what he'd call it. Careless, maybe. Distressed, certainly. Risky, especially if she was still being followed. And entirely his fault. He'd only needed to be civil. He'd only needed to let her know that she was welcome. And instead he'd given her a bitterly cold shoulder.

"Shall I let the billeting officer know the room is free again?" his mother asked.

"No," Tom had said. "Not yet."

But work had to be finished first. They had three people to get decently to their rest that Christmas Eve. And the roads were treacherous and the ground was frozen and everything took longer than it needed to. He'd managed to place one telephone call mid-morning, another around lunchtime. Throughout the day, his father watched his white-knuckled, tight-jawed frustration, and came to a new understanding. When they had pulled in with the hearse at last untenanted, it was already dark, and his father had said, "Do you need to borrow the car, son?"

And Tom had said quite simply, "Thanks."

But now, having actually found her, all his churning feelings—all the fear and guilt and worry—curdle into something else. In the moonlight, she looks ghostly, eyes shadowed and dark, skin as pale as wax. It is so very bloody difficult indeed, he thinks, to care for someone who doesn't care for themselves at all.

"What do I *want*?" he asks. "What do you think I want? I mean, what on earth were you thinking? Disappearing like that. You worried the hell out of us—"

She wraps her arms around herself. "You didn't want me there."

"Well, that's . . ." He shifts his balance, uncomfortable, his anger already fading. "That's not true."

"No, it is," she says. "And I understand. I completely understand, I really do."

And her tone is so sincere that his remaining anger just collapses.

"I didn't want you to *leave*."

"It's all right. It doesn't matter."

"It does." He shivers. "Look, it's cold; do you think I might come in?"

"Better switch off that torch," she says, "before Hermann Göring sees."

He hesitates. She realises that this is not a simple thing for him, to pick up something that's fallen on the ground. Rather than let him feel it, she sweeps up the torch, clicks it off and hands it over, then stands aside to let him in. He slips past her. She closes the door. Her hands are cold, and shaky with the aftermath of adrenaline. She was never going to see him again and now he's here. He was furious with her; it was clear that he was furious. But now he seems concerned, conciliatory. She can't keep up with this.

The kitchen table is washed with moonlight. He stands in front of it, a dark upright line.

"What time is it?" she asks, leaning back against the door.

He peers at luminous watch hands. "Just after seven."

"P.m.?"

"Yes—"

"And," she says, hesitant, "what day?"

"Still Christmas Eve," he says gently.

"I see."

"You left last night. Or early this morning."

She is quite adrift, but he has found her, and she seems calm now, so that's a start. But still he feels like he's three steps behind her, that she's racing away into the darkness, and will soon be completely out of reach. He touches the back of a kitchen chair. "May I?"

"Please."

He sits down, easing out his stiff leg. She stays standing in the shadows by the door. Her face is pale, her body wrapped in a grey coat. He can't make out her expression. He takes off his hat, tugs his cuffs down over his hands.

"Where did you learn to pick a lock?" she asks.

"I didn't," he says. "It wasn't going very well."

A flash of a smile. This gives him hope.

"Please believe me," he says. "I didn't want you to leave, nor did any of my family. On the contrary. If any harm had come to you—"

She moves towards him, into the moonlight; she sits down opposite him. This too seems hopeful. But she's a mess. Her hair a cloud, eyes huge and shadowy, thin hands folded on the tabletop. She's tense and watchful. Which is understandable. He busies himself with his bag, stowing his torch and the awl with which he'd been attempting to pick the lock. He's afraid of giving too much of himself away.

"I don't mind," she says.

"I do. It wasn't easy, I'll admit it. But that doesn't mean—" His voice catches. "It's been months, Charlotte. Months since I last heard from you. All it took was one stupid argument and you cut me dead. And then there you were yesterday, dropped on my doorstep out of a clear blue sky. And I just had to swallow all that down in one big pill, and it stuck a little. It was too much."

"They'd locked me up."

She says it so calmly that it's all the more of a shock. "What?"

She tells him about Francesca, about her father, about Summer Fields. About the treatments. From time to time he whistles softly through his teeth. He'd love more light; he'd love to see her properly. But he begins, he thinks, to understand her now. This is what happens when her father decides that she's been making a nuisance of herself.

"I'm sorry."

Her eyes shimmer, full; she turns her face away from him.

"I thought about you," she says, her voice congested. "While I was in there. I wondered how you were, and what you were doing. I thought about you a lot."

He is afraid his voice will betray him entirely. "It's like a coal mine in here, isn't it. I can hardly see you."

"The electric's off."

"Two ticks. Let's see what we can rustle up."

Glad to have something to do, he fishes out his torch, shines it downward so as not to dazzle her, illuminating a patch of worn chequerboard tiles.

"I'll fix the blackout first," he says.

He closes the blinds, then rummages in cupboards, clinking things around. He returns from the scullery with a paraffin lamp; she can hear the oil slosh as he tips it back and forth to check the fullness.

"Matches?"

She slips hers from a pocket. "Here."

He reaches for them. His fingertips brush her palm.

"Thank you."

"You're welcome."

Her hand falls to her lap; she wraps the other round it. They lie there, curled one inside the other, like a bud. She watches as he scratches up a flame, sets it to the wick and clunks the glass chimney back into place. He takes his seat again. The light is warm on his thin face.

It only now occurs to her: "How did you know where to find me?"

"I was here before, remember," he says. That strange, uneasy day.

"You knew I'd come here?"

"Well, I knew she mattered to you an awful lot." And then he smiles. "Also, I'd already tried everywhere else."

In the lamplight she looks so lovely and so haunted that he has to look away.

"Everywhere?" she asks.

"I telephoned your work. And your digs." The landlady was a little more forthcoming when he told her he'd actually seen Charlotte just the previous day. "Did you know that they'd been burgled, Mrs. Callaghan's, I mean?"

"Oh no. That's awful. Did they lose much?"

"It could have been worse. At least they weren't bombed out."

Warmth begins to flood her cheeks. And if he's spoken to Mrs. Denby, then he'll know she doesn't have a job at all, let alone an essential one.

"I'm sorry," she says. "I would have explained, if I'd had the chance. All I wanted was to talk to you. But he insisted it be done that way."

He frowns. "He?"

"Harris."

"Who's Harris?"

She still doesn't exactly know. "You remember, I told you I was being followed?"

"That man? The one who hurt you?"

"No, that wasn't him. Captain Harris is something else, something official. There's someone leaking at work; something's gone astray. That's why he'd been following me, and that's why he got me out of Summer Fields; he thought I could help him find it."

"And could you?"

"Course not. Not a clue. I never paid enough attention." She pauses for a moment, and he expects some new revelation, but all she says is, "Do you know, I believe I'm dying for a cup of tea."

And this gives him more hope still. He gladly gets to his feet again and limps over to the stove; the cold has got into him now; it makes muscle contract hard, makes tendons shrink and tighten. Makes him all the more self-conscious. He's walking across black-and-terracotta tiles and you'd think he was sailing the high seas.

"Are you hurt?" she asks.

"I'm fine." He tries the gas burner with a match, but it just gives off a tiny pop and ball of blue and then goes out.

"Gas is off too," he says.

"We could try and get a fire going."

"Good, let's. Can I stow the car for a while, though? If I pick up a fine for leaving it out after dark, Mum will lose her nut."

"There'll be keys for the old stable—" And then it occurs to her: "How did you get into the garden?"

"Jimmied the back gate. I'll fix it though. I might be lacking in the lock-picking department, but I can manage that. No one will ever know."

"You didn't think to walk up to the front door and ring the bell?"

"I wasn't sure you'd answer. And the neighbours might have noticed."

"I doubt there are any neighbours left."

Charlotte sends him out into the mews, with the bundle of keys from the hall console. Then she just sits, listening to the voices. They come quietly, from the other side of their door, which stands just ajar. They are talking to each other now, not to her. They are talking about Tom.

Well, you see, the thing about him is . . .

And what matters most is . . .

Because she never really ever before, did she, but now with Tom . . .

They seem, unusually, to be in complete accord, but she can't make out exactly what it is that they're agreeing. She wafts them away, gets up and moves around the kitchen, opening cupboards. She's hungry. Now that she realises it, she has never felt a hunger like this. A jittery, nervous, pleasant kind of hunger. She finds an inch of powdery tea-leaves in a crumpled bag. A can of sardines. A biscuit tin which she levers open to reveal a clutch of lemon puffs. She presses a fingertip into one, and it gives, flaking: only slightly soft. She pops one in her mouth, offers the tin to Tom as he returns. He takes a biscuit, bites, then sets the remaining crescent down on the tabletop.

"They had the gas put in the parlour," she says. "But there's still an open fireplace in the morning room."

He lifts the kettle from the stove and limps over to fill it at the sink. He nods to the biscuits. "That makes it theft now, as well as trespass."

"Oh, I have permission."

"Do you?"

"An open invitation."

"Well, that helps."

"Also they'll never know."

"Cups?"

"I'll get them."

She finds a tray and sets it out with kitchen china, along with food-stuffs and the lamp; the baize door is nudged open with a hip, the weight of it passed to him. He follows her up the corridor, carrying the filled kettle, steadying his way along the wall.

In the morning room, the lamp reveals shuttered windows, furniture shrouded in sheets. She puts the tray down on a low table and carries it over to the fireplace, then drags the dust sheet off the settee, shifts it closer to the fire. He leans over the hearth. There's kindling, and a scuttle half-full of coal.

"Oh, and two ticks." She heads towards the door.

"Where are you going?"

"Just fetching something," she says.

Because it's hard to be still. She feels a stirring inside her that makes her want to stretch, to run, to shake herself like a dog. She leaps up the stairs two at a time. And as she climbs, the sensation grows, till she's split open, her ribs pulled wide, her beating heart exposed.

Dear God, she thinks. What is this?

She pauses on the threshold to El's room, facing the shadows and the shaft of moonlight from the sash window. And so—

Fais comme chez toi. And there's a warmth and ease to El's voice that she hasn't heard in an age.

Charlotte drags the quilt and blanket from El's bed, bundles them up and carries them downstairs. At the drawing-room door, she pauses. Mr. and Mrs. Hartwell were never big tipplers, but . . . she dumps the covers on the floor and heads straight for the sideboard, lifts the dust sheet aside. A bottle of green ginger wine, considered by them to be medicinal. It's a third full. Bingo. She scoops up two liqueur glasses, manages to gather up the blankets again and carry everything through to the morning room.

Which is quite transformed. It glows. Tom kneels beside the fire, adding coals to the flames. She drops the covers over the back of the settee, sets the glasses and bottle on the table beside the lamp. Light catches in the green bottle, on the glasses' ruby stems and gilded rims. She sits on the floor beside him.

"Not tea then, after all?" he asks.

She grins. "We can have both."

He will remember this throughout his life, usually when things are at their most tangled and difficult. The straightforwardness with which she just sat beside him then, so close that her shoulder brushed his arm, just as they had sat together on cold benches all that autumn. The way it had felt at once astonishing and comfortable and right. It was so new to him, the excitement and the ease; he didn't know then that it could not be replicated. He did not know then that it was so rare as to be unique.

She uncorks the bottle, pours the ginger wine and slides a glass towards him. He shifts to take it, winces.

"You are hurt," she says.

"It's just the cold."

"But it hurts you?"

He makes a face. "It makes things more difficult."

"Then we'd better get you warm."

She gets to her feet in one enviably easy movement. She reaches out a hand, ripples her fingers for him, and then, when he just looks at it unmoving, she closes and opens her hand. *Come on.*

He takes her right hand in his left. His senses shift entirely to the pressure of her grip. He doesn't want to be helped. He stumbles to his feet, not letting her bear his weight. Good for her, that she has this grace and strength, but he won't lean on it.

He lets go of her, moves around, and sinks onto the settee. Flame licks from the kindling; the coals begin to catch. The kettle sits unused on the hearth. She lays a quilt over his shoulders, moves their glasses closer, then sits beside him.

"Thank you," he says.

"Do you remember, you were cross with me," she says, "when you said I thought I was all alone with things?"

"What do you mean?"

"Well, you're always helping me," she says, lifting her glass, "but you won't take any help yourself."

"I've had a bellyful," he says. "I've had a lifetime. I'm sick of it."

"No *quid pro quo* then? If you dish it out, don't you have to take it?"

He laughs and shakes his head. "There are no rules," he says. "It's entirely ad hoc. I'm just making it up as I go along."

"Quite right too."

She sips green ginger wine, swallows, and he can hear the wet in her mouth. His body stirs shamefully. This is not need, he tells himself, this is want; he should know the difference; and he won't die for wanting.

She toes off her battered tennis shoes, curls her legs up on the settee, tugs the spare blanket around her own shoulders. Her stockinged feet are tucked there, right beside him. It would be naturalness itself to open out his quilt and wrap her in it too, to share their warmth. He would do that for a friend. For Fliss. It would make more sense than just sitting like this, separately, her leaning away against the arm of the settee. He keeps thinking that he's going to do it; he can see it so clearly, as if it's a memory rather than a possibility, his arm lifting up the cover, Charlotte shuffling closer and being enveloped in warmth; but he doesn't move, just stares at the fire, the red coals and crumbling ash, and sips the sweet burning wine, and feels its warmth spread through him.

Then she yawns, so wide that her jaw creaks; she pulls the blanket up to her chin, shuffles around, restless, unable to get comfortable. "Excuse me." She slides her legs out behind him, spreads her blanket over her lap; he is acutely aware of the silk and warmth of her.

"Well," he says, and gets to his feet.

"Oh."

"Good night." He does lay his quilt over her now. "I'll come back in the morning, see how you're getting on."

She rolls her head against the arm of the settee. She looks sweet and sleepy. "Don't go."

He has to. He looks away. "I could find an armchair."

"It's too cold," she says. "You'll freeze."

Oh come on! El says.

I'll be good. I promise.

I'll believe it when I see it.

It's Tom. I couldn't hurt Tom.

Nonsense. You already have.

"The cold's not good for you, you said so."

I'll behave myself.

Oh for goodness' sake.

She says, "Stay with me."

His eyes go wide.

"I mean—I just don't want you to go. I don't want—anything—from you." A nervous laugh. "I just want you to be here. Please. Stay. We can keep each other warm. That's all."

He makes a small movement as if to leave, but his mind and body now seem to have fallen out entirely; they are no longer speaking to each other. He clicks his tongue. Then he sinks back down on the end of the sofa at her feet. He unknots his tie. He undoes his cuffs and loosens his collar. He slips off his belt and, still in shirt, sweater and trousers, sits down at the far end of the sofa. He lifts his left leg up onto the settee, and then, with a trembling numb effort, obliges the right leg to join it. He does it all as if an automaton; if he were to let himself think about what's happening, he'd be unable to move at all. Now, he lies rigid, his heart racing. She shifts the quilt and blanket so that the two of them are covered with both, then she turns on her side, away from him, facing the back of the settee.

"Will that do?" she asks, muffled.

"Yes."

"Do you have enough space?"

"Plenty."

"Warm enough?"

"Yes. Thank you." He sounds ridiculously formal.

He remains rigidly awake. He can see the curve of her shoulder and neck, the delicate curls regrowing at her nape. He remembers that first time, in Russell Square, when she'd walked right up to him, so vibrant and so lovely, and he'd assumed that she'd go skimming past, had not for a moment thought she would ever stop and actually talk to him. And now there she is. So close that they are almost touching; the covers hold their collective warmth. Her breathing slows. He reaches for the lamp and blows it out. He rests his head back, closes his eyes. His parents will be worried. But they are always worried. This, at last, seems worth the worry.

There is no way, he thinks, that he will get a wink of sleep.

She is strapped down; she can't move; they will slide the needle in. They will smash holes into her brain. They will break her up to pieces just to put her back together again and she won't even know which bits of her are missing.

She gasps awake in darkness.

But there is peace, warmth; someone softly breathes beside her.

And she remembers. She cranes her head to look; that's his delicate right arm thrown over her ankles. His head is pillowed on her eiderdown-wrapped feet. She is not strapped down; she is held. Her heart slows. This is good, she thinks. This, in fact, is perfect.

In the dark, the room begins to take shape around her. There are flecks of red in the hearth. The bottle and glasses catch a little light. She can feel the swell and sink of his chest.

Then the glint of a luminous watch.

"It's midnight," he says. "You're quite safe. Go back to sleep."

When she wakes a second time, there is a greyness to the room which means it's day outside. The light seeps through from the hallway where the blackout isn't up. She shifts round to him; he looks back at her, rumpled and soft with sleep.

Remember.

I do. I said I would be good and I was good and I am good and I will be good. I promise.

He lies there as though this moment were made of glass and to move or even breathe too deeply might make everything shatter. All the household clocks have run down to silence.

"Morning," she says, pushing herself up to seated.

"Morning," he says. "Merry Christmas."

"Oh goodness, yes; Merry Christmas. I forgot."

He sits up, teeth gritted.

"You all right?"

"I'll be fine," he says. "Once I get moving."

She holds herself back. His shirt is open at the neck, and she can see the curve of his throat and the dip in his collarbone and the shift of muscle under skin.

"We never made that cup of tea," he says, getting to his feet.

He lowers himself stiffly down at the hearth, busies himself with the embers and the kettle.

"We're here in her house, but I don't really know anything about your friend."

"El?"

"Yes. I mean, obviously we've spoken about her, but not really about *her*. What was she like?"

"Ha. El." Charlotte rubs her face. "She was . . . well, she was the best."

He smiles round at her.

"And I mean it. Just the best. Utterly loyal, but completely unreliable. Clever. Funny. Always just entirely herself. And *good* at life; good at being alive in the world. And it's just so bloody awful that she's gone."

"You loved her."

"Yes." Her nose prickles.

"You were friends since you were girls?"

Her brows knit. She doesn't answer. Her thoughts slide off and away to Regent's Park in September, the day before El died. *Sweets till we're sick, cigarettes smoked out the window, and scaring ourselves witless with ghost stories.* And then El had said, *I was thinking more gin and confidences.*

Charlotte's suddenly struggling to her feet; the covers fall away.

"What is it?"

She wades over the fallen blankets, tugging her skirt straight, retucking her blouse and yanking her sweater down. "Excuse me—"

"Are you all right?"

"I just remembered."

"Remembered what?"

"About El."

There you go, you clever girl. I knew you'd get there in the end.

She runs up the stairs. The landing is flooded with pale light; it fills El's room too; the blind is up, only the bones of the tree screening the window. Charlotte remembers sweets and chewing gum and scribbled notes and crushes and plaits dangling over scrapbooks. She remembers cigarettes and matches, bobbed hair, lipstick and eyeblack. She remembers leaning out of the open sash to fling dog-ends like fireworks into the night. She remembers shoes kicked off and stockings rolled down and earrings unhooked and set aside, gowns dropped to the floor and stepped out of, pyjamas pulled on, bottles of gin and glasses lifted clinking, an inch poured in each; the two of them reclining on pillows, seventeen years old and ever so sophisticated, and if Mrs. H ever found out what was going on, there would be hell to pay, so everything—the notes, gum, lipstick, eyeblack, matches, cigarettes, gin and smeary glasses—was stashed away before they crashed into sleep, where El's mother wouldn't find them, not in a million billion years.

Charlotte shunts the bed out of the way, then scans the floor— Lily'd be for the high jump if Mrs. Hartwell were to see these tumbleweeds of dust—for the board that's shorter than all the others; the one with a knothole. The secret stash. There. She dips a finger in, and lifts the plank away.

I knew you'd get there in the end.

An envelope.

It has El's careless open handwriting on the front, the loops and dashes of Charlotte's own name. She lifts it out. She holds a letter from her friend. But there's something else there too, between the laths.

No sweets now, no make-up or gin bottles. Just a small round tin. She picks it out. It sits in her palm with an uneasy familiarity. She clicks it open. Inside is one of the clever rubber devices that saves a girl from certain consequences. And there, too, lying on the boards, is the accompanying tube of Volpar gel. They are not easily achieved, these items, not by an unmarried woman; they do not come cheap.

I hope you had more actual fun than I did, El.

She puts the tin back. Turns the letter over in her hands again.

"What's that you've got there?" Tom asks.

He leans against the doorjamb, hair falling in his eyes, jacket pulled on over open-necked shirt. She feels a deep pleasure-pain, teasing and delicious. It's dull, being wanted; it's always the same. But this, this tug of desire; it's keen, it's compelling.

She raises the envelope. "From El. She left it for me."

"Blimey." He pushes away from the doorjamb, but doesn't move towards her. "I'll go out for a while, shall I, leave you in peace? I need to telephone home anyway."

"Use theirs."

"It's dead."

"There'll be a front door key on that bunch."

"Right you are then. Take your time."

Outside, the world is radiant. Frost sparkles. Fine flakes fall from the trees and catch the light. He walks down the pavement, enjoying the quiet, the way the cold air makes his nose tingle. Telephone boxes are rare creatures in wealthy neighbourhoods, where anyone who wants one has a telephone of their own, but he marches on contentedly. The world is different today. No less difficult, no less treacherous and slippery. But more vivid. In sharper focus.

He takes a turn for the High Street. The last time he had been in that poor Hartwell girl's room, she was lying on the bed, fully clothed and covered with a single blanket, as though taking a nap. At the time, he had been struck by the wrongness of it; of her perfect stillness, and of their presence in her room. She should have flung aside the cover, leaped to her feet, shocked, *outraged,* to find Tom and his father intruding there. But instead it was they who had lifted, then folded the blanket, and the two of them had moved her into her coffin. He remembers the weight of her cold flesh, her calves in his hands. However sad it had ever been before, however distressing, this was the first time that dealing with the dead had not seemed right. Perhaps because it was one of the first Blitz bodies he'd had to deal with. Perhaps he wasn't at all inured to it by then. Or perhaps it was a premonition, of how much it would come to matter to him, this one death; the woman who was loved by the woman he'd go and fall in love with.

Because that is it, he thinks. That's what I've gone and done. And what on earth am I supposed to do about that now?

On the High Street, two grey-painted phone boxes stand side by side. The usual red must be too vulgar and conspicuous for this part of town. He yanks the door open, wedges it with his right foot and swings himself in. He tucks the receiver against his jaw, feeds in coins and dials the code, then his home phone number. After the usual clicks and buzzes, his father picks up at the other end. Tom jabs at the button.

"Find her then?" his father asks.

In the phone box, all by himself, he grins. "I did."

"Everything all right?"

"I think so, yes."

"Good. Will you be back for your dinner?"

"I don't know yet. Is Mum climbing the walls?"

"Don't you worry about your mother. You do what you need to do, my lad. I need you back first thing on Friday is all; we're booked solid till New Year."

The Most Love Always

Dearest girl,

I am perfectly wretched that you're reading this. I'd hoped I'd have the chance to tear it up and burn it in the fire. But since you have this letter in your hands, things can't have gone that way.

Having found this, you will also have found my device. Its use was begun too late and inconsistently for it to serve. I want you to know that I was not unlucky, or led astray. I was foolish, yes; but I was also a willing and active participant in my own disgrace.

If I'd confessed my situation to you today, as we rambled round the park, I know that you would have tried to help. You always do. You would have come up with some scheme. You'd have us playing at war widows in some cottage by the sea, bringing up baby between us. Or you would have insisted on coming with me tonight. You'd have held my hand. But I don't want to be helped. I don't want company. I don't want to implicate you in the crime. And I don't want to be forgiven. I simply cannot bear to have my life, much less yours, sideswiped by this, while he can just walk away from it whistling and scot-free.

Mother doesn't want me going out at all this evening; she says it's not worth the risk. But life goes on, I tell her; it must go on, especially for the young. If we don't live our lives as best we can, then the enemy has already won. But I'm lying to her again, just as I have been lying to her for months. This is not a date I'm going on. He has made me an appointment, he has given me the money. I am assured that a medically trained person is waiting to relieve me of my difficulty. I do not know if they are man or woman, a doctor, nurse, a dentist or a vet. But I hope to walk away myself, not whistling, and far from scot-free, but knowing that it's over; that part of it at least.

Anyway. You've found the letter. You've read it. And so I never got the chance to tear it to pieces and burn it in the fire. And we never got to go to

Galloway, to swim and hike and raid the wine cellar. I'm sorry. I'm sorry that I left you with this, Lotts; with whatever it's like to lose a best friend. However shabbily I have treated you these last few months, I always thought we'd have each other forever. I messed that up. Usually it's you who's the disaster, so you can enjoy that at least, that in the end it was me who made the worst show of things. You're going to have to do something brilliant with your life now, Lotts, to make up for mine. I wish I could see you, before I have to grit my teeth and go through this. I miss you. This letter will be waiting for you, just in case; there's that small comfort, that you might understand at least why I'm gone, and why I couldn't say, and that I didn't want to leave you. You'll know where to find it.

The most love always
From your friend,
El.

Charlotte reads it the first time, breath held, eyes roving back and forth and up and down for the sharpest, brightest bits of information. The second time, she reads it steadily, greedy for her friend's voice, eyes welling and quickly wiped.

So this is what you had to do that evening, instead of gin and confidences. This was the knot in your forehead. This is why your head was full of flies.

But El does not reply.

Charlotte folds the letter. She slips it back into the envelope. She gets up from the floor, goes downstairs. Tom has returned already; he has opened the shutters in the morning room; the light through the high windows is cool and pale; the fire crackles in the grate and the kettle gives off a steady steam.

He sees her, comes towards her, with a look of sharp concern.

Charlotte presses her eyes, sinks down on the edge of the settee.

She can see it: the cottage by the sea; she and El playing at war widows; it would not have seemed a sacrifice to her. Or she would have gone with El that evening, if she'd been wanted; she'd have held El's hand through the blood and pain. She'd have taken on the risk; she'd have lied and lied and lied and lied and lied for her. And she'd even have accepted that El didn't want to be stopped or helped; she'd have waited steadily for a time when El did want her again. She'd have done whatever El had needed, whenever El had needed it, if she'd been given half a chance. El must have realised this. So what Charlotte still doesn't understand is why she was not allowed to know. It's not as though you love a person any less for making a mistake.

"She was in trouble," Charlotte says. "The kind of trouble only unmarried women can get into."

"Oh." His face goes red.

"She . . . had something done about it."

"I've seen that," he says. "I've seen the . . . consequences."

She looks up at him. She asks, tentative, "What's it like?"

He sits down beside her. He takes her hand. He doesn't want to say. "Please."

"It's always different," he says. "And it's always the same."

"Tell me."

"One woman, I remember, she left half a dozen kids; they were all lined up on the one bed, watching us, as we . . . They ended up at the Foundling Hospital. Their dad just wasn't up to it, with her gone. Another one, there was just a girl lying cold and a small suitcase in a lodging room. The landlady spitting venom."

"There'd be, I imagine—there'd be a lot of blood?"

"Sometimes. Sometimes it's infection."

There are other cases too, dozens, scores of women that they'd buried, on insurance and on charity. Their pale unblemished corpses.

"But what's the same is the fear," he says. "Every time. Whatever took them, whoever's left to mourn, it's the fear that is the same."

After a moment, Charlotte says, "It doesn't stand now, does it? What they said about how El died."

He isn't far behind her: "The paperwork was quite correct."

The kettle begins to sing. He lifts the teapot lid and pours leaves from the packet. Charlotte watches him retrieve the bubbling kettle with a folded cloth. He fills the pot.

"Mrs. Hartwell laid her out, you said. Did her make-up. All of that."

Tom wafts that aside. "The doctor, though." Tom leans to set the kettle on the hearth, sits in beside her. "If it ever came out. He'd be struck off. If he lied, just to cover something up."

"An old family friend though. At the end of his career."

Tom shakes his head, gives a low, breathy whistle.

"Or maybe not lied," Charlotte concedes, remembering the old soldier, too tired for this new fight. Knuckling his eyes, swigging vile coffee. "He said he knew what'd happened to her at a glance. So maybe that's all he did."

"What?"

"Glance."

"Christ."

Charlotte closes her eyes. She sees Lily nudging into El's bedroom with a breakfast tray that Sunday, wishing her good morning. No response. Sets the tray down to open the blind, lifts it again and turns, and sees, in morning light, El lying strangely still. The tray falls, china smashes; a scream. Mrs. Hartwell hurries in, tying her dressing gown; a cry; the rush to help, to revive; but the body, touched, is cold. The blankets, pulled back, are deep in blood. Call the doctor—and then distress blooms into fear—no, wait—no. Strip the bed, soak those sheets. Bring soap and water. Wash her down and change her clothes. Get that feather-bed out of here. And take away those breakfast things. All this in panic and through tears. And then knocking on the front door—ignore it. *Ignore it.* More knocking. No. Go, Lily. Tell them that we're not at home.

And once it was done, the tidying up of El, and the sending of Charlotte on her way, Mrs. Hartwell had gone down to the telephone, and placed a call to Dr. Travers at the hospital. They've just brought her home, my darling girl; she was caught out in a raid; there was nothing they could do. And he, blinkered by trust, and by experience, and to spare them any further grief, had come straight there from the worst night of his life, to write out the death certificate.

Or he was complicit in the lie. Charlotte remembers the two of them, Mrs. Hartwell and Dr. Travers, heads together, conspiratorial, at the funeral. Whether it was error or deceit, she finds she can't blame him: knowing the truth hasn't helped a bit.

Either way, the relief, as Mrs. Hartwell watched him uncap his pen, must have tasted bitter.

To learn that much about your child, and to know you'd lost her in the same moment. To exploit the loyalty or trust of an old friend, and jeopardise his reputation. Then to live with the fear of discovery, both of the scandal and the lie. No wonder; no wonder any of it. No wonder Mrs. Hartwell had been so steely afterwards—not just grieving, but also angry and afraid. No wonder she'd go to any lengths to get Charlotte to stop asking questions.

Charlotte presses her eyes. She recalls Janet's wrists draped in old lace, her joy at the prospect of a sticky bun with a friend, all her other hours sucked into a pit of poverty and privation; Saskia's wheedling voice from behind the apartment door, the drink and the carelessness and the casual unkindness; Vanessa's black-and-white photograph sliding from a stack of newspapers, an image of someone she had hardly known, of someone who really had nothing to do with her at all. Those wildly disparate lives. She sees the dark shape dragging itself out of the blackout, which had, in the light of an incendiary, become just a ratty little man with a moustache. And the shadow man himself resolving into the very solid Harris, his thick hands on the steering wheel as he sped her away from Summer Fields; these had turned out to be the safest hands of all. And she begins to understand, and as she understands, all the pieces she has been trying to fit together turn to smoke and twist away.

Tom pours tea, hands her a cup; she takes it, thanks him.

"They're not connected," she says.

"What?"

"El, Janet, Vanessa, Saskia. Their deaths are not connected."

"Aren't they?"

"Well, they are, yes. But only by me. I'm not the cause, I'm just what they have in common. I should have seen it sooner. I should have seen it ages ago. That this is just what happens. This is the price you pay."

"You mean in war?"

"No. I mean, for love."

"Love?"

"I mean, it's a big stupid risk, isn't it?" she says. "It's easily the most stupid, risky thing that you can ever do, is love someone."

"Do you think so?"

"It is. It always is. There's this whole other being who's also at the same time a piece of you, and they're out there just wandering around in the world and anything could happen to them. Because people are just so bloody fragile. People are so easily damaged. So easily broken. And you can't do a thing about it; you can't keep them safe. So why would you go and love someone when they can just . . ."

She pauses. Her eyes are shining. She doesn't look at him.

"And because it hurts so terribly, when you lose someone, you think it has to mean something. It can't just be pointless and stupid and awful—and that's what I was doing, I was trying to make it mean something, when really it doesn't mean anything at all."

And then her eyes close, tears run. She covers her mouth and crumples into him; she sobs. He holds her, feels the warmth and softness of wool and the sharpness of her bones beneath her clothes and the press of her against his chest and the way she's shuddering. He feels the weight of it all. The tenderness. The responsibility. He does not feel at all adequate to this, but he holds her till she stops shaking.

She moves away. She wipes her face. Touches the damp on his jacket. "I'm sorry."

He tries to speak, has to clear his throat: "You don't need to be sorry."

"No, I do. I've been unkind."

"You haven't. Not at all."

"No, I have, and I'm sorry, I've been stupid and careless and unkind."

"You've been sad, and preoccupied, and misled, you've been lied to; that doesn't make you any of those other things."

She touches his cheek. His eyes go wide. This makes her smile. "Thank you," she says. She leans in, and she kisses him.

He startles. Then he closes his eyes. For a moment, there is just this. The warm touch of their lips. When she moves away, he opens his eyes. His smile is soft, lopsided; it pulls at her. She, still raw with tears, smiles back.

"Hello," he says.

"Hello."

They don't know what else to say to each other. They both laugh and turn away.

And not a word from El. Or from anybody else.

They set the morning room to rights between them, shunting and lifting the settee and table back into place, wafting the dust sheets over the furniture again. Each small domestic exchange is imbued with novelty and promise, as though they're children playing house.

She rakes the ashes through and carries them outside, returns the bottle of ginger wine to the parlour and brings the glasses through to be washed. She leans against the kitchen table, watching as he soaps and rinses the glasses and teacups, then dries them. She is filled with the clarity that sometimes follows tears.

"I'll have to go to the police now," she says.

"Can you?"

He passes the cups and glasses to her, one by one, his left hand to her right, and she hangs the cups from their hooks and sets the glasses down on the table. How astonishing it is, he thinks, to be happy, with the world the way it is.

"That man, in the blackout. They need to know about him."

"But what about your dad?"

"I'll send a letter. An anonymous tip-off."

"Good."

She goes to put the liqueur glasses back where they belong, then climbs the stairs with the covers bundled in her arms and remakes El's bed. She tucks it in neatly, smoothing down the covers.

Who was it, El? she asks. Who did you fall for so hard? Who was it that made you always too busy to see me? Who walked away whistling and scot-free?

She puts El's tennis shoes back in the wardrobe, tucks the laces in. Then she peers under the bed, to make sure the loose board is lying flush with the others. She blows dust clots over the bare plank. El's secrets can rest there undisturbed, until the house is atomised or burned to cinders; or, if better times should ever come, until other children grow up here, and hunt out hidey-holes and secret places, and are baffled to find a perished rubber Dutch cap and rusted tube of spermicide beneath their bedroom floor.

Charlotte gets back to her feet and goes to the window.

One last smoke for old times' sake. What do you say, El?

But El does not reply.

"I've never been in a hearse before," she says, sinking into the leather seat.

"Most people only do it the once."

He drives well, his frail right hand sufficient to steady the wheel while he changes gear with his left. They glide through the quiet streets. It has a stateliness, this car, unlike the rattling Austin Ruby that had strained for speed along the country lanes. To think that was only two days ago; it seems like a lifetime. In the spring, Charlotte will turn twenty-one, but gaining her majority will make no difference. She will have to steer clear of her father forever if she is to stay out of Summer Fields. It is good, she realises, to have a straightforward reason to never see him again.

They drive on in silence, he remembering the boy she was in slacks and trilby, the cropped head and burst lip. She had wanted to pass as someone else, to find another way to be. And she was already living in cheap digs and working as a stenographer when he met her. She didn't have to live like that, if she hadn't wanted to. She chose it all. And she chose him. It really is Christmas now.

The car glides along Woodland Road. The gaping hole where a hundred and twenty-two used to be is now fenced off, and sloping walls shored up with timbers. Her eyes fill. She presses her lips tight.

"What is it?" Tom asks.

All this time, her own voice whispering at her to kill herself. All this time, when desperate millions were battling to keep on going for another day.

"Charlotte?"

She finds a handkerchief. She presses her eyes and nose, but the tears keep coming.

"What is it, Charlotte?" He touches her arm. "Is it too much? If it's too much, you don't have to. I can just take you home."

She shakes her head, gives a hiccupping sob.

"What's wrong?"

Her chin dimples dangerously, but she steels herself and says, "I'm all right. Thank you. I'm all right."

"Shall we go in?" he asks.

She checks her face in her compact, tuts at the state of herself, does her best to tidy her distress away.

"I want to be different," she says.

"In what way?"

"All kinds of ways."

"Don't be too different," he says. "Please."

She rings the bell and waits. Tom stands at her shoulder, right hand pocketed, his left hand moving instinctively to check and tidy. He straightens his tie, touches his hat and collar, brushing his lapels, and then, thinking again, takes his hat off. He couldn't feel more awkward if this were a first visit to new in-laws.

There are hasty footfalls inside and then the door is flung wide: Mrs. Callaghan stands there, wrapped for the occasion in a festive cherry-red cardigan, delight dawning, arms opening to receive Charlotte.

"Oh, my darling. Oh, my wee dote. Come here till I see you."

"Mrs. C."

Charlotte takes two halting steps and is received into Mrs. Callaghan's embrace.

"I can't stay," Charlotte mumbles into wool. "Father, and Francesca; if they found out—"

"You'll stay a wee while," Mrs. Callaghan says, rubbing her back. "You'll stay for a cup of tea."

Mr. Gibbons comes down the stairs. "Hello there."

Charlotte lifts her face to him, and grins.

He rolls from toe to heel and back again, hands clasped behind his back, beaming. "I am glad to see you."

"You'll be the chap who telephoned. Well done." Mrs. Callaghan winks at Tom over Charlotte's shoulder. She gives Charlotte an extra squeeze, lets go. "He your young man, then?"

Charlotte turns to catch his eye.

"I think he might be, Mrs. C. If he doesn't mind."

They sit in at the kitchen table. Charlotte and Tom staunchly refuse a share of the scanty Christmas dinner Mrs. Callaghan has got boiling soft and parching dry on and in the stove. They accept a cup of tea, with a dab of milk, which seems strain enough to put on anyone's household. The news is scanty too: Mr. Gibbons has been moved onto day shifts at the warehouse, and Mrs. Callaghan's sister has not only survived the bombing but has become a grandmother.

"What about the burglary, Mrs. C? That must have been awful."

"There really wasn't that much took," she says. "And, thankfully, Mr. Gibbons is back on days now, so I do feel a lot safer in my bed. Or in a deckchair in the kitchen, more often than not."

"Would you mind if I went up and collected my things? While we've got the car here."

"Oh—"

"If you have them packed away somewhere, I don't mind hunting them out."

"No, but—"

"Only I've been travelling rather light. I'm afraid it must show. I've been living in these same clothes for I don't know how long."

"Oh, my dear, I'm sorry. All your things have gone."

"Gone? You mean in the burglary?"

"No, it was before that. Your sister; she stripped the room quite bare."

Everything she owned. Everything she'd worked for. Her books. Her Olivetti. All her clothes. Without so much as a by-your-leave. But with the clear assumption that her feelings on the matter were irrelevant. It is a blow.

Mr. Gibbons clears his throat. "I have a few bits and pieces I can spare," he says, "if that's any help."

"You," Charlotte says, "really are an angel."

· · ·

"Your mother, though," Charlotte says to Tom, back in the car, as they now face the immediate prospect of returning there.

"She'll be fine."

"No, I mean, she shouldn't have to put up with me."

"It's not you. It's nothing particularly about you. It'd be the same with anyone."

The hearse creeps down Woodland Road, and turns left onto Gipsy Hill. There's no traffic, but the gradient is steep, and the surface black with ice.

"The imposition, having a stranger in the house?"

"Not even that." He keeps his eyes on the road. He has long known this but never articulated it before: "It's me."

"You?"

She watches him; he watches the road, adjusts his steering, changes gear.

"She's on guard." There's a pragmatism about the way he says it, but there's also a stiffness; this is difficult for him.

"Against what?"

"She wants to keep me safe," he says. "But she's beginning to realise that she can't. And that's hard going for her."

She looks down at her folded hands, her bright but soft blue gloves. They drive on in silence for a while, sweeping through the quiet, damaged city. She feels as though she has been handed something infinitely precious and fragile. She is not sure that she can take proper care of it.

"What'll we do?" she asks.

"She'll get over it."

She can feel her cheeks begin to burn. "I mean, about us."

"You're asking *me*?"

"Yes."

"I don't know." And there's an edge to his tone which unsettles her. "I'm a total novice at this. This was not on my agenda. I haven't got the foggiest idea."

A Season for Dying

Midwinter into early spring; that always used to be our busiest time of year. Anyone old or weak or ill, that's the lowest ebb, that's when they're most likely to slip away."

She takes the last plate off him, wipes it dry.

"So there's a season," she says. "Like with asparagus. Or blackberries."

"There used to be," he says. "But not any more. Now people die out of season; midwinter is no different to June."

He slips a pan into the water; they watch the suds bubble in.

She thinks, I am happy, right now, in this moment. Just us, in the scullery, talking about anything at all, and taking forever to do the washing-up. His rolled sleeve by hers, their hands moving in tandem, sometimes touching, the door closed on the belting-hot kitchen, where Mrs. Hawthorne sits and knits and keeps an ear out for whatever the young people might be getting up to. They get up to nothing, and keep on getting up to nothing; their behaviour has been *impeccable,* Charlotte thinks, accenting it in the French way in her thoughts, as though addressing it to El. It cannot be pecked. So, see, El: I can be good, if I put my mind to it. But El isn't replying, nor are the other voices; the door is closed, and though she catches murmuring, the odd phrase, nobody says a word to her.

"Ask her if she'd like more tea," Tom suggests.

"Okey-dokey."

Charlotte carries the stacked plates through to the kitchen. She arranges them carefully on the dresser, while Mrs. Hawthorne, sitting with her feet on the fender, knits something in a lovely soft plum-coloured wool. She feels the cold, Mrs. Hawthorne; her hands go white and numb; that's why the kitchen is kept tropically warm, and why it is always safe to escape to the freezing scullery; she won't follow anyone out there, unless she really has to. The china is thick, and a queasy Germolene pink, but Mrs. Hawthorne treasures it, having made up her collection piece by piece since her marriage, and so Charlotte treats it with a tentative respect.

"Thomas asks would you like another cup," Charlotte says, as she finishes setting out the plates. She glances round. Mrs. Hawthorne is watching her closely; she now drops her eyes back to her knitting, and counts stitches.

"No, thank you."

Whatever Tom says, Mrs. Hawthorne does not seem to be getting over anything at all.

The bombing resumes, and Tom's work intensifies; he still has shifts firewatching, and has college and essays and lab time, and now he also has Charlotte just *there;* it keeps him in a fizzy, unsettled, unresolvable state. He is happy, but it is not comfortable; it is not easy. They barely touch; they barely have a moment privately; his thoughts are scattered and his sleep is destroyed. At night, knowing that she lies alone just up that short flight of stairs, he levers himself around on his lumpy mattress and fights with the blankets. They cannot go on like this, and yet he cannot think how things could change for the better. Marriage is impossible. The idea that she might commit herself to him—crippled, only a meagre scholarship to his name, and with an uncertain future ahead of him—is beyond ridiculous. And any other kind of love is equally impossible. Naturally, it crosses, in fact it lingers in his mind, but only as a tormenting guilty dream. If the world could pause, and stay like this, in this strange abeyance, so that he can pass her on the stairs, or stand beside her at the scullery sink, or walk with her to the grocers and catch her hand and hold it for a while, that would be sufficient. Even if it destroys his sleep and nerves. It's not perfect, but what is perfect in this world? If the world could pause at this, he would, he tells himself, be content.

But the world spins on.

Planes rumble overhead as they bed down in the hallway. The tiles are ice; a draught rages under the door and up the stairs. Charlotte curls up on her pallet, in blankets safety-pinned together to form a bag. Her designated place is near the front door, just next to Fliss, who chatters away nervously, and grabs at Charlotte's arm whenever something gets too close. Nell, who unlike Lady Jane seems oblivious to the thunder, likes to amble around in circles before settling down between the girls with a harrumph. The dog's breath is dreadful, but she is stolid and warm and keeps the draughts at bay. Tom lies on the other side of his parents, at the foot of the stairs. Mrs. Hawthorne says it's because it's harder for him to make his way through the sleepers if he has to get up in the night.

But Charlotte sleeps now, extraordinarily; the dog, often as not, curled in the crook of her knees, and the family cat sometimes a slight weight on her blanket. She sleeps deep and when something wakes her—a close call; the morning's stirring—it is always from the same dream: a blank black room with a patch of empty light, and voices from behind a door that's now completely shut. A murmuring. They are talking to each other quite intently, the voices; they pay no attention to her at all. She knows they are talking about El's lover, the man who kept her too busy to see her friends. The man who made the appointment, gave her the money, and sent her here, to the blank black room and the closed door.

El, she thinks. El? Are you there?

Why didn't you ever tell me about him?

Not at the start, when you were happy? Not at the end, when it all went to pieces?

Were you ashamed of him?

She waits, but El doesn't speak to her; the voices just murmur on.

Was it the grocer's boy? Your father's foreman? Was it a married man?

Because you know I've been as bad. I've probably been worse. You know because I've told you. All that gin, all those confidences. How we've roared and sobbed at my missteps. I would never have begrudged you yours. You know that, surely?

But not to tell me. Not even in your letter. When it no longer mattered if I knew.

Unless it does still matter.

Unless—

That afternoon in Regent's Park. You were exhausted and out-of-sorts. At the time, I just thought you were overworked, suggested that you talk to my father about changing roles. And you said you wouldn't dream of asking him.

Then I said: Just you wait till he wants something off *you*.

And you just went silent. You didn't say a word.

Charlotte shivers.

You didn't, did you, El?

El?

You wouldn't, would you? It wasn't him; please say it wasn't him.

From behind the door now, there is utter silence. El does not reply.

I never really told you what he was like.

It took me too long to work it out myself. It took me years.

I am sorry. If he's what happened to you. I am sorry.

It is surprising, Mrs. Hawthorne observes, how much time off Charlotte has, given the nature of her job. Charlotte can only agree. It is not only surprising, it is unrealistic. It is becoming clear that this situation cannot be sustained. She is in limbo. She has no income, no work, no references with which to seek work; she daren't draw money from her bank, in case it also draws her family's attention. She has only one mauve-and-grey ten-bob note and a handful of coins left in her purse after contributing to the housekeeping, and that's due again on Friday. The voices are ignoring her; they just murmur together behind that door. Her sense of purpose has deserted her too; there was no great mystery, no meaning, and so now she must just accept the chaos, and that's far harder to face. El and her father; her father and El; she keeps sidling up on this thought and shying away from it again.

She'll have to enlist, she thinks. She just hasn't decided where. The Land Army, or factory work, the ATS, the WRNS, or she could join the WAAF and learn to fly. Any one of them, though, could send her to the other end of the country, and she can't bear the thought of that.

But she has to do something; she can't presume upon the Hartwells' goodwill forever.

"Ah, Miss Richmond, there you are," Mrs. Hawthorne says, pausing halfway up the stairs, looking up at Charlotte on the landing. Angled thus, she becomes smooth-faced and lovely, the girl she once was, despite the silver wing of hair.

"Charlotte, please," Charlotte says yet again, standing aside to let Mrs. Hawthorne come up. "Or Lottie. Or Lotts. I really don't mind." Just not Lolo.

But Mrs. Hawthorne, who is clutching her plum-coloured knitting, stands aside herself and waits.

"I wonder if you'd give me a moment of your time," she says.

"Of course." Charlotte hastens down to her.

Mrs. Hawthorne ushers her to the front parlour. The room is full and uprightly furnished, with a card table, upholstered wing chairs, a baby's tears plant trailing from a stand. The walls are greenish, cluttered with prints; there's a studio photograph of two Victorian ancestors over the fireplace. This can't be good, Charlotte thinks. One can't be asked into rooms like this and it be good.

"The light is better here," Mrs. Hawthorne explains.

"I see."

Charlotte doesn't see at all. She stands just inside the door. No question of making oneself comfortable here.

Mrs. Hawthorne must know, Charlotte thinks; she must have found out. Not only about the lies and deception; she knows about what kind of person Charlotte is, or was; she knows about the Dutch cap and the Volpar gel and all the things that she has done and been, and that she is tainted and will taint everything she touches and so must go. Must stay away from Tom.

Charlotte should never have come here, she thinks; she should never have inflicted herself on these good people.

"I'm sorry—" she begins.

"You see, I know you lost so many of your things, with that awful bomb of yours, and so I thought . . ." Mrs. Hawthorne moves to spread her knitting on the card table. The needles are gone, and the pieces made up into a neat crew-necked sweater, just Charlotte's size, but with the simplicity and practicality of a man's garment. "Will it do?" Mrs. Hawthorne asks.

Charlotte touches the wool, looks up at Mrs. Hawthorne.

"Because a gift can sometimes feel like an imposition, I do understand. And I wouldn't want you to feel that way. But I thought it would be to your taste; you like your things simple, don't you? But if you don't like it, Fliss can have it. It'll be big on her, but there's no harm in that; she's growing so fast at the moment, I can hardly keep up."

"Thank you," Charlotte says.

Belsie, brightening, holds it up against Charlotte, to check for size. "There we are. Good. We had nothing for you at Christmas, you see, which I didn't like at all, though it couldn't be helped."

"It is so very, very kind of you." Charlotte is entirely wrong-footed. She had no idea.

Belsie hands the sweater to her, then indicates a chair. "Please."

And so Charlotte sits.

"I had determined not to ask. But I should like to know. Just one thing. If you don't mind."

Now it's coming. And she owes her the truth.

"Do you really, dear, have no one?"

"Sorry?"

"Because if there was anyone, who you might want to ring up, to let them know how you are, we would not mind at all, if you were to use the telephone."

Charlotte goes to speak, but finds herself unable.

"Just because, if you'll forgive me. If you were my child, whatever upset or misunderstanding there had been between us, if I didn't know where you were, or what was happening to you, it would be pure torture to me. I'd want to hear from you, more than anything, whatever the disagreement or trouble might have been. So if there's anyone, who might be feeling like that right now, and you might ring them and set their mind at rest . . ."

"Thank you," Charlotte says, "but there isn't, I assure you. Not now. Not any more."

"Oh, my dear." She reaches towards Charlotte, stops short of touching her. "I am sorry."

Charlotte strokes the sweater. Blinks.

"You have been so very kind," she says. "I am quite bowled over."

The last Saturday in January, it snows all morning. Mid-afternoon, and there is a knock on the Hawthornes' front door. This itself is not unusual—it is a coming-and-going sort of household, with friends and neighbours, the exhausted old assistants, members of connected trades, and sometimes the recently bereaved dropping in for a moment and staying for an hour—it's just that this knock is unique in that it has to do with Charlotte.

Fliss comes bounding back from answering the door, making Nell go giddy and attempt a frisk.

"It's an old man," Fliss announces.

"What name is it?" Belsie asks, getting to her feet.

"Didn't ask. He's not here for us, he's here to see *you*"—with a nod to Charlotte—"and he's got a car!"

Charlotte rises automatically, tugs her plum-coloured sweater straight. She feels numb. Her ears are ringing. It was bound to happen, wasn't it. He's found her.

"Oh Fliss," her mother says. "Your *manners*."

Fliss plants herself in a chair. "*His* manners more like. Wouldn't even come in. Wouldn't hear of it. Prefers to wait outside in the cold."

"You're not expecting a caller?" Belsie asks.

Charlotte's voice is dry. "It'll be my father. Or someone that he's sent."

"Ah," Belsie says. "I see."

Charlotte heads for the door. The cold sky through the fanlight. Her footfalls on the tiled floor. The intense black of Tom's coat hanging from the rack. Everything seems slowed down, her senses heightened, the mind's device to allow a chance to catch the last handhold before the fall. But there is nothing to catch hold of here. He has come for her again. But this time she isn't scared. She is angry.

"Charlotte . . ."

She turns to see Tom coming down the stairs towards her, his face a question.

"It's all right," she says.

"I'll go," Tom says.

"I have to face him sometime."

"Don't let him persuade you of anything," he says. "Don't get in his car."

"I won't."

She lifts her coat off the rack.

Belsie comes out into the corridor, forehead knotted, treading into her outdoor shoes and wrapping her cardigan tight. "I'll go and get your dad," she tells Tom. She touches Charlotte's arm. "Sweetheart. We'll get the neighbours out. We'll call the police if we have to. You're not going anywhere you don't want to."

"Thank you."

But when Charlotte opens the door, the figure waiting in the snow is not her father, nor even one of his proxies. There, looking even more slumped and fatigued than ever, hands tucked into his armpits, nose puce with cold, breath a fog, is Harris. He gives her an upward jerk of the chin by way of greeting. All her anger falls away.

"Bad time?" he asks.

"Not at all." It's a genuine delight to see him.

"Good. Quiet word?"

She moves to join him. There's a messy collective exclamation from behind her. She turns to see a phalanx of Hawthornes at her back. Tom glaring, fierce; Fliss baffled and worried and tugging on Tom's sleeve, Nell nosing through; Mr. and Mrs. Hawthorne hastening down the hall, Fred drying his hands on a towel, open-mouthed, astonished at the goings-on.

"Sorry. Sorry," Charlotte says. "It's all right. It's not Father after all."

Harris snorts, making a dragon plume in the icy air.

"This is Captain Harris. He just wants a word."

"This is him?" Tom asks.

"This is him," Charlotte says.

"Right." Then, with a sudden adult directness, he addresses Harris: "Thank you, sir."

Harris looks at him a moment. Then he dips his head in acknowledgement.

"It's fine," Tom says to his family, ushering them back. "She's safe with him."

Once Tom's closed the door, voices immediately break out within, questions gabbled and hissed; Tom doing his best to quell or answer them. The two of them, though, are silent in the street.

Harris turns and walks back towards the car. Charlotte follows. The car ticks as it cools. The snow has only just stopped falling, so his tyre tracks and footprints are the only marks until her own trail joins them. Harris stops, gestures her close; he's positioning the two of them away from the Hawthorne door, and angled so that their conversation is screened from the view of nearby windows.

"Got something for you," he says.

He reaches inside his coat, unbuttons the jacket underneath, as though reaching for his holster; she takes an instinctive step back.

"Oh come on," he says.

He withdraws his hand, and presents her with a small black box. It has become scuffed and rubbed around the edges since she last saw it. She would almost, she thinks, have preferred the gun.

"Go on." He rattles it; the pearls knock against each other inside.

No.

Because Francesca had her things packed up and sent away. Because they should, by rights, be back in her father's possession by now. The earrings her father gave her, to give to her godmother. They can't be here; Harris can't have them. Because if they are sitting there on Harris's broad palm, that means—

"Come on now," he says. "I came all this way."

She can't dive into this dark water. She can't tolerate this cold. She wraps her arms around herself. She shakes her head.

He flips the box open, turns it towards her. "There."

The pair of black pearls lie hooked into the satin backing. They are oily, slick and flawless. But the lining of the box has been cut, and now lies loose against the card. Something had been hidden in there, and something has been found.

"This is what you thought I had," she says.

"To be fair, you did have them."

She touches a pearl with a fingertip; it rolls against the satin. It was never anything to do with work at all.

"What was in the lining?"

"I'm not at liberty."

"Something very small," she says. She looks up at him.

"Physically," he says. "Yes."

The light caught in the pearls is coloured by the street; a wash of cold white, a smudge of blue from the car, all rendered in miniature and on silk.

The documents that cross her father's desk. The conversations he is privy to. The projects he signs off on. The accounts he keeps, of the limited and vital resources this island still has at its disposal. And his keen interest in photography. He could still get the chemicals, after all. She finds that, when it comes to it, she is not surprised at all. What else, really, would she have expected of him? The man who always knew better than anybody else had pitched in with the enemy. Of course he had.

"Not Sas, though?"

"She had no idea that he'd co-opted you," Harris says, "if that's any consolation."

It's too terrible to believe, the idea that Saskia might have wanted to hole the ship, and watch it sinking. "Mary; it must have been Mary's fault. Mary must have corrupted her."

He shakes his head. "I'm afraid Lady Bowers had her own particular ideas about what England means."

Charlotte waves this aside. "But you should have seen the way Mary was. Feeding Sas with drink. And that Eugenics business. She wasn't *nice* . . ."

A suggestion of a smile. "Maybe not. But she's very good at her job."

Charlotte's thoughts hit a wall, crumple and slide.

That same woman, on the Underground. The same woman, but with a different air. Who'd pretended not to hear her name yelled right at her, because it was not her real name.

"Did Saskia ever find out?"

"At the end."

The shift in Harris's expression is so slight as to be almost imperceptible. A tightening of the eyes, a narrowing of the lips. She knows him well enough by now to see it. Sees too the upturned table, the smash of crockery, the scuff on the parquet floor. He and Mary Clarke, between them, rearranging the debris.

"We'd have had a very demoralising scandal on our hands. And we can't afford that. Not with the way things are."

But from his tone it's clear that he isn't quite at home with what he's saying. With what he is obliged to do.

"And my father?"

"He panicked, if that helps at all," Harris says. "He got wind of us; that's when he handed the package off to you. And then he put you in Summer Fields, well out of the way. So you might say he was protecting you."

"You're wasted in your line of work," she says. "You could go on stage with that material."

"Well."

"Not a shred of doubt then?"

"We have a girl in his office."

The mouse, Charlotte thinks; the mouse who'd have had Parkin leaping on a chair.

The air stirs. A spindrift of snow tumbles across the street towards them. He reaches into his pocket; keys jangle. He's on the verge of leaving. She wants to keep him there, hold on to him.

"What on earth will I tell Francesca?" she asks.

"Nothing."

"Nothing?"

"There'll be an accident. Something simple. The nation can mourn the loss of a loyal servant, your sister can grieve, and then we can all just get on with the task in hand."

Charlotte feels like a balloon that's been let go of, careening up into the sky. Endless distance, space; hurtling speed.

"And you can go home now," Harris says. "If you want to."

He offers her his empty hand, and she clasps it. Then his grip shifts and he grasps her wrist, turns it, and places the box directly into her palm. She looks up at him. Her fingers close around the box. He lets her go. She remembers that wound, the livid pit in his side. And in those pale eyes she sees disquiet and regret. She wants to tell him that she really sees him now, but she can't pick her thoughts apart enough to speak.

"Good luck," he says.

She nods.

She watches him walk back to the car and get in. The engine coughs and sputters into life. He doesn't look at her again. He slips the car into gear, pulls out from the kerb.

She turns and follows the trail of their overlapping prints back towards the door. Their footfalls have compacted the snow; here and there they've dragged it back to reveal the stone beneath. This is how it's been all these tangled months, she thinks: her steps blundering over Harris's, Harris's blurring hers, as they traced the same routes around London, and out across the countryside. Their paths were always intertwined, but with such different purposes, and to such different ends. But this moment, this pinprick on the map, is where they'd both been heading all along. From here they're spinning off in different directions, the distance growing with each step.

She reaches for the door, but the handle dips before she touches it, and the door swings wide. Tom searches her face, then peers past her, to the car turning in the street. Harris is just a shape in the driver's seat, misted by condensation.

"Are you all right?" Tom asks.

She looks back with him. The Austin reaches the corner, rounds it and is gone. The engine noise fades away. They're left in silence. The snow sits deep, covering the cobblestones and pavements. A cat sits inside a window and stares out sleepily. Children pelt down the street, yelling, coats flying. This threadbare, scratched-together place is beautiful, she thinks. There's a life to be lived here, if they're but given half a chance.

She turns back to Tom. She takes his hand.

"I will be," she says. "Yes."

Acknowledgements

Years ago, I completed a PhD on the work of the Anglo-Irish writer Elizabeth Bowen. It was really more about the hyphen than anything else; the see-saw gap she inhabited between the Anglo and the Irish. Bowen was also a writer of the war years, and I was fascinated then, as now, by her exploration of the strange states that war generates, whether psychological, physiological, or psycho-geographical. *The Midnight News* owes a great deal to the years I spent absorbing this extraordinary, not-entirely-placeable woman's work.

She isn't the only fiction writer I've been haunted by; I've soaked myself in stories from that time. I also grubbed through contemporary diaries and letters, hungry for turns of phrase, for different flavours, textures and colours. Histories too, for both the wider sweep and the small detail. This is a novel, not a PhD, and so, thank God, nobody's marking my bibliography, but these are the sources I turned to most frequently throughout the writing of this novel: Richard J. Aldrich's *Witness to War,* Paul Addison and Jeremy A. Crang's *Listening to Britain,* Mike Brown's *Put That Light Out!,* Juliet Gardiner's *The Blitz,* Joshua Levine's *The Secret History of the Blitz,* and E. H. Warmington's *A History of Birkbeck College.* Alongside these, Brian Parson's *The Undertaker at Work* and Andrew Scull's *Madness in Civilization* were both invaluable.

Thanks are due too to Rebecca Brown, to whom *The Midnight News* is dedicated, for reading early drafts, for guiding me to the reality of life lived with a condition like Tom's, and for all the gin and confidences down the years. Daragh Carville, for your clarity, insight and unstinting support. Clare Alexander: I am so grateful for your perseverance with me. Anna Stein, too, for always being in my corner. Francesca Main and Diana Miller: it is my extreme good fortune that I get to work with you. Georgia Goodall and Jade Craddock, for sparing my blushes. To Sarah New and Sara Eagle, to Jenny Carrow and Cassandra Pappas, and to Ellen Feldman and Peggy Samedi, for all the care, creativity and attention to detail you have brought to the book. To Eamonn Hughes, who all those years ago let me pause that PhD, and write another thing entirely. To Penny and Beth for their company in cold water; and to Cathy and Liz, for helping me towards an understanding of the shapes and patterns of families like the Richmonds. Thank you.

A NOTE ABOUT THE AUTHOR

Jo BAKER was born in Lancashire and educated at Oxford University and Queen's University Belfast. She is the author of the best-selling novel *Longbourn,* as well as *The Body Lies; A Country Road, A Tree; The Undertow; The Telling; The Mermaid's Child;* and *Offcomer.* She lives in Lancaster, England.

A NOTE ON THE TYPE

This book was set in a version of the well-known Monotype face Bembo. This letter was cut for the celebrated Venetian printer Aldus Manutius by Francesco Griffo, and first used in Pietro Cardinal Bembo's *De Aetna* of 1495. The companion italic is an adaptation of the chancery script type designed by the calligrapher and printer Lodovico degli Arrighi.

Composed by North Market Street Graphics,
Lancaster, Pennsylvania

Printed and bound by Berryville Graphics,
Berryville, Virginia

Designed by Cassandra J. Pappas